Int

Sunday, May 6, 20
9:17 a.m.
Bonita Beach, Florida

MW01131297

The Mimosa twins began their day strolling north and south from their usual spot on the beach, near the boardwalk from the Collier County parking lot, Jill going south, Carie north. Jill glanced into the gazebo with the AA meeting and saw that all seemed to be going normally there. She walked on down to the southernmost gazebo and turned back north, scanning the slowly growing crowd, ignoring the men ogling her young, lush body. As she neared the boardwalk, her sister's voice came over the earbuds of her modified MP3 player.

"Jillybean, got a possible situation up here near Pop's, by the volleyball net. A young couple just set a beach bag down and turned back north, where they came from. It may be nothing, but they're acting a little hinky, so I'm gonna follow them. Got your tool kit with you?"

"Rodger Dodger, Carie Berry. Want me to check out the bag?"

"Yup. It's the yellow one right by the post."

"I see you. Ah, got it. Be there in a sec."

"Okay. Keep me posted."

"Will do." Jill meandered up to the bag, opened it, lifted up a corner of a folded beach towel and looked inside.

"Oh, geez, CB, it's a bomb, all right; C4 and ball bearings, with a timer set for noon and a backup cell phone detonator."

"Can you defuse it?"

1

The Devlin Deception

Formerly titled "The Donne Deal:
How One Man Bought and Fixed the USA"

With an Homage to Bonita Springs, Florida

By

Jake Devlin

with Bonnie Springs

www.JakeDevlin.com

JakeDevlin@JakeDevlin.com

First Edition: September 2012

This is a work of fiction

... unfortunately.

Dedicated to those who are
desperately seeking complacency.

- PREFACE -

This novel began purely as the story about Gordon Donne buying and fixing the country, but as it evolved, the events occurring in Bonita Springs, Florida, took on a life of their own, as you, readers, will discover as you wend your way through this work, especially when you meet Pamela93 in Chapter 4.

For those of you who are familiar with Bonita, don't be dismayed at seeing new names for familiar locations. I've fictionalized those throughout, except for the few whose permission I sought to use their real names. (If you do know Bonita, you might start a list of the fictional and actual names; that may come in handy near the end of the book. Word to the wise, okay?)

As for the scenes where I'm involved, those are as close as I can get to what actually happened, but my memory is not always running at a hundred percent; a friend of mine named that condition Quarterheimer's, but sometimes it feels like Thirdheimer's, even Halfheimer's on occasion. I did check the local newspapers' archives and some transcripts, so I believe those scenes are fairly close to the actual events.

And for those of you who expected to find your name somewhere in here but can't find it, I offer a sincere mea culpa. I've tried to put in as many as possible, but I may have left some of you out, and the fault for that is purely mine. Perhaps if I write another, I can find a place for each of the rest of you, if and when I can find and/or get my notes organized. In any event, I enjoyed chatting with each and every one of you along this journey ... or just on the beach in Bonita.

WARNING!!!

Some chapters in this novel contain obligatory but gratuitous erotic content and may be inappropriate for the young, the prudish, the anal-retentive (more fiber should help with that, BTW) or the humorless (like a woman named Kathi I dated back in the seventies, who did not appreciate my suggesting that her name should be pronounced "Kath-eye" if she insisted on spelling it that way; I think we dated for a total of a week, maybe two. But I digress.)

I have marked the chapters where that is the primary content with an upper case "R" after the chapter number for your convenience (and because I don't want to hear a lot of complaints about that stuff). Use your own discretion. Word to the wise, okay?

- *PROLOGUE* -

Friday, December 9, 2011
10:17 a.m.
The Oval Office
Washington, DC

Immediately after President Obama signed the sixth Save The Economy Act in a videotaped ceremony, the United States was sold, thanks to three clauses that had been covertly inserted into the bill, which no one in the Congress read before voting it into law.

The price was a grand total of 82.7 cents ... about eighty-three pennies, and that was significantly above market value.

The buyer was a reclusive billionaire named Gordon Olin Donne, who was present at the ceremony.

He handed the Treasury Secretary a one-dollar bill and said, "Keep the change, Tim."

He then handed the Attorney General his termination papers and replaced him with his own personal attorney, who, immediately after being sworn in, signed an opinion declaring the sale absolutely legal and immune from being contested.

He then turned to the President, said, "You're fired," and handed him his termination papers.

The Vice President and Majority and Minority Leaders from both the House and Senate, all of whom were in attendance for the signing, were surrounded by the Joint Chiefs of Staff while Donne told them they were all fired, handed them their termination papers and told them to surrender their cell phones and all their electronic devices and ordered them to sit quietly in the couches and chairs in the center of the room. Spluttering, but intimidated by the military presence, they all complied.

Donne then sat in the chair just vacated by the flabbergasted now ex-president, glanced around the Oval Office and began a lengthy, exhaustive restructuring of the federal government.

He issued orders firing the entire Congress and the Supreme Court and declaring his own absolute sovereignty. By noon, he had signed 257 pre-prepared directives, by six p.m. he had met face-to-face with the directors of the FBI, CIA, Secret Service, IRS and the US Mint, with the Secretaries of the Treasury, State and Defense, the Joint Chiefs of Staff, the Chairman of the Federal Reserve and with the entire White House staff, and at eight p.m. sharp, preceded by intense media speculation, Gordon Olin Donne held his first live broadcast to the nation.

But all day long, he kept reminding himself that only the first step on his long road to vengeance was now behind him.

-1-
Six Months Earlier

Sunday, June 12, 2011
4:17 a.m.
Bonita Springs, Florida

In total darkness, a silent, black, amphibious helicopter landed briefly at the shoreline of Bonita Beach. Six men and one woman slid wraith-like onto the sand with their equipment, and within ten seconds the helo disappeared into the night in near-total silence.

An hour later, still in darkness, a small red skiff, piloted by an acne-scarred teenager wearing a Master Bait & Tackle T-shirt ("You Can't Beat Our Bait"), stopped about thirty feet offshore from the helo's landing spot, only long enough for the teenager to quickly and carefully slide a beige box perhaps eight feet long, two feet wide and one foot tall into the water, parallel to the beach, where it sank to the bottom, about ten feet below the surface. The skiff motored off, only to return as the sun rose, landing perhaps a hundred yards south of where the box had been dropped. The teen pulled a tackle box and a fishing rod from the skiff, set the box on the shore and began casting into the quiet surf, giggling to himself.

In North Naples, also at dawn, a few miles south of the fishing teen, a heavyset middle-aged man clad in brand-name running shorts (size XXXXL) and an Overeaters Unanimous T-shirt waddled from a luxury beachfront hotel and along the beach, scattering exactly a thousand small objects from his fanny pack into the near-shore waters for a few hundred yards north and south of the hotel. He returned to his room, called room service to order a huge and outrageously over-priced breakfast, picked up his cell phone and texted a three-word message: "Vanderbilt Beach completed."

An hour or so later, a frail elderly woman wearing a T-shirt that read "Proud Member of the Batteries for Life Club" walked with some difficulty onto Bonita Beach and opened a bag of popcorn, which she scattered on the sand. Perhaps twenty seagulls immediately flew in and started fighting, squalling and swarming to get at the treat. When all of it had been devoured, the woman went slowly back to the parking lot and drove herself to a senior citizens center in her gated community, where she spent the morning peeing, playing mahjong and gossiping with her fellow seniors.

-2-

Friday, December 9, 2011
10:37 a.m.
The Capitol
Washington, DC

A fat, gay Representative from Massachusetts was enjoying his daily massage in the House gym in the basement of the Capitol with his favorite masseur, Eric, when he found that he was no longer a Congressman, but not due to his recent announcement of his retirement. Twenty minutes after Donne bought the country, two armed Marines in battle fatigues appeared in the doorway of the massage room and handed him a paper informing him that he had been fired. They escorted him to the House chamber, where he, along with all the other Members of Congress still in town, was held incommunicado until eight p.m. (They let him get dressed first.)

The Justices of the Supreme Court were also escorted to the House chamber and held incommunicado. Congressmen and women who were not in DC were located and also sequestered.

Just before eight p.m. EST, after catered lunches and dinners had been served to all, the Members who were in the Oval Office when the bill was signed and had been sequestered separately were brought into the chambers and joined their colleagues. Televisions were turned on and tuned to Donne's address.

-3-
52.6 Years Earlier

Sunday, May 10, 1959 (Mothers Day)
5:27 a.m.
Houston, Texas

In the pre-dawn dark, a small female figure left a cardboard box on the front steps of the Prescrott Street Children's Home, then disappeared into the morning fog.

A few minutes later, when the weekend custodian arrived for his regular shift, he looked into the box, saw a pale, sickly newborn infant wrapped in a ragged old blanket, coughing weakly, and carried it into the building. He called for the charge nurse and gave the box and the little boy to her; he then changed into his coveralls and began the day's work. At 3:30, finished for the day, he clocked out and headed home, giving no further thought to the baby or the box.

A year and a half later, after PSCH had nursed the baby back to health, the little boy was adopted by a local graduate student and his infertile wife. After a night of heavy drinking and pot-smoking, they had decided on a name for the boy, and that name, Gordon Olin Donne, appeared on the official substitute birth certificate prepared by the PSCH and filed with the State of Texas along with all the adoption paperwork. The boy's date of birth was estimated to be May 6th.

When the little boy was four, his father finally received his PhD in Religious Studies, specializing in comparative religion, and began what would become a relatively undistinguished career in academia, teaching and doing research at multiple different colleges, ending up in the education department of a small university in southern New Hampshire. The couple had no other children, natural or adopted, and generally lived a lower-middle-class life, occasionally needing to borrow money from their families to pay bills.

Gordon's mother and father divorced in 1974, and she obtained full custody of the boy, now age fourteen. She received her BA in art history a year later and went on to become an assistant curator at an art museum in St. Petersburg, Florida, when it opened in 1976. She suffered a fatal fall while re-hanging "The Martyrdom of St. Kevin" after its annual cleaning in 1978; a corner of the frame fractured her skull, but the painting itself suffered no damage, and the frame was cleaned quickly and easily.

Gordon's father died of hypothermia in 1977 when he and six other customers in a Manchester supermarket were locked in a walk-in freezer with nineteen clerks and managers during an armed robbery that turned into a 37-hour standoff. The autopsy showed that he also had a terminal case of cirrhosis of the liver and would have been dead within a year in any event.

The boy earned the nickname "Scrappy" in first grade, after some third-grade bullies teased him because of his name and stole his lunch money. His adopted mother's father, a former Texas Ranger, taught him to stand up for and defend himself, in spite of his diminutive size. He never again lost his lunch money or a schoolyard fight, and he also stood up for other kids who were being bullied for whatever reasons. No kids at any of the seven grade schools he attended ever lost their lunch money ... or if they did, they got it back, doubled ... and sometimes tripled.

When he was in the third grade, using a kick his grandfather had taught him, he shattered the left knee of a particularly large sixth-grade bully who was and had been tormenting many smaller first- and second-graders. Unfortunately, the sixth grader was the son of a wealthy friend of the school principal, so it was Gordon who was expelled. His parents scolded him at length, but his grandfather

4

quietly yet clearly supported him, reminding him many times in future years that that bully would always walk with a painful and awkward limp and would remember his humiliation at the hands -- actually, foot -- of a boy half his size.

Gordon was usually more comfortable talking with adults than with kids his age, and his IQ was measured several times, with an average of 143, in the genius range. While his father was not a particularly positive role model, with his drinking and his frequent loud arguments with his wife's father, Gordon was never abused, either verbally or physically, but he bonded more closely with his grandfather, who taught the boy how to shoot, hunt and fish, as well as passing on the powerful moral code that all Rangers lived by.

One thing (perhaps the only one) that Gordon's father and grandfather shared was an interest in chess, and Gordon took to it like a fish to water, winning a local tournament at the age of six, less than a year after his introduction to the game. In later life, Gordon credited that game for much of his success in business, especially in his hedge fund and in venture capital, which evolved into Donne Enterprises International (DEI) in the early eighties and beyond.

Gordon and his grandfather remained close until the latter's death in 1998 after a long battle with lung cancer, which he fought with what his fellow Rangers called "sheer orneriness." But at the age of 89, he'd had a fine life, was lucid to the end and had taught his adopted grandson many, many valuable lessons, which stuck with him for the rest of his life.

One that Gordon particularly remembered and often applied in later life was "The clever cougar hides his claws."

In addition to chess, Gordon showed an interest and talent in math and the stock market, which his mother and grandfather encouraged; his father was disinterested, if not openly hostile, to the boy's interest in the market, but he supported his mathematics, even though he himself was terrible at it.

On his ninth birthday, in 1968, his grandfather, thanks to some Ranger connections, was able to introduce Gordon to a legendary investor from Omaha, who gave the boy signed copies of two books by Benjamin Graham, "The Intelligent Investor" and "Security Analysis," which the boy devoured over the next seven months, taking copious notes.

For his tenth birthday, his grandfather gave Gordon five thousand dollars to do with as he wanted. Gordon, balancing instant and deferred gratification, kept five hundred dollars in cash, which he spent for gifts and entertainment over the next year, and invested the rest, using what he'd learned from the Graham books and his other studies of the markets. His portfolio more than doubled by his twelfth birthday, and grew more than twentyfold by the time he graduated from high school.

5

He also showed entrepreneurial spirit, especially with his math skills. He developed several algorithms that he then built into a software platform for financial transactions, which he sold to a major computer company in 1979 for fifty-five million dollars, just weeks before he turned twenty.

That platform formed the basis for all bank transfers for the next eight years, until Donne developed a competing platform, which became the de facto standard and still remains in use to this day; but instead of selling that one outright, he licensed it to clearing houses and kept maintenance contracts through one of the companies in Donne Enterprises International. So to this day, ALL bank transfers around the world are handled by the DEI platform.

Donne won a full scholarship to a major Ivy League university, but dropped out in his junior year with his fifty-five million dollars and began building his own hedge fund and private equity/venture capital businesses. He took financial care of his grandfather, and also set up generous annuities for eleven teachers who'd had the greatest positive influence on him in elementary, junior and senior high school. He felt that it was a great tragedy that his parents had both died before his windfall.

But he carried all of that history and experience with him when he entered the Oval Office on December 9, 2011, filled with anticipation that his plans for that day would work.

-4-

Sunday, June 12, 2011
11:03 a.m.
Bonita Beach, Florida

Another placid, brochure-perfect day on the Gulf: overnight low, 72 degrees, the high forecast to be 91, a mild easterly breeze, a Gulf temperature of 86 degrees and not a cloud in the bright blue sky.

By late morning, the beach was maybe a quarter full with locals and some tourists, mostly Europeans. The AA meetings in the gazebos at the south end of the beach had dispersed an hour before, and the parking lots were only half full, unlike February, March and April, when every available legal parking space was full by 9:30 and many cars took their chances at getting ticketed and towed from illegal ones. "Season" was a time when residents mostly stayed home, but now they were coming out in force, renewing lapsed acquaintances and reclaiming their habitual spots on the sand. They mostly knew each other only by first names; last names just added to the information they might forget, since many of them had what they sometimes called Quarterheimer's, also known as senior moments.

Millie, Fran and Alvina, friends for sixty years, each weighing well over 300 pounds, were lying together on their usual red blankets, gossiping at length about all the annoying newly-retired "young'uns" in their over-55 trailer park. When you're over eighty, you've got a right to your opinions ... and to be offended by anything and everything; or so they continually told themselves. Some folks on the beach called them "The Triple-Ton Threat," while others referred to them as the "Antique Elephant Parade," and still others just called them the "Beach Balls." They were all paging through the latest issues of three of the top fashion-and-relationship magazines.

A dozen or so of the Beach Potatoes, a self-named group of locals, ranging in age from roughly 30 to 50, gathered in their usual spot a bit south of the boardwalk from the Collier County parking lot, some reading, some swapping jokes, others exchanging recipes, and still others heading into the water with their noodles. A nicely tanned woman named Carole, who was known as the Sweet Potato for her gentle and pleasant disposition, was talking with Jim, the Scalloped Potato, about his plans for dealing with his severe hair loss.

In the water, the Barefoot Beach Babes, also self-named, bobbed and gossiped, mostly about their husbands, who were all off golfing.

Norm and Janet headed to their regular spot near the high tide line, where Norm used a long-shafted drill and then a sand anchor with spiral flanges to put up their umbrella, which cast a shadow on empty sand, since both of them sat on their macramaed beach chairs in the sun, never in the shadow. That irony never entered their minds as Janet worked on her sudoku and Norm on his crossword puzzle after finishing their sausage-cheese-and-egg breakfast muffins.

A bit south of Norm and Janet, a crewcut, extremely pale but well-muscled young man was sitting in a plain beach chair under an umbrella, facing north, talking on his cell phone, but so quietly that no one could hear a word he was saying. His aviator sunglasses hid his eyes from anyone's view. The Beach Potatoes commented about him, calling him another Mashed Potato, while Carole, the Sweet Potato, walked down to him and said she hoped he was using lots of sunscreen; he simply nodded and went back to his cell phone, but his eyes followed her shapely figure as she returned to her group.

The Hat Squad had been in the water for two hours, floating on noodles and bobbing up and down, back and forth, soothing their arthritis and osteoporosis, gabbing away. They'd lost two members over the winter, so now they were down to only thirteen. Alice was still the leader and moderator; she also usually won in their weekly poker games in their gated community, where she was president of the homeowners association. All the members agreed that she had the best hats; today, it was a huge purple cloche with a wide brim and several multi-colored peacock feathers dangling all around it.

Up very close to the stairs to the showers and rest rooms, the

Incontinentals gathered for convenience and quick access, in separate clumps, since, while they shared the same affliction, they had never made connections with each other, so there was no inter-clump conversation.

Carie and Jill, the Mimosa twins (brunette, 30-ish, very cute) were sitting on their towels in their usual space next to the boardwalk from the Collier County parking lot, towel-dancing and people-watching.

Most of the current popular authors were well represented in the hands of multiple readers, and a few ebook readers were scattered around the beach. One guy even had his in a plastic bag and was reading in the water, up to his waist. He called it "aqua-literating" and claimed his reader had never gotten even slightly damp.

But he nearly dropped it when he glanced up and saw a tall, lissome, extraordinarily well-built blonde meandering south on the shoreline. Wearing a near-thong gold bikini a few shades lighter than her tan and a tiny, nearly sheer sarong around her waist, she could have been a former Miss America ... or with her figure, maybe a Miss September. From a distance, she looked to be about 23, but she was actually just weeks shy of the big 5-0. As she walked, not strutting or flouncing, but totally self-confident, heads turned and eyes ogled.

Even the teenagers playing volleyball near Pop's at the north end of the beach stopped their game; one of the boys let the ball loose and chased it to the shoreline, getting within ten feet of the object of his immediate hormonal affection, eyes and another part of his anatomy bulging. When he returned to the net and said, "Definitely a MILF," the other boys snickered and one of the girls rolled her eyes and punched him in the shoulder.

Next in line were the Incontinentals, three of whom reached into their bags for binoculars, seven for their cell phone cameras, and all the rest of the men rapidly cleaned their glasses, except for the ones who'd had cataract surgery, who silently thanked their doctors for giving them such clear vision. The women looked on enviously.

In the water, Alice pushed the feathers away from her face and glared at the blonde, and the rest of the Hat Squad followed, glaring and adding their own catty comments to Alice's.

Still further south, Millie poked Alvina and hissed, "Do you believe that? Doesn't Lee County have a law against thongs?"

Alvina replied, "Yup, but it only requires that the back be at least two inches wide."

Millie persisted, "Well, that one may be legal, but it's disgusting."

Fran muttered, "I'll bet she's airbrushed."

Alvina looked down her substantial nose at Fran. "That's only in the magazines, dumbo. You can't be airbrushed live."

Millie sneered.

Fran blinked several times, then looked at Alvina blankly. "Are you sure?"

Alvina waved her off. "Sure, I'm sure. Geez."

Seven of the Beach Potatoes pulled out their phones and started shooting video. Jim, the Scalloped Potato, took off his hat, rubbed his scalp and said to nobody in particular, "This is not a bald head; it's a solar panel for a sex machine." Carole, the sweet one, looked at the blonde and thought again about getting implants, even though to others, she had a great natural figure; three of the guys in the group had already named her the Hot Potato.

When Norm turned to ogle the blonde, he stubbed his toe on the drill sticking out of the ground next to his chair; Janet glanced at him, then at the blonde, then back at Norm, and said, "She IS gorgeous, isn't she?"

Norm quickly replied, "Not as gorgeous as you are, my love."

Janet smiled as she reached into their beach bag: "Good comeback, Norm. I'll get a bandage for your toe. It's bleeding."

The blonde, who had been scanning the crowd from behind her high-fashion sunglasses as she strolled, but never making eye contact, stopped briefly to chat with an elderly couple, who shrugged, but pointed further south.

A moment later, she stopped to ask something of a nondescript but deeply tanned older man, who was lying on what looked to be a homemade PVC lounge with a six-inch white fringe hanging down all around it. He was reading one of Milton Berle's joke collections and was known for his self-defecating humor. A T-shirt with a picture of a man lying in a hammock and the words "American Idle" was hanging off the end of his lounge.

In answer to her question, he shook his head sadly and pointed further south. As she continued on, he heaved a deep sigh. His eyes took a long time to return to the book.

The Mimosa twins glanced at the blonde, nodded to each other and activated the miniature sound-and-video recording equipment embedded in their beach bags. Jill whispered to Carie, "I hope we look that good when we're her age." Carie smiled and nodded, but kept her eyes on the blonde.

The blonde then sauntered up to another older man reclining on a three-way beach lounge maybe fifteen feet further south, also near the waterline; he was writing in a small spiral notebook.

In a gentle, melodious voice, she said, "Excuse me."

Startled, the man looked up and saw a face with high cheekbones, full lips and either no or very natural makeup, a true movie star face, framed in lustrous, luxuriantly wavy honey blonde hair. He didn't -- couldn't -- ignore her anatomically very correct figure, of course.

Perflutzed, he held up an index finger, then pointed to his mouth, finished chewing a chocolate chip cookie, swallowed and mumbled, "Mm-hmm?"

She waited, but when nothing else was forthcoming, she asked, "Are you Jake Devlin, by any chance?"

He swallowed one more time and said, "Yes, I am, but not by chance; that's the name I was given."

"You're writing <u>The Donne Deal</u>?"

Jake licked some crumbs from his lips. "Yup."

She held out her hand and Jake took it. "I'm Pamela93; I've sent you some suggestions through your web site, back when you only had Donne's speech up there."

"You're Pamela93? You don't look at all like I pictured you," Jake said, thinking that she actually looked precisely as he'd pictured her. "But I loved your idea on the minimum tax; that got me thinking."

"Minimum tax? That wasn't mine. I did the Roth IRA and the capital loss offset increases."

"Oh, geez, I'm sorry. My memory isn't what it used to be."

"No problem. You missed a bit, there on the right. May I?"

She reached down and brushed a final crumb off the corner of his lip. "Got it."

"Thanks."

"May I sit and talk with you for a while?"

"Sure. Right here on the other side of my cooler okay?"

"Great. And just call me Pam." She set her beach bag down, unwrapped her sarong, flipped open a chair and slithered into it, giving Jake a winning smile and batting her dazzling blues at him over her elegant sunglasses.

-5-

Friday, December 9, 2011
7:55 p.m. EST
Bonita Springs, Florida

Slinky Joe's is a popular restaurant and bar in Bonita Springs, Florida, with a live band every night and a diverse clientele of retirees, bikers, rednecks and tourists, a true cross-cultural local icon. Debbie Jackson, in a skimpy red halter and denim short shorts that revealed the top of a red thong and a "tramp stamp" tattoo, sat at the bar, nursing her sixth beer of the night, looking around to see who she might con into buying her her seventh, when Pete, one of the owners, took the mike from the band and spoke to the crowd.

"Folks, we're gonna take a vote here. I know you've been loving Salt and Pepper's music, but there's apparently a MAJOR announcement about the future of our country coming on the TV in five minutes. Joe and I have been seeing the promos all afternoon and evening, and we know many of you have seen those, too. This sounds like something that'll probably affect all of us, so we're gonna do a mini-democracy exercise here. Brittany and Justin are due for a break at 8:30, but if we move that up half an hour, we can all see just what this announcement is all about.

"So let's see some hands. First, those who want them to break now and watch the announcement? Okay. And now those who don't want that?" At that, Debbie put up both hands and yowled a loud Confederate yell, then saw that she was the only one yelling, so she sat lumpily back down on her barstool.

"Okay," Pete continued, "looks like about three-quarters of you want to watch. So let's have a BIG round of applause for Brittany and Justin" -- and the crowd whistled, hollered and applauded -- "and let's see what's gonna happen."

Debbie turned to a mullet-cut guy in a wifebeater T-shirt who had just returned to his stool next to hers and mumbled, "What the fuck? I LOVE Brittany; she's got a great voice, better'n Whitney Houston. And now we gotta watch that lyin' (N-word deleted) AGAIN? Buy me a beer, Darryl, so I can get through this shit. I'll make it worth your while later." She leered suggestively at him.

Darryl, five beers into his usual twelve, and having been the recipient of Debbie's well-practiced favors several times in the past, debated with himself for perhaps two seconds and then agreed; he'd just settle for eleven beers tonight.

Seventy-nine-year-old Marion Herman and her eighty-four-year-old hubby, George, retired co-CEOs of a custom steel manufacturing company in Indianapolis, were sitting at a table in the front corner of the dining area, far away from the bar, pool tables and the stage. Visiting Slinky Joe's for the first time, they felt completely out of their element, but had been enjoying Salt and Pepper's music, on the recommendation of their neighbors, Ron and Eileen Roderick.

Marion looked at George and said, "Honey, have you got your hearing aids turned up?" George nodded and murmured, "Tuesday." Marion sighed and rolled her eyes.

Pete grabbed the remote, changed all the TVs to the 24-hour news channel and ran the audio through the band's amplifiers, catching the news anchor in the midst of his commentary:

" ... -itzer, and we're on pins and needles here. The White House has not issued any hints of what this speech is going to be. We don't even have an early release of it, so we're completely at sea on what he might say."

He paused, listening to his earpiece. "I'm just hearing that we're ready to go live to the Oval Office. So here we go."

At that point the picture shifted to the Oval Office, but instead of President Obama's well-known visage, a stranger smiled awkwardly at the camera. He looked to be in his early fifties, smallish, bald with a light fringe around the sides and back, a bulbous nose, ears too big for his head, an overbite and a weak, receding chin.

Debbie leaned over to Darryl and said, "Geez, who the fuck is this guy? He looks like a fuckin' munchkin."

George whispered to Marion, "Is that Harold Lloyd?" Marion whispered back, "No, George; Harold Lloyd is dead." George whispered, "Did we go to the funeral?" Marion whispered, "Shh."

"Good evening, my fellow Americans. I know you expected to see President Obama sitting here, but I've just fired him, along with Congress, the Attorney General, the Solicitor General and the Supreme Court, and it's all perfectly legal."

At that, a collective gasp arose from the crowd, and Debbie looked at Darryl and mumbled, "What the fuck? What'd he say?"

"Shhh," hissed the matron sitting to her left.

George took Marion's hand in his and said, "This isn't Friday Night Live, is it?"

On all the TVs, the stranger said, "My name is Gordon Donne, D-o-n-n-e, and up until right this moment, I was the owner and CEO of Donne Enterprises International, a private multinational corporation which may be familiar to some of you. For the rest of you, there's a lot of information about me and my company on the Internet."

At that point, journalists, hedge fund managers, CEOs, and heads of state all around the world typed his name into their search engines, which nearly crashed those search engines' servers.

"This morning, after President Obama signed the 1500-page Save The Economy Act, three clauses in which authorized my actions, I bought the federal government, lock, stock and barrel, and I've taken over the executive, judicial and legislative responsibilities. Since I'm taking on all three of those roles, my salary will be triple what I would ask for just one, so you taxpayers will be paying me three dollars a year instead of one.

"Before I go further, I want to acknowledge something that I have no doubt will be uncovered and exploited in the next few days. I have suffered for my entire life from a mild form of Asperger's Syndrome, which I have worked diligently, but with sometimes limited success, to overcome. That syndrome has made me much more comfortable with numbers, systems and macro concepts than with words and social interactions, but in my new position as owner or whatever title people wind up giving me, I will work even more diligently to overcome that difficulty. So I apologize in advance if that syndrome surfaces as you and I have our conversations over the next several weeks, months and years, but especially tonight as you all get to know me a little bit for the first time.

"Over the next year, I'm going to make our government work efficiently and productively, something that our Congresses and Presidents have not been able or willing to do for decades, as most of you probably know already. They've just been 'kicking the can down the road,' burying their heads in the sand and outright lying to the American people."

Several people at Slinky Joe's murmured, "That's right" and "F'sure" and "Right on." Joe and Pete, watching in their cramped office behind the bar, exchanged skeptical looks and then focused back on the 13-inch black-and-white TV sitting on their file cabinet. Joe, the more mathematical partner, reached for a notebook and a pen. "I think we need to take some notes, Pete." Pete just nodded.

"In fact," Donne continued, "many of you have realized that our political system has almost completely hijacked and corrupted the so-called 'representative democracy' envisioned by our Founding Fathers, and that both the Democrats AND the Republicans have put the interests of party ... and the special interests they serve, and themselves ... above the country as a whole, using all of our citizens as unwilling ... or sometimes willing ... pawns in their political power plays. It's like the Democrats and Republicans are children sitting in a sandbox, throwing sand at each other, but that sandbox is on the back deck of the Titanic, with no one up in the wheelhouse steering the ship away from the icebergs that they've all been warned about.

"Like many of our citizens, I've become disgusted with the continuous political posturing and the inability of our politicians to set aside their constant quest for reelection and come to agreement on MAJOR issues confronting the United States. Just look back to how the President and Congress dropped the ball and virtually ignored the ideas from the Simpson-Bowles commission and the incongruously named Super Committee, and don't forget the idiot brinksmanship and mudslinging in the debates about raising the debt ceiling this past summer; to finally come to an agreement just ONE DAY before the deadline was not only irresponsible, but should have been criminal. And don't forget that that debacle triggered a ratings downgrade of the United States, the first ever in our history.

"Of course, any sort of REAL fiscal responsibility would cut off the taxpayer funding for the trough at which our elected politicians have been feeding so greedily for decades, lining their own corrupt pockets and those of their cronies. I swear, every time I watch the Congress in action, I'm reminded of seagulls squalling and shrieking around a handful of popcorn tossed on a beach. Or pigeons in Central Park, for those of you who've never been to a beach. Just take a moment and picture that.

"And that popcorn, my fellow taxpayers, is YOUR money. But Congress and Presidents have thought that it's theirs. Remember Willie Sutton, the 1920s bank robber who was asked why he robbed banks; apocryphally, he said 'That's where the money is.' Wherever there's a big pile of money, there are lots of people trying to figure out how to get their greedy little paws on it, and when some of those people have the power to write the laws to make that legal, watch out.

13

"Now, I'm not going to spend a lot of time tonight on dragging politicians through the mud and trying to place blame for their past failures; we'll be dealing with that over the next several months. I will say that BOTH parties and their supporters, and, of course, lobbyists, have brought this country nearly to its knees. And I use the term 'nearly' deliberately. That is about to change in many ways, and for the better, in the short term, the medium term and the long term, and the 'full faith and credit of the United States' will stand as a rock-solid underpinning of our country once again. Are you listening, (names of three rating agencies deleted; trademark issues)?"

Marion turned to George and whispered, "He's not using a teleprompter, is he?"

"Nope," George replied, "and no notes written on his hand, either." He paused, then, "Is that Walter Cronkite?" Marion sighed and rolled her eyes.

Debbie slurred to Darryl, "Who the fuck is Fitchmoodies?"

"Shh," the matron to her left said again.

"You got a fuckin' problem, bitch?" Debbie mumbled, raising her fist, but Darryl restrained her and switched seats with her.

"Many of my compatriots have told me that I'm taking on an impossible task, but I don't believe that. If we wait any longer, kick the can down the road again, we may well have passed the point of no return and it WILL be impossible. But by applying some common sense and solid business principles, and the innate creativity and ingenuity of the American people, which we will be encouraging through some public-private partnerships, mostly private, I believe that by working together, we can accomplish this task.

"Today, I've fired all of President Obama's so-called 'czars,' but I've appointed two, one as what I call the Czar of Anti-Hubris, to advise me when and if she feels I'm overreaching in any way, and a Czar of Unintended Consequences, which should be self-explanatory. Each of them has agreed to serve for a salary of a dollar a year, and I'm sure we're going to have some pretty spirited discussions.

"I've also met with the directors of the FBI, CIA, Homeland Security, Secret Service and the IRS, as well as the Joint Chiefs of Staff and the Secretaries of State, Treasury and Defense, and I've signed and issued over 250 directives, which have the force of law, and which will begin an accelerated process of America's long-delayed job-creating recovery. Those directives will all be posted on a web site at precisely ten o'clock Eastern Standard Time tonight, and I'll give you the link at the end of my time with you this evening. They are less than three pages each and they're all written in plain, direct English, so you don't need to be a lawyer ... or hire one ... to understand any of them. That, by the way, will be a hallmark of my administration: plain, direct English, no opaque legalese.

"Some of those directives will take effect immediately, some on January 1st, 2012, about three weeks from today, and others will implement changes more gradually, and there will be winners and losers, as in any change or restructuring. Generally, the losers will be the folks who've enjoyed special perks and privileges from riding on the backs of others, and the winners will be the folks who've borne the burden for those privileged ones for far too long.

"Over this weekend and through next week, I'll be meeting with all Cabinet members who have not been fired to let them know exactly what I expect them to do on behalf of the country ... on your behalf ... and in the months to come, you will all see major changes as we restructure the entire federal government and its relationships with the individual state and local governments, as well as with the rest of the world ... but most importantly, with you, our citizens and taxpayers.

"One of the first directives I signed today declares that, effective January 1st, 2016, the official language of the United States will be ... Norwegian. No, just kidding; I have to admit I'm a fan of that nerdy Manhattan filmmaker and clarinet player. It'll be English.

"Now, I know many Americans have become accustomed to problems being solved in half an hour or an hour on television, and I'll tell you right now that this all is not going to happen that quickly. It will take some time, and there will be advances and setbacks along the road."

(Author's note: from here to the end of Chapter 5, readers who have little or no interest in Donne's actual policies may find this part a bit tedious and detailed; feel free to skip it and turn the pages to near the end of this chapter, perhaps the middle of Page 24. On the other hand, adults and policy wonks will find this to be much of the crux of how Donne fixes the country and may want to take notes. JD)

"First, on the economic front, this country is facing three major challenges, one long-term, one medium-term and one short-term. Long term, our national debt, including unfunded liabilities, looks overwhelming; projections vary between 65 and 80 TRILLION dollars. Today, our debt, NOT including the unfunded liabilities, stands at about 15 trillion dollars, and it's projected to reach 24 trillion dollars in just three years, at the beginning of 2015, if we continue on our current path. Using today's figure of 15 trillion dollars, that works out to about $48,000 per citizen, using the latest census figures. By the beginning of 2015, that'll rise to about $73,000 per citizen. And if we add in the unfunded liabilities for things like Social Security, Medicare, Medicaid and federal retirement benefits, that figure is so big that I won't even bother to try to explain it. But it's HUGE. And fixing all those problems has to start now, should have started years ago, because if WE don't get started, our children, grandchildren and GREAT GREAT grandchildren are going to be saddled with an even bigger burden, one that will make what's going on in Greece, Italy, Ireland, Portugal and Spain these days seem miniscule.

"My long-term economic goal is to get the current national debt down to around two trillion; I'd aim for lower, but I don't want to keep investors and traders from having that fixed-income choice available.

"Medium term, the challenge is the budget deficit, the amount we spend above and beyond our revenues each year, which we're now covering by borrowing. Every dollar of deficit adds a dollar to our debt, and the only way we're going to start paying down the debt is to not only balance the budget, but create a surplus, where our revenues exceed our expenses. That surplus can then be used to start chipping away at the debt.

"The short-term challenge is an economy that is still in the doldrums, maybe showing a tiny bit of growth, but nowhere near enough to bring in enough revenues to start bringing down the deficit, never mind getting to balance and certainly not enough to generate a surplus. A BIG cause of the slowness of economic growth is and has been the uncertainty that the back-and-forth political sandboxing has created for American businesses and individuals. I'm going to change that to CERTAINTY.

"I need to give a huge thank you to the Simpson-Bowles Commission for all their hard and unappreciated work, and I've used their recommendations as a starting point, but the strategies and policies in my directives go far beyond theirs in many respects.

"So my immediate goal on the economic front will be to get the economy growing and to take the dampers that the government has put on it off its back. One part of that will be totally restructuring our ridiculous tax code.

"So on January 1st, 2012, MANY changes will take effect, which will allow most individuals and couples to fill out a simple two-page tax return like the one I'm holding here, a copy of which will also be posted on the web site by ten o'clock tonight. We'll also be making significant changes to Social Security, Medicare and Medicaid, none of which will affect anyone who is currently enrolled in those programs or who will be enrolling in the next fifteen years. Younger people will have a variety of choices available to them, and the younger you are now, the more choices you will have.

"Business taxes will also change on January 1st, designed to make American businesses much more competitive in the global economy and to incentivize businesses to repatriate the trillions of dollars they have kept overseas ... and to do that within the first six months of 2012 ... and begin investing in American enterprises and creating jobs in this country. At long last, the playing field will be leveled for all American businesses.

"Now, I know those sound like buzzwords that you've heard over and over again from politicians ... hmmm; I just can't keep the contempt out of my voice when I say that word, in case you haven't noticed ... but you'll be seeing specifics over the next days, weeks and months. Some of you will like some of them, others will hate those same things, but when you see the whole package as it develops, I believe that you'll see how all the pieces fit together to put the US on a sustainable and reasonable road to recovery and growth well beyond anything you've been able to expect since the financial and housing crisis that finally caught up with us about three years ago, when the chickens of bad policies came home to roost.

"As for my domestic priorities, first is the taxpayers; I will ensure that the monies we take from you ... and I do mean 'take,' since that IS what taxes do ... are spent efficiently and well, with minimal waste, corruption, fraud and abuse (I know, more of those buzzwords, but I mean them and you will see them really minimized). I'll be especially hard on institutions and programs that were created to serve people, but have grown to think that people exist to serve them.

"One of my first directives orders that all federal employees and contractors have a mandatory fiduciary duty to the taxpayers and will be personally accountable for failures in dealing with YOUR money.

"My second priority is business, especially small business and entrepreneurs, to finally give them some degree of certainty for at least the next ten years, and the economy, since that's what gives our citizens a much broader range of choices and opportunities to live the kind of life most of us dream of living (yup, more buzzwords; but note that I said 'opportunities,' not 'guaranteed outcomes').

"My goal for the economy is to achieve a 10% annual growth rate in GDP within eight years, and many of my policies have been and will be based on a simple criterion: will this policy advance or hinder that goal? As just a few examples, I have issued directives abolishing the National Labor Relations Board, repealing the Davis-Bacon Act, decertifying the AFSCME at the federal level and establishing a federal Right to Work law, as well as eliminating the federal Civil Service Board.

"I have issued another directive banning strikes, both by ANY public employees and by private employees for a period of three years, during which time I will work with both business and labor with a goal of cooperative solutions, not adversarial ones, as we have now. I have also frozen all union strike funds. No lockouts, either.

"Also, we will be loosening a lot of the overreaching, byzantine regulatory grip that agencies like the EPA, EEOC, OSHA and several others have had on the throat of businesses and individuals for far too long; we will return to levels of sensible, reasonable regulation, not ideologically driven, and we will also pay very little attention to agenda-driven science. I have issued an immediate moratorium on

ANY new regulations and will be going thru each and every existing one, eliminating those that have kept businesses from expanding and/or locating in this country. Several of those are already in directives that you'll be able to find on the web site at ten p.m.

"Now, none of that means that we'll be ignoring the 'safety nets' that our truly vulnerable citizens need, but there will be changes in that area, as well, since our government has done a pretty abysmal job there for several decades.

"On the international front, we face a plethora of issues, both economic and security-related. First, as to our foreign aid policy, we will insist on reciprocal agreements AND performance for every dollar of foreign aid we send out, and renewal of each of our commitments will be based on performance-based criteria. And I will be VERY quick to cut off foreign aid to countries that do not live up to their agreements and promises.

"Our defense department will not see many serious changes in the immediate future, but the Joint Chiefs and I have come to several agreements in which the defense budget can be reduced significantly but wisely, mostly by eliminating the political influences that have controlled many of their past decisions, and without changing either our readiness or our security posture. Our goal there is to be lean, mean and nimble."

Donne frowned at the camera, narrowing his eyes, intimidating everyone watching. "I'm sure that our defenses will be tested in the very near future, but I assure anyone who wants to do that that we will stop any attempts with quick and powerful force, not necessarily proportional. Word to the wise, okay? And on the remote chance that any attempts succeed, our response will be totally out of proportion. I trust that is clear, plain and direct.

"Here in America, most of us are familiar with hearing moms telling their misbehaving kids, 'Just wait till your father gets home.' Well, for anyone who's been misbehaving, inside or outside our borders, I have just two words for you: 'Daddy's Home.' And for those of you who know how I've run Donne Enterprises International, you know I do NOT mess around. Another word to the wise. Got it?

"For some of the biggest bloodsuckers who've been feeding their egos and their bank accounts from the federal trough, that gravy train comes to a halt right now; that includes all lobbyists, PACs and political analysts, because there will be no federal elections for the foreseeable future. As a side benefit, we won't be assaulted with all the negative ads that most political campaigns bombard us with.

"For some others, who've benefited from federal largesse, but not to the bloodsucking level, that ol' gravy train will either come to a halt this January 1st or slow down quickly until coming to a full stop on January 1st of 2013; and that includes ALL business and agricultural subsidies, the so-called 'loopholes' in the now-defunct tax code and the special non-taxable status of most so-called 'nonprofit' institutions. Again, for the truly vulnerable, you will find some changes to the 'safety nets,' but nothing that you won't be able to handle.

"And for the many people in this country who have gotten spoiled, coddled and pandered to by politicians seeking only to be re-elected and refusing to make unpopular but necessary decisions, I will tell you frankly, those days are over. I will not make decisions simply because they'll be unpopular, but I will also not shy away from making needed decisions because they may be unpopular. I don't plan to play Santa Claus, and I will be insisting that Americans start the process, if they haven't already, of growing up.

"There will also be many changes on the social front, most of them designed to increase your personal freedoms and choices. You'll find all of these on the web site at ten p.m., but just for a few quick examples, marijuana will be decriminalized on January 1st, 2012, and production and sales of it will be licensed and taxed, beginning in July 2012, and ..."

Debbie, Darryl and many of the other regulars cheered.

"... gay marrage, abortion and assisted suicide (using the Oregon law as a model) will all be legalized as of January 1st, 2012, about three weeks from today. The same goes for prostitution, using the Nevada laws as a model there. Pornography, too, but not child porn."

At that, a variety of applause and boos resonated through the whole restaurant. Of course, booze circulated, too.

"Additionally, although I am not and never have been a smoker, all federal, state and local laws, statutes, regulations and ordinances restricting smoking in outdoor areas are now repealed, other than within ten feet of entrances to highly trafficked buildings, and local business owners, including, but not limited to, restaurants, bars and retail establishments or any business open to the public, may decide for themselves whether smoking will be allowed in and on their premises."

Debbie, Darryl and many of the others cheered even more loudly. In the back office, Joe and Pete exchanged glances and smiled. Joe made another note.

"As for Donne Enterprises International, some of you know that I've become a multi-billionaire over the past three decades, but as of today, I've severed my operational relationship with the company, leaving it in the capable hands of my COO, chief operations officer, Wes Farley. And, Wes, I have to let you know that you'll be getting no favors and no inside information from me. You're on your own, and I know you'll do right by the company, its clients and employees.

"And as a tiny sign of my confidence in my plans for the country, I'm immediately donating two billion dollars from my personal wealth toward the 2012 deficit, and I encourage others on my economic level to do similarly. Together with (ready for another buzzword?) shared sacrifices, we will be able to pull this country not only back from the brink and up by its bootstraps, but forward into a successful and sustainable growth trajectory and to return to our rightful place as a shining beacon to freedom- and success-seeking people around the world.

"Now, putting all the needed policies in place is sort of like putting a huge jigsaw puzzle together, and a lot of smart and dedicated people have been working with me on these policies for months as we've prepared for this occasion, and so far tonight, I've spoken mostly in generalities. Now I'm going to give you some of the details -- not all of them, 'cause I don't have the time and I doubt many of you watching this do, either -- but here are a few of the major ones, mainly on income taxes for businesses and individuals.

"But first, since I've fired the President and the entire Congress and there'll be no more federal elections for the foreseeable future, I will be confiscating all campaign funds, all PAC and SuperPAC monies and all lobbying funds held by registered or unregistered lobbyists and applying them to the deficit."

Everybody in Slinky Joe's cheered, other than Debbie Jackson, who had fallen asleep with her face on the bar; she awoke enough to give out a groggy "Yay" and then closed her eyes again, a little bit of drool sliding onto her forearm.

(Author's note: Here come the numbers. Policy wonks: notepads ready? JD)

"Now, as to taxes, major changes. Here to my left is the current tax code, totaling more than 72,000 pages. Here's the new one, three pages for individuals, ten pages for businesses. Here's some details.

"Effective January 1st, 2012, there'll be a maximum rate of 21% of GAAP earnings for businesses with over $10 billion in revenues, with no subsidies or so-called 'loopholes,' 100% expensing, with a territorial system, and dividends will be fully deductible; in fact, dividends paid in 2012 will be granted a 150% deduction, not just a hundred. This will apply no matter what form of business structure you have, be it corporate, partnership or sole proprietorship. For businesses with less than a million dollars in revenue, the rate will be 10%; between a million and 10 million, 12%; between 10 million and 100 million, 14%; between 100 million and one billion, 16%; and between one billion and ten billion, 18%. The maximum rate of 21% kicks in when revenues are above $10 billion. Those rates will apply to all earnings, not tiered, as with individual tax rates."

In the back office, Pete said to Joe, "That's good, right?" Joe nodded and said, "I think so; I'll have to run the numbers to be sure, but it sounds good."

"And since businesses will have no more lobbying expenses, they will give the government the average annual amount they've spent on lobbying, including campaign contributions, over the last five years, in addition to their taxes. Since there will be no more federal lobbying, I'd encourage all businesses to get refunds, to the extent they can, of any prepaid lobbying expenses.

"Also, to encourage the repatriation of the trillion-plus dollars held overseas, we will only charge a 5% tax rate on funds repatriated in the first six months of 2012.

"For individuals, the top rate will be 27% of all income, earned and unearned, with NO deductions or exemptions and only two tax credits: the foreign tax credit and a new charitable tax credit of 50%, limited to 40% of your income tax liability. So if you donate a thousand dollars to your favorite charity, you'll be able to take five hundred bucks off your tax bill, which is much more generous than the current charitable deduction. Lower rates of 6, 12, 18 and 24 percent will apply at income levels below $1,300,000 for individuals, and the first $20,000 is not taxed at all. Incomes from 20 thousand to 40 thousand will be taxed at only six percent. From 40 thousand to 100 thousand, you'll pay a flat 12 percent; between 100 thousand and 300 thousand, it'll be 18 percent; and it'll be 24 percent on the next million. That's for individuals. For couples filing jointly, double those numbers and subtract one percentage point from the tax rate; that should help balance out the 'marriage penalty.'

"The capital loss offset against ordinary income will be raised from the current $3,000 to $25,000, and then indexed for inflation in future years; again, double that for couples. No change to the carryover provisions. Also, as of January 1st, there will be no differentiation between short- and long-term gains or losses, and neither you nor your broker will have to report all your individual trades; you'll be able to rely on your broker's summary of capital gains or losses and report that on a single line on your tax return.

"Social Security benefits will not be taxed, but welfare, unemployment payments, food stamps and other federally-funded benefits will be.

"There will also be a minimum tax of a little under two bucks a day for every resident, other than those who are listed as dependents on another taxpayer's return and those under age 18 or over 80, beginning in 2013, but only half of that, a bit under a dollar a day, starting in 2012.

"There will be no alternative minimum tax nor any estate tax.

"And since Democrats have generally tended to call for higher taxes, we'll give you what you want; everybody who is registered as a Democrat will pay a 20% surcharge on their income tax bill. Registered Republicans will pay a 15% surcharge, since they've generally called for lower taxes, but have also increased spending on a near par with Democrats. Registered independents will pay a 10% surcharge. This will be based on your registration as of today, so there's no point in rushing to change that. If you are not a registered voter, there'll be no surcharge. I will reconsider these surcharges for the 2014 tax year, but you can count on them for 2012 and 2013.

"There will be a national sales tax, on everything except labor, energy, medicine and consumer medical equipment, of 4%, beginning on April 1st, 2012, with an offsetting nonrefundable tax credit of $375 for those whose total income is at or below 125% of the poverty level. On January 1st, 2013, that credit will increase to $500. Again, double that for couples filing jointly. This tax will also apply to all online retailers who deliver to customers within the USA.

"The amount that triggers a 1099 will be increased to $1,000.

"The limit on contributions to the tax-free Roth IRA will be doubled to $10,000 for 2012 and go up by 1,000 dollars each year after that for the next ten years. I would strongly encourage each of you to contribute that maximum, if you can.

"One special additional tax will only apply to people who've worked at high levels in the federal government and then gone on to leverage their position into a high-paying job in the private sector, what we've come to call the 'revolving door,' or to demand big bucks for speaking, writing or other celebrity pursuits. And that tax will be 50% of any income they make as a result, in addition to their regular income tax. This tax will also apply to anyone who has been entitled to Secret Service protection since the year 1990.

"As for non-profits, all 501(c)(2, 3, 4 and 5) institutions with revenues of over a million dollars a year will be taxed at the greater of 50% of gross donation and/or grant revenues OR 50% of their average annual gross donation and/or grant revenues over the past five years; it'll be 20% for those under a million, 10 percent on those under $100,000 per year, and zero on those under 20,000. Local governments may also begin charging them property taxes; no more tax exemptions there. And they will also have to pay the national sales tax, as well as state and local sales taxes.

"Combined with the charitable donation tax credit AND the fact that as of this moment, the federal government will no longer be giving grants to ANY nonprofits, donors will be able to exercise much greater freedom of choice as to those institutions they want to support. Which nonprofits thrive and which don't survive will be up to the PEOPLE, not bureaucrats.

"We will be creating an app for filing your simplified tax returns, which will work securely across all platforms; that'll be ready by mid-2012, so you'll be able to file your returns on your smartphone, PC or any mobile device.

"Individuals will also have the choice of filing their 2011 taxes under the new rules or the current ones, whichever is more advantageous for you.

"And to combat identity theft and tax refund fraud, individual

22

taxpayers will need to provide a thumbprint on their paper form or in the app that we'll be creating for the digital platforms. Obviously, we'll have alternatives for amputees and others unable to provide a thumbprint, and we'll work hard to address any privacy concerns.

"Also, when our GDP growth rate has reached five percent, halfway to my goal, I will look very seriously at lowering both business and individual tax rates. But we've got to get there first, okay? Another word to the wise.

"Another tax, but one with which I expect near-zero compliance, is a 150% tax on all revenues from criminal activity, especially drug dealing, combined with much tougher penalties for failure to pay that tax at a local bank or police station within 12 hours of receiving the revenues. While that may not generate many dollars directly, it will give prosecutors a new tool to fight serious crime, and penalties will include confiscation of ALL of the criminals' assets, using the same burden of proof the IRS uses, and as you all probably know, the IRS can be relentless. I call that the Al Capone tax, and it begins right" ... Donne snapped his fingers ... "now."

"Also, lawyers, individual or as business entities, will pay double the tax rates I outlined earlier, and major penalties, again with the IRS burden of proof, will apply if any lawyer does not comply."

At that, the entire crowd in Slinky Joe's erupted in applause and cheers, other than from one table in the corner, where two attorneys were dining with their mistresses, and from one woman, Colleen, the wife of an ambulance-chasing lawyer, who was at another table with her lover, Keith, a local developer, whose wife, Damin, was having a torrid affair with Bill, a local dentist; Bill's wife, Deirdre, was involved in an equally torrid affair with Tom, an ex-councilman.

Tom's wife, Nicole, was having an affair with Isabel, the wife of Karsten, a local Elvis impersonator, who was currently belting out a gratingly off-key rendition of "Blue Suede Shoes" at The Coach, a competitor of Slinky Joe's across US 41 in the hardware plaza, whose owners had not even mentioned the speech to their customers.

Karsten, in turn, was having his own affair with Ned, the owner of a closet-organizing franchise. Karsten and Isabel's marriage was clearly a double-beard.

Ned's wife, Sandy, was at that moment sharing a bouncing bed at a local motel with Anthony, the president of the local branch of a national bank and deeply involved in money laundering for the Sinachoa drug cartel, while Anthony's wife, Jessica, was shrieking with fake delight in Colleen's bedroom with Colleen's husband, Joe.

"Double the tax?" Colleen muttered to herself. "I'd better divorce that sleaze bag now, while the getting is good."

Donne continued, "Additionally, both sides of settlements in any divorce at or above $200,000 will be taxed at 20 percent."

Colleen reconsidered briefly, but only briefly.

On the following Monday, she met with a high-priced divorce lawyer, as did thousands of lawyers' spouses all around the country. Thousands of domestic violence complaints were lodged against lawyers over the weekend and in the following months.

Donne continued, "You'll be able to find all the details of the new tax code in Section 2 on the web site at ten p.m. tonight.

"When you get to the web site, you'll find an index by subject, like energy, education, health care, insurance, defense and tort reform, just for a few examples, so you can quickly find the directives that are of particular interest to you. None of the directives are more than three pages long and, again, they're all written in clear, straight-forward English. You'll also be able to find a 'Download All' link where you can download and save or print all of the directives I signed today; they're available in a variety of formats. And each and every one of my future directives will be uploaded by midnight of the day I issue them.

"There's also a link there for feedback, and I personally want to encourage anybody to use that link and tell me what you think about the directives I've issued so far and make any suggestions you want for future policy. I know that opens us up to lots of nutcases and passionate malcontents, and obviously we'll screen those out, but if you've got some reasonable and well-thought-out ideas, I want them to reach me so I can consider them. I particularly want to hear from people who have firsthand information and opinions about absurdities, corruption and inefficiencies in government that need to be fixed, especially in the regulatory arena.

"We'll also be setting up teams here to utilize all forms of social media and get good back-and-forth communications going.

"And I'll give a very public hint to you investment types: do a lot of analysis of ALL the pieces to help you decide what you want to do when the stock, bond and currency markets open on Monday. I will make no predictions on that, other than that I would expect some volatility during the early part of this transition.

"But I will let all traders and investors know that as of midnight tonight, the uptick rule will be reinstated, and as of February 1st, 2012, the wash sale rule will be repealed. As of January 1st, naked shorting will be rooted out and SEVERELY punished. So if you're holding any naked shorts, you've got three weeks to unwind those. Yet another word to the wise.

"Now, I know many of you watching this have interrupted your Friday night entertainment, so I'm going to wrap this up with just a few final thoughts.

"First, the web site with all the directives I've issued today, as well as a replay of this speech, which will be active at precisely ten p.m. tonight, is www._____.gov, as you see here on the screen. It is hosted on Donne Enterprises servers, with multiple mirror sites, so anyone who wants to dig into those details can do so, with no worries about the servers crashing, even if those Anonymous clowns try one of their cyberattacks.

"Second, while this has been a very general speech, with only a few specifics, by noon tomorrow, I will have posted a series of videos going over all the details of today's directives, section by section. Those videos will also be available on Donne Enterprises servers, and the web address is www._____1.gov, as you see below. So just add the number 1 to the other web address.

"Third, I'll be looking forward to the Sunday morning talk shows, and I fully expect to see all the usual spin doctors, poll dancers (that's p-o-l-l, by the way), pundits, special interest people, professional mudslingers and possibly even a few reasonable analysts, and if you watch any or all of those shows, I'd encourage you to carefully consider their biases, constituencies and/or clients as you listen to what they say. Keep your eyes and ears open for hints of greed, direct or indirect; another word to the wise, okay? And watch how they play with the word 'fair.' Oh, remember the sandbox on the Titanic, too.

"Finally, I'll be conducting a televised press conference on Tuesday afternoon, starting at one p.m., for all journalists with White House credentials, so I'd suggest you gather your thoughts and questions and be prepared for an interesting afternoon. I hope all of you can come up with some great 'gotcha' questions, which I will certainly welcome, other than questions which try to get me to play in that sandbox on one side or the other.

"Oh, a few quick additional things I almost forgot. First, no more anchor babies, and for those anchor babies who are now under ten years old, the rights and benefits given to them and their relatives have been revoked as of this moment.

"Second, if you remember when the dollar was on the gold standard, we're going to do the same thing, but instead of gold, we'll use oil. So the value of the dollar will now be one-sixtieth of one barrel of West Texas Intermediate crude oil, or sixty bucks a barrel, and one-seventieth of one barrel of Brent North Sea crude, or seventy bucks a barrel, as of right now. Sorry, longs; and shorts, don't gloat.

"Third, speaking of oil, and energy in general, I have issued directives that ensure that drilling on federal lands and waters and the construction of nuclear power plants will require only NOTICE, not permits and approvals and environmental impact statements and other bureaucratic delaying tactics. I've also approved the Keystone pipeline, with a few restrictions.

"Fourth, Obamacare, mostly gone; Dodd-Frank, totally re-evaluated, mostly gone; cap and trade, never."

A mixture of applause and boos filled Slinky Joe's.

"Fifth, I will have a budget prepared by February 1st, 2012, for the rest of this fiscal year that will reduce spending by a minimum of 20 percent, and by May 31st, we'll have a budget for FY 2013 that has a minimum 33 percent reduction. And that is based on current spending, NOT projected baselines. The FY 2014 budget will be balanced, with possibly even a slight surplus.

"Finally, I would also invite all the economists out there to submit their analyses of the economic impact of the policies I've put in place, including everything that will be on the web site this evening, and to include charts of their predictions of GDP, deficits and debt over the next 20 years, using both static and dynamic analysis. The CBO and OMB will be doing that, as well, all to be in my office by close of business this coming Monday.

"With that, I wish you all a very good evening, and for those of you who will want to do your analyses, a very busy and productive weekend. And a very happy holiday season to all. Good night."

In the back office, Joe turned to Pete and said, "Well, looks like it's gonna be a long weekend. Wow."

Pete replied, "Yup, but you're the numbers guy. I'll get back out there and see how the customers are taking that all in and get Salt and Pepper back onstage, get things going again."

Marion leaned over to George and said, "Honey, let's pay the bill and get home; I need to look at those directives as soon as they're online." George smiled, reached for his wallet and said, "Omaha." He dropped a twenty on the table, heaved himself out of his chair, grabbed his walker and shuffled toward the door. Marion did a quick calculation in her head, opened her purse, dropped another twenty, sighed, rolled her eyes and headed after George.

Darryl poked Debbie, who was still asleep and snoring, and said, "Let's go out to my truck." Debbie opened her eyes groggily, slurred, "Mmm, okay," and they staggered out of the bar. They returned ten minutes later.

-6-

Saturday, December 10, 2011
2:25 a.m. (8:25 p.m. EST)
St. Tropez, France

A man with many names clicked from a 24-hour news channel to the local French news channel, checked the time on his diamond-encrusted watch, took another sip from his glass of the most expensive wine in the world and smiled at his reflection in the window of his villa overlooking the marina in St. Tropez. In the light of the full moon, he could just make out the imposing silhouette of his 39-meter yacht, custom built to his precise specifications. But that was not why he was smiling. What curved the corners of his mouth slightly up was the certain knowledge that his skills as the world's most talented assassin would soon be called for, and aside from his standard fee of 20 million euros, he knew he would enjoy the challenge. He had no doubt as to the target; his only curiosity was who the client might turn out to be.

But as he settled back into his hot tub with the latest novel by the author who put Sanibel on the literary map, he had no inkling that before everything was over, he would have contracts from nineteen discrete (and, of course, discreet) clients, all with the same target ... and the same fee, of course. So he would make a real killing by making a real killing.

-7-

Friday, December 9, 2011
8:45 p.m. EST
Cyberspace

As soon as Donne's speech concluded, hackers both in and out of Anonymous began spreading the word that at precisely 9:58 p.m., the most massive Denial of Service (DOS) attack ever attempted would begin, and by 8:45, the instructions for that had spread to over five thousand individual hackers, each of whom controlled an average of 178.3 computers scattered all around the world. In gleeful anticipation of shutting down the servers at Donne Enterprises, many of them ran upstairs to raid their parents' pantries and refrigerators for provisions, mostly corn chips, potato chips and chocolate sodas, and then scurried back down to their basements.

*   *   *   *   *   *

8:45 p.m. EST
Bonita Springs, FL

Marion headed to their riverfront mansion on the south side of their luxurious gated community. Once she got inside and got George comfortably settled in his recliner, she got on the phone and called all of her friends in her book club, investment club and even a few of the Bonita Hookers (they hooked rugs) to make sure they all knew what had happened and were ready to go online at ten and watch the replay, as well as digging into the directives.

*   *   *   *   *   *

8:45 p.m. EST
Bonita Springs, FL

Back at Slinky Joe's, Joe was in the office, going over his notes, Pete was out front, going table to table, chatting with the many people who remained, Salt and Pepper were back on stage, and Debbie was alone on the dance floor, unsteadily shaking and wriggling her scrawny body as provocatively as she could. Darryl was sitting bleary-eyed at the bar, sipping his eighth beer; three to go before he'd try to drive the nine miles back to his trailer park, hoping to avoid another DUI.

* * * * * *

8:45 p.m. EST
The Capitol
Washington, DC

On the House floor, now-ex-Members of Congress and Supreme Court justices had been heatedly discussing the events of the day and ways in which they might resist Donne's surprise takeover. Never in the history of the building had the decibel level come anywhere near what it was this evening ... and it was bipartisan.

At 8:45, the doors opened and hundreds of side-armed Marines in battle fatigues swarmed the chamber, and, in pairs, escorted each Member to his or her office and oversaw the removal of all personal items and the exit of each from the premises, during which all phones were given back and notices not to return were distributed.

A similar process was followed with each Supreme Court justice, and with absent Members of Congress over the next few weeks.

-8-

Friday, December 9, 2011
9:59:59 p.m. EST
Donne Enterprises International Server Farm

The duty technician flipped a switch and all the sites and mirror sites went live. On the home page, just below the "Replay Speech" link, the First Directive stated that "Each and every directive issued by this office shall include by reference the following: 'Any and all constitutional provisions, statutes, case law, common law, executive orders, regulations, ordinances and/or rules of any type, at any level of government, federal, state or local, are hereby declared null and void as they run counter to this directive only, but shall remain in effect for all other purposes.'" Below that was an index by topic.

In the security office, the duty technician watched as DEI's anti-hacking algorithms recognized the DOS attacks and automatically and rapidly disabled the IP addresses involved in the attacks; all the mirror sites stayed online. Nobody accessing the sites experienced any difficulty. This event also provided feedback for DEI's cybersecurity staff in defending against cyberattacks from China, Iran and other countries in the future.

But in nearly five thousand basements around the world, corn chips, potato chips and chocolate soda dropped and/or spilled on keyboards, mice and floors.

* * * * * *

Friday, December 9, 2011
9:01 p.m. CST (10:01 EST)
Dothan, Alabama

Steven O. Burns, Esquire, logged on from his office at the national trial lawyers society's headquarters, clicked on the link for "Legal Reform," read the entire section, downloaded and printed it all, then picked up the phone and dialed.

"Speak."

"It's bad, John. Not only has he doubled our tax rate and banned advertising, he's ordered 'loser pays,' and he's limiting any lawyer in federal courts to a 5% contingency fee, 2% for class actions, and a max of $100 per hour for individual clients, $200 for businesses, with a max of two lawyers per side."

"WHAT? That's price-fixing!"

"Not only that, but any lawyer who files a frivolous or nuisance lawsuit will be fined 10% of his total assets, NOT net worth, for the first offense, 30% for a second and 50% for a third and beyond, and that's NOT billable to clients. And he can unilaterally declare ANY lawsuit frivolous or a nuisance, even in state and local courts."

"Jesus."

"Same thing goes for what he's calling 'egregious delaying tactics' and for over-billing and double-billing. He's also cutting off lawsuits under the Americans with Disabilities Act, as well as environmental suits, even below the federal level."

"Christ."

"And he's encouraging the states to follow his examples."

"Shit. We've got to do something. We'll sue the sonofabitch."

"We'll figure something out. But I've got a lot more to do on all of these directives. I've just scratched the surface."

"I've got the site split between all our top guys, so you just stick

29

with the section you're on and we'll all go over the whole thing Sunday afternoon at headquarters. Two o'clock."

"Got it; two o'clock. See ya then, John."

"Keep at it, Steve."

*   *   *   *   *   *

Overnight
Cyberspace

Within minutes of Donne's speech, the brouhaha that had engaged the blogosphere and all social media since early in the day, when a few leaks came out about something happening (although no one seemed to have a clear handle on the actual facts) transformed itself into all-out chaos and full-blown polarization, both with paid bloggers from every special interest and with amateurs. It quickly degenerated, as it usually did, into personal attacks by one commenter on another ... or on all the others. "SSDD," as one comment read.

-9-
Six Months Earlier

Sunday, June 12, 2011
11:08 a.m.
Bonita Beach, Florida

Eight men and one woman were working the beach and the shallow waters with metal detectors. The two men in waist-deep water were methodically repeating the grid patterns they'd run every weekend day for several years, but the six men and one woman on the beach appeared to be total newbies, wandering aimlessly, awkwardly swinging their detectors back and forth, finding nothing. But if one listened closely to the two in the water, one could hear them muttering to each other as they passed, "Goddamn penny pitchers."

Pam set her beach bag down, flipped open a chair and slithered into it, giving Jake a winning smile and batting her blues at him over her elegant sunglasses.

"Just call me Pam."

"And you can call me Jake, okay?"

"Okay, Jake."

Jake reached into his beach bag briefly, then into his cooler, pulled out a plastic sandwich bag, held it out to her and said, "I've always wanted to say this. Want a cookie, little girl?"

Pam laughed, a deep, open laugh, and said, with an exaggerated Southern belle accent, "Why, suh, I hardly know you." Then, dropping the accent, "Don't mind if I do. Homemade?"

"Not by a long shot. Closest I come to the C-word is heating cinnamon rolls from a tube in a convection oven."

"The C-word?"

"Hard for me to even say it ... c-c-c-cook."

"Oh." Pam chuckled as she reached into the bag. "But wouldn't that be the B-word?"

"The B-word?'"

Pam chuckled. "Bake."

"There's a difference?" Jake said, looking blank and naive.

Pam looked at him quizzically.

"Sorry, just pulling your leg. They're from a dollar store, a buck a bag."

Pam took a bite, carefully licking all the crumbs from her lips. "Mmm, that's good. Thank you."

"You're welcome."

Pam glanced at the water over Jake's shoulder and giggled. Jake turned and saw a little girl, maybe a year and a half old, putting wet sand in her mouth. A teenaged girl, maybe her older sister, said, "Tara, don't eat the sand. It's not dinnertime yet." Jake chuckled, and when the girl and the toddler came past him on the way back to their chairs, he asked the girl if he could use her line in his novel. She said, "Sure." Jake wrote briefly in his notebook.

Then he turned back to Pam and smiled.

"So, Pam, what brings a gorgeous young woman like you to visit an old fart like me?"

"Well, thanks for that, Jake, but I'm not that young. And you don't look that old." She paused, wrinkled her brow and continued, "I guess after the emails we've swapped, I just wanted to meet you in person and, well, see what makes you tick and how you came to be writing this book of yours."

"Hmm. Okay. Long story or short?"

"Whatever you want; I've got all day."

Jake smiled. "Okay. But first I've gotta tell ya that it's incredibly hard for me to be serious for very long. My record so far is three and a half minutes. All right. So here goes.

"About four, five years ago, I was living in Myrtle Beach, South Carolina, hanging out at the beach, and I thought I'd write a book about all the stuff I was seeing and hearing about, like the history and people's experiences and anecdotes of life there. There was all kinds of interesting stuff on the beach, too. So I got it all done and ready for publication, with the title 'Myrtle Beach Memories.'"

"Nice title."

"Yeah. And then another guy up there put together a lot of photos of women in bikinis, called it 'Myrtle Beach Mammaries,' and started selling it to tourists. So when I started to try selling mine ... well, let's put it this way. The boobs were more interested in boobs."

Pam stifled a laugh. "Oh, I'm sorry. That must have hurt."

"Yup, and after a while, I quit trying to sell the book.

"But as I was talking with people up there, many of them were also saying a lot of political things, mostly angry with the government, similar to the stuff in the first part of Donne's speech."

"And this was when again?"

"Um, '05 until maybe early '08 – no, middle of '08, fallish, just after TARP and the Lehman bankruptcy and all that stuff.

"So I started asking people up there more political questions, and as we moved toward the election, people's opinions got more and more polarized and sometimes downright vicious, but most all of them were pretty angry, on both sides. And they were VERY emotional, but not very rational and reasonable."

"I remember that, all around the country, not just Myrtle Beach."

"And it got even worse after the election."

"So are you a Republican or a Dem- – oh, I'm sorry. I shouldn't be asking that."

"Neither, actually, but I don't tell anybody who I vote for."

"No problem; I can understand that. Sorry."

"Anyhow, then I decided to go somewhere else and do the same kind of thing. I bumped into a web site, DiscoverBonitaSprings.com, liked what I saw and moved here in, um, April? Yeah, April of '09. And I found the same kind of political anger here. And then --"

A somewhat heavyset woman in her mid-fifties, jogging by near the waterline, waved and said, "Hi, Jake."

"Oh, hey, Dr. Deb. How ya doing?"

Dr. Deb paused, jogging in place. "Fine, fine. You?"

"Mostly sunny. Pam, this is Dr. Debbie Jackson; Dr. Deb, Pam."

"Nice to meet you, Pam."

"Same here."

"See y'all later." She jogged off.

Pam looked back at Jake. "Dr. Deb?"

"Yup. She's a psychologist, private practice. She let me use her for the Debbie Jackson character ... well, her name, at least."

"That's the skanky one in Slinky Joe's?"

"Right."

"Cool." She paused. "So then?"

"Well, then I started trying to think about all those opinions and a lot of the anger, get some perspective on it all.

"You've seen the approval rating of Congress, right?"

"Oh, yeah. Low teens, like 13 percent, somewhere in there."

"Yup. And probably headed lower. And remember the Speaker of the House saying, 'We've got to pass the bill to find out what's in it'? I think that was on Obamacare."

Pam laughed. "Yeah, I remember that."

"And remember that idiot Congressman who was worried that if the Marines added eight thousand troops to their contingent on Guam, the island might tip over?"

Pam laughed even harder. "Oh, God, yes. Totally embarrassing."

Jake laughed along, and then frowned. "But somebody elected him. Ever watched the nighttime talk show segment where the host interviews people on the street who are so ignorant?"

"Yeah."

"It's frightening, frankly, 'cause these people can vote. In fact, I think he should rename the segment as 'And These People Vote?' -- or make that a tag line after each segment."

Pam chuckled and said, "And they reproduce."

Jake nodded and then said, "Oh, did you ever see that movie ... oh, what was the title?" He rubbed his forehead. "Damn. Silly plot, but the first three minutes were great. Had a yuppie kind of couple having a serious discussion about holding off on having children until their careers were in good shape, and then a trailer trashy couple yelling and popping kids out one right after the other ..."

Pam said, "Oh, yeah, I did see it ... the one with the incredibly stupid rapper as President later on?"

Jake said, "Yup, that's the one. Oh, what was the name? Damn."

Pam shrugged. "It'll come back."

Jake continued. "Okay; we'll see.

"Anyhow, then you've got the Democrats and Republicans playing what I'd call 'Politics Over Policy,' and we've got that sandbox analogy that I had Donne give in his speech."

"Oh, on the back deck of the Titanic?"

"That's the one.

"So as I was thinking about all this stuff, I began wondering what could happen if we got politics out of policy-making and got rid of the whole election-to-election pendulum and uncertainty."

"Impossible."

"Probably. But remember, this is fiction. Anyhow, I got thinking, what about a complete do-over, a blank slate?"

"Tabula rasa."

Jake looked a little more closely at Pam. "Exactly, but I wasn't even thinking about writing anything yet. But I realized that a do-over might call for a dictator of some sort, who didn't have to pander to the voters to stay in office. So I started talking about that idea with people, asking the ones who bitched the most about the government what they would do if they were in total charge and could make whatever policies they wanted to. And not one of them actually had any real policy ideas; they just kept bashing the government in general and the party they opposed in particular and with lots of passion. But the idea of a benevolent dictator kept running around in my tired old brain. So the next question would be how to get from here to there."

"Like a violent overthrow of the government?"

"Thought about that, but that's such a cliche."

"And treasonous."

"But even worse, not practical. Look at what's been going on with the Arab Spring. Nope. But I thought back to Pelosi's comment and figured somebody could sneak something into a must-pass bill that declares someone the boss and get in that way, all nice and legal. Bingo. Basic setup done. Then it's just a matter of deciding what he's going to do and who or what is going to be the antagonist or antagonists, and there's the story. But not as simple as it sounds."

"Hmm; I'd guess not."

"So I added that to my list of things to talk about with people here in Bonita. We've got lots of retirees and many of them have run businesses, some have worked in union jobs, a whole spectrum of folks, and lots more in tourist season than are here now. And when I started asking the right questions, they gave me lots of ideas from their experiences, and round about January, I think, I wrote a first draft of Donne's speech and put it online, started getting some feedback and new ideas, including yours."

"But not the minimum tax."

"Nope; I don't remember who that came from, but it's a pretty cool idea, especially trying to figure out the 'what ifs' that would spin out from that.

"Anyhow, it all sorta morphed into the idea of doing a novel.

"But then there was one guy on the beach, kind of a sarcastic, arrogant --"

A shrill female voice broke through their conversation, "Billy Lee, Stevie Bruce, kit thowin' sand!" Jake and Pam looked toward the water and saw two young boys, maybe six and four, doing exactly that, with each other as the target.

Pam stifled a laugh and mouthed the words, "Stevie Bruce? Thowing?"

Jake shrugged and laughed quietly.

"Billy Lee, Stevie Bruce, I said KIT IT!!!! You wanna whuppin'?"

Jake smiled. "From Lehigh; lotsa rednecks out there. Her name's Ginny May."

Pam giggled again, "Ginny May what?"

"No, just Ginny May; Ginny for Virginia, and May is her last name. Her hubby is Frank May; everybody calls him Frannie."

"Really?"

"Really. Met 'em about a year ago. And see those heavy ladies

34

with her? That's her sis-in-law, Sally, and her mom, Lurlene."

"Lurlene? No way."

"Way. She's a great cook, I've heard."

"Wow, Frannie May, Ginny May, Sally, Lurlene and ... Stevie Bruce." Pam started to giggle, then a full-out laugh. "Stevie Bruce."

Jake put on his own deep Southern accent and drawled, "Who'da thunk it?" And he started to laugh, too.

Then he paused, got his laughing under control, scratched his head, and said, "I forgot. Where was I?"

Pam, still chuckling, scrunched up her face, paused a moment and then said, "Something about a sarcastic guy?"

"Oh, right.   There was this one guy named Alan, who sometimes fishes here from the beach, kind of a sarcastic, arrogant asshole ... oh, pardon my French ..."

Pam waved it off and smiled.   "No problem; that's one of my favorite words."

"Really? Cool. Anyhow, way back, probably in early February, this clown said something like 'If you write something like that, the black helicopters'll be coming for you.'   And even though I was thinking of this all as a sort of silly exercise in total fiction, that did kind of scare me some, 'cause people in power don't like to hear anything that might rock their boat, fiction or not. So I kinda backed off for a while, pushed all those thoughts down, and went back to just being the guy on the beach who tells good bad jokes and doesn't take too much too seriously ... and doesn't get taken too seriously, either."

Jake shivered, took a deep breath and said, "Then a week or so later, I had my first black helicopter nightmare."

-10-

Saturday, December 10, 2011
7:10 a.m. EST
New York City, New York

Jonathan Payne picked up his usual papers as he returned to his Park Avenue penthouse from his morning jog, glancing at the headlines as he rode up in his private elevator.   One blared "BILLIONAIRE BUYS AMERICA," with the subhead "Disaster or Opportunity?" Another read "OBAMA OUT, DONNE IN," another read "DONNE DID IT," another went with "DONNE DONE IT," one went even further, with "DONNE DONE DID IT," and the bottom one in the stack, the only paper to remember Donne's middle name, read "G.O.D. BUYS U.S.A. W.T.F.?"

Back in his penthouse, Payne perused each paper patiently and persistently, making notes on a yellow legal pad, occasionally double-checking Donne's directives on his PC, until he had 27 pages of tightly written analysis and had downed seven large mugs of his favorite coffee.

When Jennifer, his trophy wife (the third, and twenty years younger than his second), blonde, with one of those squeaky voices that's cute at first, but grates badly after about four months, brought him an eighth mug, Jonathan leaned back, stretched and groaned as she massaged his neck and shoulders.

"Poopsie, don't you think it's time for a break? You've been at this for three hours straight."

"Oh, that's good, Jenn ... yeah, right there ... a little higher on the neck ... ahhhhh, nice ... hey, you remember Gordy Donne?"

"Gordy, Gordy? Oh, you mean that awkward little guy who came to our wedding? With the three Amazons with him?"

"Yeah; those were his bodyguards ... oh, good; you got it ... maybe a little harder, right there. He's the guy who just bought the country."

"Oh, I heard something about that; Marsha and Pat were talking about it at the gym this morning. That was last night, right?"

"Right."

"And he really bought the whole country?"

"Right. I can't believe he finally pulled it off; he's been wanting to do that for years."

"So is that good or bad?"

"Some of both, but mostly good, from what I've looked at so far."

"Okay."

"I've got to start calling the board, let them know we're not going to build those new plants in Brazil and China; we'll be better off building them right here, probably in Florida or Texas, maybe Indiana or Wisconsin."

"Oh, I love Florida. Are we gonna go back there soon?"

"Maybe in January. But I'm going to be pretty busy for the next few weeks."

"More than usual? You're already working too hard. I'm afraid you're gonna give yourself a heart attack."

"Oh, Jenn, you worry too much. And you know I get bored when things are just ... ahhh, that feels great. Where did you ever learn to do that?"

"Massage school. Those spots right behind your ears are super-sensitive. And I've got good thumbs, of course."

"Best thumbs on the Upper East Side."

"Don't you know it, Poopsie."

"Love you, Jenn. But I've got to get to the phone now."

"Oh, damn, I was hoping to entice you into the bedroom before I

have to get ready for that charity lunch at the Bernsteins'."
"Feeling a little frisky, huh?"
"Oh, more than a little."
"Maybe when you get back, okay?"
"Okay, Poopsie. Your neck feel better?"
"Absolutely, Jenn."
"Maybe I'll need you to zip me up after I shower."
"Maybe I'll do that. Off you go now."
"Okay, lovey. Remember, don't work too hard."
"Okay."
"Promise?"
"Cross my heart."
"Okay, then. Ta-ta for now."
Jonathan stretched one last time and picked up his phone.
"Hey, Phil; it's Jon ... fine ... have you been studying Donne's stuff? Me, too. Look, I think we need to reconsider the China and Brazil plants ... right ... oh, you, too? Good. And we might think about bringing more of our overseas profits back and paying a big dividend in Q1 ... yeah, a big one. And we might look at buying some plants here instead of building; lots of vacant stuff around ... right. I was thinking that one in Tampa; we could get a good deal on that if we move fast. But I think a lot of CEOs are thinking like I am now, and I don't want to get into bidding wars ... precisely. Look, have your staff get a proposal done on those three issues and we'll get it to the board Monday, so put a rush on it, okay? What? No, I've been focused on Donne's stuff, haven't had it on. Hang on ... oh, geez. Is that those Occupy gangsters again? Look at 'em. Christ, haven't they learned anything? 'Gimme, gimme, gimme.' Like little spoiled teenagers ... I know, I know; right. Oh, that reminds me. How are we doing on setting up those intern and apprenticeship programs? Remember, my goal there is thirty cities by the end of next quarter, thirty thousand new ... oh, good, nineteen? Good progress, Phil. Okay; give me a buzz whenever. I'll be available. Bye."
Jonathan stretched again, rolled his neck and made another phone call.
"Hi, Amber. It's Jon Payne. Very good, thank you. I'll need a guard for my wife in about an hour; she's walking over to Fifth Avenue, and that Occupy movement may be on her route ... no, she insists on walking ... I know; can't live without 'em, either ... no, I think one'll be enough ... Wayne? Yeah, he'll be fine. About eleven. Just have him buzz when he arrives and I'll let him into the elevator. And she'll be coming back later ... hang on a second."
Jonathan hit the mute button and walked into the master bath suite, where Jennifer had just started her shower.
"Hey, Jenn, how long will that lunch take?"
"Oh, Poopsie, I can leave early if you want me to."

"No, no, no, take your time; I just need to give the bodyguard a rough idea of how long you'll be there."

"Ohhhh, shucks. Why do I need a guard, anyhow?"

"The Occupy gang is out again."

"Damn. Okay. I think we'll be done around two, maybe two-thirty."

"Okay."

"Can you get Wayne and Linda? I like them."

"Okay. Holler if you need a zip."

"I may need more than that, Poopsie, and I'll do more than holler."

"Okay."

"Be sure to take your little pill about two-thirty, Poopsie, okay?"

"Okay."

"Promise?"

"Promise."

Relieved that he'd hit the mute button before talking with her, Jonathan returned to the living room and hit it again.

"Hey, Amber, can we get both Wayne and Linda? Jenn likes 'em … great. And it looks like she'll be in there till about two-thirty or so… ah, the Bernsteins … yeah … oh, they do? Good; so they can just wait in there, then, with the others, okay? Good. By the way, do you still have that no-tipping policy? Okay. But your folks are so good, sometimes I'd like to tip 'em. Okay. Thanks, Amber. I'll keep an ear out for them about eleven. Bye."

-11-
Six months earlier

Sunday, June 12, 2011
11:19 a.m.
Bonita Beach, Florida

Jake shivered, took a deep breath and said, "Then a week or so later, I had my first black helicopter nightmare."

Pam smiled gently and said, "Just from that asshole's comment?"

Jake laughed. "And some other folks, too. It was running around in my subconscious for a while and finally resurfaced. And it kind of fit in with a joke I'd made up a year before or so, that by 2020, someone in this country would be arrested for smoking a cigarette in their own home by a SWAT team that was high on legal marijuana."

Pam chuckled. "We may be headed that way, I guess."

"Yup. But it wasn't a SWAT team in the helicopter; I think that would have been overkill."

"Standard overkill procedure, of course."

"Oh, yeah. But it was two FBI agents, one old and fat and kinda dull and the other an eager, gung-ho, arrogant young punk, probably just out of the academy. They jumped out of the helicopter wearing business suits and sunglasses right into the water, sank in up to their knees, and finally clambered up to me, right here." Jake paused, reached into his cooler, pulled out a water bottle and a tube of lip balm, took a long sip and then put some balm on his lips.

Pam pulled a bottle out of her bag and took a sip.

Jake asked, "Want me to put that in my cooler? Plenty of room."

"Sure; thanks."

Jake put it in his cooler, and then Pam asked, "So what did the FBI guys do?"

"Oh," Jake replied, "they came at me with guns drawn, and the young one accused me of being unpatriotic and divisive, and then they argued about whether that word was pronounced 'div-eye-sive' or 'div-ih-sive,' with a long I or short 'I.'"

Pam laughed and said, "You know, I've heard it both ways ... sometimes in the same newscasts."

"So have I. So I guess the word itself is divisive; it does what it says, makes people argue about it. Anyhow, then I told them that this was MY dream and I could make them into gargoyles or give them clown noses if I wanted to. And suddenly they both had clown noses. And then they were walking back into the water toward the helo, yelling at each other: 'Div-eye-sive,' 'Div-ih-sive,' back and forth, and when they got in up to their chests, I woke up."

Pam laughed and then said, "So do you think your book will be unpatriotic and divisive/divisive?"

"Unpatriotic, no; Donne is totally about genuinely fixing the government for the benefit of the country and its people. Divisive/divisive? Absolutely. And he's got to do stuff that pisses off a lot of powerful people in order to motivate the assassination plots."

"Assassination plots?"

"Sure; got to have some drama in there to offset the tedium of him talking about policy stuff."

"So are you still worried about the black helicopters coming for you in reality, here?"

"Hmm; for a silly little novel, compared to all the real anti-government stuff on the Web? Not really, but I guess it's always a possibility ... not helicopters, but maybe a visit from the feds, one way or another. But that would be politically motivated, and depending on the IQ and bias of whoever might show up, I don't think I'd have a real problem. Plus there's the whole free speech issue. As an aside, I've actually been thinking about doing another one about a guy who's sort of an anti-Donne, does exactly the opposite of what he does, opposite policies; a bad guy. I may actually do that after I finish this one, just as a kind of experiment. I haven't mentioned that to anyone till now, and I haven't tried writing anything on that, either.

"But, Pam, I've just been blabbing away here. What about you? What's your background? I'll bet you've done some modeling. And those sunglasses aren't cheap."

Pam furrowed her brow and said, "Well, that's a long --"

Just then Jake's arm shot up and he managed to catch a football inches before it struck Pam's head. Pam, startled at Jake's quick movement, started to reach to block his forearm, then stopped herself as she saw what was happening.

The teen who'd been trying to catch the football ran over, casually mumbled, "Sorry," and reached for the ball.

Jake held onto the ball and said, "Just a second, son. Before I give this back, let me tell you about a little beach rule we've got here. If this comes this close to us again, it's mine for ten minutes, and after that, if it gets this close once more, it's mine forever. Okay?"

The teen shrugged, said, "Okay," and reached out for the ball again.

Jake kept the ball, held out his hand and said more sharply, "Deal?"

The teen shook Jake's hand tentatively and said, "Deal."

Jake said, "Okay. Now go have fun. But be careful where that thing goes."

The teen and his buddy consulted briefly, then moved a long way down the beach.

Pam said, "Is that really a beach rule?"

Jake shrugged. "Naw, I just made that up, maybe a year ago; but it works. So far I've got maybe six or seven footballs and nine or ten frisbees at home."

Pam laughed, "Verbal contract, huh?"

"Yup."

"Good idea."

"Thanks. And I used that kind of contract in the book."

"Really? How?"

"Two ways that I can think of. First, anyone who comes in to see Donne has to sign a release that says if they lie, dissemble, deflect, demonize, demagogue or hyperbolate to him, they face big penalties; and second, in a tradeoff with business guys, he quits micro-inspecting and micro-regulating their operations, but if they screw up and don't take care of the damages and fix whatever problem caused the screwup, BIG penalties, tripled if they try to cover it up."

"Interesting," Pam said. "Let me think about that for a minute."

Jake said, "Take your time," reached into his beach bag and pulled out a cigarette and a magnifying glass, sat up on his lounge, facing the Gulf, and stretched his shoulders, rotating his neck and head right and left. Then he focused the sunlight onto the end of the cigarette, which almost immediately began to smoke. Once it got going well, in about six or seven seconds, Jake puffed on it and put the glass back in his bag.

Pam said, "That's cool. May I try it?"

Jake handed her the magnifier and said, "Go for it."

Pam aimed her ciggie at the sun, put the glass right on the end of it and then pulled it up until the focal point got very small and smoke started. In a few seconds, she puffed on it and gave Jake the glass back. "Thanks."

Jake said, "You know, Pam, you're the first person I've ever seen who's done that right the first time."

Pam shrugged and said, "It's just optics." She smiled and said, "I'll let you in on a little secret, Jake. I may be blonde, but I ain't dumb."

Jake smiled. "Didn't that blonde country singer say that?"

Pam said, "Not quite, but close. Someone asked her if she was offended by dumb blonde jokes, and she replied, 'Naw, 'cause I ain't dumb ... and I ain't blonde.'"

Jake laughed. "I'd forgotten that one. But that reminds me of the blonde joke to end all blonde jokes. Wanna hear it?"

"Sure."

"Okay. Why are blonde jokes so short?"

"Why?"

"So brunettes and redheads can remember them."

Pam laughed. "Oh, I've gotta remember that." Then she laughed harder, uncontrollably.

Jake joined her, not quite understanding why, but her laughter WAS contagious.

Finally, with tears running down her cheeks, she managed to burble out, "Stevie Bruce, Ginny May. Sorry; can't get that outa my head."

Jake also managed to control himself and said, "Don't forget about Frannie May," and that set Pam off again. "And Lurlene."

After a solid minute of gales of laughter, they both breathed deeply and controlled themselves, at least for the moment. Pam took off her sunglasses, set them on Jake's cooler, pulled a small towel out of her bag and began wiping her face. Jake picked up her sunglasses, opened his cooler and offered her her bottle of water. As she swigged from it, he took a closer look at her sunglasses, then handed them to her as she gave him the bottle, which he put back in the cooler. After a bit more stretching, he put his cigarette out, put the butt in an empty pack, then reached into his cooler and pulled out a container of ice cream, took one spoonful, and then a gulp of water, put some more lip balm on and lay back down.

"Ahhh. I think the main reason I smoke is to give me an excuse to use some ice cream to soothe my throat after each one."

Pam, chuckling and smiling, said, "Can I ask you something, Jake? Something I've been wondering about since I sat down."

"Sure; go ahead."

"How did you get that scar on your left thigh? Looks like a knife wound."

"Nah, just sheer dumb luck. Second week I was sitting on the beach, some idiots left their umbrella up while they went walking, and it blew loose and hit me. 13 stitches."

"Pretty close to the femoral artery."

"Yup; more dumb luck that it missed. That's why I always check to see who's got open umbrellas upwind of me when I'm stretching. And if you see Norm over there ... hey, Norm."

Norm looked up from his puzzle and waved. "Hey, Jake."

"He uses that drill and the sand anchor to hold the umbrella down, even in strong winds."

Pam looked over and winced slightly, then recovered her composure. "Good idea."

"Yup; Norm's pretty clever. He's a retired dentist."

"Ah-ha."

"Speaking of doctors, I see you had a great plastic surgeon."

"No, no; these are real."

"No, I'm sorry; I mean that bullet wound over your left collarbone."

"Oh, that. A long time ago, different life."

"CIA, FBI, DIA, military, what?"

"No, no --"

"C'mon, Pam. I saw the DS380/17 in your sunglasses. That's Top Echelon only, no civilian uses."

Pam's eyes widened. "You know about --"

She didn't finish, as a loud roar came from the water and shrieks and screams broke out all over the beach, everybody staring and pointing at the Gulf.

Pam's eyes widened even further, and Jake turned to look over his right shoulder.

"What the --"

Then gunfire erupted and all the beachgoers began running toward the parking lots, except for the Mimosa twins, who reached into their beach bags and adjusted the zoom on their equipment.

-12-

Saturday, December 10, 2011
3:15 p.m. EST
New York City, New York

The Occupy people began occupying the Upper East Side about noon, marching up, down and across all the streets and avenues, waving the usual hodgepodge of signs that had become familiar to anyone who paid any attention to any news programs, with a few new additions: "Down With Donne," "No Miminum Tax," "Money is a Shitty Regilion" and "No Tax on Non-Profets." There was another which read "We Have Passionate Vague Demands" and another claiming "We Hate Self-Defecating Humor."

Wayne and Linda, at Jennifer's request, accompanied her up the private elevator to the Paynes' penthouse on their return from the charity lunch. When the doors opened, Jonathan gaped at the sight before him.

"Jenn, are you okay? What happened?"

"It was awful, Jon. They threw, they threw --" She broke down in tears and fell into Jon's arms. Jon looked at Wayne and Linda.

"What happened out there?"

"We had no problem getting to the Bernsteins', but on the way back, it looked like it might be difficult. So Linda changed coats with Jennifer -- I mean Mrs. Payne -- and moved ahead of us as a decoy. Mrs. Payne stayed with me and we followed about eight feet behind. The protesters were all over Fifth Avenue, the street, the sidewalks, scores of them, marching and chanting. We made it through that crowd and the ones on the cross street, but when we turned onto Park, somebody splashed red paint on Linda and yelled at her about wearing fur."

"He swore at her, Jon. It was awful," Jenn wailed.

"Are you hurt, Linda?" Jon asked.

"No, but that clown sure is. He won't be using that arm again for a long, long time," Linda replied.

"With that melee distracting everyone, I rushed Mrs. Payne here to your building and we got inside; nobody followed us or touched her."

"Wayne was wonderful, Jon," Jenn whimpered.

"And Linda cleared from the crowd and joined us inside after a few minutes."

Linda said, "I made sure I wasn't followed, went way past this building, around the corner, turned the coat inside out, wrapped it into a ball and came back on the other side of the street with my hat

43

inside out. When the way looked clear, I came across the street and Wayne let me in. Then we hustled into your elevator.

"And we've got a cleaner who can probably get that paint off the coat, if we get it to him soon."

"Oh, that'd be wonderful. I love that coat," Jennifer said, perking up a little.

"If you've got a trash bag or two, that'd be great," Linda said.

"I'll get some," Jennifer said, and headed off to the kitchen.

"You two have done superbly," Jon said.

"Just our job, Mr. Payne," said Wayne.

"Well, you do it exceptionally well, as always."

"Thank you, sir."

"I'll be sure to mention that to Amber when I talk to her."

"Again, thank you, sir."

"And if you ever want to think about making a change, I would love to make you both a very lucrative offer."

"Well, thank you, Mr. Payne, but OP-US has been very good to us both and we'll probably stick with them till death do us part."

Jennifer returned from the kitchen with two large trash bags. "Will these work?"

"That should be fine. Thank you, Mrs. Payne," Linda said.

"Did I hear you say 'Opus,' Wayne?"

"Yes, you did, Mrs. Payne; Optimum Protection, U-S, the company we work for."

"Oh, right; I forgot. Sometimes I can be such a ditz."

Wayne held one bag open while Linda stuffed the coat inside, and then they used the other to double-bag it, careful to avoid dripping any paint on the expensive carpet.

Linda added, "I'm pretty sure I didn't let any drip in the foyer or the elevator, but I'll double-check on our way out. And we'll call you as soon as the coat has been cleaned."

"Anything else you need us for, Mr. Payne?" Wayne asked.

"Not right now, Wayne. But if you want to bash a few of those damned animal rights idiots out there, feel absolutely free."

"I'd love to, Mr. Payne, but only defensively."

"Oh, well; too bad. And from now on, feel free to call me Jon, okay?"

"Okay, Mr. – I mean Jon."

Linda said, "I guess we should be on our way and get the cleaner started on this coat."

"Be sure to send me the bill."

"Okay, Mr. – I mean Jon. But that won't be much at all."

Jennifer gave each of them a hug and whispered, "You two are real life-savers. Thank you so much."

"Glad we could be there for you. Bye," said Linda, and they both got into the elevator and headed down.

"They are so cool, Poopsie."

"They're amazing, Jenn.   And thanks for not calling me Poopsie in front of them."

"Oh, I know that's just between us, Jon."

"You feeling better now?"

"Lots better. They both really helped calm me down."

"How about a drink?"

"I've got a better idea. Did you take that little pill?"

"I told you I would, so of course. But you're sure you're okay?"

"I'm fine now, really. Let's go see if that pill has worked its way down to Stevie Bruce. Ginny May is getting anxious for a visit."

"Okay, Punkin. Let's go."

And they headed off to another room in the penthouse.

-13-
Six Months Earlier

Sunday, June 12, 2011
11:26 a.m. EDT
Bonita Beach, Florida

BANG! One gunshot, then two more: BANG, BANG!!!

Who was shooting?   Jake and Pam saw that It was the pale, muscled young man south of Norm and Janet, holding a handgun in a two-handed stance, firing out at the Gulf.

Then three M-16s joined in, as three Marines in sand camouflage suits burst up from the sandy beach where they'd been buried since before dawn, sighted on the target the pale young man had first shot at and fired on full automatic.

Millie, struggling to get her rotund self up from her red blanket, along with Fran and Alvina, cried out, "Something just goosed me!!!"

The man on the PVC lounge pulled his right hand back out from underneath the fringe, scratched his left elbow and calmly watched events unfold.

Pam, still in her beach chair, but with a handgun of her own in her hand, shouted in a stentorian, commanding tone, "Cease fire, Marines, cease fire!" The gunfire immediately stopped. Jake looked at her in amazement.

A hundred yards further south, the teen in the Master Bait T-shirt hurriedly closed his tackle box, tossed it and his pole into the skiff and motored at full speed south toward Naples, no longer giggling. A small metal box with a small red button, a toggle switch and a green light on it bounced about on the bottom of the boat.

45

Jake looked out at a rapidly deflating and shredded King Kong head, about fifteen feet tall and ten feet wide, as it fell back into the Gulf, floating on the light chop, about ten yards south of the Hat Squad, who were all paddling north as fast as they could with their noodles, boogie boards and lifebelts.

Fifty yards further out on the Gulf, a jet ski had stalled out and was smoking; the kid who had rented it had disappeared.

Millie fell over as a fourth Marine finally emerged, M-16 at the ready, from his hiding spot directly under where she had put her blanket two hours earlier.

The Incontinentals and others on the beach pulled out cell phones and began taking pictures and videos of what was going on.

The four Marines converged on Pam and Jake, their weapons all pointed at Jake, who cowered, his arms crossed in front of his face.

"No, no, no," Pam commanded. "Weapons down!" The Marines complied. "He's clear."

The Marine who'd been under Millie looked at his fellows and asked, "Where's Ron?"

The pale young man pointed toward Norm and Janet, who had run toward the parking lot when the gunfire began and were now coming back to their chairs. "Danuski? I think he was somewhere in there."

Pam pointed at two of the Marines and said, "Hunsucker, Babcock, see what's going on with him. Miller, Schwartz, crowd control ... PEACEFULLY, no weapons." She looked at the pale young man, "Murphy, get out there and see what the hell that thing was. I'll hold your weapon." Murphy nodded, handed Pam his handgun and his sunglasses, revealing pinkish-red irises, and headed for the water and the deflated gorilla head.

Hunsucker and Babcock ran over to Norm and Janet, calling for their compatriot both aloud and into their throat mikes, getting no response. They pulled Norm's drill out of the sand and saw blood on it, about a foot up from the tip.

Janet said, "That's Norm's; he cut his toe on it." Norm showed them his bandage.

Hunsucker threw their chairs aside, then reached for the umbrella. He pulled up on the shaft, but it wouldn't budge. He reached down to pull up on the handles of the sand anchor; still no movement.

Norm said, "Twist it ... no, the other way."

Hunsucker twisted and the anchor slowly came up, exposing more blood mixed in the sand on the blade. He and Babcock began digging in the sand with their hands, revealing the top of a helmet, then even more blood mixed with the sand.

"Oh, shit," Hunsucker muttered.

"Oh, Ron, no," Babcock cried.

Norm looked on as more sand and blood came out in the Marines' hands; he covered his mouth, looked at Janet, and croaked, "Oh, my god."

Babcock and Hunsucker finally got enough sand out to be able to pull Ron up and onto the beach. They rolled him over, revealing a mangled, bloody throat. Hunsucker checked for a pulse, found nothing but dried and drying blood. Babcock started crying.

The beach crowd shrank even further back, but several kept their cell phone videos recording. Janet turned away and vomited. A flock of twenty or thirty seagulls swooped in and began gobbling up her breakfast muffin.

Babcock leaped to his feet, grabbed his weapon and pointed it at Norm. "You killed him, you killed him," he screamed, tears still running down his cheeks.

Norm cried out, "I didn't know he was there!"

Pam yelled, "Stand down, Marine. STAND DOWN, dammit!"

Hunsucker jumped up, grabbed Babcock's weapon and forced it down to the ground. "Cool it, Babs; cool it."

Pam ran directly between Norm and Babcock, got right in Babcock's face and in a measured but intense tone said, "I said, STAND DOWN, Marine!!!"

Babcock, snarling at Norm, looked back at Pam, said, "Yes, ma'am," and backed away.

Pam said, "It was an accident. How could he know Ron was down there? Think, Marine." Hunsucker pulled Babcock away from Norm and Pam, toward the water, talking him down as best he could.

"Goddamn Cheney," Pam muttered. Jake wondered why she was cursing the former vice president, but before he could think further about that, Murphy hollered from the Gulf.

"Ma'am, I think you'd better see this."

Pam responded, "Any immediate danger?"

"I don't think so, ma'am."

"Okay. Give me a minute. Babcock, help Miller and Schwartz with the crowds. Hunsucker, cover him up with something."

Norm said, "Here, take our towels."

As Hunsucker covered the body, sirens sounded in the distance, rapidly approaching the beach.

"Oh, shit; locals," Pam said under her breath. She pulled a radio from her beach bag, flicked it on and said, "Chopper One, Beach Gang. We need you back here right now."

"On our way, Beach Gang; ETA, five."

"Make it two."

"We'll do our best, ma'am."

"We also need a body bag."

After a brief pause, Chopper One responded, "One body bag, confirmed. Chopper One, out."

Pam turned to her men and ordered, "Marines, prepare for backup." The Marines arrayed themselves in a semicircle behind her, facing the parking lots, M-16s at the ready, but pointed slightly toward the ground.

Three Lee County and four Collier County sheriff's cars pulled into the parking lots and a dozen deputies emerged, running onto the beach, some guns holstered, some drawn. The onlookers moved even further away, cameras still recording.

Pam reached into her beach bag, pulled out a leather wallet and stepped in front of her men, holding the wallet up in the faces of the approaching deputies.

"Secret Service; holster your weapons!"

A huge, bald hulk of a man with Collier County sergeant's stripes lumbered up to Pam and reached out to grab her wallet. She pulled it back and said, "Look, don't touch, Sergeant."

"Lady, I don't care who you are or what that badge says, you're in my county and you need to tell me what's going on, why you've got Marines on my beach, right now!"

"Back down, Sergeant. This is a national security issue. Marines, with me NOW!" Hunsucker and Babcock immediately moved up to Pam's side and aimed their weapons at the sergeant's feet. Miller and Schwartz casually but pointedly swept their weapons back and forth, covering the other deputies, two of whom were still pointing their sidearms at Pam and the Marines.

Pam got directly in the sergeant's face and spoke coldly and forcefully, "Stand. Down. NOW. Sergeant."

The sergeant, his face now flushed, hesitated, then turned to the deputies and hollered, "Holster your weapons, deputies!" They all complied, both Lee and Collier.

Pam lowered her voice, backed slightly away from the sergeant, and said, "Now, Sergeant, here's what's going to happen. A helicopter will be here soon ... hear it? ... and we will take our dead Marine ... accidental death, by the way ... and leave. My eyes are up here, Sergeant. Thank you."

She hollered over her shoulder, "Murphy, come here." Murphy swam to shore and jogged over to Pam.

"What did you find out there?"

"Well, ma'am, there's a box on the bottom, with several scuba tanks and a remote relay to open them all, to inflate that gorilla balloon, plus a speaker that floated to the surface and made the sound, the roar. Nothing else down there, nothing that looks dangerous. I'm sorry for letting it startle me."

"We'll deal with that later, Murphy." She looked at the sergeant again, "Now, Sergeant ..." she looked at his name tag "... Dooley, is it? ... that is something you CAN investigate. I'll expect to see a copy of your report. My office will contact you."

At that moment, the helicopter returned and set down, half on the water, half on shore, and three more Marines in full BDU's exited, one with a black body bag. They ran to Danuski's body, zipped it into the bag and carried it back to the helo.

Pam turned to Jake and said, "Jake, I have now officially cleared you of any national security issues. Good luck with your book. Sergeant Dooley, this is Jake Devlin, who is a witness, along with everybody on the beach, to that ... inflatable event. But as for that Marine we've just carried from your beach, that is off ... and I emphasize 'off' ... limits to you, and if I hear anything ... ANYTHING ... about any inquiries you make or harassment of anyone on this beach on that issue, I will have your job AND your certification, and you will wind up as MAYBE a mall cop, if you're lucky. Clear?"

"Yes, ma'am."

"Good. Jake, I will be in touch, and you let me know how it goes with Sergeant Dooley here, okay?"

"Yes, ma'am, I will."

"Sergeant, for my records, what's your first name?"

"Thomas, ma'am."

Pam smiled slightly, for the first time since the deputies arrived. "My sympathies, Sergeant."

Sgt. Dooley's face reddened slightly; he did not smile.

Pam then reached into her beach bag, removed a full-body coverup and wrapped it around herself. Miller folded up her beach chair, and she and the Marines, still keeping an eye on the deputies, all boarded the helo.

A little boy ran down to the shore, waving at the helo. Ginny May's shrill voice rang out, "Stevie Bruce, no!!! Get back here or you'll get a whuppin'!" The little boy ignored her and kept waving.

Pam looked out at the boy and then at Jake and burst out giggling again, mouthing "Stevie Bruce?"

The helicopter took off and headed back north, toward Fort Myers Beach, leaving Jake with a final vision of Pam's laughing, gorgeous visage surrounded by grim Marines and the helo's side door sliding shut.

Sergeant Dooley muttered, "Bitch," under his breath, then turned to Jake and said gruffly, "So, Jake Devlin, what the hell happened here?"

Trying to suppress his own laughter, Jake said, "But only as to the inflatable event, of course?"

Dooley glared at Jake and hissed, "Of course."

-14-

Sunday, December 11, 2011
Morning, afternoon and evening

All of the Sunday morning talk shows were filled, as Donne had predicted, with political and economic pundits, from both sides of the aisle, as well as the usual mudslingers and malcontents. Keynesian economists predicted the immediate demise of the country, with charts, graphs and statistics to back up their positions. Austrian school economists refudiated *(that actually is a pretty fun word; JD)* each and every one of the Keynesians' assertions and doomsday scenarios, in spite of the Keynesians' constant attempts to interrupt, out-talk and out-shout them.

On one of the roundtable shows, two of the participants, both female, actually came to blows over the correct pronunciation of "divisive." The video went viral and had over a million hits within two days. The apologies each of them issued five days later received minimal news coverage, but when they returned to the show the following week, they agreed that both pronunciations were acceptable and that that word absolutely applied to most of Donne's policies. They could not agree on their opinions of Donne, which they continued to argue strenuously, but they did manage to restrain themselves from creating another viral video.

In cathedrals, churches, temples and mosques all around the country and the world, Donne's policies on abortion, gay marrage, assisted suicide and marijuana legalization were variously denounced and excoriated by passionate priests, pastors, rabbis and imams. All of them, however, agreed that his tax on nonprofits was a despicable, antisocial, even demonic money grab. Televangelists were especially vocal and passionate on that issue, continuously and passionately pleading with their followers to contribute before New Year's to avoid that tax.

In Rome, the Vatican issued a scathing attack on Donne and his policies and excommunicated him, even though he wasn't Catholic. A British newspaper's Monday morning edition's headline read "POPE CURSES G.O.D." Privately, the inner circle debated whether to call Donne the Antichrist, but the heads of the marketing, legal and financial departments objected vociferously, so that discussion was tabled.

Unsurprisingly, no organized crime figures complained about the Al Capone tax in public, but it certainly was a dominant topic of angry discussions in English and a wide variety of non-English languages throughout the United States and around the world. None of those

50

discussions were in Andorran, though.

National union leaders burned up the phone and internet wires having similar angry discussions and working to energize their membership bases against Donne's anti-union policies.

Up and down K Street in Washington, DC, and in their satellite offices in other major cities, lobbyists were scrambling to spread anti-Donne talking points to their paid bloggers and to multiple PR firms, as well as to their hired-gun talking heads, columnists and radio talk-show hosts.

Nearly all leaders of all types of social justice and environmental groups spoke with their top groupies and supporters and started developing strategies and plans for marches, demonstrations and other ways of objecting to the tax on nonprofits.

At two p.m. Central Standard Time, Steve and John and the other members of the trial lawyers society's board of directors met in their headquarters in Dothan, Alabama, and went over all of Donne's policies that affected their profession, progressively getting angrier and angrier as they discovered new restrictions on their ability to control (and fleece) their clients and pad their own paychecks.

Bankers around the world, especially central bankers, used their backdoor communications channels to spread a single message, which boiled down to this: "We have GOT to stop him from paying down the debt. That would kill our plan to bankrupt the US, along with all the other countries we've loaned money to, and we'll also lose the interest payments we planned to receive. Strategies, ideas? Time to advance the plan for the 2019 India-China-Arab war? Raise US interest rates immediately? Do a Biddle? Bust the bond bubble early?"

Back in Washington, both the Democratic and Republican national committees movers and shakers had been shaking in their boots ever since Donne's speech, and in their all-day meetings both Saturday and Sunday, they were also unable to come up with any strategies to counter his policies, and their frustration levels rose, along with the blood pressure of many of their senior members.

Predictably, most of those individuals and institutions with funds that would be confiscated put in transfer requests to their banks and other financial repositories, well aware that each of those requests violated Donne's Directives Numbers 213 through 217, but unaware that each of those transfer requests was routed through DEI's funds transfer platform, which flagged and rerouted them all to a special government account Donne had established on Friday, and equally unaware that each of those requests was noted in a report which landed digitally on Donne's desk Monday morning and was updated hourly thereafter.

As he read them, Gordon Donne smiled and said to himself, "And the second step of my vengeance has begun."

-15-

Monday, December 12, 2011
Morning, afternoon, evening and overnight
New York, New York

With the Asian and European stock markets in disarray overnight from Sunday to Monday, US investors and traders were in near-panic mode, and the futures indicated a market opening down between eight and thirteen percent, with extremely high volatility.

On the three morning network shows, stock pundits both roiled and calmed the emotions of viewers, but all of them agreed that the tax preparation services should be sold and that any pullbacks in the near future should be thought of as buying opportunities, but only in American-based companies. None of them were convincing in their forex predictions, some claiming the euro would go up versus the dollar, others taking the opposite view. Those who had been long oil, betting its price would go up, universally criticized Donne's putting the dollar on the oil standard; the shorts, who'd bet that oil would go down, cheered, but internally raged at the loss of that very profitable trading market.

On the investment shows on cable, all of the talking heads tried valiantly to sound reasonable, logical and rational in their analysis of Donne's policies' effects on the markets as they interviewed traders and brokers, all of whom were "talking their book," meaning what they said was driven in good part by the positions they held at the time.

When the market opened at 9:30 EST, all three of the major indices immediately fell between seven and nine percent, the tax preparation companies between 65 and 80 percent, oil companies between 11 and 14 percent and the euro fell nearly 16 percent versus the dollar. But since oil was down nearly 35 percent in dollar terms, it was actually down in euros, as well. And since speculators could no longer trade oil futures in dollar terms, the euro's fluctuations versus the dollar would be affected in good part by supply and demand in the oil market. The same would prove to be true with the other currencies that traded against the dollar in the forex market.

On the positive side, airlines, railroads, trucking and utility companies saw significant bounces, as did restaurant and many retail stocks, as well as the stocks of other companies whose input costs were significantly oil-related.

By late morning, it looked like the markets were bottoming, as the shorts started covering, and the indices began moving up. By noon, they had all regained about a third of the morning's losses, and the sense of relief continued for the rest of the day, but the markets still closed down. At least the indices were only down between one and three percent, and the volatility index, which had spiked up in the morning, was only up a couple of points at the close.

After the close, all three rating agencies announced that, although they were affirming the United States' current credit rating, they each anticipated that as Donne's policies took effect, they would all be inclined to raise the rating back to the highest level, where it was prior to the downgrade after the debt ceiling debacle last August.

In after-market trading, all three indices regained all their losses, and by eight p.m., when after-market trading ended, they were actually positive, and the futures showed a decent upward bias for Tuesday.

On the first of the two fake news shows on cable that night, the host began the show with his typically sophomoric trivialization of the weekends' events, with an overly caricatured cartoon of Donne, emphasizing his large ears and short stature, wearing a Napoleonic uniform, in the typical Napoleonic stance, but holding a pistol to a much taller cartooned Uncle Sam, cowering in fear. His satirical correspondents "reported" from a green-screened Capitol, White House and Supreme Court building, suggesting that Donne planned to lease those out to an entertainment company which would install animatronic robots and turn all three into tourist attractions with historical nostalgia.

His guest, a left-leaning professor of constitutional law at a noted university in Cambridge, Massachusetts, was treated with the host's typical highly intelligent second-half style, and argued with all his proud, pedantic and patronizing bluster that Donne's takeover of the government was absolutely, clearly and positively unconstitutional.

The show after that followed a similar theme, with the tongue-in-cheek conservative host satirizing Donne's tax policies with fake interviews with greedy billionaires flaunting their newfound wealth and buying ostentatious yachts, limousines, watches and wines.

But then he went into a raving rant against Donne's confiscation of his SuperPAC, which he'd planned to use in satiric fake ads in the Republican primary and in the general election.

His guest was a noted conservative political columnist, who barely managed to get three words in edgewise due to the host's usual raised-eyebrow interruptive style. The point he was trying to make was to object to Donne's social policies on individual choice, but that was overpowered by the host's continuing rant against the confiscation of his SuperPAC.

Overnight, the Asian and European markets stayed relatively stable, fluctuating a few points above and below unchanged.

Everyone was awaiting Donne's press conference at one p.m. on Tuesday.

-16-
Six Months Earlier

Sunday, June 12, 2011
2:37 p.m. EDT
Bonita Springs, Florida

When Jake got home from the beach after an early afternoon rainstorm, he found an email from Pamela93 in his inbox: "Sorry about the chaos this a.m. I need to see you as soon as you get this. URGENT!!!!! Let me know where and when and I'll be there. Pam."

Jake debated for a while, but finally responded. "Seabreeze Cafe, off Forester, in the tiki hut, five o'clock. JD" Then he went in to take a shower. When he came out, he found a reply from Pamela93. "See you then. Be careful and watch your six. Pam."

Jake made a couple of phone calls, reviewed some emails, then got to the Seabreeze Cafe an hour early, drove around checking all the cars in the front and back lots and finding them all empty of passengers. Only then did he park his car and duck quickly through the drizzle into the restaurant, noticing two older couples sitting at the counter, six booths full of retirees and families, and as he headed out into the tiki hut area, he noticed the Mimosa twins, now wearing coverups over their bikinis, sitting at one of the tables in the back. He took a chair at a table where he could keep an eye on both entrances, the door from the restaurant and the steps from the back parking lot, the two choke points, staying alert to all the comings and goings. He saw nothing that aroused his suspicions, so he pulled his notebook out and started outlining Donne's press conference, glancing up frequently to check the doors.

Chelsea, the only waitress on duty, came out of the restaurant and said, "Hi, Jake, the usual?"

"Nah, Chel, just ice water for now. Thanks."

"Okay," she said, "one draft ice water coming up. Want some lemon in that?"

"That would be great, Chel."

A few minutes later, when she set the glass in front of him, she said, "Did you hear about the excitement at the beach today? "

"Oh, yeah; I was there, and I'm still shaking from it all. Never had bullets flying so close to me before."

"You were there? Holy crap! What happened?"

"I'm still not sure, but it was scary as hell. The cops asked me not to talk about it; I guess I'm a witness. But I can tell you that they evacuated the beach and brought in the bomb squad, interrogated everybody they could before the rain came and cut it all short. There musta been fifty or sixty deputies and thirty or forty cop cars. It was a madhouse, even more of a mess than when the Marines were firing at the ... oops; probably said too much already. Sorry. Keep that just between us, okay, Chel?"

"Sure, Jake."

"But if you search for 'gorilla head Bonita,' you'll probably find a video that got uploaded."

"I'll do that; thanks. Are you gonna be okay?"

"I think so. But I'm still shaking."

Chelsea patted him on the shoulder and said, "Good luck with that. And I'll leave you alone; I see you're writing."

"Just making some notes; it helps, keeps my brain occupied and my body a little less shaky."

"So how's the book coming?"

"Kinda slow, but I'm still hoping to finish it by December; I've got his first speech set for then. But I get stuck a lot."

"How about a quick joke? Think that'd help?"

Jake perked up and said, "Go ahead; try it."

"Did you hear about the two Irish guys who walked out of a pub?"

Jake rolled his eyes around, but came up with nothing, "Nope."

"It could happen."

Jake chuckled. "Not bad, Chel, not bad at all; I'll add that to the repertoire. And thanks; that did help."

"It's the beta-endorphins. Hang in there, Jake."

"Will do. Thanks again, Chel." Jake went back to his notebook, but kept checking the door and the steps.

At about 4:30, Jake saw a tall woman coming through the indoor restaurant, in loose khaki bermuda shorts, a baggy shortsleeved sweatshirt and a large black hat covering all of her hair, carrying a big beach bag. She was shambling along and wearing those big wraparound sunglasses people get after cataract surgery, and it took Jake a moment to see through her disguise and recognize Pam. He could also tell she was exercising good tradecraft, unobtrusively alert to her surroundings. When she came through the door out to the tiki hut and looked his way, he waved and she came over and sat in the chair beside him, setting her sunglasses on the table.

"Okay, Secret Service lady, what the hell is going on?"

"Shh, Jake; keep your voice down. I'll tell you everything I know. But not here; we're being watched."

"No, we're not; I checked."

"Not well enough. See those two girls at that table over there? They were on the beach this morning."

"Yeah, they were. But I know them; they're regulars. I think their names are, uh, Carie and ... um ... Jill, I think. They're okay."

"Are you sure? They look like pros to me."

"Pros? Nah, just some cutesy young kids; been on the beach for three or four months. And I'm sure they saw you talking with me and heard you tell the sergeant you were Secret Service. And Sergeant Dooley interviewed them as witnesses, I'm pretty sure."

Pam paused, then said, "Okay, but I'm gonna keep an eye on 'em."

"Fine. Now, lady, what the hell is going on? Why all the Marines this morning? And what was with that gorilla head?"

"The gorilla head, I have no idea. But I was totally against having the Marines along. That was all my boss's idea."

"So are you really Secret Service?"

"This morning, yes, but as of this afternoon, I'm on suspension. He's just CYAing."

"Who is?"

"My boss, Chaney."

"Dick Cheney, the ex-VP?"

"No, Randy Chaney, who set up that whole op this morning."

"Wait a minute; let's back up. Just start at the beginning and tell me what happened this morning and what's so urgent now."

"Okay."

"And what was that about some national security issue?"

"Okay. I don't know for sure how it happened, but your name came up as a possible security risk, and my boss tasked me with checking you out. But I'd already been looking at your website and the speech you had up there, and I was intrigued, and I made those suggestions and then you and I got into that first email exchange. And that was long before I got tasked."

"Yup; I looked back at those first emails this afternoon. And the second round, too; but there the tone had changed a bit."

"That was after I got tasked -- you know, I think that was probably after you put up the first bit about the assassin, and maybe the NSA computers flagged it then."

"NSA? Seriously?"

"Well, I'd guess that word would trigger something. In fact, I'm sure it did."

"Maybe because it was near the President's name?"

"Maybe -- no, I'd say probably."

"Hmm."

"Now, I don't know exactly where the order came from, but it got to me from my boss, Chaney, so that's all I have. But he's a lot more political than I am, kind of a suck-up, so it may have come from the political people in the White House."

"Geez. Because of an innocuous, stupid little novel?"

"Well, you gotta admit that some of the stuff you have Donne proposing could be pretty controversial."

"Well, yeah, but that's mostly for the assassination plots."

Just then, Chelsea came over and asked Pam, "Can I get you

something, hon?"

Pam smiled up at her and said, "Just some ice water, please."

"Lemon in it?"

"Sure; thanks."

"Coming right up. Anything else, Jake?"

"Sure, I'll have another, Chel."

"Be right back."

"You come here a lot?" Pam asked.

"Yeah, I guess so." Jake paused a moment, looked closely at Pam and said, "Is your name really Pamela?"

"Yes, it is. Really."

"Last name?"

"Robertson-Brooks. But I just go by Brooks usually."

"Robertson-Brooks? Married?"

"Widowed. Want to see ID? I don't have my badge anymore."

"Sure."

"Okay." Pam dug into her bag, pulled out a wallet, extracted a Virginia driver's license and showed it to Jake.

"Satisfied?"

"Okay -- wait a minute. You were born in '61?"

"Yup, July 29th."

"You really do not look that old. But go on. You were saying your boss is political and he ordered you to --"

"Tasked me to check you out."

"Tasked you; okay."

"Well, that whole email exchange of ours led me to the conclusion that you were no security risk, but Chaney insisted that I meet you face to face and ... well, he wanted me to interrogate you. And then he insisted that the Marines go with me. Like I said, overkill. And I objected, told him I could do it alone. But he overruled me and ordered them along; he even drew a diagram of where he wanted them in the sand."

"And that got your Marine killed."

"Right. And now he's trying to blame me for that. So he had me suspended pending the outcome of an investigation."

"Geez, what an asshole."

"Got that right, Jake. At least I put my objections in writing and they're logged."

"That's good."

"I can handle that. But I emailed you because he's gonna want to justify himself, and that means he might be coming after you to prove that you are a security risk."

"What? Because of a silly little piece of fiction?"

"Yup; you can't believe the ego this guy has, and he's got to save face. That's part of why I wanted to get together with you now."

"Oh, geez."

"To warn you."

"Oh, geez."

At that point, Chelsea returned with their glasses, put them down, looked at Jake and asked, "You okay, Jake?"

"Yeah, Chel, fine, fine," he choked out, taking a big sip of his water.

"Okay, hon. You need anything, just let me know."

"I will; thanks, Chel." As Chelsea went back into the restaurant, Jake pulled out a cigarette and lit it, his hands trembling.

"Geez, Pam, you've got me paranoid. Now I'm even wondering about them." He gestured subtly toward the Mimosa twins, who were looking at a cell phone and giggling loudly.

Pam glanced over at the twins, shrugged and said, "Like I said, they look like pros to me, and pretty skilled at hiding it."

"Oh, geez. I've been thinking of them as just cute little sun bunnies."

"Well, I could be wrong, Jake, but I don't think so. I can tell you they're not with us."

"Us?"

"Secret Service. Could be FBI ... or CIA ... or somebody else."

"CIA? Oh, geez. But they're so young."

"Some agents look even younger."

Jake took another puff of his cigarette and coughed deeply, then took a big gulp of his water and started coughing even harder. Pam reached over and patted his back, but that didn't help; he kept coughing.

The Mimosa twins looked over, concerned looks on both their faces. Carie (or was it Jill?) dug in their beach bag, took out a box of cough drops and held it up, offering it to Jake. He shook his head, but steepled his hands in front of his face and nodded his thanks, still coughing.

Pam, who had been digging in her bag at the same time, pulled out an identical box, offered it to Jake, who looked at her suspiciously, until she shook one out into her hand and put it in her own mouth. Then he accepted one and popped it in. He stubbed his cigarette out in the ashtray and took a small sip of his water, and his coughing gradually subsided.

"You gonna be okay, Jake?"

"Just went down the wrong pipe, I think. Geez. Sorry."

"Don't worry about it. Happens to me sometimes, too. That's why I always carry these with me."

"They DO work, but, god, they taste awful."

"You get used to them. Here, keep these; I've got more in my car."

"You sure?"

"Yup, no problem."

"Thanks – wait. No little high-tech tracking device in there, right?"

Pam crossed her heart and smiled. "Nope; I promise."

"No eavesdropping ... ah ... thingie?"

"Thingie? Nope, no listening device, either. Nothing like that."

"You have got me paranoid now – but what about that DS380/17 in your sunglasses?"

"Chaney insisted on that. It recorded everything, video and audio. And I made a copy for myself before I gave it to him. Like I said, you're off the hook as far as I'm concerned. But how did you know about that? It's supposed to be classified."

Jake shrugged, glanced over at the Mimosa twins, who were back to giggling with their cell phones, then said, "I don't think so. I read a lot of defense and spy stuff ... research, you know; Donne will have assassins and surveillance people after him ... and that little device was very clever. I don't remember just where I read about it, though."

"Hmm. Maybe I'm wrong. Okay."

"You said you made a copy. Can I get a copy of that?"

"Oh, Jake, I can't. I've probably already told you too much. Maybe when my suspension is over ... or when I retire. And with what's going on right now, I'm gonna do that as soon as I hit 50 next month; I've got enough time in and I've just about had it with all the BS and the egos."

"Like your boss." Jake shivered.

"Yeah. He's been hitting on me for years and he's pissed 'cause I've rejected him each and every time, even filed a few complaints, but nothing's ever come of them. He's too well connected."

"What an asshole."

"Absolutely. Lots of them around ... in every agency, too."

"Lots of 'em out in the civilian world, too."

"Yeah."

"But with the way you look, I would guess you get hit on a lot."

Pam shrugged and sighed. "Yeah, it happens."

Jake took a small sip of his water, coughed once, and then said, tentatively, "Can I make an admission?"

"Sure." Pam looked at him expectantly.

"When I first saw you, the very first thought that crossed my mind was – well, actually the second; I'm always concerned about some other author or publisher ripping off my idea – was that you might be setting me up for a honey trap."

Pam blanched. "Wh- – why would you think that?"

"First, no wedding ring, and then look at you, look at me. Women that look like you don't just come up to guys that look like me and are as old as I am ... well, unless they're looking for a sugar daddy."

"I'm not looking for that; promise. But a honey trap?"

"Well, it sorta was, wasn't it?"

Pam took a sip of her water, ran her fingers through her hair, and finally said, "I – I guess you could see it that way. And I'm sure my boss would think that way, too. But it wasn't like that in my mind; looks aren't everything. I just wanted to prove that you were <u>not</u> a risk. Really."

Jake looked closely at Pam, frowning in concentration as he scrutinized her face, and said, "Look me in the eyes and tell me that again, okay?"

"Okay." Pam looked directly at Jake and said, "I just wanted to prove that you were <u>not</u> a security risk." She paused. "Really."

Jake, after a brief pause, said, "Okay. I believe you."

Pam sighed and smiled. "I'm glad."

"Or maybe they taught you how to lie really well in the CIA."

"How did you – oh, shit."

"Just a shot in the dark, Pam. And I'm sorry for that. But I had to know."

"That was a long time ago, Jake. I've been with the Secret Service since '93."

"And how long with the Company before that?"

"You know I can't discuss that, Jake."

"Or you'd have to kill me?"

"That's just a bad movie cliché."

"Whew."

"Of course, it's true."

"What?"

"Kidding, Jake, just kidding. Gotcha."

"Oh, geez, Pam. My nerves are on edge enough right now."

"Sorry; really. But you set that up so nicely, I just couldn't resist."

"Geez."

Jake pulled out another cigarette, but just fiddled with it for a moment, then put it back in the pack, took a deep breath and sighed.

"So, Pam, seriously, how much danger am I in from your boss and his cohorts?"

"I don't know for sure, Jake. He's a devious sonofabitch and he can manipulate the government in all kinds of ways to get at you."

"Like how?"

"Shhh. What's this?" She looked up as Chelsea approached their table with a small piece of paper in her hand.

"What's up, Chel?" Jake asked.

"Sorry to intrude, Jake, ma'am, but some guy asked me to give this to you." Jake reached out and accepted the paper from her.

"Okay; thanks, Chel."

As Chelsea returned into the restaurant, Jake looked at the paper, then read it to Pam. "Search the internet for 'Jesse Jackson Al Sharpton Extortion' and for 'Sinclair Young Obama Murder.' Wonder what that's about."

Pam leaned in to Jake, dropped her voice and said, "Oh, Jake, you don't want to touch that second one. It's a VERY dangerous subject."

"What? Why?"

"Take my word for it. You'd be in a lot more danger, and not only from my boss."

"Me? More? Geez ... wait a minute. Don't we have free speech in this country?"

Pam shook her head. "Oh, Jake, you are so naive. Politics is a LOT dirtier than anyone, even you, could imagine. People die and disappear."

"Oh, geez." Jake dropped his face into his hands. "So what now? I should get one of those long-handled mirrors to check for bombs under my car? Get a remote control to start it? Put a heavy-duty security system in my house? Video cameras? Hire a bunch of bodyguards to watch my back wherever I go? Maybe a sniper on the roof of the condos across the street from the beach? Anti-aircraft guns?"

"I don't think you need to go that far, but if I were you, I sure would NOT do anything with these," Pam said, tapping the paper, "and I'd sure keep an eye out for anything that looks at all hinky."

Jake dropped his voice to a whisper. "Like the twins over there?"

"Yup, like that."

"Oh, geez."

"One idea. When you're doing that stretching thing on the beach, looking for upwind umbrellas, you should also pay more attention to the people you see, especially if they seem out of place or hinky."

"I can do that, I think."

"Look, Jake, you're a nice guy and I like you, but I'm afraid you may get in way over your head if you're not careful."

"So I need to be paranoid?"

"Well, not really paranoid, just a lot more cautious."

"Watch my six, huh?"

"Exactly."

"Maybe I can do that. Thanks."

Pam dug into her bag, pulled out a business card and wrote a number on the back.

"Here, Jake. You've got my email, but if you run into anything or just want to talk, here's my cell number. Call me, okay?"

"Okay."

"I've got to get back to DC, see how I can fight Chaney on this."

She reached for her sunglasses and started to get up, but Jake said, "Wait a second. Let me give you my number, too. No cell, but I've got voicemail." He wrote a number on a page from his tiny notebook and gave it to Pam.

"Thanks, Jake. No cell phone? Really?"

"Nope; never bothered with that."

"Wow. Maybe you are that old ... oh, sorry."

"No problem; I'm used to it."

"Okay. Now you take care, okay?" Pam leaned over and gave Jake a quick peck on the cheek, gave his shoulder a quick squeeze, then stood up, smiled, glanced at the Mimosa twins and left. The twins seemed not to notice her, as Chelsea was setting large sandwiches in front of them.

"Okay," Jake said to Pam's receding backside as she opened the door into the restaurant. Then he pulled his notebook out of his shirt pocket, wrote "BS and ego," put the notebook back, looked over at the Mimosa twins, saw that Chelsea was still talking with them, sipped the last of his water, put a ten on the table and got up. He caught Chelsea's eye, pointed to the table and waved goodbye.

Carefully checking his surroundings, Jake headed toward the restaurant's door, but instead of going inside, he turned left into the atrium in the center of the tower, saw it was empty and headed in.

He pulled out the box of cough drops Pam had given him, popped another one in his mouth and started to put the box back in his pocket. Then he held it up close and looked it over from all angles, shook it a few times and palmed it.

When he got to where he could see his car, parked on the north side of the building, away from the restaurant's front entrance, he noticed an old pickup truck parked a couple of spaces away, between him and his car. He held up for a moment, looking around carefully, then used his remote to start the car. He then jogged through the drizzle, passing the pickup, unobtrusively dropped the cough drop box in the bed, got into his own car and headed out.

But instead of heading straight home, he took a left from Forester, drove east to the closest convenience store, where he bought a few boxes of cough drops, then drove randomly around several blocks in Bonita Shores for a few minutes, keeping an eye on his rearview mirror, and when he saw no one following him, turned west on Bonita Beach Road and headed home.

-17-

Tuesday, December 13, 2011
9:15 a.m.
Bonita Springs, Florida

On the Tuesday of Donne's first press conference, commuters awoke to a series of freshly painted decorations in the right-hand lanes of Bonita Beach Road, eastbound and westbound, repeated approximately every mile between I-75 and the beach.

Paul and Gayle Rutledge and their three children, aged six, nine and 13, left their hotel, stopped at Dotty's for a to-go breakfast and headed to the beach on this, the fourth day of their two-week vacation from Paul's job as an advertising agency CEO in St. Paul and Gayle's much more demanding job as a full-time mom.

Cindy, the oldest, riding shotgun, was the first to notice. "Look, Dad," she whooped, and started laughing loudly.

Paul looked over and saw the word "OLD" stenciled in white paint in the right lane, then about thirty feet farther on, the word "FART," and another thirty feet on, the word "LANE," all in letters at least six feet tall.

Cindy said, "You better switch lanes," and laughed again.

Paul chuckled and said, "Why me, smartass? You're the old fart."

"No, I'm not. You are."

"No, you are."

"No, you are."

Jordan, the nine-year-old, piped up from the back seat, "You're the old fart, you're the old fart," and Skyler, his six-year-old sister, joined in, "You're the old fart, you're the old fart."

And with that, all three of the kids joined in, singing the phrase over and over in fully uncoordinated disharmony, until Gayle finally said, "That's enough; pipe down, everybody."

Then Cindy saw another set of the words and, in an only slightly subdued voice, said, "Better switch lanes, Old Fart."

Paul gave her a surreptitious glance and smiled to himself.

Jordan, irrepressible, started up again, "Daddy is an old fart, Daddy is an old fart," then Skyler, after squinching up her face a bit, came out with, "Cindy is an old fart, Cindy is an old fart," again singing in their childish disharmony, both kids singing over each other, with Cindy yelling "Shut up, shut up!!" until Gayle finally yelled, "Stop it, stop it!!! That is ENOUGH!! If you all don't settle down, we're turning around and going back to the hotel and you won't get to build any sand castles."

At that point, a sulky silence settled over the entire car, until Paul asked Gayle, "You've got my tablet, right? I want to watch that press

63

conference this afternoon."

Gayle said, "Yeah, I've got it right in the bag, and it's all charged up."

"Great, hon. So now all of this old fart family is ready to have a great time at the beach."

Gayle rolled her eyes and shot daggers at the back of Paul's head as they continued west toward the Gulf.

As they rode over the bridge onto the island, Cindy piped up, "From now on, I want to be called 'Montana.'"

"Last week it was 'Idaho,'" Skyler chirped. "Idaho, Idaho, Idaho!" Jordan joined in, "Udaho, Udaho, Udaho."

Gayle growled, "Everybody, QUIET! Shut up!!!"

They continued in sulky silence, arriving at the beach ten minutes later.

-18-
Six Months Earlier

Monday, June 13, 2011
2:53 a.m. EDT
Bonita Beach, Florida

Jake awoke instantly from a light but restorative sleep, grabbed his .38 Special from under the pillow and was on his feet within three seconds, sweeping his weapon and his vision quickly across the spartan loft bedroom, noticing the red light on the security control box, indicating the system was in secure mode. He padded silently across to the sliding glass doors to the balcony overlooking the Gulf, checked that they were secure, then crept to the locked door to the rest of the house. Quietly turning the deadbolt, he slowly opened the door and took a quick glance out, then ducked back behind the doorframe. Seeing and hearing nothing, he moved out fast and low, nearly on his knees, but maintaining flexibility, and again swept his weapon and vision quickly back and forth. He saw nothing amiss.

He glanced over the banister and again saw nothing in the open living area below. Breathing deeply and slowly, he made his way down the stairs, carefully avoiding the ninth step from the bottom, which he'd booby trapped. Reaching the floor, he scanned each corner of the room, then moved to the door to the study and went in high and fast. But again, nothing. He also found nothing in either of the ground-floor bedrooms, the kitchen or the bathroom.

Creeping silently to the front door, he deactivated the alarm and opened the door, glancing down the stairs to the ground below. Again, nada.

"Pull yourself together," he mumbled to himself, closing the door and reactivating the alarm system. He crossed to the sideboard on the north wall and retrieved the power cord to his computer from the hidden drawer, then headed into the study, where he plugged in and booted up his computer while rewinding the security tapes to ten minutes before he awoke. Forwarding at double speed, the only thing he saw was a slow-moving dark SUV traveling south on Hickory at 2:52:43, passing in and out of view from left to right in about six seconds. Freezing the video, zooming in and advancing frame by frame, he was only able to make out a dark face looking out the passenger window at his house as the vehicle passed by; he couldn't tell if it was male or female. None of the other cameras showed anything out of the ordinary.

Jake breathed a small sigh of relief, but he knew he probably wouldn't be able to get back to sleep, still somewhat shaken from all the gunfire on the beach the previous morning, from Pam's warning about her boss and his ongoing suspicions, and especially from the appalling allegations he'd found on the internet from the paper Chelsea had given him.

Once his PC finished booting up, he checked the curtains to be sure no lights could be seen from the beach side, since it was turtle nesting season, and only then did he turn on the desk lamp, settle into the chair and check his emails, finding two that needed replies. He sent those and then began typing from the notes he'd made while waiting for Pamela at the Seabreeze Cafe: "... -itzer reporting from the White House Press Room, where we're expecting Gordon Donne to appear at any minute for his long-awaited first live press conference. You can feel the electricity ..."

-19-

Tuesday, December 13, 2011
Midday
New York, New York

As the morning wore on and the markets all hovered only a bit up or a bit down, volume stayed near an all-time low, but the buzz of conversation and arguments was near an all-time high.

But as one p.m. approached, a hush of anticipation settled over the entire trading floor and everybody looked to the televisions and their tablets with rapt attention.

* * * * * *

12:55 p.m.
Bonita Beach, Florida

Paul Rutledge finished up the sandwich Gayle had made for him and stuffed the wrapper into their trash bag. Then he pulled his tablet from their beach bag and started searching for the online broadcast of Donne's press conference.

Cindy, Jordan and Skyler were happily building a huge sandcastle down near the shoreline, occasionally singing out "Daddy is an old fart." Gayle kept a close eye on them while she chatted with an Italian couple, Salvatore and Rafaella, and an octogenarian Canadian woman, Lucy, who'd been snowbirding in Bonita for the past fifteen or sixteen years; she wasn't clear on which. Lucy had also seen the OLD FART LANE stencils and wondered if those had been installed by the City and how that could possibly be enforced. She also said in no uncertain terms that she was not going to be forced into that lane if she didn't want to go there. "Nobody tells me where to drive my Jaguar," she grumbled.

Paul finally got to an online site with Donne's press conference, but only after a great deal of frustration, and even then, the screen was difficult to see in the bright sun. He managed to get the screen tilted to where he could sort of see what was going on, his earbuds in, volume adjusted, and settled in just as the press conference was beginning to get underway.

"... -itzer reporting from the White House Press Room, where we're expecting Gordon Donne to appear at any minute for his long-awaited first live press conference. You can feel the electricity of anticipation coursing through the room, and again, we have received no prepared statement from his office, nor has there been either a demand or a request from Mr. Donne's office for advance notice of any of our questions. So it looks like it's going to be a free-for-all, and from some of the conversations we've had while we've been waiting, probably a pretty wild one.

"We've also noticed a couple of additions on the stage: that big touch screen on the right and a chair and side table on the left -- okay, here we go, right on time."

At precisely one p.m., Donne, dressed in jeans and a tropical shirt, entered the Press Room, preceded by two bodyguards and followed by a short, thin and very prim woman and a stout man, both in business suits, who sat in the fold-down chairs along the left wall. Donne strode to the podium and faced the assembled crowd.

"Ladies and gentlemen, before I begin, I want to introduce my Anti-Hubris Czar, Cecily Fusi, F-u-s-i, pronounced Fyoo-si, not Fussy or Fyoo-zi. Cecily has been with me for twelve years and has always acted as a trusted sounding board, sort of like my conscience.

"Could you stand up, Cissy?"

The female stood and the press applauded politely.

"Next to Cissy is Cody Harbison, my Czar for Unintended Consequences. Cody has a phenomenal ability to take any set of facts and predict an entire spectrum of both intended and unintended consequences with uncanny accuracy. Cody's been with Donne Enterprises International for seventeen years, and he's the only guy who's ever been able to beat me at chess."

"Just once, Gordy, in '96," Cody said as he stood up. The press corps laughed and applauded.

"Thanks, guys," Donne said as they sat back down. Then he smiled at the press corps and held up a sheaf of papers.

"Ladies and gentlemen, a couple of announcements and then I'll take your questions. First, I'm holding 173 letters of commitment from big businesses all around the world, pledging to open offices or manufacturing plants here in the United States, with projections of over 1.1 million jobs by the end of next year."

A gasp rose from most of the hard-crusted, cynical journalists in the room, and on trading floors around the world, millions of buy orders were executed, and in a matter of seconds, all three US stock indices spiked up between one and one and a half percent.

On Bonita Beach, Paul tented a towel over his head and his tablet and was able to follow the market action on the ticker and summary windows on the bottom of the screen.

Donne continued, "That's just in the past three days. Furthermore, a survey conducted by a major pollster yesterday and last evening shows that 77% of small businesses in this country are now planning to add new employees in the first quarter of 2012, which works out to be another 2.3 million jobs."

At that, the three indices shot up another percent and a half. Paul let out a too-loud "Yessss!" Gayle pulled up a corner of his towel tent and held a finger to her lips to shush him. Paul nodded a silent okay, but quickly returned his eyes to the screen as Donne continued with his comments.

"I know a few of the pundits on the Sunday morning talk fests wondered why I only mentioned the word 'jobs' once in my speech last Friday. I hope what I just told you all made up for that omission. Creating private sector jobs is one of my major priorities, but I know that the role of government, using that word in its most generalized sense, is not to do that directly, but to create the kind of environment that supports job creation, and in my admittedly biased opinion, that is better done with carrots than with sticks, metaphorically speaking, although some of both are needed. It's a question of balance.

"Next, as most of us know, the whole world is going to be facing a serious situation with water as the population rises beyond seven billion, but that does not give any government the right to restrict its citizens' private property rights, which as of now includes the right for any property owner in this country to deal with any precipitation that falls on his property in any way he chooses, without any kind of restrictions. Sorry, Colorado and Utah, but now your residents can now have rain barrels, and people everywhere are free to use their own creativity in any way they choose. That's Directive 318, which, along with many others, has been posted on _____.gov.

"Now, a VERY important and special announcement. As you all know, interest rates are very low, and many of our seniors can't get a decent return on their retirement savings without taking substantial and often dangerous risks. In part to help with that, and in part to provide some investment capital for the country, I am creating a USA Sovereign Wealth Fund, which will be a private institution, NOT a government one.

"Among the many ways institutions and individuals can invest in this fund, it will offer a guaranteed minimum rate of five percent on a five-year CD, with an annual withdrawal option; for example, if you invest a hundred thousand dollars, each January 15th, you'll get a check for five thousand dollars, and after five years, you'll get your hundred thousand back. So after five years, you'll have collected 25 thousand dollars and can also get your hundred thousand back.

"On a ten-year CD, the interest rate will be eight percent, if you take the annual withdrawal option. So each January, you'll get a check for eight thousand dollars, or eighty thousand over ten years, and then you get your hundred thou back.

"Now, if you don't choose the annual withdrawal option, your rate will be one percent higher on each of those CDs, compounded daily.

"There will also be longer-term CD's available, and the minimum investment will be as low as five hundred dollars.

"In addition, with my hedge fund and private equity experience, I know that our return will be significantly higher than five, six, eight or nine percent, and those excess returns will be split 70/30, with the 70 percent going to infrastructure repair and development and other types of projects and the 30 percent into a pool which will be added to the return each investor receives, to be distributed or reinvested, at the investor's option, at the end of the CD's term.

"I have created this fund under Directive 251, and we'll have the details in the form of a prospectus available online in PDF format by Friday of this week.

"I do have some other announcements to make, but I'll defer those and we'll get right to the Q&A, since there'll probably be some overlap there." Donne moved to the chair and settled comfortably into it.

"Okay, first question? Let's see. Yes? Please use the mike."

"Good afternoon, sir. Barbara _____ from _____ News. Have you decided on what title you want to have us call you?"

"Nope; not one of my priorities. How about this? For now, let's go with Mr. Donne and after we've gotten to know each other better, we can go with Gordon or Gordy. I know that's not a title, but my focus is on policy, not little stuff like that. Fair enough?"

"Yes, sir, Mr. Donne."

"Oh, geez, can we drop the 'sir'? I'm pretty informal, in case you all haven't noticed. I don't stand on protocol much."

"Okay, Mr. Donne."

"Thanks. Next? How about a tough one?"

"Kestyn ____ from ____. How can you justify lowering taxes on millionaires and billionaires?"

"Oh, that's not a tough one. Two ways to answer that. First, we get as much revenue from a ten percent tax on one guy making a hundred thousand as from a five percent tax on two guys making a hundred K each. And I would rather see two folks making a hundred thousand each than just one. That's a goal of many of my policies.

"Second, I would rather that we collect 27 percent from ten of those millionaires and billionaires than 39 or 45 or even 80 percent from the one of them who's either too stuck or too stupid to move out of the country. Remember, the rich have a LOT of choices. Think of the folks moving from New York to Florida and Texas to escape New York's high taxes, or moving their wealth to both legal and illegal offshore tax havens. Okay. Next? Yes?"

"Savannah ____ from ____."

"Oh, I can tell this is gonna be a tough one already."

The group laughed, albeit somewhat guardedly.

"I'll do my best, Mr. Donne. As you know, several commentators on Sunday called you 'heartless.' How do you respond to that?"

"Well, as I was watching them and hearing that, I just thought that their sense of 'fairness' was a lot different from mine. I believe you've gotta have a balance between reason and compassion, or head and heart, and that'll be a bit different for each issue. But as for me, I will never go so far in the heart direction as to be a sucker. Word to the wise, okay? Next?"

"Avery ___ from ___. I've got a photo here of you and Mohammar Gaddafi together, smiling and shaking hands. What's the story on that?"

"Oh, that. You have a copy I can see?"

"Sure, Mr. Pres- – Mr. Donne."

"That's okay, Avery; old habits die hard. Thanks. Oh, right. This was in ... ah ... 1993? Yes, '93, when one of our companies built an automated brick factory in Libya. He was one sneaky, devious bastard, I'll tell you. So we had to be even sneakier and deviouser – I mean more devious; sorry. I'm a fan of win-win solutions, but he was like a dog with a bone trying to make it win-lose. So we made sure he lost, I think it was to the tune of about half a billion bucks on that deal. And knowing that that was money he stole from his people and would otherwise have gone into his personal fortune somewhere, we put that into a separate account in our hedge fund in anticipation of his departure; that account is now worth in excess of forty billion dollars and belongs to the <u>people</u> of Libya."

Avery spoke up again. "Did you say forty billion dollars?"

"That's correct, Avery. That's what half a billion can grow into over eighteen years, prudently managed, as we have. Go ahead and do the math yourself. I can also tell you that since Gaddafi's death, Wes Farley and a team at DEI have been working with governments and claimants around the world to track down the billions he stole and hid away. Next? Yes."

"Sondra _____ of _____. I'll try for a tough one, Mr. Donne."

"If anyone can, Sondra, it's you. Go for it."

"You were accused of being unpatriotic and anti-democratic on one of the talk shows. Are you anti-democratic and unpatriotic?"

"Oh, I heard that on Sunday, and it came from one of the very best and most practiced mudslingers, and he can sling vague and highly emotional terms around like a short-order cook slinging hash in a dirty diner kitchen. But I do like his Loosiana accent.

"First, I am NOT unpatriotic; he is dead wrong on that score. I am concerned about making things better for this country and for as many of its people as I possibly can. In my opinion, that's pretty darned patriotic.

"As for the anti-democratic bit, I am definitely opposed to what our, quote, representative, unquote, democracy has become, where it seems your representatives do NOT represent you, but use crony capitalism and earmarks to enrich themselves and their friends and campaign contributors, at YOUR expense. If they were in the private sector and pulled the kind of stuff most, if not all, of them pull, they'd be in prison for life. Oh, that's my opinion.

"Also, I do think that democracy, and by that I mean mob democracy, can be destructive and often illusory. I much prefer plurocracy, which means individual choice in as many areas as possible.

"Just for an overused example, if our breakfast cereal choice was determined democratically, there would only be ONE cereal on supermarket shelves, and about half the people wouldn't like that one cereal. Plurocracy is what gives us the many choices we have there. Our Founding Fathers were appropriately leery of direct democracy and set this country up as a republic, with an electoral college, to protect against ochlocracy, another word for mob democracy.

"Then there's the whole issue of minority rights. In a country as large and diverse as ours, it's difficult in a democracy to restrain people who want everybody else to believe and behave the way they do and can lobby a few powerful representatives to accomplish that. But we have to recognize that controlling everybody's behavior is not a goal that we should support. Democracy can lead to tyranny just as much as military force can, even by a 51-to-49 percent vote, and if we look at how easily opinion can be swayed with propaganda, I think a strong case can be made against mob democracy.

"My highest value is freedom and individual choice for 'the people,' and that can be tromped on by democratic tyranny as much as by any other kind of tyranny. I think you'll find as you look at my policies and directives, freedom and plurocracy is the underlying principle.

"Also, with elections every two years, there's a huge loss of certainty. It makes it very hard for people and businesses to do much long-term planning, when the rules could change with each election. We have got to stop the pendulum from swinging so far to the right and then to the left and let it settle down in one spot. And what we have now and call democracy, but has gotten so corrupted, just doesn't cut it when it comes to that need. Okay. Next? Yes."

"Dennis _____ from _____. In an interview in yesterday's issue of our paper, one of your competitors called you, quote, a "ruthless negotiator." Are you ruthless?"

"I read that interview and I want to thank him for the compliment, but that particular fellow is prone to understatement. Okay. Yes?"

"Doris _____, _____. In your directives, you have eliminated the National Labor Relations Board, the Equal Employment Opportunity Commission, the Minority and Women Business Enterprise and Affirmative Action initiatives, as well as the Americans with Disabilities Act. How can you possibly defend those actions?"

"Well, Doris, I don't need to defend them, but I'm more than happy to explain the philosophy behind them, and that boils down to three words: Merit, Choice and Opportunity. While all of those ideas were well-intentioned at first, they have all become little more than full-employment-for-lawyers policies, as well as shakedown vehicles for certain greedy and self-aggrandizing activists. Preferences and quotas have come to overpower qualifications and merit. That's over and done. The ONLY hiring preference that will continue is for veterans, but even that will not outweigh merit and qualifications.

"As for the ADA, that piece of well-intended legislation has been used by hundreds of money-grubbing lawyers simply to shake down thousands of small businesses and to literally kill thousands of good developments. That's over. Next? Yes."

"Charles ___, ____. Have you seen the report on the $800,000 GSA party in Las Vegas in October of 2010?"

"I haven't yet, but I've been briefed on it. And I understand there are some videos, as well. If it turns out that what I've heard is accurate, <u>everybody</u> involved in the decisions about that event will be summarily fired AND held personally accountable for all taxpayer money that they wasted on that fiasco, and I do mean <u>personally</u> accountable. Furthermore --"

A rumble of voices was heard in the hall outside the press room, and a uniformed Marine walked swiftly to Donne's chair, saluted and handed Donne a sheet of paper. Donne read it briefly, then looked at the press corps.

"I'm sorry, folks. We're gonna have to take a brief break here, not more than ten minutes, and we'll continue this right after that." He stood up and the journalists did, as well. "No, no, no, don't bother standing; I don't need y'all to do that. I'll be right back."

The break actually lasted nearly 15 minutes, during which the press corps milled around the room, a few heading outdoors for a quick smoke break. But notes and attitudes were compared and contrasted, especially after Donne's last answer. Many arguments centered around the correct pronunciation of "divisive."

On Bonita Beach, Paul glanced at Gayle and Lucy, just as Lucy noticed a middle-aged guy casting his line into the water.

"Hey, idiot, no fishing in the swimming area," Lucy bellowed.

-20-
Five Months Earlier

Sunday, July 3, 2011
4:54 a.m.
Vienna, Austria

The Carnivore (one of his many names) had arrived on a private jet at four a.m. local time. A driver stood by a black SUV, which had been chartered anonymously through a cutout.

As soon as the Carnivore had settled himself in the back seat, the SUV left the airport through an open back gate. The driver had been instructed to engage in no conversation with his passenger, so he drove in silence to the Bahnhof Wien Meidling, where his passenger left the SUV, watched it drive off and then entered the station, favoring his right leg. But he wasn't there to board a train.

Inside, the Carnivore went into the men's room and into a stall, where he turned his jacket inside out, removed a set of scraggly teeth, pulled off his blond wig and replaced it with a black watch cap, stuffing the wig into a pocket with the fake teeth. As he left the men's room, favoring his left leg, but only slightly, he checked for watchers and, finding none, returned outside and climbed into the last taxi in the line, giving the driver an address on Pottendorfer Strasse, a short drive from the station. He got out there, paid the driver and walked slowly toward the house, still favoring his left leg.

Once the taxi was out of sight, he went back to the street, limped to the corner of Pottendorfer Weg and turned north, walking with no limp to the safe house a bit up the street, eyes constantly checking for anything out of place. Again seeing nothing, he stopped on the sidewalk and used his remote to deactivate the alarm system and unlock the door, then hurried up the walk and inside, closing the door and reactivating the alarm system at the keypad in the foyer.

"Welcome back, Carnivore," a raspy female voice echoed from the living room.

The Carnivore pressed a red button on the bottom of the keypad and a rapid swoosh, a muffled shriek and a loud clunk came from the living room. The Carnivore chuckled quietly, walked from the foyer into the living room and turned on the lights. When he saw what awaited him, his chuckle expanded into a full-blown laugh.

The Sniper squirmed in an easy chair, but she and the chair were both encased in an all-plexiglass half-wheel about two feet wider than the chair, arching over the chair from front to back. As she realized what had just happened, she started to laugh along with the Carnivore.

"Very funny, Carnivore. I like it. Now get me out."

"Of course, Sharon," the Carnivore replied, still laughing. He crossed to the couch, lifted a part of one of the end tables and pressed a button. The half-wheel quickly rotated forward, sliding into the floor in front of the chair, where its edges merged imperceptibly with the hardwood flooring.

Sharon slid out of the chair, got down on her hands and knees and examined the interstice.

"Damned near invisible, and definitely very clever. How did you come up with that?"

"I saw a tire half-buried in a garden in Sorrento when I was on the Grianchi job. Of course, that one had a Madonna underneath the arch. So maybe I'll call it the Madonna cage."

"I like that. What makes it work? Hydraulics?"

"Springs to swing it up, winch to pull it back down. And check this out."

He pushed another button and a tiny nozzle slid out from the left side of the back of the chair.

"Any kind of spray you want in that, incapacitating to fatal."

"Nice."

"You're the first chance I've had to really test it."

"Thanks for skipping the gas."

"You're quite welcome, my dear. This is just a prototype. The final will also be bulletproof and soundproof and we'll make a key fob remote."

"Very, VERY nice.

"So how'd it go in Copenhagen?"

"Pizza cake. The DX201/6 worked perfectly."

"Details, Carnivore, details."

"Okay. Picture this. Ten minutes after midnight, full moon, just outside the Rosenborg Palace Garden. I'm slouched over, in full disguise, doing my drunk act, leaning against the fence near the Gothersgade entrance when I see the target, with three heavy-duty guards. He's waddling around the corner from Kronprinsessegade, one BG in front and one on each side, slightly behind him."

"No fourth guy to fill out the diamond?"

"Nope; stupid lapse in tradecraft."

"And fatal?"

"Absolutely.

"Once they passed me, I lurched up from the fence, staggered out to where I was about 15 feet directly behind the fat fuck, got a clear shot between the two heavies, and took it. The dart ran right into his big butt and he reached back to pull it out, but the barbs kept it in. The two rear BG's moved in to try to help get it out, and just after I'd gotten back around the corner to safety, I pushed the boom button."

"How big a boom?"

"Same as in our final test on the first prototype.

"The BG on point survived, barely, but the other two and the target are now splattered over a big part of that intersection; they'll be picking up bits of them for months, if not years."

"But you're okay?"

"Yup. I only got a bit of blow-by, mostly the BGs, probably. Got away clean, dropped the gun and the costume with Hailey at the safe house and flew back here on the jet. Pizza cake. And zero collateral damage, other than some of the fence, maybe a few bushes and trees."

"Well, one less bad-ass human trafficker."

"And our client will move up and take his place. So what have we really accomplished?"

"20 million euros, for one."

"Yup, from another bad guy. And we'll probably get a contract on him from HIS assistant in a month or two."

"Right," Sharon said. They both laughed.

"Great technology. I think we can move it into production now.

"Meanwhile, you're heading back to Florida, right?"

"Right. Flying out tomorrow afternoon – I mean this afternoon."

"Good. See you there sometime, maybe."

"Probably not. I'm on the top floor all day every day."

"Right. Anything else we can get for you up there?"

"Nothing I can think of; it's comfy and cozy, nice furnishings. I'm pretty well set."

"Well, if you do need anything, just let Amber know."

"Will do; thanks."

"Okay. I gotta get a quick bite and some rack time; getting too old for even this mid-distance stuff. So g'night, Sniper."

"G'night, Carnivore."

-21-

Tuesday, December 13, 2011
1:35 p.m.
The White House Press Room
Washington, DC

At 1:30, a Marine had come into the press room and given the press corps a five-minute warning, and exactly five minutes later, Gordon Donne returned to the podium and nodded at everybody.

"Sorry for the interruption and the delay, folks. Sometimes things need to be decided, and this was one of those times. Thanks for your patience." He moved over to the chair and sat back down.

"Now, I think we're ready for the next question. Yes?"

"Marissa _____ from _____, Mr. Donne. I'd like to follow up on Doris's question."

"Go for it."

"How can you eliminate the preference for women in particular when their earnings are only 78% of males' earnings?"

"It's easy; I just sign a directive. Seriously, that number has been bandied about for years and it ignores lots of factors that go into it, like women leaving the workforce to have kids, just for one example. My goal is to absolutely level the playing field and opportunities for all people, regardless of gender, race or any other characteristic other than qualifications. And the MWBE has been gamed too much.

"Now, Marissa, this is going to be an extreme example, but in your field, would you hire a woman who couldn't spell just because she's a woman? I would hope not. And my government is not going to try to make employers do that kind of thing. We encourage both the public and private sector to simply hire the most qualified, and get rid of unqualified and/or unproductive employees. In particular, we have abolished all quotas, whether by statute or in practice to satisfy some implied or inferred standard.

"Along those lines, if you read all my directives, you'll have seen that we will be offering green cards to foreign students who earn advanced degrees in math, engineering and the physical sciences. It will be their choice, but we are no longer going to force them back out of this country when they graduate. Nor will we continue to force the children of immigrants who've opened businesses here under E2 or EB-5 visas to leave the country once they turn 21. And we will be loosening the requirements and getting rid of most of the bureaucratic red tape for those two types of visas, and expanding the availability of H1-B visas.

"We want to attract and keep talented, educated and creative people, regardless of their national origin, as well as keep families together ... as long as they add to our growth and economic health.

"Now, for those who would object to all those evil immigrants coming in and taking American jobs, I would suggest that you all encourage your constituents to improve their own skills so they can compete effectively.

"On the other end of the spectrum, we will no longer encourage slackers and system-gamers to come here or stay here. Next? Yes."

"Terry _____, _____. I'm sure you saw the editorials in our paper today, especially the one from our Nobel Prize-winning economist, that pointed out that your economic policies are exactly the wrong thing to do in the midst of a recession. How do you respond?"

"Well, Terry, someone once said that the reason astrology was invented was to make economics look scientific."

Many in the audience laughed aloud, although a few, including Terry, did not join in.

"Now, you may remember that at the end of my speech Friday night, I invited economists to submit their predictions based on their analysis of my policies. Well, we received over 200 of those in time to include a few of them in some charts that we've prepared. Here's one that combines their GDP growth projections over the next 20 years."

Donne then tapped on a tablet PC on the table beside him and a graphic appeared on the screen on the other side of the podium.

"Oh, I'm sorry; that's a spaghetti plot of hurricane paths in the Gulf of Mexico. Yup; there's Texas, and Florida's over there."

This time, the entire audience joined in laughter.

"Let me change that a little. Let's see. If I just pull on the ends of the Gulf Coast, like this, so it becomes a straight vertical line, or axis, on the right end, then change the units to percentages, and we make the bottom line a time axis, you can see that we now have a lot of lines squiggling up and down, and ending up in a range from minus 23% ... that's your guy's, Terry ... to plus 19% in 2032. And look at all the squiggles each one takes in the near term. Which of these is most accurate, only time will tell.

"Now, I've looked at LOTS of economic forecasts, 90% of which are downright wrong. And many of them are ideologically or politically driven. So I don't give a whole lot of credibility to any of them, especially the Keynesians your paper seems to prefer to hire.

"As to the guy you mentioned, Terry, I think Paul could do a great service for this country just by buying a big, luxurious motorcycle with a sidecar, some leathers and a helmet and taking a year off from your paper and traveling the country, talking to lots of regular people.

That would be both a small contribution to GDP growth and a great contribution to his education in the real world, where he apparently hasn't been living ever since he got the Nobel Prize. Next? Yes."

"Leslie ____, ____. Mr. Donne, what you do think about the Tea Party and the more recent Occupy movement?"

"I think that both of them are a result of the frustration that most of our population feels about 'business as usual' in both the public and private sectors. As for the Occupy people, in my opinion, they are MUCH less than one percent of the population claiming to represent 99 percent, and that's downright false. I think they probably speak for maybe five percent. Think about it. Look at someone at, say, the 70th percentile; they're doing just fine. At the 40th percentile, maybe not that well, but they're getting by okay. But it's easy to look at in black and white, especially if you're loud about it, as they sure manage to be. But frankly, I don't get a sense that they have any concrete and realistic ideas to put forth. If they ever do, I'd be happy to discuss those with one or two people they want to send over here ... but just one or two; more than that and it tends to deteriorate to a lot of noise and not much significant give and take.

"The Tea Party, when it comes to taxes, has got it about right, maybe a bit too extreme. But when they get into the theocratic stuff and demand that the government force everybody to behave as if they believe the same way the tea party social conservatives do, that's where I have a problem. Again, it's easy to look at stuff in black and white and miss the nuances, the multiple shades of gray, and it's easy to want to limit other people's freedom of choice. Okay. Next? Yes."

"Danielle ____, ____. Several of your critics on the Sunday morning shows complained that your background was primarily as a hedge fund manager –"

"Owner."

"I'm sorry; owner – and that the public has a pretty low opinion of hedge funds. What can you say to those critics?"

"Well, Danielle, I'm actually quite proud of our hedge fund. One of the best things we did was price our services well. When most hedge funds were two-and-twenty funds, in other words, charging clients two percent a year on their account plus taking 20 percent of the gains, we attracted a lot of money by simply taking a zero annual fee and fifteen percent of the gains, reducing that to ten percent on funds a client kept with us for five years. Our clients' ten-year average annual return, after our fees, was 26.7 percent, way above the second place fund, which averaged 14.9 percent. And we were managing over 1.8 trillion dollars, with fewer than a hundred direct employees.

"And by investing some of that money as venture capital or private equity funding, we started or acquired hundreds of businesses all over the world, which is what developed into Donne Enterprises International.   And in all of our businesses, we've instituted generous profit-sharing plans, so we've never had unions in any of them. In many of the businesses, those profit-sharing plans were used by the employees to buy the companies back from us after we'd turned them around; DEI keeps ten percent and the option to go back in and fix new problems as they arise, as consultants. And we still have given our investors generous returns. Okay. Yes?"

"Stephanie _____, ____. Mr. Donne, are you going to release your tax returns?"

"No. Okay. Ye- --"

"Why not?"

"Because I'm not running for anything, Stephanie. And I'm not going to release DEI's returns, either. Okay. Yes?"

"Brenna ____, ____. Last night's talk shows and fake news shows had a lot of jokes at your expense. How do you feel about those?"

"I've sent black helicopters for them all. Just kidding. But I could if I wanted to." He glanced over at Cissy, who shrugged and nodded. Donne smiled.

"Actually, I've got a pretty thick skin, even on this little body, and I know I'm no Charlton Heston, sort of charisma-free. I also know that until they start to see how my policies are going to work in reality, ad hominem jokes are about all they can do. So I don't really mind in the slightest.

"In fact, I really liked the cartoon of me on that first fake news show. You know what they say about men with big ears, don't you?"

The press corps tittered a bit nervously.

"Well, it's true, absolute fact."

The crowd tittered even more nervously.

"Yup. We really do listen better than the poor guys who only have little ones."

A few in the crowd broke into audible chuckles.

"But I do pay attention to all those late night shows, even if I can't watch them all myself; I get summaries and clips each day. They shouldn't think they'll have much impact on my policies, of course.

"But I have to say I'm intrigued by John's idea of animatronic robots in the Capitol and the --"

Just then, the Marine officer entered again, saluted and whispered into Donne's ear. Donne whispered back briefly and stood up.

"I'm sorry, gang, but I've got to go, and this will probably take a lot longer. So with my mea culpa, I've got to suspend this press conference right now. But we may have an announcement later this afternoon; we'll let you know on that. Thank you all for coming."

With that, Donne followed the Marine officer out, followed in turn by his two czars. The press corps murmured, mumbled and mingled, finally dispersing back to their offices to file their stories and await further developments.

-22-
Five Months Earlier

Thursday, July 7, 2011
9:15 a.m.
Bonita Springs, FL

A rare rainy day in Bonita Springs. Jake lolled on his bed with his laptop, consolidating and organizing notes that he'd made in his tiny beach notebook, and reminding himself that he should quit using spiral notebooks and get some that didn't have those annoying little stubs of paper, several of which had gotten away from him when he ripped the sheets out and were now fluttering around in the breeze coming in from the Gulf during a break In the downpour.

"Geez, I hate these things," Jake mumbled as he threw back the covers and began a search-and-recovery mission, which took him all of six minutes, two minutes of which involved scrambling after one recalcitrant piece that had lodged far under his bed and caused him to deeply scratch his right shoulder on the bottom of the bedspring.

While he was in the bathroom, dousing the wound with hydrogen peroxide and putting on a large bandage, the rain and wind picked up again and Jake hurried out to close the sliders. But he slipped on some rain that had blown in on the tile floor and fell through the screen, cutting his right thigh on the frame of the screen door and scraping his cheek, hands and one forearm on the river-rock balcony floor.

Back in the bathroom after closing the slider, with more peroxide and bandages, Jake muttered, "I am not superstitious, I am not superstitious. I do not believe in omens. This is just a coincidence. Just a coincidence. Guess I'd better get a tetanus booster, at least. Geez. What a klutz. Damn, damn, damn."

An hour later, Jake limped out of an urgent care clinic on Bonita Beach Road, his wallet 412 dollars lighter, but with a tetanus shot, four stitches in his shoulder and eight in his thigh, fresh bandages and a prescription for an antibiotic, which he filled (to his surprise, for free) at a supermarket on his way home. He also had a prescription for a heavy-duty painkiller, which he didn't fill, a choice he later regretted. The doc had also told him not to go in the water for two weeks and to come back in ten days to get the stitches out.

He did pick up three small non-spiral notebooks, some over-the-counter painkillers, a couple packages of hot dog buns and a bag of his favorite half-ounce meatballs, which he noticed now only had 65 in the bag, instead of the 80 that each bag had previously held, but the price was the same. A quick bit of math and Jake concluded that that worked out to an inflation rate of about 23 percent in a few months.

As he went by the frozen food section, he noticed that the ice cream he'd bought the previous week for $5.75 for one, then get one free, was now not on a BOGO, but was now priced at $4.89. He didn't bother to do the math on that, but it seemed that a true BOGO should still be at the lower price.

"Geez," he muttered to himself, "I gotta find some way to put those in the book. Wonder what Donne would do? Hmm; what would Donne do? Cool. WWDD. Or ... hmm ... WWGD? Hmm. Do I dare?"

Chuckling, Jake left the supermarket, where he saw two tables set up, one with a pro-Obama sign and one with a pro-Republican sign, both attempting to register voters, and he debated only briefly before approaching the Obama table, where he told the two people manning it that he thought Obama was the biggest liar ever to be elected President and then mentioned the book he was writing and challenging them to read what he had online; he gave them the web address.

Then he walked over to the Republican table and told them that he was writing a book about a guy who buys the country and legalizes gay marriage, abortion and marijuana, and challenged them to read what he's got online, also giving them the web address.

He walked to his car, again chuckling about the WWGD idea, but then he reminded himself about Pam's warning, so when he left the parking lot, he stopped for a small tub of ice cream at the Princely Dollop on 8th Street, then drove around some random streets in Bonita Shores, saw nobody following him and returned home, getting there a bit past eleven.

He mopped up the water on the tile floor and used hydrogen peroxide to remove the bloodstains on the white shag rug around his bed, careful to avoid aggravating his new injuries. Half an hour later, finally satisfied with his cleanup, he settled back on his bed and continued consolidating his notes, adding "WWDD" and "WWGD" to the batch. He also added "MBs, +23%" and "$5.75 vs. $4.89" and "MD, $412!!"

By noon, Jake's butt hurt from the tetanus shot, so he popped a couple of the OTC painkillers, told himself, "There's a nap for that," rolled over on his side and took one.

-23-

Tuesday, December 13, 2011
3:55 p.m.
The White House Press Room
Washington, DC

By a quarter to four, rumors about something going on in the Mideast were circulating among the members of the press corps who had returned to the room. Some of them were on their cell phones, frantically trying to get the latest information from their main offices and Mideast correspondents, for the most part unsuccessfully.

At five minutes to four, the screen to the right of the podium came to life with a shot of the Situation Room, showing Donne and several military and civilian personnel gathered around the table, most staring intently at something slightly to the left of the camera aimed at them. All the journalists either shut off their phones or held them up to record or transmit what was on the screen.

Donne looked up at the camera and smiled at the milling press corps as an aide handed him a microphone. Donne fumbled with it for a moment, then found the on/off switch and clicked it on.

"Ladies and gentlemen, I'll be joining you there in a few minutes, but I just wanted to let you know that we have just wrapped up three operations in the Mideast, capturing or killing three senior-level Al Qaeda leaders, with no American casualties and no collateral damage, as far as we know at this point.

"I can't tell you more than that, other than that it was a joint military/CIA operation and that it was the culmination of several months of cooperative intelligence gathering by many, many agencies in our government and others. At least that's what I was told in the briefings I've gotten on this since Friday morning.

"In any event, I'll be back with y'all in a few minutes, ten at the most. Smoke 'em if you got 'em." Donne handed the microphone back to the aide and then said to Cissy, who was seated next to him, "I've always wanted to say that," apparently unaware that he hadn't turned the mike off. The screen then went to black.

-24-
Five Months Earlier

Thursday, July 7, 2011
2:55 p.m.
Bonita Beach, FL

Jake was startled awake by a bright flash and a loud clap of thunder, which seemed to come from right outside his window. Automatically reaching under his pillow, he grabbed his .38 and leapt to his feet, sweeping the gun from left to right. Another clap of thunder, this one further away, and Jake realized what had awakened him, so he relaxed, but only a little.

Limping a bit and being careful not to disturb his stitches, he did his now-routine check of the alarm system and the house, this time going carefully down the inside stairs from the first floor to the ground level, where he checked the garage doors, the extra fridge, the hidden safe and his car. Finding nothing amiss, he returned to his loft bedroom and secured his weapon back in its hiding place.

Padding carefully over to the sliding glass doors, he looked out at the screen flapping in the breeze and, seeing that his fall had only pulled it from the frame, he decided he'd try to fix it himself once the rain stopped.

But he also noticed that one of his southern neighbor's trees must have been struck by the lightning bolt that had awakened him and was now lying across their pool, stretching toward the shoreline.

The surf was huge, some of the waves cresting at seven feet, maybe eight, and the stakes and tapes around most of the turtle nests in front of his house and his northern neighbor's McMansion were gone.

But he also saw that a few surfers were out, braving the rain and seeming to be enjoying riding the big waves.

"Idiots." Jake shook his head, went back to his bed, took another couple of painkillers and pulled his laptop and his notebook off the side table and continued with his organizing and consolidating. But he was much more careful with the spiral notebook, just crossing things off rather than tearing the pages out. He was also careful about putting pressure on the wrong place on his butt, but within half an hour, he was again lying on his left side, fast asleep.

-25-

Tuesday, December 13, 2011
4:05 p.m.
The White House Press Room
Washington, DC

As he'd promised, Donne returned to the press room, preceded and followed by his retinue, and he smiled a bit grimly at the crowd.

"Before I take any more questions, we're preparing a release for y'all on the operations we just finished, including the names of the AQ we killed and the two we captured. So I won't have to try to pronounce their names. You should have that release in just a few minutes, on your phones, tablets and on our web site.

"Now, I've got time for only a few more questions. Yes?"

"Yani _____, from _____. On these operations, do you give President Obama credit for those?"

"Of course, to the extent he authorized the original intelligence ops, as did President Bush before that. But as for actual credit, that goes to our military intelligence agencies, especially the CIA, and other countries' intelligence agencies, as well as the military people who participated in the actual ops. Beyond that, I won't be able to go into any operational details. Classified. Okay. Yes?"

"Samantha _____, _____. In your directives, particularly Numbers 148 through 161, you've eliminated OSHA, the Occupational Safety and Health Administration, and many functions of the Food and Drug Administration, the Federal Communications Commission and the Securities and Exchange Commission. Could you explain how you plan to accomplish their missions?"

"Well, Samantha, in general, I'm getting the government out of micromanaging and microregulating and replacing those with a freer rein, but absolute responsibility and accountability on the part of companies that have been regulated.

"Specifically as to OSHA, the biggest problem with that agency has been petty-minded and inadequately trained inspectors with massive checklists going into businesses with a mindset of finding tiny violations, most often in some part of the byzantine paperwork, and assessing fines. Like the EPA and EEOC and several other agencies, it's had a distinctly anti-business bias. So I've dissolved it, replacing it with a pro-business safety agency, which only goes into a business after there's an injury, fatality or environmental incident, on a consulting basis, paid for by the company, and remains there until the contributing problems, if any, are corrected.

"If the company reports the incident, compensates any and all victims adequately and fixes the problems, there will be no fine. If someone else reports the incident, there will be a fine equivalent to the assessed damages. But If the company tries to cover it up, shame on them; not only will damages be assessed, but the fine will be triple the damages assessed <u>and</u> the officers, directors, counsel and any other personnel involved in the coverup will be personally liable for two thirds of that fine ... PERSONALLY liable.

"This is sort of like a solution for the problem of reckless driving that I heard about years ago. If you got rid of all the seat belts, air bags and other safety devices, and installed knives that flip out from the steering wheel in an impact, in EVERY vehicle, I know I'd drive more carefully, and I'd think most sensible people would. I know that's not a practical solution to that problem, but the principle is worth looking at. And it's that principle I'm applying to OSHA.

"As to the other agencies you mentioned, we are not eliminating them, but they have become so bureaucratic and ineffective that they need a total culture shift. We will no longer tolerate SEC attorneys spending their days downloading pornography, and we're going to be replacing much of the legal staff there with top-notch forensic accounting people who can actually understand the data that they look at.

"We will be revamping the FDA to follow the European model and eliminating most of the byzantine bureaucratic hurdles that keep promising drugs in the pipeline for way too long. And the FCC will also be totally revamped and will lose the crony capitalism image that it's had, because it will no longer be involved in crony capitalism. Period.

"And ANY agency that's been involved in anything even remotely smacking of that will be totally restructured and completely culture shifted, to a culture and attitude of selfless and efficient service for its customers, the people. Okay. Yes?"

"Carmen _____, _____. Mr. Donne, how can you justify allowing the resumption of embryonic stem cell research?"

"Because stem cell research has already saved thousands of lives and discovered cures for hundreds of diseases. To limit this kind of scientific research, even with embryonic stem cells, on the basis of some religious belief, is not something my government will support. Okay. Yes?"

"Dell _____, ____. How is your crowd-sourcing going? Are you getting any good suggestions from the people?"

"It's very early, but we've received several hundred messages so far, which get screened for the nutjobs and the pointless, and the rest get passed up to my staff, who do a further screening, and then they get passed to Cissy and Cody, who decide which ones come to me. At this point, I've only seen about forty of those. I also take a random sample of the ones that have been screened out, just to check the process.

"The underlying principle is that while I own the country, I don't know everything, as Cissy reminds me every day ... that's her job ... and the innovation, creativity and problem-solving abilities of the American people can be boundless. Out of the forty ideas that I've reviewed, about half are surprisingly innovative, and about half of those are actually doable and will probably be implemented, and the folks who sent them in will be rewarded. Okay. Yes?"

"Jessica _____, _____. What kinds of rewards do you mean?"

"I'm still sorting that out, but in some cases, we'll be giving a percentage of the total we save each year, probably with an annual max of a million dollars or so, and in some cases, where financial rewards aren't valuable to the person, we'll figure something else out, maybe like naming something after them. I'm also open to any ideas or suggestions that any of our citizens have."

Donne looked directly into the camera. "So any of you watching this, by all means use the link on our website, _____.gov, and send in your ideas, okay?

"Time for one more. Yes?"

"Keira ____, _____. Regarding the national debt, do you blame Bush or Obama more for that?"

"That's a sandbox-on-the-Titanic question, a political one, and I'm not going to get into it. I will only say that both parties and both presidents share blame. We'll be going after the wrongdoers over the next few months, and you'll know about that when it happens. And no, I'm not going to go into any details now.

"But I took this challenge on as it exists, and my focus is on fixing what's wrong and going forward more effectively, and that's just what I'm going to be doing.

"Okay, folks, that's all the time we have now. Thank you for coming, and mea culpa for the interruptions. But I think they were worth it. Oh, the press release has been posted and distributed."

At that, Donne left the press room, followed by his retinue, ignoring the many questions that were shouted after him.

In Bonita Springs, Paul, Gayle and the three kids were driving back to their hotel from the beach, Cindy "Call Me Montana" still riding shotgun and the other two children sound asleep in the back seat, Skyler with her head on Gayle's lap and Jordan with his head against the window. So Paul wasn't able to watch the last segment of the press conference. But Cindy laughed out loud as she saw that the white stencils had also been painted in the eastbound right lane.

* * * * * *

The top stories on the major networks that evening and in the morning newspapers were "Donne Refuses to Release Tax Returns: What Could He Be Hiding?," "Donne Guts Regulators," "Donne

85

Encourages Smokers," "Donne Defends Hedge Fund Background," "Donne Calls Tea Party 'Too Extreme,'" "Donne Likes Robots in Capitol," "Donne/Gaddafi Connection? Donne Holding $40 Billion of Libya's Money," "Donne Accusations: Heartless, Ruthless, Hates Women, Minorities, Unions, Churches, the Unborn and the Disabled," but the news on the Al Qaeda operations was only covered by one lone newspaper in Kalamazoo, Michigan, and then got only three paragraphs on Page 8, surrounded by large ads for a local supermarket, two dentists and three urologists. Donne's news on businesses pledging to move or build plants and create jobs in the US went totally unreported.

Sound bites on the major networks included, "It's easy to see things in black and white," "It's easy to want to limit other people's freedom of choice," "Democracy can lead to tyranny," "I've sent the black helicopters for them all," "Mea culpa" and "Smoke 'em if you got 'em."

-26-
Five Months Earlier

Thursday, July 7, 2011
4:30 p.m.
Bonita Beach, FL

Jake's eyes slowly opened to a bedroom even darker than it had been earlier in the day. Sunset was still four hours away, but the clouds were so black that almost no light came in his doors and windows. There was no wind and only a gentle sprizzle of rain, part sprinkle, part drizzle.

Jake reached under his pillow, stretching the stitches on his right shoulder slightly, so he glanced at the alarm box, saw the red light and pulled his arm back. He stumbled into the bathroom, splashed some cold water on his face and neck, brushed his teeth, gargled and began to feel almost human.

He popped another couple of OTC painkillers, got dressed in a sweat suit and slippers and meandered down the stairs with his laptop and notebook, only remembering to avoid the ninth step at the last minute, and nearly tumbling down the stairs when he did.

He retrieved the power cord from the sideboard, walked into his study, plugged in his PC and booted it up. He closed the curtains and turned on the lights, then out to the kitchen, where he made a quick meatball sub, nuked it, brought it back to his study and started munching.

Once the PC finished booting, Jake checked his email and found one from Pamela93, sent earlier that morning: "Hi, Jake. I was down in Bonita this past weekend, looked for you on the beach, couldn't find you; hope you're okay. I'll be back this coming weekend and I'd like to meet with you again. Got some news that I think you'll like to hear; might help you relax some. Please call or email if you can find some time to chat. Pam."

Jake leaned back to think, but bumped his butt where he'd gotten the shot and leaned forward quickly, gritting his teeth. He got a pillow from one of the guest bedrooms and put it on his chair, sat down carefully and sighed with relief. Then he started a reply to Pam.

"Hey, Pam. Sorry I missed you, but sure, I'd be happy to see you this weekend. I had to get some stitches (klutz!) and can't go in the water, so no beach for me for awhile; too hot on shore. How about we meet at the Seafood Shack on BBR, about a mile east of the beach, out on the covered lanai? My schedule is pretty open, so let me know what time works for you. Maybe lunch Sat? Jake."

He sent it and then composed and sent several emails with attachments to several separate recipients, using several anonymous mail servers scattered around the world.

He then settled in to work on the timeline for Donne's tenure as owner, finishing his sandwich when he got to the spring of 2012.

Half an hour later, as he was listing some likely candidates for the many assassination plots, his PC pinged, indicating a new email, which turned out to be Pam's reply: "Lunch Sat at the Seafood Shack works for me. Noon? Pam."

Jake replied: "Noon Sat. See ya then. Jake." He went back to his list of assassination plotter prospects, adding lawyers, human traffickers and drug cartels to the list.

-27-

Thursday, December 15, 2011
1:30 p.m.
The Oval Office
Washington, DC

Donne, in jeans and another tropical shirt, got up from his desk and welcomed Jim Ferguson, head of Health and Human Services' Office of the Inspector General (HHS-OIG), with a big smile and a hearty handshake, guiding him to one of the couches in the center of the room, and taking his own seat on the opposite one. There was a clipboard on the coffee table between them, which Donne picked up and set to his side.

"Jim, I'm glad to meet you. Kathleen tells me you're damned good at what you do."

"Thank you, sir."

"Now, relax, Jim. I want us to be totally informal here, since you and I will be working pretty closely for a good long time."

"I look forward to that, sir."

"Okay. First, let's cut the 'sir' shit. Just call me Gordy, okay?"

"I'll try, si- – Gordy."

"Good, good. Now, one of your primary missions Is to track down Medicare fraudsters, catch them and shut them down, right?"

"Medicaid fraud, too. And build cases for prosecution."

"Right.

"What's the most frustrating part of your job, Jim?"

"Seeing them right back in business within days of our making a bust, especially if they're mob-related, and a lot of them are."

"And why does that happen, do you think?"

"Lawyers, and our system doesn't usually let us keep them in custody; they make bond and go right back to work. Or they close down in one location and open up again in another."

"Right. But now you've got some new tools to use."

"That Al Capone tax you announced Friday?"

"Exactly. Now you can hit 'em where it hurts, in their wallets. With IRS cooperation, you can arrest them twelve hours after they receive a payment, seize <u>all</u> their property and possibly hold them indefinitely. And you'll know when they're getting a payment, because their account will be flagged as soon as you have probable cause from your investigations."

"So we just do the investigations and turn it over to the IRS?"

"Oh, no, no; it's cooperative. See, we're freeing up thousands of IRS agents, since they won't be looking at all those Schedule D trades anymore, and we'll be assigning many of those thousands to work with you, help your accounting folks out, running fraud-discovery algorithms and all that stuff. And since those fraudsters now have not only fraud charges against them, with all that innocent-until-proven-guilty BS, they ALSO have tax evasion charges, and there the burden of proof is reversed. Not only that, but their lawyers can't charge them more than 200 bucks an hour in federal court, so attorneys will be less motivated to work for those folks ... or ANY folks, for that matter. Not as much of a cash cow as it has been for those shysters."

"Wait, please. I'm trying to get my head around all that."

"Take your time, Jim."

After a long pause, Jim asked, "Maybe if you could just run me through an operation and explain how the IRS is involved, that would help."

"No problem.

"Right now, you gather some evidence to reach probable cause and then go for arrest and search warrants, right?"

"Generally, yes."

"Once a judge grants those, you set up an armed arrest op, with some other agencies and local police?"

"Secret Service, FBI and locals, right."

"And you go in heavy and make the arrests and do the searches, right?"

"Right."

"Well, three changes so far. First, some of the IRS agents work side by side with your accounting folks to find and build the evidence for the warrants. Second, when you get the warrants and go in for the arrest, you've got notice of their receipt of funds, so you go in twelve hours after that. And third, you've got some armed IRS agents with you, and they make a second arrest, this one for tax evasion, of the Al Capone tax, unless they can prove that they paid that within twelve hours of receipt of the funds. And they won't be able to do that, because they didn't.

"Then, since the penalty for that kind of tax evasion can range from the tax due up to immediate seizure of ALL the evaders' assets, they have the authority right then and there to seize everything."

"Okayyyyy," Jim said hesitantly. "I think I get that."

"So then, in order to try to get their property back, they have to go into Tax Court and prove that their activities were NOT criminal, but the judges will normally delay that trial until the conclusion of the criminal fraud trial, which is back in your bailiwick, with the DOJ, as it is now. But now they have an incentive to get that trial concluded quickly, and your side can ask for continuance after continuance. Meanwhile, they have no assets; the IRS has them. And if they do try to go back into the business, you and the IRS just go after them again and again, using the Al Capone tax as the basis.

"Now, I know that's an oversimplification, but I think you've got the idea."

"Yup, I think I do. And I like it."

"Now, one warning. Be VERY careful about abusing those powers you've got. And I'll be telling the IRS director the same thing. It's a very powerful law, and it'll be tempting to abuse it. Don't."

"No, sir."

"Gordy."

"Gordy."

"We're on the same side here, Jim."

"Yes, si- – I mean, you bet, Gordy."

"Good. Any questions?"

"Let me think."

"Take your time. Oh, you can also have a DVD of this chat we've just had, if you want."

"DVD?"

"Yup. We record all of these conversations. You can take it with you when you leave and show it to your whole team, or even put it on the web, if you want. I have no problem if the bad guys see it; that'll put them on notice."

"Hmm. I'll show it to my team, but I'll have to think about putting it out to the public."

"Well, after your next high-profile case, that should give them enough notice ... I don't mean legal notice, of course. I just want some alarm bells to go off in that community."

"Deterrence."

"Exactly."

"So what do I do now?"

"I'll be seeing the IRS director later this afternoon, and I'll have her or one of her people contact you and y'all can figure out just how you want to coordinate and get this ball rolling ... quickly."

"Good."

"Check with Emily on your way out for a copy of the DVD."

"Will do ... oh, I do have one question."

"Sure."

"Will we be able to get a budget increase?"

"No."

"Oh."

"Worth asking, though, wasn't it?"

"I guess so," Jim said hesitantly.

"Ah, but we'll also be making some of the military available to you when you need extra manpower."

"But I thought they weren't allowed to operate inside the US to make arrests. Posse comitatus and all?"

"As of last Friday, that's gone, and they're now allowed, but with extremely limited authority. Check out Directives 83 through 88."

"I'll do that."

"You're a good man, Jim. Keep it going."

"Will do."

"And feel free to get in touch with me or Emily, Taylor, Alex or Maria whenever you have any questions or concerns."

"Will do ... Gordy."

"Good." They stood and shook hands. Ferguson headed out the door and Donne returned to his desk, leaving the unused clipboard on the coffee table. He continued with the papers in his overflowing inbox, laying them in one of two piles when he had finished with them. The smaller pile was for the ones he'd approved, and the far larger one was for those he'd denied or disapproved.

-28-
Five Months Earlier

Saturday, July 9, 2011
11:10 a.m.
Bonita Springs, FL

Jake arrived early at the Seafood Shack and did a quick but thorough parking lot check before he parked. He walked through the patio, noticing nothing that seemed hinky, and went on in to the covered lanai, sitting (tenderly) at the table at the far end, his back to the corner, and carefully checking out the half-dozen or so other early customers. Again, nothing suspicious.

"Hi, Jake," Beverly, the waitress, said as she got to his table. "Haven't seen you in a while. Been okay?"

"A little under the weather, Bev. How 'bout you?"

"Same-oh, same-oh. What can I get for ya?"

"Just ice water and lemon; I'm meeting someone later."

"Comin' right up. Nice shirt; bright red looks good on ya."

As Beverly headed back inside, Jake pulled out his notebook and a copy of Machiavelli's "The Prince" and picked up reading where he'd left off, occasionally jotting some notes.

When Beverly came back with his drink, she noticed the book and said, "Ooooo, I read that back in college. Scary guy, huh?"

"By today's standards, yup. But back then, he made a lot of sense."

"But executing all your enemies?"

"Sometimes. But again, that was centuries ago. And that was way before the French Revolution and the guillotine. "

"Oh, yeah. Hey, my new boyfriend told me a guillotine joke. Wanna hear it?"

"Sure."

"Okay; I hope I can remember it. Okay; here goes. They're bringing three at a time up to the guillotine; this group is a priest, a drunk and an engineer. They tell the priest he's got a choice: face up or face down. He says, 'I want to see where I'm going, so face up.' He lies down, face up, and they pull the blade up and let it go. But it stops four inches above his throat. The crowd yells, 'It's a miracle, a miracle,' so they let him go.

"The drunk is next, gets the same choice, but he just falls over with his face down in the block. They pull the blade up, let it go, and it stops four inches above his neck. So they let him go, and he staggers off and passes out behind some bushes.

"The engineer is next, and he chooses face up. He lies down,

91

they pull the blade up and he says ... let me make sure I've got this right ... he says, 'Oh, wait; I see the problem.'"

Jake laughed and Beverly beamed.

"Did I tell that okay?"

"You did just fine, Bev, just fine," Jake said, giving her an okay sign. "I'll add that to my repertoire. So did you meet the new guy on that online dating service, MisterRightForYou dot info?"

"Yup."

"Do you think this guy is your Mr. Right?"

"Well, so far he's Mr. Tolerable. "

"You're a beauty, Bev; I'm sure you'll do fine."

"Thanks, Jake; I needed that."

Beverly beamed again and headed back into the restaurant. Jake made some notes, glanced around the lanai again, then went back to his book and his notes.

About 11:30, Jake saw Pam coming out from the restaurant. Her hair was loose, she was wearing denim shorts and a light blue Fishbuster Charters T-shirt ("They Hatch 'Em, We Catch 'Em"), and had the cataract surgery sunglasses on again. All the male heads turned to follow her. She saw Jake, walked right over to him, pulled off her sunglasses, gave him another peck on the cheek and sat down across from him, smiling broadly.

"Hi, Jake."

"Hey, Pam."

"Sorry I missed you last weekend."

"I was a little under the weather," Jake said, looking closely at her. "So what's the good news?"

"You're clear; I got Chaney off your back, at least officially."

"Chaney, your CYA-ing boss?"

"Ex-boss now; he's been suspended and I've been reinstated. And I've put in for retirement as of the end of this month."

"And he's off my back? That's a relief. I've been on edge, maybe even paranoid since you left last time."

"I can understand that, but now you can ease up some, I think."

"Okay. Now tell me the whole story. Last I knew, you were suspended and that asshole was pissed off at you and maybe coming after me."

"Right. So when I got back to DC that night, I called his boss and told her the whole story, sent her copies of my video of our conversation and my objections; remember, I'd logged those."

"Yup."

"Well, she set up a meeting with me for Tuesday after she met with Chaney on Monday. And I gave her a full sworn and notarized statement, with copies of my objections and his diagram."

"Of where to put those Marines."

"Right.

"And we got a few anonymous videos of the whole thing, from the time I walked up to you until I left in the helicopter. And another showed Norm using his drill, with some resistance at one point; we think that's when he hit Danuski's neck."

"Oh, geez; I remember him doing that, but I had no idea what that was. That was the one named Ron, right?"

"Right. Your memory is better than you think, I guess."

"Hell, I've seen him being dug up a lot in my dreams since then."

"Me, too."

"And that other guy pointing his gun at Norm, yelling at him."

"Oh, Babcock."

"What was with him?"

Pam paused and crinkled her brow. "They were lovers."

Jake's eyebrows rose. "Gay?"

"Yup. Babcock and Hunsucker had been together for a few years, and Danuski was trying to break them up."

"Really?"

"Really. Used to call them Hun-Bab."

"Hun-Bab?"

"Right.

"Anyhow, after seeing all that stuff, she called my boss in and tore him a new one, since he'd placed all the blame on me. And she reinstated me and gave him a two-month unpaid suspension, mainly for lying to her on the previous day."

"So why didn't you tell me that back then?"

"Because he appealed, and that took some time, until Mark, the director, cut that off and affirmed my reinstatement and his suspension. That was last Thursday, a week ago. And on Friday night, I headed down here to surprise you on the beach."

"Damn; wish I'd been there."

"Me, too. So are you feeling better now? You said something about some stitches?"

"Separate issue. Last weekend I had some kind of flu, I think, four days in bed; couldn't even get any writing done, just a few notes here and there. And the stitches, day before yesterday; did some pretty klutzy things, got some cuts on my shoulder and thigh, and had to get a tetanus shot."

"Oh, I'm sorry."

"Yup, makes it a little uncomfy to sit the wrong way."

"The stitches?"

"No, the shot; he gave it in my butt,"

"Not in the arm? I thought that's where they give 'em."

"Really? I thought that doc was kind of a sadist."

"Oh, yeah; had a few of those myself. The stories I could tell."

"I can only imagine. Maybe someday I can pick your brain for some inside info from your time in the Service."

Pam smiled demurely. "Maybe someday you can, but not now; after I retire, that's a definite maybe. Could probably fill a book."

"I'll cross my fingers."

"It's only three weeks away."

Just then, Beverly came out of the restaurant, saw Pam and came right over.

"What can I get for you, ma'am?"

Pam thought for a moment, then said, "Can you do a cranberry Mimosa?"

"Sure 'nuff. Jake?"

"I'll have a white zin, and no, I'm not gay."

"Oh, Jake, you always say that," Beverly said, laughing.

"And, Bev, can you bring us some menus? You want to have lunch, right, Pam?"

"Sounds good to me."

"Be right back." Beverly headed back to the restaurant.

"Do you really always say that?"

"Yup. It cuts off a common reaction with a joke; something I call joke-jitsu. And I really just like white zin."

"Not an oenophile, huh?"

"A what?"

"Sorry. A wine connoisseur."

"Far from it. And I really don't drink much."

"Hmm."

"In fact, that T-shirt you're wearing?"

"It's not mine; I found it in the condo I'm using, kind of liked the name."

"Oh. Anyway, Marti and Captain Dave are friends of mine. That's how she pronounces her name, Mart-eye, long I. They live over on the Imperial River, and I've gone to their boat parade party the last two Decembers, and she kids me about bringing a bottle of strawberry zin along, calls it my limeade. She actually uses a different word, one that starts with a K, but that's trademarked, so I had to make it 'limeade.' I take it home and finish it off around August. I've still got about a third of it in my fridge from last December."

"It doesn't go bad?"

"Not that I can tell. But then I'm not a – what was that word?"

"Oenophile."

"I can probably use that." He made a note.

"No, Jake, it's o-e-, not e-e."

"Oh, thanks." He made the correction, just as Beverly returned with their drinks and menus.

"I brought you some ice water and lemon, too, ma'am, and another for you, Jake. And here's the menus."

"Thanks, Bev. Oh, Bev, this is Pam."

"Hi, Pam. Nice to meetcha."

94

"Hi, Bev. Same."

"Hey, Bev, you got a blonde joke for Pam?"

"Hmmm. Okay, here's one. What's a brunette's mating call?" She paused, looked around quickly. "'Have all the blondes left?'"

Pam cracked up. "Oh, I love that one."

Jake laughed, too. "Another good one from the fabulous Bev."

Bev beamed and bowed. "Thank you, thank you very much."

Pam said, "And that's a damned good Elvis impression, too."

Bev looked at Pam and said, "Thank you, thank you very much, ma'am."

Pam said, "Oh, no, thank YOU very much, Bev; I'll definitely get some use outa that one. Made my day."

"Cool. Let me know when you're ready to order, okay?"

"Okay."

As Bev walked away, Pam inadvertently (or was it advertently?) brushed Jake's forearm with hers as she reached for a menu, and then asked him, "So what's good here, Jake?"

-29-

Thursday, December 15, 2011
2:30 p.m.
The Oval Office
Washington, DC

The four union presidents followed Emily, Donne's chief of staff, into the Oval Office. Emily carried four sheets of paper over to Donne at his desk, handed them to him and whispered in his ear. Donne looked at her, then at the four standing in front of his desk.

"Gentlemen, I understand you have objections to signing these releases, correct?"

They all nodded, but stayed silent.

"You need to answer aloud, for the record.

"Richard?"

"Yes, I object."

"Bob?"

"I object."

"Andy?"

"I object."

"Lee?"

"Me, too."

"Then I have no time to listen to you. Good day, gentlemen.

"Emily, please show them out."

"Follow me, gentlemen, please."

Richard objected first, "But, Mr. --"

95

"Gentlemen, you heard me. Please leave now." Donne spoke it quietly but forcefully. "That is a direct order."

All four stood their ground, until Donne stood up, all five feet five inches of him, and strode over to them, looking up at each in turn.

"Richard, leave now. Bob, leave now. Andy, leave now. Lee, leave now."

Again, all four stayed put.

"Emily, get the guards in here and arrest these four gentlemen for trespassing and contempt."

"Yes, sir, Mr. Donne." She stepped out.

Again, Richard spoke up. "You can't --"

Donne cut him off. "Actually, Dickie-boy, I can. You four will be held in our basement cellblock for seven days, incommunicado."

Lee turned to the door and spluttered, "Sir, I will --"

Donne whispered, "Too late, Lee."

The door opened and four security guards entered, followed by two Secret Service agents. Donne moved back and leaned on the front edge of his desk.

"Escort these gentlemen to the cells in the basement. Seven days incommunicado. But treat them well, feed them well and give them appropriate sleeping gear. Thank you."

As the guards took the four men into custody, handcuffing them and confiscating their phones, Donne said, "Emily, please put out an immediate press release, Type 3, with these four gentlemen's names in the appropriate blanks. Thank you."

"Yes, sir, Mr. Donne."

The guards escorted the four out of the Oval Office through a different door from the one through which they had entered. Once the door had closed, Donne looked at Emily and shrugged sadly.

"Geez, Emily, I hated doing that. But I figured those four would be the first to try."

"Yup, Gordy. I thought so as soon as they came in."

"Well, let's see if that gives us the result we want."

"Hope so."

"Now, send copies of Directives 127 and 241 down to the four of 'em, and then --"

"And then we play it like Munich, right?"

Donne smiled. "You are good, Emily. But not till Monday."

"C'mon, Gordy; I know how your mind works after all these years. Four-day wait."

"But even if they fall for it, we'll probably have demonstrators outside tonight, so alert the Secret Service and pull in some soldiers per Directives 204 to 209. Full audio and video, containment nets, but no live ammo."

"Yes, sir."

"And you'll probably want to bunk here tonight."

Emily smiled. "Absolutely, sir."

"And Harry and Julie, too, if you want."

"Nope; they're still back in Macon with their dad and stepmom."

"Ah, that should be okay, then.

"What's next?"

"Nothing till three; that's the Cardinal from Rome."

Donne frowned and drummed his fingers on the desktop. "Well, that should be interesting. Thanks, Emily." He returned to his chair and picked up a stack of papers; Emily headed back to the outer office.

-30-
Five Months Earlier

Saturday, July 9, 2011
11:55 a.m.
Bonita Springs, FL

"Mmmmmm!!!! Pam moaned. "Ohhh, that's positively orgasmic! Oh, oh, ohhhhhhhh!"

Jake smiled and said quietly to himself, "Wait for it."

Pam continued moaning, smiling at Jake.

"Good, good," he whispered. "Still waiting. And --"

Finally, an elderly woman who had just sat down at the table behind Pam turned around, caught Jake's eye and said, "Excuse me. What is she having?"

"-- there it is," Jake whispered, and then replied to the woman, "It's the shrimp and lobster pasta, ma'am."

"Thank you, sonny.

"George, call the waitress. I want some of that."

"Sure, Marion. Where's my cell phone?"

Marion rolled her eyes and waved to Beverly, who came right over and took her order.

Pam looked at Jake and whispered "'Sonny'?"

"Guess I look young for my age. Maybe I'll go to a plastic surgeon, get some wrinkles added." Pam chuckled.

Jake continued, "So you're enjoying your pasta?"

"Oh, my god; best I've ever tasted. Really."

"I'm glad."

"How's your Angus burger?"

"Great."

"But you're just picking at it."

"I don't eat a lot; probably take most of it home. With a half pounder, I'll maybe get three more meals out of it."

"Three more? Wow – oh, here, have the last bit of this. It really is delicious."

"You sure?"

"Yup."

"Oh, surf 'n turf."

Pam chuckled quietly. "Ready?" Jake nodded.

Pam speared the last chunks of lobster, shrimp and pasta, swirled up the last bits of the sauce and held the fork out to Jake's open mouth as they both leaned in across the table.

As he began chewing, Pam said, "By the way, you have great looking teeth. I noticed that when we first met."

Jake held up a finger apologetically, chewed, finally swallowed, then said, "Thanks; they go in a glass at night."

"No. Really? They look positively natural."

"Need proof? Wanna see my 90-year-old redneck impression?"

Pam grimaced. "Ah, no; I'll take your word for it. But they do look good."

"Thanks."

After an awkward pause as Pam finished her pasta, Jake cleared his throat and said, "Pam, would it be okay if I use you in the book?"

"What do you mean?"

"I don't know; maybe like Secretary of State. Donne's gonna need a whole new Cabinet and ... oh, wait; even better. How'd you like to be Director of the Secret Service?"

"Oh, no, no."

"I'd change your name, of course; last name, anyhow. But I'd love to have a character like you in a senior position."

"I don't know, Jake. I --"

"Look, Pam, you're smart, you're gorgeous, and you sure knew how to deal with that sergeant and those Marines on the beach, so all I'd do is build a character sort of like you. Hmm. But I'd have to ugly her up some, maybe drop your eye candy rating five or six points. And I wouldn't have to use your name; it'd just be between you and me."

"Maybe – I guess as long as – I mean – Jake, you've got me speechless, and that doesn't happen often."

"Look, I'm sorry. No need to rush this. Just think about it for a while. I just like the idea ... and I also like the name Pamela. And remember, it's just fiction."

"I know; I just – you caught me totally off guard with that."

"I'll do it," Marion said, turning around and looking at Jake over Pam's shoulder. "I'm sorry; I couldn't help but overhear you. You're writing a book?"

"Yup," said Jake.

"What's it about? Well, if you don't mind my asking."

"No, that's fine. It's about – well, a guy buys the US government, declares himself dictator and fixes it all."

"Fixes it? For real?"

"Yup."

"Wow. Oh, yes, I'll do it. You can use me and George any way you want."

"Marion and George. Cool. Your last name's not Kirby, is it?"

"No; it's Herman. And no, we don't have a dog named Neil."

"I'll bet you get that a lot," Jake said, writing in his notebook.

"Not so much anymore, at least not from the kids these days. This is my hubby, George."

"Hi, George; I'm Jake."

"And I'm Pamela; nice to meet you both."

George looked at them vacantly and smiled, then looked at Marion.

"They're a nice looking couple. Who are they?"

"They're new friends, George."

Jake said, "Oh, we're not a couple, just friends."

Pam got up, gently took George's hands in hers, looked him straight in the eyes and said, "Hi, George. We've never met before. My name is Pamela, but you can call me Pam, okay?"

"Okay, Pam." George beamed at Pam, squeezed her hands tightly, tears welling in his eyes. "You're a good daughter, Patty, and I hope you're as happy with your new husband as I've been with Martha."

Pam kept her eyes on George's, sighed deeply and finally whispered, "Thank you, Daddy; I hope so, too."

Marion leaned across the table and said, "George, it's Marion."

"Oh, hi, Marion. Are we heading home now?"

"No, George, not yet – ah, here comes our meal."

Pam gave George's hands a final squeeze and stood up, as Beverly arrived and placed the Hermans' orders in front of them.

Jake gathered up his things and said, "Bev, we're gonna head out to the patio for a smoke," looking to Pam for her agreement; she nodded. "Can we take our drinks out there, and get a doggie box?"

"Sure, Jake; I'll pack up your burger. Anything else?"

Jake glanced at Pam, who shook her head absently, still looking at George. "Nah, we're fine, Bev; thanks. And don't pack the pickle."

Pam touched George's shoulder and said, "Enjoy your meal, George," and then smiled at Marion. "And I'm sure you will, Marion."

"I sure hope so. Nice to meet you, Pam." She nodded at George, who was meticulously cutting his first conch fritter into four pieces. "And thank you so much." Pam smiled and nodded as she and Jake headed out to the patio, drinks in hand.

-31-

Thursday, December 15, 2011
3:00 p.m.
The Oval Office
Washington, DC

At the stroke of three, Emily led the Cardinal, in a black cassock, scarlet fascia and scarlet skullcap, into the office, where Donne was seated behind his desk, still dressed in jeans and tropical shirt. Emily gave Donne another piece of paper, whispered in his ear, nodded at the Cardinal and left the room.

Donne glanced at the paper, set it on his desk, stood up and walked over to the Cardinal, who had his hand extended, palm down. But instead of kissing the prelate's ring, Donne shook his hand and said, "Welcome, Your Eminence; good to see you again. It's been what, four years?"

"I believe so; when the curia signed the contract with DEI."

"I trust the software and maintenance are all going well for you."

"Technically, all is working fine."

"Well, if you have any problems with it, just call Wes; I'm sure he'll be glad to take care of it. As you know, as of last Friday, I'm no longer involved with the company."

"Yes; I watched your speech."

"Please, let's sit over here," Donne said, as he guided his guest to one of the couches and took a seat on the opposite one. Again, he took the clipboard off the coffee table and set it beside him.

"I understand the Pope is not happy with me and my policies here, from what I saw in the papers over the weekend."

"He certainly is not."

"And you are here representing the entire Church, and speaking directly for the Pope?"

"I am."

"Well, let's get down to brass tacks, then. What are the Church's specific problems with my policies?"

"You're not a religious man, are you?"

"Not relevant. Go on."

"Do you even believe in God?"

"Again, not relevant. Go on."

"But I need to understand the man to whom I'm speaking."

"That didn't seem to keep the Pope from excommunicating me, and I'm not even Catholic. Go on."

"We have concerns for your everlasting soul."

"I appreciate that, but that is frankly none of your concern. You are here talking to the guy who owns the whole friggin' government of the US of A, and I have faith that your agenda has more concrete items on it than my soul. So let's get to it."

"Well --"

"Oh, before you do, I also have faith that you read and understand the document you signed before you came in here."

"I did and I do."

"Okay. Now you can go on. Brass tacks, padre."

The Cardinal glared at Donne, then pulled several sheets of paper from a briefcase at his feet.

"First, the Holy Church strenuously objects to your condoning and encouraging the sin of murder of the unborn."

Donne picked up the clipboard, made a note and said, "You're talking about my legalizing abortion."

"Murder."

"As you call it. Are you referring to abortion or not?"

"I am. Murder of the unborn --"

"All right; Church objects to legalizing abortion. Next?"

"We strenuously object to your condoning and encouraging the sin of same- --"

"Gay marrage; got it. Next?"

"We strenuously object to your condoning and encouraging the sin of self-murder."

"Assisted suicide; got it. Next?"

"You have no responses to those?"

"Not yet. What else has your panties in a bunch, padre?"

"Mr. Donne, you are speaking to a Cardinal of the Holy Catholic Church. I do not appreciate your flip attitude on these issues of major importance to all God-fearing Christians."

Donne leaned forward and pointed toward his desk. "See that sign, the one that says 'No BS Zone,' and the one next to it that says, 'No Ego Zone'? That means I'm here to get this country back on its feet and not to pander or massage anyone's ego, and I don't tolerate any BS at all. Zero tolerance on both scores.

"So you and I can dance around semantics and philosophy and talking points and ego, or we can dig in, roll up our sleeves and get down to brass tacks, down to the bottom line, and get something sorted out, man-to-man. Your choice."

The Cardinal simply stared at Donne, expressions of shock, anger and confusion alternately fleeting across his face.

"Or maybe we could just arm-wrestle and settle it all, padre."

Suddenly, shock predominated the Cardinal's face, then he laughed aloud, but nervously.

"I heard you weren't big on protocol, young man."

Donne chuckled. "Well, that's progress; okay.

"I'll bet you guys are pissed off about the tax on churches and nonprofits, too, of course."

"We object to that as unconscionable and an assault on religious freedom, as guaranteed in your Constitution."

"Okay; abortion, gay marrage, assisted suicide and the church tax. Anything else on your list there?"

"Legalizing marijuana and encouraging smoking of tobacco."

"Anything else?"

"We are concerned about the moral decay of this country and will be opposed to any policies that support or continue that, and to any further assaults on our religious freedom."

"Anything else?"

The Cardinal looked at his papers and finally said, "I believe that's it … for now."

"Okay. I've noted your objections, but all of those policies will stay."

"But --"

"No buts, Your Eminence. My government is not a means for you to impose your beliefs on everyone else and control their behavior, just as it won't do that for Muslims or Jews, Hindus, Buddhists or atheists … or voodoo priestesses, for that matter. You'd agree, I trust, that not everybody in this country believes what you believe?"

The Cardinal fidgeted, puffed up his chest, then let it sag, but he stayed silent.

"Yes or no?"

Cowed, the Cardinal muttered, "Yes."

"Well, you and your church will have freedom of religion, as you have always enjoyed here, but there will also be freedom from religion for non-believers. My government will always remain neutral on that issue. It will never be a theocracy … of ANY brand. That is not our role. And we will not set foot on the slippery slope on those issues you brought up. My policies there will stand."

"And you are also firm on the tax on the Church?"

"Absolutely."

"But our work for the poor will suffer."

"Well, Your Eminence, if that is really as important to you and the Church as you want me to believe it is, you will come up with some creative solutions to keep that from happening, perhaps by finding other ways to economize, MAYBE at the upper management levels of the Church. Word to the wise."

The Cardinal glared at Donne, who stared right back. The silence continued for a good thirty seconds, and then the Cardinal spoke.

"I will advise His Holiness of your position."

"You do that, Your Eminence."

"And may God have mercy on your soul."

"I'm pretty sure She will, padre. Good day."

The Cardinal angrily gathered his papers, stuffed them into his briefcase and started to head for the door.

"Oh, Your Eminence, if you would like a DVD or audio CD of our discussion here, just ask Emily or Jodi for one. No charge."

The Cardinal glared one last time at Donne and then left the Oval Office, trying to slam the door, but was prevented from doing so by the hydraulic door closer.

"Pompous sonofabitch," Donne murmured to himself as he returned to his desk and the stacks of papers on it, which he got separated into the two piles in a little less than an hour.

-32-
Five Months Earlier

Saturday, July 9, 2011
12:15 p.m.
The Seafood Shack
Bonita Springs, FL

As soon as Jake and Pam found a table at the far end of the outdoor patio, overlooking the canal, Pam tore a paper towel from the dowel in the middle of the table, took off her sunglasses, dabbed at her eyes and blew her nose.

"I'm sorry, Jake. He was so dear, and it's so sad."

"You were very good with him," Jake said, patting her hand, which she turned up to grip his tightly.

"God, I hate Alzheimer's." Her tears welled up again and she began sniffling.

"Someone close to you?" Jake asked.

Pam nodded and said, "My father."

"I'm so sorry, Pam."

"His name was George, too, and he looked a lot like him."

"Oh, geez, I'm really sorry. How long has he been gone?"

"Four – no, five months now. And my mom died two weeks after he did. So it's just me and my sister Judy now. I haven't seen any of them much, but when the two of them went so close to each other, it leaves a kind of emptiness behind."

"Oh, Pam."

Pam pulled her hand away, took another paper towel and dabbed at her eyes and blew her nose again.

"I'm sorry, Jake."

"No, no, Pam, that's okay. Take your time."

Pam took a long sip of her drink and dabbed a few final tears from her face, then sighed and smiled weakly at Jake.

"Okay. Can we talk about something else?"

"Sure."

"Anything else."

"Okay." Jake took a sip of his wine, wiped his lips with his thumb and then said, "How about your plans after you retire?"

"Oh, I don't know yet," Pam said, still sniffling a bit. "I do want to take a few weeks or months and just unwind, and then who knows? I've got offers from a forensic accounting place and a private security firm. Or maybe I'll finish my master's."

"Master's? In what?"

"Physics."

"Physics? Really?"

"Yeah, that was my bachelor's, but it was a long time ago."

"And the accounting?"

"MBA in finance."

"And you did some modeling, too, right?"

"Even a longer time ago, but yeah."

"And sometime in there in the CIA."

Pam glanced sharply at Jake. "How did – oh, right. Yeah, also a long time ago."

"Now, if you were a piano or violin virtuoso, you'd be a real Renaissance woman."

Pam looked at Jake in total surprise, then saw the expression on his face, and laughed.

"Amazing. Piano, but far from a virtuoso. But how did you guess that?"

"Long fingers," Jake said as he held his hand up to hers, palms together. "See?"

"Okay. But yours are pretty long, too. Which was it for you?"

"Guitar and banjo, but also no virtuoso, and it was a VERY long time ago."

"Do you still play?"

"Geez, no, not in maybe ten years. And since I've been doing the book, I haven't really done anything; too focused, I guess."

Jake glanced out at the canal next to the patio, then back at Pam.

"Like two weeks ago at the beach, there was a herd of manatees mating right at the shoreline, lots of people gathered around taking pictures and videos of it, and my only thought was how to put that in the book, even though it's mostly set in DC; no manatees up there."

"Mating? Wow. I've never even seen a manatee."

"Oh, they come by the beach a lot when the water's warm enough. And some of the people sent me pics and videos of them mating; I can forward those to you if you want."

"Yeah, I'd like that."

"Okay. Manatee porn for Pam." He wrote in his notebook while Pam laughed, then glanced out at the canal again.

"We get a lot of dolphins down here, too, and sometimes they put on quite a show."

"Dolphin porn?"

"No; sorry. Just occasionally jumping all the way out of the water and once in a while chasing fish really close to shore."

"I'd like to see that sometime."

"Summer before last, we had a guy on vacation from the East Coast, Miami, I think, who was a marine biologist at one of the research places over there, and he taught us how to call dolphins and manatees."

"Really?" said Pam, incredulous. "How?"

"Well, you stand in the water up to about mid-stomach, facing away from shore, concentrate, hold your hand out like this, and then you go, 'C'mere, dolphins!' and beckon them in."

Pam looked at Jake quizzically.

He continued, "Now, for manatees, since they're so much bigger, you go like this, 'C'mere, manatees,'" in a much deeper voice.

Pam laughed and then, deadpan, asked, "And just how often does that work?"

"Oh, maybe five percent of the time," Jake deadpanned back.

Pam chortled. "Oh, Jake."

"Had you going there for a minute, didn't I?"

"Yup; definitely a gotcha."

Just then, Beverly came over with Jake's doggie box, laughed and said, "Now, now, Jake, are you calling manatees again?" Jake just smiled and nodded … and shrugged very slightly.

"Okay. Can I get you some refills?"

Jake nodded at Pam, who nodded back.

"Sure, Bev; thanks."

"I'll bring some more ice water and lemon, too."

"Thanks, Bev; you're a love."

As Beverly headed back into the restaurant, a huge body-builder type in a tight T-shirt, accompanied by a stunning brunette, came in under the archway from the parking lot and took an empty table two down from Jake and Pam.

"Hey, Joe, Angela," Jake called after they got settled in.

"Oh, hi, Jake. Didn't see you there," the body-builder replied.

"Got my camouflage shirt on."

Angela smiled and asked, "So how's the book coming?"

"Coming along. Angela, Joe, this is Pam."

Angela and Joe chorused, "Hi, Pam."

"Hi, Joe, Angela; nice to meet you."

Jake said, "Joe coaches over at Silva's Gym. Right, Joe?"

"Right."

"You known Jake a long time?" Pam asked.

"Maybe … what? … a year or so," Joe replied. "Remember what you told me the first time we met?"

"Um …"

"The bench press?"

"Oh. Oh, yeah."

Angela said, "What was that?"

Joe said, "He told me he'd bench-pressed 700 pounds the week before."

Angela looked at Jake's body skeptically. "Really?"

"Yup. And what did you say, Jake?"

"Two five-pounders, ten reps a day, seven days; 700 pounds."

Pam laughed loudly, while Angela looked puzzled, then giggled tentatively and looked at Joe, who whispered in her ear.

"Oh," she said, and laughed louder, blushing a little.

"And I built this whole body without any steroids."

Pam and Joe cracked up, but Angela again looked puzzled and blushed.

"So," Joe said, "you found a place for us in your book yet, Jake?"

"Still working on that, but I'll find something for you; promise."

"I think Joey would make a great general," Angela said, caressing his bicep. "He loves to drive his boat."

The deafening silence that followed was broken, mercifully, by Bev's arrival with a tray of drinks for Jake and Pam. As she set the last glass down, she glanced out at the canal, then at Jake, and said, "Oh, wow, Jake. Look at that." All four turned in their chairs, Jake very carefully, and stared at the water.

-33-

Thursday, December 15, 2011
10:25 p.m. local time (4:25 p.m. EST)
The Papal Chambers
Vatican City, Rome, Italy

Hanging up the speakerphone at the end of the report from his emissary to Donne, his neck and face as red as a Cardinal's fascia, the Pope turned and glared at the five members of his inner *inner* inner circle and roared in his native language what could best be translated into English as "Who the fuck does this prick think he is?"

(Author's note: A second translator watched the tapes of this meeting and came up with this: "What does this zucchini believe is his real identity?" A lip reader then reviewed them and claimed he'd said, "Who's gonna bring me a banana? I'm hungry." Frankly, I can't tell who's right on this, and the same goes for all the dialogue in this section, so I've just gone with sort of consensus translations. I don't suggest that any reader take any of this as absolutely accurate. JD)

The four Cardinals and one military officer in the room all buzzed with shock at the Pope's choice language. Never before had they seen him so upset, and considering his age, they were appropriately concerned that he might give himself a heart attack or stroke.

"Half? He wantsa HALF?" the Pope continued, seemingly verging on apoplexy. "Sonovabitcha. We gotta kicka hizza ess."

The financial Cardinal spoke first, "Bennie, Bennie, calm down. We'll take care of that. Let me get you some water."

"I don't wanna no wine-a. I wanna deas onna how to deal with this pyla peanudda butter." He glared at each in turn.

Finally, the marketing Cardinal took a deep breath and said, "I've been thinking since we met last Saturday, and maybe we could go with denouncing him as the Antichrist."

The legal Cardinal piped up, "No, no, no, we can't do that. You can't imagine how much liability we'd open ourselves up to."

"Liability, schmiability; I could sell it. I've studied gobbles and all his techniques. I can sell anyzing."

The doctrinal Cardinal said, "No, the Antichrist plan doesn't come until 2022, after the India-China-Arab war."

The financial Cardinal put in his two euros. "No, you're all seeing the problem wrong. How do we get Donne to rescind the tax on the Church? That's the real challenge. Focus, people, focus."

The Pope cut in, "Hey, you watcha you language!"

"No, Bennie, I said, 'focus.'"

"I told you to watcha you language and you justa say it again. Whassa matta you?"

"Oh, Bennie, I – never mind. I apologize," the financial Cardinal said, rolling his eyes. "How about we just refuse to pay the tax?"

The Cardinals and the Pope all spoke over each other, until the military officer spoke up. "Gentlemen, gentlemen, your attention, please." All eyes in the room turned to him.

"I will take care of the problem. Do not ask me how; you do not want to know."

The room went completely silent, until the Pope nodded and whispered something unintelligible, but which was translated by the two interpreters as "Fruit" or "Suet," and by the lip reader as "Duet," at which point the butler left the room and the recording ended.

-34-
Five Months Earlier

Saturday, July 9, 2011
12:45 p.m.
The Seafood Shack
Bonita Springs, FL

As Jake, Pam, Joe and Angela turned toward the canal, a crowd rushed from the restaurant and clustered on the docks and the patio, all staring at the water.

Beverly looked at Jake and said, "Well, well, well, Jake; you finally did it."

Pam said, "Is that what I think it is, Jake?"

Jake just nodded and smiled.

"First one I've seen live." She stood up and walked to the edge of the patio; Jake got up carefully and followed her.

Bev went over to one of the docks and turned a faucet on, and a dark brown nose rose from the canal, snarfing up the fresh water running from the hose hanging from the end of the dock. A large brown body floated up to the surface behind the nose and rolled over, the two front flippers sloshing in the brackish canal water.

"My god, it's huge," Pam muttered to Jake.

"Maybe a fourteen-footer," Jake replied.

"Fourteen feet? More like fourteen inches." Pam pointed.

"Oh, that; yeah, it's a male," Jake said. "Must be a female somewhere nearby."

"He's so ugly, he's kinda cute."

"Yup, and they're very gentle, quiet beasts."

"Wow. I've got to get some pictures." Pam went back to the table, rummaged in her bag and pulled out a cell phone. She came back to the edge and took several photos, including a few of the crowd gathered around the docks and patio. Jake noticed that two people, a man and a woman in their mid-forties, turned their faces away from Pam as she aimed the camera in their direction; he took note of their appearance, then went back to the table, sat tenderly, lit a cigarette and wrote in his non-spiral notebook.

When Pam returned, she was beaming and smiling. "That was SO cool, Jake."

"You're welcome," Jake said, smiling back.

Pam laughed, pulled a cigarette out of her bag and said, "Five percent?"

Jake nodded, laughed, lit her cigarette and then said, "I've got another admission, Pam."

"Yeah?"

"I saw him coming from the bay before I told the story."

"Ah-ha. I wondered what had caught your eye."

"We call him Steve. He shows up for a drink a couple of times a week. They don't drink saltwater, but they can go for a couple weeks before they need --"

Pam had been laughing as Jake was talking, and she said, "I'm sorry, what was that?"

"Just that they can go a couple of weeks without fresh – okay, what's so funny?"

Pam kept laughing, but managed to blurt out, "Steve ... every time I hear ... that, I ... think of ... Stevie Bruce." Her laughter took over and she started snorting, shaking uncontrollably and tearing up. Contagious, that got Jake laughing, too.

Finally, Pam grabbed a paper towel and wiped her tears away and managed to slow the laughter.

"Well, looked like Stevie has a big bad Bruce," Jake managed to spit out between laughs.

"Oh, god, Jake, he does." Pam's laughter changed to a mix of cackling and snorting. "Jesus, my stomach hurts."

Jake, still laughing, said, "Maybe the pasta?" which got Pam going again. Jake continued, "You know you're supposed to wait at least an hour after eating to laugh. Or is it an hour after swimming to do any eating?"

"Oh, Jake, stop, please." Pam's laughter turned into coughing and she held yet another paper towel up in front of her face. Jake immediately quit laughing.

"Are you okay, Pam?"

"Excuse me." She grabbed her bag, got up and headed quickly into the restaurant, holding the towel firmly to her mouth and nose. Jake followed her with his eyes and then noticed the couple that had turned away from Pam's camera getting up from their table and following her.

"Hey, Angela, can you keep an eye on our table?"

"Okay."

"Joe, can you come with me?"

"Sure, Jake."

Jake got up and headed into the restaurant, with Joe right behind him.

-35-

Thursday, December 15, 2011
9:35 p.m.
The White House
Washington, DC

The four union bosses sat around a table in fairly comfortable chairs in one of the ten cells in the basement, picking at the remnants of the large plate of cold cuts and buns that had been delivered to them three hours earlier, along with a plate of cheese cubes and a cooler of soft drinks, milk and water. A container of hot coffee and a package of tea bags were also in the cell.

"I still can't believe this shit," Richard hissed, throwing the two directives on the table. "Personally fuckin' liable? Permits? Fees? For demonstrating? This fuckin' sonofabitch!!"

"On top of taking all our PAC funds," Andy snarled.

Bob added, "And closing out our insurance scams – I mean plans. And fuckin' around with the pension plans."

Lee's two cents: "And making the whole country 'right to work.' Shit."

Richard said angrily, "But this is the part that pisses me off the most. 'Organizers, inciters, communicators and supporters, direct or indirect, of any activities including, but not limited to, demonstrations or protests, shall be personally jointly and severally liable for any damages inflicted on any property, public or private, by any participant in such activities and for any cleanup and any extra security costs.' And it goes on to say that each and every participant will also be personally liable for those damages and/or costs."

Andy hissed, "The sonofabitch."

Bob said, "Who cares about the demonstrators? Fuck 'em. But to hold <u>us</u> liable? Bastard."

Lee pointed to another paper. "And this one, 127? Strikers may be summarily fired? And any interference with scabs is a felony? What the fuck is that? And more personal liability for us? Shit."

At that moment, a heavy door outside their cell door slammed open. All four bosses got up and went to the bars of their cell. They saw two men pulling and pushing a large arched plexiglass object on dollies past the cells. The arch was about five feet tall, ten feet long and four feet wide.

Richard whispered, "What the fuck is that? A half-wheel for half a giant hamster?"

The door slammed shut.

Andy asked the men, "What's that?"

One of the men answered, "Can't tell you. Classified."

Bob piped up, "Are you guys union?"

The other man laughed. "Are you kidding? If we were, there'd be six guys doing this job."

The first man laughed and said, "Maybe a dozen. Have a nice few days, guys."

Another heavy door slid open and the men moved the object on through it. The door closed behind them with another slam.

Lee said, "That's under the Oval Office, right?"

Richard said, "Yeah, I think so."

Bob added, "Yup, it is."

Andy said, "Weird."

They moved back to their chairs around the table, except for Richard, who paced the room and then said, "So what the fuck do we do now?"

"Go to bed, guys," an electronic voice said. The lights went out.

-36-
Five Months Earlier

Saturday, July 9, 2011
1:05 p.m.
The Seafood Shack
Bonita Springs, FL

As Jake and Joe hurried through the restaurant, they saw the guy from the couple that had followed Pam standing by the windows in the front wall opposite the restrooms. Neither Pam nor the woman were anywhere to be seen; Jake assumed, which he rarely allowed himself to do, that they were in the women's restroom.

When Jake and Joe started to go past the man, heading for the men's room, he backed up against the wall, letting Jake pass by, but when he saw how closely they were looking at him, one on either side of him, he blanched and said, "Oh, God. Did my wife hire you?"

Jake said, "No, buddy. We just want to talk to you." Joe blocked the narrow hallway with his muscled body.

With no warning, the guy reached behind his back, but both Jake and Joe moved quickly, Jake getting a solid hold on the guy's hand and bending the fingers back, while Joe grabbed the semi-automatic pistol lodged in the guy's waistband under his loose shirt, which he handed to Jake.

"Well, well, well," said Jake. "That's some pretty heavy weaponry there, buddy. Are you that scared of your wife? No, no, no; quit squirming or I'll break your fingers. Settle down, now."

"I got him, Jake," said Joe, as he put the guy's right arm into a hammerlock.

Jake knocked on the women's door. "Pam, are you okay?"

Pam's voice came from the other side of the door. "Yup, I'm fine, Jake. Do you see a guy out there, hanging around?"

"Yeah. Joe's holding him and I've got his gun."

The door opened and Pam looked out. "Yup, that's him. Get him in here, quick."

Jake stood back as Joe pushed the guy into the room, still keeping the lock on his arm. Jake followed them in, noticing the woman sitting on the floor with a bloody nose, her arms around the sink drainpipe and flex ties on her wrists. Pam was holding a smaller version of the gun Jake had.

"Okay, Joe, turn him around." Joe complied and Pam put flex ties from her bag on his wrists in front of him and pushed him onto the floor next to the woman, saying, "Sit. Stay. No, no, don't say anything." She pulled some paper towels from the dispenser, gagged them both, then pulled out her cell phone and speed-dialed.

"This is Pamela Robertson-Brooks, Secret Service, Badge _____. I need a soft pickup in Bonita Springs ASAP. I'm holding two federal fugitives in the women's restroom at the Seafood Shack on Bonita Beach Road, about a mile east of the beach. How soon can you get some marshals and transport here? No, I can NOT hold. Hello? Shit.

"Jake, get his wallet and ID, would you?" Jake reached behind the man, pulled his wallet from the pocket of his bermuda shorts and gave it to Pam. She opened it and pulled out a driver's license, which she held next to another one, which she'd apparently gotten from the woman, while keeping the couple covered with the small gun.

"Well, well, well, Nick and Nora Dunn? Geez, if you're going to use aliases, why not go all the way and make it Charles?" She gave the wallet and IDs back to Jake. Jake looked at the IDs closely.

"Hello? Yes, I'm still here. Oh, Tristan? Yup, it's Pam. Look, I've got the Fischers ... yup, Dylan and Emma ... no, just happened to see 'em at a restaurant ... yup, got 'em flex tied, but I need transport, a soft pickup. How soon can you get some marshals here? I need 'em ASAP ... no, no locals ... five? Guess that'll have to do ... right, in the women's restroom ... call me when you're in the parking lot and we'll get 'em out to you ... no, I've got some civilian help ... no, they're cool ... okay." Pam closed the phone and turned to Jake and Joe.

"Thank you, guys. Five minutes. How did you know?"

Jake shrugged. "Just something hinky about them when you were snapping pics, and then they followed you. So I asked Joe to help and we followed them. He's an ex-Marine."

Joe shook his head, "Not ex. Once a Marine, always a Marine."

"Oh, right; sorry, Joe.

"Anyhow, when he went for his gun, I grabbed his hand and Joe got his other arm pinned. Then we knocked on the door. That's it."

Joe said, "I didn't know you could move that fast, Jake, and that hold you put on him, good one. How'd you know that?"

"Oh, I learned it from a woman on the beach who teaches martial arts; I thought it might be useful somewhere in the novel. It's got some Japanese name that I don't remember, but I've got it in my notes. Guess it was just a response when he reached behind him.

"So, Pam, who are these Fischers?"

"Fugitives, counterfeiters, Number 43 on the Most Wanted List. I thought that was them as soon as I saw 'em out there, so I faked that coughing fit and headed to the restroom. Split 'em up so I could confirm who she was. And it worked. She made a big mistake by pulling this little gun when I wouldn't give her my phone. I was about to come out and get him when you knocked. That's it on my end."

Pam glanced down at the two sitting on the floor; Dylan was trying to pull the towels out of his mouth, but Pam shook her head and he stopped, glaring angrily at her. Emma was whimpering. Pam put another paper towel in her hands, which she held to her nose to try to control some of the bleeding, but she, too, glared hatefully at Pam.

"I think there's a reward for these two, and I can probably work it so you two can split it."

Joe's eyes lit up and he said, "Really? Cool."

But Jake said, "Oh, none for me. Let Joe have it all, if there is one."

Pam looked quizzically at Jake. "Really?"

Jake nodded. "Really."

Joe said, "Jake, are you sure?"

Jake nodded again. "Absolutely, really."

Pam said, "Well, okay. Jake, got your notebook with you?"

"Of course. And my pen."

"Joe, if you would, name, address, email and phone number."

Joe asked, "No Social Security?"

"No need for that now. Once I get it all set up, then we will."

"Okay." Joe wrote in Jake's notebook, ripped out the page and gave it to Pam; she slid it into her bag and looked at her watch.

"Two minutes." She pulled a small knife from her bag, slit the flex ties on the woman's wrists, pulled her arms from around the pipe and used new ties to bind her again, hands in front of her body. The old ones and the knife went into her bag.

"Hey, Pam," Jake said, "this just gave me an idea."

"Yeah?"

"Yeah; I like the name Dunn that these two used."

"Not as good as Charles woulda been. Dunn is okay, but ... eh."

"But Dunn is a lot better name than what I came up with for the guy that buys the country, O'Hickenfrankenofskiopoulostein."

"Yeah, I wondered why you'd picked a name like that."

"Well, I think I'm gonna change it to Dunn now. Just run a 'find and replace' function, and that'll work much better, I think. Lots more possibilities with that one, too. Of course, I'll have to take out that multicultural joke that Debbie Jackson made, but that's no big – hey!"

Pam casually slammed her elbow back into Dylan's face, breaking his nose, just as he was reaching for her bag and the knife she'd used to cut his wife's ties.

"Now, now, Dylan, Dylan, did you think I'm so easily distracted?" She pointed to the back of her head. "Eyes back here, always. But thanks, Jake. And Emma, don't you get any ideas now. Here, Dylan." She gave him a paper towel, which he held up to his nose.

Jake chuckled. "Now they match."

Pam held another paper towel out to Jake and said, "Here, Jake. You're bleeding." She pointed at his shoulder.

"Damn, I musta pulled the stitches." He gave Pam the gun and wallet he'd been holding, which she put in her bag, and then pressed the towel against his shoulder under his T-shirt. "Ow. Damn."

Dunn, still holding his paper towel to his nose, smirked and chuckled. Pam glared at him, then lightly slapped the side of his head.

"No Schadenfreude from you, Dylan, you --"

Pam's phone buzzed and she picked it up.

"Robertson-Brooks … oh, good, Tristan. Who? Lydia and Kirk? Great. Send 'em in and we'll be right out." She slipped her phone back in her bag and pulled out two more flex ties.

"They're here. On your feet." As they stood up, held by Joe and Jake, Pam ran the new flex ties between the ones on their wrists, tying the two of them together. She pulled their arms down to waist level, took another paper towel, dampened it and wiped the remaining blood from their faces, but she left the towels in their mouths.

She picked up her bag, opened the door, looked toward the front, then took the Fischers from Joe and Jake, holding them by the flex ties between them with one hand and carrying the small gun in the other, and moved them out into the hallway just as a youngish couple, clad in beach clothes, came toward them from the front door. Pam walked her prisoners up to them and the five moved quickly out into the parking lot to a silver SUV parked close by the front door. Jake and Joe watched through the windows as Pam spoke briefly with the driver, handed him the two guns, signed a paper on a clipboard, which he also signed and kept, and then nodded as the SUV drove slowly up out of the lot, heading west on Bonita Beach Road.

-37-

Friday, December 16, 2011
9:30 a.m.
The White House
Washington, DC

Donne's chief of staff, Emily, escorted Ex-President Obama and Ex-Vice President Biden into the Oval Office, where Donne was ...

(Author's note: The remainder of this section has been redacted at the request of certain people who wish to remain anonymous. Consideration has been provided by them to the author. Sorry; it was really eye-opening. But it was long; 23 pages. JD)

* * * * * *

1:30 p.m.
Donne's chief of staff, Emily, escorted Ex-President Bush and Ex-Vice President Cheney into the Oval Office, where Donne was ...

(Author's note: The remainder of this section has been redacted at the request of certain people who wish to remain anonymous. Consideration has been provided by them to the author. Sorry; it was really eye-opening. But it was long; 18 pages. JD)

* * * * * *

-38-
Five Months Earlier

Saturday, July 9, 2011
1:25 p.m.
The Seafood Shack
Bonita Springs, FL

As the SUV left the parking lot, Pam came back in and said, "Okay. Let's go finish our drinks, guys. I've got a few minutes before I'll need to head up there and get started on the paperwork."
Jake said, "Oh, geez, I completely forgot. I asked Angela to keep an eye on our table."

Pam said, "Let's hope she didn't take that literally. Oh, sorry, Joe."

Joe said, "I'm sorry. What?"

Pam said, "Nothing; never mind."

Jake said, "How do you do that, Pam? I'm still shaking and you're calm as a zucchini and making a joke."

"Cucumber, Jake, not zucchini."

"Oh, sorry; old habit, old joke."

"Compartmentalization, Jake, that's all. It's another old habit of mine. From the job."

As they got to the table, Angela saw them and said, "Nobody touched anything, Jake."

Jake smiled, "Thanks, Angela."

"So what's going on?"

Joe looked at Pam, who nodded and said, "Sure, it's okay."

"Me and Jake helped Pam catch some fugitives."

Angela smiled. "Sure you did, honey; sure you did."

"No, really, baby."

Pam interjected and said, "Yes, Angela, they did." Jake nodded.

"Really? You're not pulling my leg?" She looked up and around the patio, fluffing her hair. "Okay. Where's the cameras?"

"No, baby, no cameras; it's for real."

"I'm Secret Service, Angela."

"For real?"

"For real."

"Wow. And my Joey helped?"

"Yes, Angela, he did."

"Oh, cool. Honey, are you okay?"

"Yeah, I'm fine. But Jake got a little --"

"Oh, Jakey, Jakey, are you hurt? Is that your blood?"

"Yup; but I just pulled some stitches. I'll get it treated soon."

Pam glanced at Jake and mouthed "Jakey?" Jake shrugged and sipped the last of his wine, focusing his attention on the bottom of the glass.

He winced and looked up as he felt a hand on his injured shoulder; it was Beverly's.

"Can I get you another, Jake? Pam?" Pam shook her head.

"No, thanks, Bev. We've got to head out. Just the check, okay?"

"No check. A lady on the lanai paid for you two, left a big tip on top of that. She said to give you a big thanks from, ah, George."

Pam gasped, then took a deep breath and sighed.

"Oh, that's very nice, but I can't accept. I'll have to go talk to her."

"Not possible; they left a few minutes ago."

"Oh, dear. I can't accept gifts. I'm a Se- – federal employee."

Jake said, "Well, I was going to pay anyway, so could you think of it as a gift to me, and let it go at that?"

"Well, that's a stretch, but ... wait, I can't even let you pay for me; I was going to go Dutch."

Jake, perplexed, said, "Oh, geez. I have no --"

Angela interrupted. "I have an idea. How about this? Pam, you give Jake whatever half the bill would have been, and that should let you off the hook, right?"

Pam and Jake both looked at Angela in amazement, and then Pam said tentatively, "I guess ... I think I could be okay with that, maybe. Jake, what do you think?"

"I think ... I think ... I think that's your call, Pam."

"Oh. Um ... okay, I guess that'd work. How much was the check, Bev?"

"Let's see." Bev pulled some checks from her pocket and thumbed through them. "38 dollars and 27 cents. That woman gave me fifty bucks in case you wanted dessert or more drinks."

"So why don't you just give Jake twenty bucks and call it even," Angela suggested.

Jake said, "Fine with me."

Pam pulled out a twenty and a five and gave them to Jake. "Works for me. Thanks, Angela.

"And Bev, the next time you see them, please, please, please pass on my sincere thank you, okay?"

"Will do. Jake, you know your shoulder is bleeding, right?"

"Yup. I'm going to get it fixed as soon as we leave."

"Which should be right now," Pam said, swigging the last of her Mimosa. "I'm sorry, guys. Joe, thanks again, and Angela, so nice to meet you."

Angela smiled and said, "Backatcha, Secret Service lady."

Bev, perplexed, said, "Secret Service?"

Pam looked at her, put a finger to her lips and said, "Our little secret, okay?"

Bev zipped her finger across her lips. "Yup. And next time you're in, I'll be your secret server. Shhh."

Pam chuckled. "Next time I'm in, I'll probably be retired."

"Oh, don't wait that long."

"Not that long; about three weeks."

"Really? Congratulations. We'll have a party."

Angela said, "Oh, I love parties. Can we come, too?"

Bev said, "Sure. But you look too young to retire."

"Why, thank you, thank you very much."

Bev chuckled, "Wow. Are you an Elvis fan, too?"

"Not as much as you, but yeah."

"Cool."

"Oh, Bev, that couple that was sitting over at that table, they won't be coming back. I'll take care of their check."

"Oh, the Dunns?"

"You know them?"

"Sure; they've been regulars here for years."

"Well, you won't be seeing 'em again. Do you have their check?"

"Sure." She pulled out another check. "Here. 57 dollars and 83 cents."

Pam reached into her bag, pulled out Dylan's wallet and took out four twenties, examined them closely and gave them to Bev. "Keep the change, Bev. But I'll need a receipt, okay? Handwritten is fine."

Bev wrote one out and gave it to Pam, who tucked it into the wallet and put it back in her bag. "That's a big tip, Pam. Thanks."

"Thank you, Bev. But now I'm afraid I really have to run. Bye, y'all." She leaned over and gave Jake a peck on the cheek, nodded at the others and headed for the archway to the parking lot. After three steps, she started giggling and turned back.

"Jake, say goodbye to Steve for me, okay?"

"Okay."

Pam then burst out laughing. "And to Bruce."

Jake laughed, too. "Okay."

Beverly, Angela and Joe all said in unison, "Bruce?"

Jake, now laughing uncontrollably, managed to say, "Long story. Another time. Thanks, all. I've got to go get this looked at. Bye. Oops." He pulled off another paper towel and pressed it against his shoulder on top of the other bloodied one.

After a minute or so, he followed Pam out of the archway, carrying his doggie box and leaving three very perplexed people behind, shaking their heads and mumbling, "Bruce?"

But when he got out to the parking lot, he saw Pam sitting behind the wheel of a dark blue SUV, dabbing at her eyes with another towel as her shoulders shook. Jake couldn't tell if she was laughing or crying, and he debated going over to see what, if anything, he might do to help or if he should just let her deal with whatever was bothering her, but then she sat up, started the engine and drove off, heading west, saving Jake from making a decision. He started his car and headed east to the clinic, briefly puzzled. Then he figured it out.

"Compartmentalization."

-39-

Saturday, December 17, 2011
10:57 a.m.
The Eiffel Tower
Paris, France

Two men in expensive business suits, one light gray, one black, strolled around the edges of the crowd in front of the Tower, chatting very quietly.

The man in the black suit, speaking English with a mild Italian accent, said, "20 million Euros is a lot, even for us."

Light gray suit shrugged. "I understand, but that's his price. Same terms: half down, nonrefundable, the remainder when the job is done, and, of course, the life of your principal as collateral."

"As usual; no problem. Guaranteed no blowback on us?"

"Guaranteed. You know his reputation for discretion."

"That's why we came to you. We need complete deniability."

"That you'll have, absolutely. He's never let you down, has he?"

"No, but he's never done a head of state for us before."

"Not for you."

"You mean -- no, I shouldn't ask, should I?"

"No, you should not."

"Can he get him even in the White House?"

"Well, obviously that's tougher, but he can do it."

"We need it done immediately, if not sooner."

"He's got one job to finish first, but he'll get to him as soon as that's done. You'll need to be patient."

"How patient? We need it done by the end of January at the latest."

"January? No problem."

"And nothing extra for the tougher security?"

"Nope. His price is always the same, no matter the target, from an unfaithful husband in Milano to any head of state anywhere. No discounts, no extras, ever."

"I guess that's why he's called The Egal- --"

"No, no, no; none of that. You know better."

"Sorry."

"Sorry? Sorry doesn't cut it. You want him to come after you?"

"No, no, please."

The man in the gray suit stared at him for several moments, then relaxed a bit, but didn't smile. He held out a business card.

"All right. See these numbers?"

"Yes."

"Memorize them."

"Okay." He paused. "Got 'em." Gray suit took the card back.

"I'll expect to see a deposit for ten million euros in that account by close of business Monday."

"You'll have it."

"Then we're done. Now walk away."

The two men parted. After a few moments, the man in the black suit pulled out a cell phone and dialed, speaking in rapid Italian, translated as follows:

"Gaetano here. Write this down." He repeated the numbers he had memorized, but too quietly for the woman with shotgun-miked sunglasses to record or hear them as she moved closer. "Repeat them back." He paused. "Good. Ten million euros to that account by close of business Monday." Another pause. "No, you don't. His (inaudible)-ness has authorized this himself -- minchia! No, that wasn't for you. Take care of it. I'll be back by tomorrow night." He closed his phone and headed toward the Metro.

The woman with the miked sunglasses pulled out her own cell phone and dialed. "Authentication 4583021. They've met and agreed. Get to the KSK Triplets and tell them we need 'em again, and this time they'll be going after The Egalitarian; they'll love that. I'll be in the office in about fifteen, and Ilario can translate the Italian stuff."

-40-
Five Months Earlier

Saturday, July 9, 2011
5:25 p.m.
Bonita Springs, FL

When Jake drove home from the clinic, new stitches in his shoulder and his wallet another $217 lighter, he did his now-habitual surveillance detection route through Bonita Shores and detected nothing.

After he'd parked the car and replenished his wallet cash from the hidden safe, he went upstairs, put the doggie box in the kitchen fridge and booted up his PC.

He found 13 emails in his inbox objecting to Donne legalizing abortion in his book, all in the same format and with exactly the same wording.

"Well, well, well, so it begins." He created a new file, named it "Abortion," and filed the emails there.

There was also one supportive email, which liked the Al Capone tax idea, and seemed personally written. Jake sent a quick thank you email to that sender.

His stomach grumbled, so he went to the fridge, cut off a third of the remaining burger and nuked it, then he settled in ... again carefully ... at his PC and continued working on the novel. He also put a sticky note on the PC tower that said, "Stevie Bruce :-) how to use?" By the time he finished his snack, he had that figured out.

-41-

Monday, December 19, 2011
11:30 a.m.
The White House
Washington, DC

Donne's chief of staff escorted the Director of Central Intelligence, Grant Costello, and his deputy, Lou Abbott, into the Oval Office, where Donne and his Attorney General, Lannie O. "Bud" Longstreet, were awaiting them, standing near the couches in the center of the room. Emily nodded to Donne and then returned to the outer office.

Donne walked over and enthusiastically shook both their hands. "Grant, Lou, again, great job leading up to last week. And you've passed my congratulations on to everybody involved, right?"

"Yes, we have, Gordy," Grant replied. Lou nodded, her jowls bouncing slightly.

"Good, good. Lannie, you remember Grant from when we did that stuff with him in Riyadh back in '05, right?"

"Hi, Grant; good to see you again."

"Hey, Lannie; been a long time."

"And, Lou, this is Lannie Longstreet, my AG. Lannie, Lou, Deputy DCI."

"Lou, good to meet at last. I've heard good things about you."

"Nice to meet you, Lannie."

"All right," Donne said, "enough blah-blah. Sit, sit, and let's get started." Grant and Lou sat on one couch, facing Donne and Longstreet on the other. Donne picked up his ever-present clipboard.

"So, Grant, have we gotten anything good out of those AQs yet?"

"Just a little bit, Gordy; they're tough nuts to crack."

"Where have you got them?"

"Are you sure you want to know that?"

"Look, I don't care about plausible deniability; that's for the politicians. So yes, I want to know. And you know Lannie and I are both cleared."

"Okay. They're in our chalet in Andorra, in the mountains north of Soldeu, only accessible by helicopter."

"Good, good. All okay with the Andorran government?"

"Yup, everything's fine. They have no idea we're there, and we're keeping the same low profile we've had for twenty years."

"Good. I don't want any international incidents this soon."

"Right. Everybody's clear on that. It's just a corporate retreat."

"Good, good. But I want you to squeeze these jihadists as dry as you can. Lannie and I have the written guidelines for you. Lannie?"

"Right here, Gordy." He gave Grant a six-page memorandum.

"You'll find that memo gives you a lot more leeway in dealing with those bastards. And it's Top Secret/USAP, of course."

"Of course."

"You'll see in there that we're getting rid of all that softy politically correct bullshit jargon that the last administration foisted on everybody. These guys are radical Islamists and terrorists, plain and simple, and we're gonna call 'em as we see 'em. No more pussyfootin' around, no more walking on eggshells for any of us. We're at war, period, and they are the fuckin' enemy, period. And my priority is intelligence over prosecution; kill or capture. This nation's security is my top priority, period. And Lannie is okay with that, and will make sure the DOJ and FBI are on board. Right, Lannie?"

Lannie responded, "Already started. I'm getting some backlash, of course. But Mere is on board."

"Keep it going, and keep me posted on that, and feel free to point the finger at me. It is my policy, and I've got pretty thick skin."

"Will do. Oh, Mere is Olivia Meredith Gwynn, FBI Director."

"Grant, you and Lou can go over that later, and if you have any backlash, same thing; feel free to make me the bad guy, okay?"

"Okay."

"Now, your people are paying special attention to anything at all around the holidays coming up and the anniversary of bin Laden's death next May, right?"

"Absolutely, Gordy; HUMINT, SIGINT and all the rest, everything lined up on that. We've already heard some things and we've closed down seventeen cells around the world that were planning attacks, some here, some in Europe and a few in Indonesia and the Philippines, even one in Australia. Got 97 AQ's in custody, and we're interrogating them in thirteen locations around the world, some with the host government's permission, some way under the radar."

"Good. Again, no incidents, okay? Keep all of your hotheads in line. But squeeze 'em hard and get the intel."

"Absolutely."

"Good, good. And I've pardoned all your guys and the soldiers that the previous AG prosecuted, and they've all been released. Politics, yecchh. I've also ordered them to be reimbursed for their legal fees and added some big bonuses for damages to their lives and their reputations."

"We and they all appreciate that, sir."

"No, no, Grant, no more 'sir,' okay? It's Gordy. And that goes for you, as well, Lou."

"Yes, si- – I mean Gordy."

"Good. Okay, anything else – oh, I know about the fatwa that's been issued on me by that nutjob in Iran. You guys are on top of that, right?"

"Of course, Gordy. But you know that a bounty like that brings all sorts of pros, amateurs and nutcases out of the woodwork. But I'm sure you've got enhanced protection around you, even beyond the Service."

"We're on top of that, Grant. Got some new technologies that even you don't know about yet."

"Really?"

"Really. Some are still only in prototype at DEI, but some are fully operational. And when you do see them, they'll blow your mind."

"Looking forward to that, Gordy."

"Soon, Grant, soon."

"Okay; I'll be patient."

"Good, good. Okay, any questions, thoughts, concerns?"

"I've got one."

"Go ahead, Lou."

"Well, sir --"

"Gordy."

"-- Gordy ... sorry ... you know the ACLU is coming after us, and they'll keep up the pressure."

"Don't you worry about them, Lou. Lannie and I have already intervened and closed down all of their lawsuits with you, and we've put them on notice that the rules have changed and they're almost out of business as far as any branch of the federal government is concerned. Another week and they'll all have gotten the message, and poof, no more ACLU problems. We are at war, period.

"Okay. Anything else?"

"Nothing from me, Gordy."

"That was it from me."

"Lannie?"

"Nope, all clear."

"Okay. Go over that memo and if you have any questions, just get in touch with Emily, Alex, Taylor, Jodi or Maria, and I'll get back to you or get you in here ASAP. Go for it. And I've got your six, okay?"

"Okay, Gordy; appreciate it."

Donne stood and shook hands all around.

"Oh, if you want a DVD of this meeting, check with Alex on the way out. Thanks, everybody. Now I've got to get back to prepping the Medicare speech for tonight."

Everybody left, and Donne went back to his desk, buzzed his

chief of staff and asked her to gather up his social media team and bring them into the Oval Office in twenty minutes.

"Will do, Gordy. Twenty minutes."

"Thanks, Emily."

Donne then picked up the printout of his speech and continued editing and rehearsing it, nibbling from time to time on a turkey-and-peanut butter sandwich, but ignoring a plastic container of sprouts, tofu and parsley which had suspiciously appeared with the sandwich.

Twenty minutes later, the intercom on his desk buzzed and Emily said, "The team is here, Mr. Donne."

"Thanks, Emily. Bring 'em on in."

Several twenty-something men and women followed Emily in and milled about the room until Donne waved them to sit and get comfortable. He also quietly handed Emily the plastic container as she gave him a stack of papers. She smiled innocently and took the container with her as she left. (She snacked on the contents at her desk for the next half hour.)

Donne came around from behind his desk and smiled.

"Good morning, gang. Everybody comfy? Good, good.

"Okay. I've only met some of you, so could the team leaders introduce their teams, please? Lexie, go ahead."

"Yes, Mr. Donne. We're the Monitors, and we have a network of over a hundred freelancers screening all the social media sites and blogs, funneling what they find to the ten of us: Susie, Ellie, Sydne, Selma, Katie, Tracey, Tammy, Riley, Ragan and me."

"Thanks, Lexie, and welcome to you all. Maddie?"

"We're the Responders, Mr. Donne. My team and our network respond to whatever Lexie's team sends us, positive or negative, with the talking points Emily has given us. We are Bettina, Birgitte, Bria, Becca, Belinda, Zoey, Dawn, Rhiannon and me."

"Good, Maddie, and welcome to you and your team. Kennedy?"

"We're the Initiators, Mr. Donne. We get daily updates from Emily and her staff and start feeding them out to the public through our volunteer network of bloggers and other social media people, plus several PR firms and media contacts. My team is Brittnie, Cassie, Kiersten, Donna, Heather, Lacie, Brian and me."

"Thank you, Kennedy, and welcome to all of you, too.

"I've been getting very good reports from Emily on how you're all doing, and I applaud your dedication and inventiveness.

"Now, tonight I'll be giving a speech on Medicare, Medicaid and health insurance, and it's definitely going to be controversial, so you'll all need to be prepared for an explosion of activity, especially from the organized health insurance companies, doctors, the pharma companies and the other special interests that are gonna be affected.

"Emily has prepared our talking points on this whole change," he said as he handed the stack of papers to the team leaders, "and as you study those, you'll see that this idea is completely and totally to put choice and control back into the hands of the people.

"So, Maddie, Lexie and Kennedy, you'll need to bring your teams and your networks up to speed on all this, so they're ready to go 24/7 as soon as I give that speech. I wouldn't expect the spike to last more than a week or so, but it'll be pretty intense, I'm sure.

"If you need more people for your teams, let Emily know and she'll be sure you get 'em.

"And one important thing I need you all to remember. We don't need to get defensive, no matter what lies and BS they shoot out. We're gonna stay just soft and neutral, so no flaming, no personal attacks, just the facts. And gentle, self-assured. Okay?"

Everybody nodded or said, "Yes, sir."

"Good. If you have any questions at all this afternoon or at any time as we go through this, I'll be available 24/7, and you can reach me through Emily or any of her staff.

"Okay. Any questions now?"

The teams all glanced at each other, but nobody said anything, until Lexie spoke up. "I guess not, Mr. Donne; I think we're good."

"Okay, that's it for now, then. I'm counting on each and every one of you to do the absolute best you can.

"So let's all get a good rest and be ready for the onslaught about 8:45 tonight. And thanks again, gang."

At that point, spontaneous and loud applause broke out as all of the teams got up and headed out, all smiles, except Brian, the only guy in the group, who was lagging behind and intensely studying the papers he was carrying, so intensely that he bumped into the closing door as he reached it. He backed up, re-opened the door and started to head out, blushing deeply, but still studying the papers.

"Hey, Brian, do you play chess? Donne asked.

Brian looked up nervously. "Yes, sir, Mr. Donne."

"Thought so. We'll talk later. For now, have at it. And thanks."

When the door closed behind Brian, Donne returned to his desk and got back to work on his speech and on his sandwich, mumbling, "Tofu equals protein minus taste."

-42-
Four Months Earlier

Saturday, August 13, 2011
10:10 a.m.
Bonita Beach, Florida

With his stitches removed ($146) and the cuts nearly healed, Jake was floating on a couple of noodles in the Gulf on this already hot day, bicycling his legs under the surface, a dead cigarette butt tucked under a bow of his sunglasses at his temple and a book in his hands. His fashion statement was completed by a slightly tattered bucket beach hat, which had originally been white, but now verged on ecru.

He'd arrived about 7:45, set up his lounge, cooler and beach bag, watched the X-Fit with Kevin exercise group until he got vicariously exhausted, exchanged "Good Mornings" with some of the early walkers and had made several notes in his notebook. But now, as he floated in the warm, clear Gulf water, he was reading a thick nonfiction paperback book, a process someone had called "aqua-literating."

"Good book?" a female voice asked from behind him.

"Can't put it down," Jake replied as he swiveled to see who was there. "Oh, hey, Ann Louise. How's the Bitch of the Beach doing?"

"Oh, so-so," she said. "You?"

"Waking up. Should be done by maybe Tuesday."

"So whatcha reading now?"

Jake showed her the cover and said, "It's a pretty scathing history of the Federal Reserve and the worldwide banking cabal, from colonial times up to now. Already raised my blood pressure up to near normal three times in the last half hour or so."

"That's nice. Listen, I got something for your book."

"Okay."

"Well --"

"Now, this will be of national significance, right, not like your last one, that people from New Jersey sit too close to other people's chairs and blankets?"

"Well, they do do that all over the country, not just here, don't they?"

"Okay, but what's Donne gonna do about it, make a law that they have to stay at least, what, two feet away? Three? Five? C'mon."

"Well, I think it's a legitimate complaint. Okay, okay. Now, you know how the Collier lot is set up so that it's a long walk from the east end to the boardwalk, right?"

"Yeah. So?"

"Well, a lot of people come early just to walk the beach, get some exercise, with nothing to carry, right?"

"Yeah."

"And a lot of families come for the day and they have tons of stuff to carry, like chairs and toys for the kids, umbrellas and coolers?"

"Yeah."

"So doesn't it piss you off that the exercisers park up front, close to the boardwalk, and take up all the spaces in the circle, so the families have to walk so much further with all their stuff?"

"Never thought about it, but it does seem ironic." He chuckled. "I guess if I had a family and a lot of stuff, yeah, it'd be annoying."

"They come for the exercise, but can't walk the little bit further to the end of the lot, get just a little more exercise."

"I guess that's sort of inconsiderate, but, again, national?"

"Probably happens everywhere."

"Could be, but a vital national interest?"

"Well, I think so."

"Tell you what, Ann Louise; I'll think about it, okay?"

"Oh, okay," she said, downcast. "But think hard."

"I will, I will; promise."

"Okay. Well, see ya later. Have a nice day."

Jake gave her a Benny Hill salute and said, "Yes, ma'am, I will."

"Oh, can you do anything to get Sonya to shut up? She runs on and on about nothing, can't get away from her. And she's so angry, on and on, bitching about (N-word deleted)s and Jews. Jesus."

"I've got some super glue in my bag, if you want to sneak it into her lipstick. But she and Herb only come on weekends, now that he's working again."

"Yeah, but – oh, shit, they're here and I think she just saw me."

"Well, don't hang around me anymore. Go, go."

Just then a harsh nasal female voice called out from shore, "Hey, Ann Louise!"

"Oh, shit."

"Go, go. I'll talk to you later."

"I'm going."

"Hey, Ann Louise! Wait up!"

But Ann Louise wasn't fast enough, and Sonya caught up with her about twenty feet from Jake and stayed with her as she headed back north as quickly as a woman of her girth could in chest-deep water.

Jake breathed a sigh of relief and started for the shore, filling a bag with water to wash his feet when he got to his lounge. Once there and with that done and the cigarette butt in an empty pack, he pulled a plastic container of ice cream from his cooler, ate a spoonful and let it slide down his throat. He followed that with a drink of water and some lip balm, then lay down and went back to his book, with a goal of staying on shore in the hot sun for at least twenty minutes. He also made a few notes in his notebook.

Eight minutes later, he was back in the water, with noodles, bag, book and a newly-lit cigarette, rotating 360 degrees occasionally.

Forty minutes later, he had walked in chest-deep water north to the volleyball net and back, then south an equal distance from his lounge and back, all in chest-deep water, negotiating pathways around other people in the water, reading and occasionally chatting with both strangers and people he knew, spreading the link to his web site to the ones that seemed to have above-average intelligence, including a few of the Beach Potatoes, some of the Barefoot Beach Babes, none of the Hat Squad, and one tourist named John who said he worked for the United Nations and wondered whether Donne would keep the US in the UN. (The Incontinentals never went in the water, nor did the Beach Balls.)

A few minutes past eleven, a gentle female voice behind him said, "Good book?"

"Can't put it – oh, hey, Pam." Then he swiveled to face her. She was chest-deep in the water, floating on a bright blue noodle, wearing a shiny black bikini top with a golden ring in the cleavage; it was a bit less revealing than the one she'd had on two months before, but still eye-catching. Her hair was back in a ponytail and her sunglasses had some gold filigree on the frame. Her face hadn't changed at all, still natural and stunning.

"So you recognize my voice after a month? Cool."

"Pizza cake; it's hard to forget. When did you get in?"

"Last night. Hope you're okay with the surprise."

"Pam, with you, EVERYTHING is a surprise. But delightful; it's always nice to see you."

"Thanks; that's a relief. Looks like you got the stitches out."

"Yup, a couple weeks ago; gonna have some scars, though. So how've you been? Two weeks of retirement treating you okay?"

"Your memory's getting better. And yup, it's been good so far, but it's tough going from being so busy to having zero responsibility. I'm still waking up at five in the morning."

"That should ease up after a week or two. At least, that's what happened to me when I retired. And I'd bet that you'll be sleeping in till seven or eight pretty soon if you want to. I mean, you're like 15 years younger than me, so I'll bet you'll adapt quicklier than I did."

"Quicklier?"

"Gets the idea across, doesn't it?"

"Yeah, I guess it does. Hmm. I like it." She chuckled.

"I think just staying in the condo for a while will help," she said, pointing across the beach. "A lot quieter than my place in DC."

Jake looked where she was pointing.

"You're staying over there? Which building?"

"The middle one."

"Really? Which floor?"

"Seventh, this side. Great view. Small, but just fine for one."

"Yeah, I've seen 'em. Very comfy, especially with the upgrades."

"And I've got it for free, till the end of October, if I want."

"Really? Nice. How'd you work that?"

"Belongs to a college roommate and her husband, but they won't be down till November, and they don't like to rent it out."

"So how long are you planning to stay?"

"I don't know yet. This seems like a great place to relax and unwind, and I do love the beach; I had no idea what I was missing. So I guess I owe you a big thank you."

"Me? Why me?"

"If I hadn't been sent to investigate you, I'd just be doing what I'd been doing, investigating other threats or counterfeiting or something in Idaho or Ohio or somewhere, never woulda seen this place and thought more seriously about retiring."

Jake thought about that for a second, then said, "Okay. You're welcome, I guess. Oh, and you're welcome; always nice to see you."

"Thanks. Nice to be seen."

Jake laughed. "Oh, before I forget, Joe got his check for the reward and said if I saw you before he did, to give you a big thanks from him."

"I'm glad it got there; I tried to expedite it. Sometimes it can take up to six months, but this was a small one."

"Twenty-five K is small?"

"As rewards go, yes."

"Wow.

"And I heard that you replaced the jet ski that one of your guys killed."

"Yeah, pretty much as soon as we heard that one of our bullets hit it. And we got some psych help for the kid who was riding it."

"So anything new with your ex-boss?"

"Raunchy Randy? He's still on suspension, I guess. Haven't heard anything about him or from him. How about you? Anything?"

"Not really; been kinda quiet since that day at the Shack."

"No more manatee porn?"

"Nope; they swim by here a few times a week, but no mating."

"You still calling 'em?"

"Yup, every morning when I get here; dolphins, too. They come by more often than the big guys."

"Really?"

"Yup, almost quotidian; probably see some today."

"Cool. So how's the book coming?"

"Slowly, but new ideas come up every day; like there was one guy I talked with maybe half an hour ago who said he worked for the UN and wondered whether I'd keep the US in the UN. Something a little hinky about him; I'm not sure. But I started the conversation, not him. So maybe that was just a coinkydink."

"A what?"

"Oh, sorry; coinkydink, like coincidence, but a bit less random."

Pam laughed. "Are you making up a lot of words for the book?"

Jake chuckled. "You got me. Sometimes I do. But I don't think I made that one up. Heard it somewhere."

"So how's the book coming? Still on target for December?"

"So far, so good. Kinda stuck on how he might fix Medicare and the whole health care thing. And a lot of other stuff, too. But I've got a rough timeline for him, and a lot of assassination plots and a few subplots outlined."

"Cool."

"And now that you're retired, maybe you can start telling me some stories from the inside."

"Maybe I can, but not right now, okay? I want to just relax for a while."

"Sure, no problem. No pressure, no stress. Me be very patient."

Pam adjusted her noodle so that it was under her arms and around her back, let her feet float up, closed her eyes and sighed. "Oh, this is heaven."

"Well, maybe the waiting room."

Jake noticed that her black bikini bottom was also less revealing than the near-thong she'd had before, but still skimpy, and had a large golden ring on each side.

Pam murmured, "You get to do this every day?"

Jake nodded. "Unless it's snowing." Pam chuckled.

"Maybe I could get used to this ... quicklier than I thought."

Jake laughed. "Oh, I'm sure you could. You're a quick study."

Pam smiled and slipped into a deep Southern accent, "Why, thank you, suh. Ah do 'preciate the compliment."

Jake said, "It's well deserved. Oh, do you know the difference between a fairy tale in the North and one in the South?"

Pam thought for a moment and then said, "Why, no, suh, ah don't."

"In the North, it begins with 'Once upon a time'; in the South, it's 'Y'all ain't gonna bleeve this shit.'"

Pam laughed, a deep belly laugh, and her taut stomach rippled, which, naturally enough, pulled Jake's attention away from her face.

"Oh, god, I love that one."

"You can just call me Jake."

Pam laughed even harder.

"Just don't call me Stevie Bruce."

At that, Pam was totally gone. She lowered her feet to the sandy bottom, brought her hands up to her mouth and alternately cackled and snorted. Jake, of course, got caught up and started laughing along.

Half a minute later, a harsh nasal voice intruded. "What's so funny?" Jake and Pam both swiveled in the water to see who it was.

"Inside joke, Sonya. Private conversation," Jake said.

"Oh. So, Jake, have you thought about --"

"Private conversation, Sonya."

"But I --"

"<u>Private</u> conversation," Jake said, a little more sharply.

"But --"

"What part of 'private' don't you understand, Sonya? Go."

"All right, all right." Sonya glared at Jake as she moved away.

Pam finally controlled herself and said, "What was that about?"

"That's Sonya, the Blabberator of the Beach. If you let her get started, she'll talk your ears off. She's very bright, but she can go on and on on the same subject beyond anyone's ability to listen."

Jake moved closer to Pam, adding, "And she has some vision problems, so she gets much closer to people than they like, to the point that they get really uncomfortable."

Pam stayed where she was and let Jake get very close. "You mean she invades people's personal space?"

"You got it."

"Like you're doing with me right now?" Pam said, smiling.

"Yup. And like you did with Sergeant ... oh, what was his name again?"

"Oh, right. Umm ... Dooley? Yeah, that was it, Dooley."

"Thomas. Poor guy. I don't think he ever knew what hit him."

Jake backed away from Pam. "You sure showed some ... uh, guts."

"I had a badge then, Jake, and some Marines."

"Well, I was impressed. Still am. And dealing with those fugitives at the Seafood Shack. You really are a Renaissance woman."

"That's the second time you've called me that, Jake." She took a deep breath and said, "My husband used to say the same thing when he was still alive."

"Well, then there's two of us who think alike."

Pam was quiet for a moment and then said pensively, almost silently, "You have more than just that in common."

"I'm sorry? What?" Jake said.

Pam blushed. "Just thinking out loud; sorry. Never mind."

After a pause, with her eyes still closed, Pam said, "I read that book you're reading, a few years ago. Quite a conspiracy theory."

"Yup, if he's got his facts right."

"Most of them, he does."

"Really?"

"Yup." She took a deep breath and dropped her feet to the

bottom. "Well, I'm ready for a little sun time."

"Me, too." Jake looked at the fingertips on his non-book-holding hand. "Looks like the botox is wearing off." Pam chuckled and they headed to shore.

-43-

Monday, December 19, 2011
1:30 p.m.
The White House
Washington, DC

Emily escorted the Surgeon General, Adam Corville, MD, and the new Secretary of Health and Human Services, Georgianne "Gigi" Maitlin, into the Oval Office, smiled at Donne, revealing a small bit of parsley stuck between her front teeth, turned around and left.

"Thanks for coming on such short notice, Doc."

"Gigi, how are you settling in?"

"Pretty well, Gordy. Kathy has been mostly very gracious and helpful with the transition, and she'll be staying on till the end of the month to consult."

"Good, good. No problems with her politics?"

"Well, a few philosophical differences, but she seems to be trying to keep them out of the mix. I can handle it."

"Good, good. If you need any help with that, just let me know, okay?"

"Will do, Gordy."

"Doc, I trust you're doing okay, as well?"

"It's an honor that you chose to keep me on, Mr. Donne."

"You've done a good job, Adam, and feel free to call me Gordy."

"Okay ... Gordy."

"Good. Now, you both know I'm unveiling the Medicare plan tonight, give folks a year's notice on how that's going to change and the new choices they'll all have. You've both looked it over, I trust, and I'm wondering if you have any questions or input."

Gigi said, "Nothing major from me, Gordy. It's about the way we planned it back at DEI, so I'm clear on it and totally on board."

"Doc?"

"Well, si- – Gordy, I'm generally okay with it all, but I think we need to do more than offer discounts to people who don't smoke and aren't overweight. They need more sticks than carrots, I think. And I thought the bans on indoor and outdoor smoking were good ideas. We've got to put more stringent restrictions on that wherever we can, some more serious behavioral controls, not remove them."

"Well, Doc, I realize that's been the way this past administration and the one before it ... well, going a long way back, all of them ... have tried to deal with things, but that whole philosophy is out, gone, dead and buried.

"Now, you and your staff can make all the recommendations you want on how to <u>persuade</u> people to quit smoking and eat more healthily ... god, that's an awkward phrase ... eat healthilier ... yeah, I like that better ... and lose weight, but it's got to be through persuasion, not mandates. I am absolutely planning to totally dismantle the nanny state, one mandate at a time, or faster, and if people on the staff can't get with that program in a reasonable amount of time, I'll be looking to replace them, like Kathy over at HHS or all the czars that Obama had.

"Spirited debates? Fine, love 'em. Intransigent ideological heads in the sand and loud voices farting talking points out their butts? Nope, sorry, not gonna fly.

"So more carrots and fewer sticks ... generally, okay? That's the way to channel our efforts."

"What about the warning labels on cigarettes?"

"No problem with those, if they're informative and realistic, not those graphic images you guys tried to mandate. See the diff?"

"Yeah, I think so."

"Now, part of it is just semantics. People get discounts for NOT doing something, not penalties FOR doing something, like with the smoking or with over-eating. That's worked for me for over twenty years at DEI and in all the businesses we resurrected and turned around, so there's a track record there.

"Now, that doesn't apply in everything. Like you may have taken what I said about replacing people as a threat or a penalty, and in a way you're right to take it that way. But I would rather persuade people to stay on the ship and help steer it in the right direction than make them walk the plank. However, there always IS a plank."

"Got it, I think."

"Good. Like I said, you've done a pretty good job, other than all that mandate crap."

"More carrots, fewer sticks."

"Right, right; good. Okay. Anything else?"

Gigi shook her head. "I'm good, Gordy."

"Me, too, I think," said Adam.

"Good. So we're done here. Thanks for coming in. Oh, if you want a DVD of this, just check with Alex, okay? Thanks again."

After they left, Donne waited two minutes, then buzzed Emily and asked her if she was alone. When she confirmed that she was, he whispered into the intercom, "Check your teeth, okay?"

There was a pause, and Donne heard a gasp over the intercom and then, "Got it, Gordy; shit."

"Good, Emily. And if I ever have peanut butter or anything in mine, be sure to let me know, okay?"

"Will do, Gordy; sorry."

"No problem, no problem. I'm back to the speech, but if anything comes up, I'll be available." He clicked off, picked up his speech and dug back into it. A few minutes later, he pulled out a pocket mirror and checked his own teeth, then continued working on the speech.

-44-
Four Months Earlier

Saturday, August 13, 2011
11:20 a.m.
Bonita Beach, Florida

Jake looked at the fingertips on his non-book-holding hand. "Looks like the botox is wearing off." Pam chuckled and they headed to shore, Pam leading the way as Jake paused to fill his foot-washing bag.

As the bottom of her bikini emerged from the water, Jake saw that it was decorated with a large golden heart in the middle of the back.

"Y'know, Pam, I've heard of women who wear their heart on their sleeve, but ..."

"I know, Jake, I know. I liked the rest of the suit enough not to worry about that." She walked over to her beach bag and chair.

"Is it okay if I sit with you again?"

"Sure. I'd like that."

Once they both got settled in, Pam looked over at Jake and said, "I've got to admit I've had you and your book on my mind for the last month, and I have a whole bunch of questions and ideas. Is that okay with you?"

"Not in any kind of professional capacity?"

"Nope; promise. I'm retired, remember? And I'm not spying for some author or publisher, either."

"Okay. I've got some questions for you, too; I've thought about you a lot ever since we met. And no, not just because you're gorgeous; I like your brain."

"And I like yours."

Jake put on his Southern drawl. "Why, thank yuh, ma'am. So y'all just go 'head and fahr them thar questions."

Pam chuckled. "Okay." She pulled out a notebook and flipped it open.

"Notes, Pam? You've got notes?"

"Yup. I've got CDO."

"CDO?"

"Yup; it's like OCD, but with the letters in the correct alphabetical order." Pam emphasized each of the last three words.

Jake laughed. "Oh, good one."

"These are in no particular order, okay?"

"Okay."

"Okay. First, have you thought about maybe having your guy get rid of the wash sale rule?"

"Oh, yeah; he does that first thing, along with reinstating the uptick rule. Isn't that in his speech?"

"I didn't see it there."

"Oh, maybe it's just in my manuscript, not online. I think I can stick that in there, maybe tonight.

"By the way, I did change his name, but I spelled it D-o-n-n-e instead of D-u-n-n; thought the poetic reference might be more interesting."

"Oh, cool; I like that. Would make the title a lot easier to say. 'Donne Buys DC' is a whole lot better. I'm not sure that other name would even have fit on a cover."

"Yeah. But I kinda liked the silliness of it."

"Hey, Jake, how about this? 'The Donne Deal'? What do you think of that for a title?"

"Oh, I love it, Pam, absolutely love it." He pulled his notebook and pen out of his bag and wrote excitedly ... well, what passed for excitedly in him. "Beautiful. I may have to give you credit for that."

"Oh, no, Jake, no need."

"Okay, I'll backburner that. But I DO love that title. How'd you come up with it?"

"No idea; it just popped up ... oh, sometimes we'd say 'It's a done deal' in the Service when we wrapped up a case and passed it on for prosecution; maybe it came from that. Jargon."

"Okay. What else?"

"Well, before I get too granular --"

"Too what?"

"Granular, down to detail level, like you did with the tax rates."

"Oh, okay."

"I guess I'm wondering how granular you want to get with things like each individual agency, department, program, and so on."

"Well, I'm not sure right now. The tax rates and that stuff were pretty granular, weren't they? And boring for the non-wonks. I mean, I sure don't want him to go through each and every nook and cranny of the whole government. I mean, I don't want this to turn into a King-sized novel, just keep it to maybe 300 to 350 pages in all. But I think being too general is ... well, is being too general

"But he will go for efficiencies and consolidations. For example, there are nearly 200 separate programs that serve poor people, each with separate staffing. Will I have him go through each of those and describe what he's doing? Nope. He'll just say something like 'I'll combine those all into a single program and get rid of the duplicate staff, flatten the top-heavy mid- and upper-level bureaucracies and cut out like 80 percent of the red tape.' Does that sound too general?"

"Hmm. Probably not for most people, but the policy wonks'll want the details. I mean, you'd be talking about programs in lots of different departments, like Agriculture, HHS, Interior, Energy, and a bunch more. It'd take a lot of pages just to list them all. But I think that kind of general statement might be enough."

"Yeah, I sure don't want to make it too boring, like just reading through the whole Simpson-Bowles plan. I did that, by the way. For me, it was interesting, and I took a lot of notes, but for somebody who just watches reality TV shows, some sitcoms and those voice and dance competition shows, it'd sure put them to sleep."

"Like Debbie Jackson?" Pam smiled.

"Well, she's a caricature, kind of extreme, but yeah.

"And there's not only depth and details, but breadth, across all the departments, and I'll tell ya I'm sure glad I'm not actually in the position of digging both down and across and doing what O'Hicken-– I mean Donne is doing."

"Oh, for sure. It's just interesting to me to speculate on how he or anyone would or could actually make the changes if they had the chance and power."

"Yeah. I feel kinda like he's a dog that's caught a car and can't quite figure out what to do with it now. But I guess I'm really that dog and he's the – oh, what's the word?"

"Don't know. Ghost dog? Character? Doppelganger?"

"Nope; it's gone. No idea. Something like 'construct.' But I guess 'character' is close enough – ah, 'alter ego.'

"I mean, you know I haven't actually written out all those 257 directives he had before his first speech, just kinda pulled that number outa my – outa thin air. I started to write 'em all, of course, but then I figured I'd just bring 'em out as things went along."

"That makes sense."

"Thanks. It's a helluva lot easier on me. But I spent about two weeks working on those, got up to about a hundred of 'em."

"Wow, that's a lot of work. Do you still have them?"

"I'm sure I do, somewhere. But in my house, having and finding are two totally separate issues."

"Even on your PC?"

"Yup. I didn't start off with much organization on – wait a minute; I think I know where I could find 'em, what the file name is."

"I would love to see those, if that's okay."

"Let me think about that. You're sure you're not spying for some author or publisher?"

Pam laughed. "Really; promise. Cross my heart." She made that gesture and Jake's eyes followed, naturally. He paused to breathe, glanced out at the Gulf and then back at Pam ... at her eyes.

"Okay, I have an idea. I think I can find the file and I'll print it out, bring it along and you can look at it with me ... as long as you're not using a DS380 or any --"

"Oh, Jake, I promise, really. But I can understand, and I don't blame you. Tell you what, I'll let you frisk me, check my sunglasses, anything you want, okay?" She paused. "Anything."

Jake felt himself blushing under his tan, took a deep breath for some control and then laughed and said, back in a Southern accent, "W'al, that's a purty open invite, ain't it, ma'am?"

Pam, in her own Southern accent, replied, "But ah do mean it sincerely, suh. I'd sho' like fo' y'all to trust me and feel safe and comfy with me."

Jake laughed in spite of himself, waggled his eyebrows and said, with no accent, "Okay. I may just take you up on that sometime."

"Ah sho' would look fo'rd to that, suh." She slid out of her chair, lay back on her towel and closed her eyes.

Jake finally dragged his gaze away from her, picked up his notebook and pen and went back to making notes.

-45-

Monday, December 19, 2011
8:30 p.m.
The White House
Washington, DC
via a 24-hour news channel

Donne, in his usual casual clothing, smiled at the camera from behind his desk in the Oval Office and held up another sheaf of papers, perhaps four inches thick.

"Good evening, my fellow Americans. Before I get into the main message I have for you tonight, I want to tell you about another 589 businesses that are moving to or expanding in this country. These are their letters of commitment, which indicate that they'll be creating another 2.4 million jobs by the end of this year. So I believe we're making progress toward the goals I set last week, good progress.

"On the other hand, this Occupy movement has gotten very much out of hand, damaging large and small business premises, hassling honest business owners and workers, destroying public property and also some private property whose owners initially welcomed them in and then changed their minds.

"We know the identities of most of the instigators and organizers of this movement, and per my Directive 241, those individuals, along with the actual perpetrators of the damage, have been and will be held personally responsible for all of that damage, both by loss of liberty and financial loss. In fact, four of them are currently resting in the cellblock in the basement of this building and will find out tonight or tomorrow morning just what that responsibility will mean for them and their bank accounts. That's all on that subject for now."

Donne reached behind the desk and placed a tablet PC on a small easel, facing the camera. The screen was blank, other than the words "MEDICARE 2013."

"Now for the main message I have for you all tonight. And while it initially concerns Medicare, especially Medicare Advantage, it will also be relevant for each and every one of you, no matter your age. It won't go into effect until next year, 2013, and we'll have lots more opportunities to go into all the details, but I would encourage all of you to pay attention to this introduction and to study the details in the months to come so you can make an informed choice later."

As Donne went through his speech, he tapped the tablet to reveal a new graphic in turn, illustrating each of his points.

"Today, the way Medicare Advantage is structured, the Medicare Trust Fund pays about 850 dollars to the insurance companies each month for each person they've enrolled in their plan. 850 bucks per person per month. And the insurance companies administer the program, standing in for the government.

"But starting with the open enrollment period at the end of next year, you'll be able to select an alternative Medicare Advantage program for 2013, and here's how it'll work.

"First, out of that 850 bucks, we'll take 500 and put it into a Health Savings Account for each enrollee. The new insurance company will issue you a debit card, which, along with a thumbprint, will be good for doctor visits, medicine, even aspirin at the pharmacy. At 500 a month, that's six thousand a year in your HSA ... for medical expenses only. If you don't use it, it'll roll over to the next year, when you'll get another six thousand dollars. That will build up until you die, and at that point it'll pass on to your heirs, at least 50% into their HSA, which will be tax-free. The remainder can go into that account tax-free, or the heir can choose to take it outside the HSA account, but it'll be taxed at a rate of 25 percent.

"Another $250 will pay the premium on a catastrophic policy, which will have a high deductible, $10,000 the first time you reach it, then down to 5,000 the second year and beyond.

"Pre-existing conditions will be covered immediately when you reach 65 and enroll.

"Now, if you're a non-smoker, you'll get a 50-dollar-a-month discount on the catastrophic policy, and that will be added to your HSA; and if you are not overweight, meaning you have a body mass index of 25 or below, you'll get another 50-buck discount, which will also go into your HSA. So that could mean an extra hundred bucks a month, twelve hundred a year, into that account if you take care of yourself.

"The catastrophic coverage will be 80/20 from the deductible up to $50,000, then 90/10 up to a hundred K, and 100% above that, with no lifetime maximums.

"The hundred bucks a month per person that we save will stay in the Medicare Trust Fund and act as a backup and reserve fund for the first few years as we see how this works out over that time.

"This subsidized combination of HSA and catastrophic coverage will also be available through Medicaid, administered nationally, not state-by-state.

"We will also make this combination available to people under 65 in age, nationally, at their own expense, with a limit of $20,000 per year for contributions to the Health Savings Account. Again, a debit card will be issued by the insurance companies for that account, and customers will have a choice of deductibles on the catastrophic policy. Premiums can also be risk-based, and pre-existing conditions will be covered, but with a five-year waiting period.

"Insurance companies may also offer other kinds of policies, up to and including what we now call Major Medical. Optional riders for other conditions and/or treatments will be available, sort of a la carte.

"My new Health and Human Services Secretary, Gigi Maitlin, and her staff and I will be working closely on several aspects of this new program, including very tough negotiations with the drug companies for much, MUCH better prices than Medicare and Medicaid have been able to get, and with medical professionals and hospitals and device manufacturers to not only start bending the cost curve, but to significantly bend it down.

"Also, the past practice of charging the uninsured up to five or six times what the insurance companies pay, that's over and done with. That practice is illegal as of right now, and in four months, all advertising to consumers for prescription drugs and medical devices will be illegal.

"We will establish an impartial rating system for all the policies that people can choose, and it'll make it really simple to compare policies and see which one is right for you and your situation.

"And since we're also allowing for national, cross-state policies, nobody will be stuck buying a higher-premium policy as an individual. Everybody will get the lowest group rate available.

"I'm also encouraging medical professionals to establish low-cost urgent care clinics in or next to every emergency room in the country, staffed by nurse practitioners and pro bono volunteer doctors. Every patient coming to the emergency room will first be thumbprinted and triaged at the clinic and treated there, if possible, and only sent to the emergency room if it's absolutely necessary.

"I'm sure that once you have your HSA, you'll be happier paying, just for example, fifty bucks at one of those clinics rather than nine hundred at the ER for the exact same treatment.

"Now, this has just been an overview, and there are lots of details to go over, and as you've heard often enough, 'The devil is in the details,' so we'll be looking this whole concept over very carefully between now and a year from now, but we'll be posting everything we have on this on the web site at ten o'clock tonight, so you'll be able to review it all and take whatever notes you might want to whenever you want to, and talk it over with your health insurance agents and your other advisers.

"Again, this won't go into effect for Medicare and Medicaid clients until 2013, but I'd expect we'll soon be seeing some pretty innovative ideas coming from insurance companies that want to get a piece of the action, and I'll have the joy of letting them all know that not only will the playing field be absolutely level, but that any chicanery on their parts will definitely NOT be in their best interests. They, like I and the entire federal government, will always put their clients' needs first. Word to the wise.

"So on that note, I'll wish you all a very happy and informative Monday evening and night, and a great rest of the week and year."

As soon as the camera was off, Donne leaned back in his chair, sighed, cracked his knuckles and stretched mightily. Then he buzzed his chief of staff.

Emily's voice came through immediately. "Yes, boss?"

"I think we're ready to do the Munich on our guests down in the basement."

"Tony's all set, Gordy, and looking forward to it."

"Good, good. Let him loose."

"Will do. And you sleep well, okay? You need to take better care of yourself; long days and nights ahead."

Donne chuckled. "I promise, Mom; off to hit the sack right now."

Emily also chuckled. "Good night, boss."

"Good night." Donne clicked off, picked up another sheaf of papers and his tablet and headed out of the Oval Office and over to the Residence, chuckling. Two Secret Service agents, the military aide carrying the nuclear football and two of his private guards followed.

-46-
Four Months Earlier

Saturday, August 13, 2011
11:45 a.m.
Bonita Beach, Florida

Pam lazily rolled over on her towel, propped herself up on her elbows and looked up at Jake, who was still writing in his notebook.

"Jake?"

"One second, Pam." Jake wrote a little more, then looked over at Pam. "Okay; sorry."

"It's okay. Just a thought here. What kind of love life does Donne have?"

"Love life? I haven't thought about that, not at all."

"Well, he's not married, is he? No kids?"

"Nope, but that's just so his enemies don't have anyone to kidnap or threaten. He's just focused on his policies."

"Well, what does he do, have an affair, bring a hooker in now and then, get a blow – I mean oral sex from an intern under his desk?"

"I don't know; it's really not something I've considered."

"Well, does he eat?"

"Yeah, and that I have thought about. He's comfortable with a simple diet; like his usual meal is a grilled ham and cheese sandwich, sometimes a cheeseburger. In fact, he let the White House chef go, since he knew he wouldn't be happy doing simple menus. But he gave him his choice of head chef positions at six of DEI's restaurants, and the guy took one in Paris. They stay in touch, and Donne occasionally invites him back to do the very rare state dinners he has to do, but they bore the bejesus outa him. And he absolutely hates getting all formal; he's been there, done that, probably has ten tuxedos. But I can't justify writing that whole scene out between the two of 'em."

"But, Jake, that does give him some personality, some regular guyness."

"Well, I'll stick that info in somewhere, just not the whole scene and the dialogue."

"Cool. And does he sleep?"

"Oh, yeah. I've got a scene where he gets awakened for some sort of emergency; still gotta figure out what that is, but it'll go in there. And his chief of staff, who's sort of a motherly type, gets on him about not getting enough sleep, eating a crappy diet and needing to delegate more."

"Well, I think you ought to give him at least SOME kind of love life, or at least some kind of a sex life."

"I guess I could throw in a line or two about that somewhere."

"Oh, Jake, you should do more than that, have a whole scene with him and someone, super-erotic and sexy. Maybe more than one scene."

"I don't --"

"He's not gay, is he?"

"No, he's – you know, I hadn't even thought about that, either."

"Well, then I think you need to put in a really erotic scene, maybe with him and a woman, or maybe a couple of women, lots of rolling around and sweat and toys and maybe handcuffs and leather and ropes and feathers and --"

"Wait, Pam, wait. Feathers?"

"Yeah, feathers. They can be really sensuous, sexy, erotic. Just imagine a really soft one, with him running it slowly and teasingly all over a naked woman's body, slowly and then even more slowly, light as a whisper, just barely touching her, running incredibly slowly across her belly, up and down her sides, under her chin, across her face, her lips ... especially her lips ... her eyes, her nose, her ears, then down to her --"

"Pam, wait, wait. You're getting way ahead of me. I wouldn't have the faintest idea of how to even start writing something like that."

"Oh, Jake, haven't you ever read a romance novel?"

"Nope, never. If there aren't car chases, CIA guys or some kind of spies, I don't bother ... well, in fiction. I do read a lot of nonfiction, especially since I started this whole project."

"It's a very popular genre. And putting some great sex scenes in would help sales, I'd bet."

"I'm not writing this for the money, Pam, just to – you know, I'm not sure I know exactly why I'm doing it anymore; it just seems pretty important to do somehow. I guess I'm just curious how his policies might – oh, and that whole debt ceiling showdown last month, and the rating downgrade, that all sure added to my motivation. That debacle got me royally pissed off, and --"

"That got a lot of people pissed off."

"And for Obama to tell seniors that they may not get their Social Security checks? Geez, I hate politicians."

"Hate? That's a pretty strong word, Jake."

"Well, both sides were using the public as sacrificial pawns, but that comment was pretty damned low; it's disgusting, all of it."

"Easy, Jake, easy."

"It's okay, Pam. I just need to talk politics at least five times a day to get my blood pressure up to near normal."

Pam laughed and Jake smiled, his anger apparently dissipated.

Then Pam said, "But back to your guy, if you make him a little more human, less nerdy, people might like him better."

"You think the union guys, the Pope, televangelists and lawyers will accept his policies more just because he --"

"The who?"

"Oh, you haven't seen that stuff yet. Those guys and a lot of others are pissed at him because he --"

"No, no, no, Jake, not them, not the characters. The readers, they might like him better."

"Oh." Jake puzzled and thought for a moment. "Hmm; maybe you're right.

"I'd thought maybe the Asperger's would help explain his style and personality, but maybe --"

"Asperger's? You gave him Asperger's?"

"Yeah. Wasn't that in the – oh, I think I put that in the press conference. Maybe it'd be better if I stuck it in his first speech."

"The one they watch at ... oh, what was the bar --"

"Slinky Joe's."

"Right."

"I don't have the press conference online. I'll move that chunk up. I thought about giving him Tourette's Syndrome, but then I had Debbie Jackson swearing a lot, to flesh out her character, so I thought his doing that might be overkill. So I just went with the Asperger's instead."

"Yeah, maybe if you moved it to the speech, that'd be good, but I really think he'd be much more interesting and sympathetic – you do want him to be sympathetic, right? Not a bad guy?"

"Well, Pam, I'm not gonna give that away yet. He's gonna be pretty complicated and I'm hoping readers will be surprised by the ending."

"You can't tell me? I'll keep it to myself."

Jake smiled, but shook his head. "Sorry, Pam, can't do that. It's a secret." He held a finger up to his mouth. "Shhhhh."

Pam looked closely at Jake. "You haven't even figured it out yet, have you?"

"Oh, no, no, Pam, you're wrong there. One of the first things I wrote was the ending and some alternate ones, and everything I'm writing now fits with the one I picked. But some of the stuff can fit with any of them."

"Does he die?"

"Oh, c'mon, Pam."

"Sorry; can't blame a girl for trying."

"Everybody dies ... sometime. But he does have a pretty clever plan for what happens to the country when he does go. At least I think it's pretty clever. We'll see."

"Well, it's your book. I'm sorry for trying to mess with it."

"That's okay, really; I'm enjoying it. This is the first ... and only ...

substantive conversation I've had about it, with anybody."

"Really? But I still think you oughta think about his sex life."

"Okay, okay. I will. By the way, do you know the difference between erotic and kinky?"

"I think so."

"No, no, you're supposed to say no."

"Oh, a joke. Okay. Geez, no, suh, I do not know the difference between erotic and kinky. Could you puhleeze enlighten me?"

"Sure. Erotic is when you use a feather; kinky is when you use the whole chicken."

Pam laughed so quickly and loudly that heads all around the beach turned to look ... some, mostly the older men, to ogle.

"I've got to remember that one," Pam said, still laughing.

"Glad you liked it."

She rolled over and sat up, slid into her beach chair and lifted her sunglasses.

"You know, Jake, I'd like to try something."

"Oh? What?"

"I'd like to write a love scene for Donne, see what you think of it."

Jake, again totally perflutzed, could only blurt out, "What? Really?"

"Really. No pressure; I'd just like to try, see what I can do."

Jake, still perflutzed, frowned, rubbed his forehead, pursed his lips and finally said, "I guess I couldn't stop you, could I?"

Pam smiled a winning smile. "Probably not. But you wouldn't have to read it if you don't want to."

Jake shrugged and dropped his hands in surrender. "Okay. And I will read it; promise."

Pam gave Jake an even broader smile and reached over to grab his hands, but from where she was, she couldn't reach them, so she put both of her hands on his shin. "Oh, thank you, Jake. You won't be sorry; promise."

"Okay."

"Cool."

Jake sighed, leaned back on his lounge and closed his eyes. Pam leaned back in her chair and closed hers, a tiny smile lingering on her face.

After a minute or so, Jake opened his eyes and looked over at Pam.

"Hey, Pam, I'm getting hungry. Want to join me for a hot dog? I'll buy."

Pam opened her eyes, sat up and stretched. The oglers ogled.

"Sure. But I thought you always had stuff in your cooler."

"Yeah, but I've got a hankering for one of Deb's jumbo dogs."

"Oh, over at the Seabreeze?"

"No, not that Deb. The one right up there in the parking lot."

"Oh, the little stand with the umbrellas? I saw that when I walked over from the condo."

"Yup, that's it."

"Cool. But didn't you say you're supposed to wait an hour after swimming before eating?"

"I did?"

"Yup, back at the Seafood Shack just before we got the Fischers."

"No kidding?"

"No, you were kidding, but you did say that."

"Boy, you have a great memory."

"Yup, nearly photographic. And you can just call me Pam."

"Okay. Pam. And by the way, noodling ain't swimming."

She got up and looked at Jake, chuckling. "Ready?"

"Yup."

"Want some help up?" She held out her hand; Jake took it and climbed up out of his lounge, knees cracking.

"Sorry; forgot to warn you to plug your ears. I've deafened nine people in the last month with those."

Pam chuckled.

"In fact, I've been thinking about getting them replaced ... maybe with hands."

Her chuckling turned into laughter. "C'mon, old man; let's go feed our faces."

As they passed the Incontinentals, Jake nodded to them, and a few waved back. But all of them leered at Pam.

"Pam, ever hear the one about the Buddhist who went up to a hot dog stand?"

"Nope," Pam said, twining her arm around Jake's.

"He said, 'Make me one with everything.'"

Pam laughed and they continued up the beach, heads turning as they went along.

Back by the Collier boardwalk, the Mimosa twins switched their recording equipment off and went back to be-bopping and towel-dancing to the music on their earbuds.

-47-

Monday, December 19, 2011
9:00 p.m.
The White House, Basement
Washington, DC

In the cellblock, the four union bosses were still rummaging in the remnants of the platter of sandwiches that had been delivered by one of the silent guards a few hours earlier, when a heavy door clanged open and closed.

Then they heard a noise of casters rolling and water sloshing, followed by a male voice humming unmusically.

Richard got to his feet and walked quietly to the cell door, looked out to his left and said, "Hey, kid." He got no response. He tried again, louder.

"Hey, kid!" Still no response. So he yelled and banged an empty soda can on the cell bars.

"Hey, hey, hey, kid!!!!!"

Twenty feet away, a young man mopping the floor jumped, looked at Richard and screamed, dropping the mop.

"Wh-wh-what are y-y-y-ou d-d-doing? No-b-b-body's su-p-p-posed to b-b-be in h-h-here."

"Take it easy, kid, easy. We're not gonna hurt you."

"B-b-but who are y-y-you?"

"We've been prisoners here for days."

"Gee, that's t-t-too b-b-bad. At least y-y-you've g-g-got the b-b-best cell, p-p-private b-b-biffy and all. B-B-But y-y-you s-s-sure s-s-scared m-m-me."

"What's your name, kid?"

"J-J-Jimmy, Jimmy C-C-Corn. And d-d-don't m-m-make n-n-no cracks ab-b-bout it, ok-k-kay?"

"Okay, I won't, promise. So Jimmy, what are you doing here?"

"I c-c-clean up every M-M-Monday. N-N-Nobody here l-l-last w-w-week. N-N-Nobody here, nobody here. Oh, I'm g-g-gonna g-g-get a s-s-spanking." He bent over, curling his arms around himself and wailing, his thick glasses wobbling on his nose.

"Hey, kid – Jimmy, don't cry. Please. Hey, kid, look at me." The kid looked cautiously over his curled arms. Richard gave him a wide smile.

"Y-Y-You're n-n-not g-g-gonna s-s-spank me, are y-y-you?"

"Of course not, Jimmy. I'm not gonna hurt you at all."

Jimmy kept his arms curled, but straightened up some.

"P-P-Promise?"

"Promise. Come closer so I don't have to talk so loud. I know it can sound scary when I have to talk loud."

"Yeah, it c-c-can. N-N-No t-t-talk l-l-loud, no loud." He started to shuffle toward Richard, arms still curled around himself.

"Yeah, Jimmy, no talk loud. That's good. Can you come a little closer?" Jimmy shuffled further, then stopped about five feet away.

"That's fine, Jimmy, just fine. Now we can just talk normally."

"N-N-Normal t-t-talk. G-G-Good. T-T-Talk good."

"Yes, it is, Jimmy, yes, it is. Normal talk good. Now, Jimmy, can you tell me how old you are?"

"H-H-How old? I'm tw-tw-twenty-n-n-nine and s-s-six m-m-months. I'll b-b-be th-th-thirty in J-J-June."

"Well, happy birthday next June, Jimmy."

146

Jimmy brightened and let his arms uncurl, then smiled a wide smile, revealing yellowed, blackened, scraggly teeth.

"H-H-Happy B-B-Birthday t-t-to J-J-Jimmy, H-H-Happy --"

"Yup, happy birthday to you, Jimmy."

"-- B-B-Birthday t-t-to m-m-me." He straightened his glasses.

"Now, Jimmy, my name is Richard and I'd like to be your friend, maybe get you something for your birthday in June. Would that be okay?

"Oh, ye-ye-yes. I'd l-l-like th-th-that ... R-R-Richard."

"What would you like for your birthday, Jimmy?"

"Oh, umm, umm ... I g-g-got it. M-M-Maybe a t-t-teddy b-b-bear?"

"That's great, Jimmy. I'll get you a really big teddy bear --"

"N-N-No, n-n-not a b-b-big one. S-S-Scary. T-T-Too big." Jimmy started to back away.

"Okay, Jimmy, not a big one. Would a tiny one be okay?"

"M-M-Medium, m-m-medium is g-g-good."

"Medium; you got it, Jimmy. That's what friends are for, isn't it?"

"I g-g-guess s-s-so."

"Would you be my friend, Jimmy?"

"I g-g-guess s-s-so."

"Say my name, Jimmy."

"R-R-Richard, r-r-right?"

"Perfect, Jimmy. And I'm your friend, right?"

"R-R-Right. F-F-Friend. R-R-Richard."

"And friends do things for each other, right, Jimmy?"

"I g-g-guess s-s-so."

"Would you do something for me, Jimmy, friend to friend?"

"I g-g-guess s-s-so."

"That's nice, Jimmy, my friend. Can I borrow your phone for a minute?"

"I g-g-guess s-s-so. I j-j-just u-u-use it t-t-to c-c-call m-m-my m-m-mom. H-H-Here, R-R-Richard, f-f-friend." He pulled an older model cell phone from his jacket pocket and gave it to Richard, who pulled it through the bars into the cell.

"Thank you, Jimmy." He checked for a dial tone and smiled.

"Whew." He dialed, waited and then said, "Dawson? Richard ... no, no, no; Donne stuck us all in a cell in the basement ... I know, I know ... yup, Thursday afternoon, totally out of touch since then ... no, some retard's phone ..."

"I'm n-n-not a r-r-retard; I'm j-j-just im-p-p-paired."

"Quiet, Jimmy. I'm talking here.

"Look, Dawson, you've got to get us out of here ... no, now, right now ... I don't care; wake one up ... me, Andy, Bob and Lee ... okay, fine; call 'em all, but get this done, now. And check all the accounts, make sure everything is still there ... what? Shit; that sonofabitch ... can you ... okay, okay. Just get us out of here, now!" He hung up.

147

"Okay, guys. Dawson's gonna get all our sharks and get a habeas corpus, tonight, get us outa here."

"C-C-Can I h-h-have m-m-my ph-ph-phone b-b-back n-n-now, R-R-Richard?"

"No; I'm gonna keep it for a while, retard."

"I am N-N-NOT a r-r-retard. I'm j-j-just im-p-p-paired. Y-Y-You're n-n-not m-my-my fr-fr-friend any-m-m-more." He started crying and ran out of the room, slamming the heavy door open and closed.

"Retard," Richard said, and dialed the phone again. "What? What? 'No connection'? What the fuck?"

"Let me see that," Andy said. "Shit, no bars, nothing." He reared back, ready to throw it against the wall, but Richard grabbed it out of his hand.

"No, don't; maybe it'll come back in a while."

* * * * * *

A few moments later, Jimmy walked into the Oval Office, pulled the fake teeth off his very white real ones and smiled at Donne.

"Pizza cake, Gordy; just like Munich. They bought it, f'sure."

"Superlative, Tony; go have a good rest. Now we wait."

"Good night, Gordy. Good luck."

-48-
Four Months Earlier

Saturday, August 13, 2011
12:10 p.m.
Bonita Beach, Florida

"Hey, Deb."

"Hi, Jake. What'll it be?"

"Two jumbo dogs. Deb, this is Pam. Pam, Deb."

"Hi, Pam. Love your suit."

"Nice to meet you, Deb, and thanks."

"Here ya go."

"Thanks."

"And there's your change."

Jake was putting ketchup and mustard on his hot dog while Pam put ketchup, mustard, onions and relish on hers when Debra pointed at a stack of bright green fliers on the table.

"Hey, Jake, Pam, what do you think about this? The Hysterical Society is doing another 'Swim With The Gator Day' next month."

"Another what day?" Jake asked, picking up a flier.

"'Swim With The Gator.' It benefits the Historical Society, you know, the ones who do the Mayor of Survey fundraiser every two years."

"Yeah, I remember that from last year, but 'Swim With The Gator'? What's that?"

"Oh, they bring a six-footer over from the zoo on Old 41, put him in the city pool by the library, and any daredevil who gets in and stays in for one minute gets a $25 gift certificate, and they charge ten bucks a head for the public to come in and watch. Last year, they raised over five grand."

Jake raised his eyebrows and said, "Wait a minute. People VOLUNTARILY get in the pool with a live alligator? That's crazy."

"Oh, yeah. Last year they had over forty guys give it a shot, and all but three came out unscathed."

"What happened to the three?"

"One minor bite, one scraped knee and one broken arm ... but he did that after getting out of the pool, tripped on his seeing-eye dog."

"Oh, geez. They all go in together?"

"Oh, no; one at a time."

"Well, at least that's -- wait a minute. His seeing- -- he was blind?"

Debra grinned. "Gotcha."

"Oh, geez. So no Gator Day?"

"No, that's for real. Just that the guy actually broke his arm tripping over his walker."

"Now you're pulling my leg again, Deb."

"Yup, you got me. So what d'ya think? Wanna give it a shot?"

"Me? Get in with a live gator? No way, Jose. I might pay the ten bucks to watch."

"Maybe Pam would; you look kinda fearless. What d'ya think?"

"I think I'd rather just watch once, Deb."

"You know what you could do, Jake? Donate some copies of your book."

"Yeah, I could do that – but it won't be out until December."

"Gift certificates. Then leave the copies at the Historical Society once it's out and they can pick 'em up there."

"Yeah, that's doable. Good idea, Deb."

"Just a thought. By the way, did you hear the one about the Buddhist hot dog vendor?"

"Nope."

"So this guy orders a hot dog, gets it, gives the guy a twenty and waits ... and waits ... and waits ... and waits ... and waits. Finally he says, 'Hey, where's my change?' And the Buddhist hot dog vendor says, 'Change comes from within.'"

Pam laughed and Jake chuckled. "Not bad, Deb, not bad. That'll go into the database."

"Thought you'd like that one. See ya later."

"Biz, Deb."

"Nice to have met you," Pam said.

As they walked back to the beach, Pam said, "'Biz'?"

Jake nodded. "Kind of our code word. Instead of saying 'Bye' for 'Goodbye,' I say, 'Biz' for 'Good biz.' Just jargon." Pam chuckled and took a bite of her hot dog, chewed and swallowed.

"Mmmm; that's good. Where does she get them?"

"She won't say; it's a secret. Maybe we should turn her over to the CIA," Jake said, smiling.

"Oh, Jake, don't joke about that. Those guys can be deadly, for real."

"SCR."

"What?"

"Sorry; Couldn't Resist. Sorry; just an acronym I made up a while ago."

"Ah. But I'd be careful about talking about those guys."

"Okay; I'll be good."

As they continued walking back to their spot, Jake nibbling at his hot dog, Pam wrapping hers for when they got back, a cute young blonde woman came by and said, "Hey, Jake."

"Morning, Laurie," Jake said, making it sound like "Morning Glory."

"Pam, this is Laurie, our beach bun-walker. Laurie, Pam."

"Hi, Pam."

"Hi, Laurie. Bun-walker?"

Laurie patted her butt. "Gotta walk this off."

"You look fine."

"Now, Jake, no flattery; I know what I know."

"Love your suit, Pam."

"Thanks."

"So how's Jeff doing up nord dere?" Jake asked.

"Fine. Got his cabin in the woods all done and he's enjoying his solitude. He'll be back late September."

"Great. Next time you talk to him, tell him hi from me and tell him you two'll definitely be in the book."

"Oh, cool. Will do. Nice meeting you, Pam."

"Same here, Laurie."

As Laurie walked on, she smiled at Jake and held her thumb and index finger out horizontally, about half an inch apart. Jake replied similarly, but holding his digits maybe an inch and a half apart. Pam looked on quizzically as Laurie laughed and continued on.

"What was that about?"

Jake blushed under his tan. "That's a VERY long story. Some other time, okay?"

"Okay. But I'm intrigued, so I'll hold you to that."

"Promise."

"And what was that about the Mayor of ... Survey, was it?"

"Oh, that was the name of this area before it was Bonita Springs, and every two years, people run for mayor, asking for votes any way they can, and it's ten cents a vote. The person who raises the most money wins and gets the title for the next two years. It's kind of fun, but I'd bet not as much as that gator thing."

"Probably not."

"The historical society also runs a kind of scavenger hunt every March, where they hide a snook replica somewhere in the city and run clues in the local paper. It's called 'Sammy the Snook,' and they have sponsors who put up prizes for whoever finds him first, usually around fifteen hundred bucks or so."

"Sounds like fun. But what's a snook?"

"It's a fish. Apparently it's got a great taste."

"Apparently?"

"I've never tasted it."

"I guess I haven't, either. Maybe we'll have to fix that sometime. I'll buy."

Jake smiled. "You're on." He held out his hand and Pam shook it, holding on a bit longer than one might expect.

She said, "Deal, then."

"Done." They both laughed as they got to their spot on the beach and settled back in.

The Mimosa twins turned their equipment back on and returned to be-bopping to the soft but rhythmic music on their earbuds.

-49-

Tuesday, December 20, 2011
10:30 a.m.
The White House
Washington, DC

Emily escorted three men and a woman into the Oval Office, handed Donne four sheets of paper, nodded to Donne and spoke to the newcomers.

"Please introduce yourself to Mr. Donne."

The woman spoke first. "Dawson Skinner, Esquire, on behalf of my client, Richard _____."

"Leonard Seacrest, Esquire, on behalf of Andy _____."

"Rollin Creek, Esquire, on behalf of Robert _____."

"Ryan Stone, Esquire, on behalf of Lee _____."

"Thank you, Emily. Have our guests all signed the release form?"

"Yes, sir, they have."

"Did they read them carefully?"

"No, sir, they did not."

"Too bad; those are binding, whether they did or not. Thank you, Emily. Please stay with us for a moment.

"Now, gentlemen, ma'am, what brings you here so urgently?"

Ms. Skinner said, "We have four orders for habeas corpus for our clients, each signed by Judge Maude Williams. We demand to see them immediately." She held out the papers, which Donne took and reviewed closely for a full minute.

"Well, these seem to be in order, and I have no problem at all with meeting that demand. But first, I have something to show you.

"Emily, if you would?"

"Yes, sir, Mr. Donne." She pressed a button on a remote on the corner of the desk and a large TV screen was revealed on the wall. She pressed another button and the screen showed a replay of the scene between Donne and the four union bosses the previous Thursday. The four lawyers watched intently, initially frowning, then clenching their fists as Donne ordered the guards in and the bosses were handcuffed and removed.

"If you are worthy of the title 'attorney,' you'll have no argument with the fact that your clients deserved the sentence I gave them. I'll also assure you that they have been treated well and are comfortable in their cell. No, no arguments now. Emily here will take you down to see your clients. You'll have two hours before we'll check in and see if you need more time. Good day."

Ms. Skinner said, "But, Mr. --"

Donne cut in. "No, Ms. Skinner, save it for after you've spoken with your client. Same for you all, gentlemen. Good day.

"Emily?"

"Yes, sir, Mr. Donne.

"This way." She led the four attorneys out of the Oval Office.

Once the door closed, Donne pressed a button on his desk, and Tony entered from a hidden doorway.

"Ready for Round Two, Tony?"

"Absolutely, Mr. D-D-Donne." He smiled sheepishly.

"Good smile, Tony."

"Thanks, Gordy. Got my toofies, glasses and wig right here."

"Great. Any problems?

"Nah; easy peazy."

"Give 'em about an hour and then have at it."

"Will do. This'll be fun."

As the door closed behind Tony, Donne's intercom buzzed.

"Yes, Emily?"

"They're on their way down with the guards. And Amy Christian is here."

"Oh, good. Just send her on in. Thanks."

"Right-o, boss."

A moment later, a 40-ish, slim, pretty, ebony-skinned woman with a briefcase and a brown paper bag entered, walked right over to Donne and gave him a hug and an air kiss, both of which he returned.

"God, Amy, you're looking good."

"Thanks, Gordy. You too ... but maybe a little tired. You getting enough sleep?"

"Not really. But there's so much stuff that just needs to be done immediately, if not sooner."

"I know what you mean. I'm getting a lot of flack and pushback from the current Secretary."

"Well, she's a tough woman, and now that she can't run in '16, I'd bet she and Bill are both really pissed."

"You got that right, Gordy."

"But you're tougher and I'm sure you can handle her. You're not doing much that's different from what you did at DEI."

"It'll probably take a couple of months, but we'll get that place flattened out."

"Of all the departments, that one's got the most excessive levels of bureaucrats I've ever seen anywhere, and most of them are just political appointees, big contributors' family and friends. 'Deputy Assistant to the Assistant to the Deputy Assistant to the Deputy Director for' ... whatever. Christ, you should be able to cut through ten or more layers, flatten it down by 50 percent."

"Oh, more than that, Gordy; maybe 70, 80 percent."

"That much, Amy?"

"Absolutely. And without losing any operational efficiencies."

"Well, you've looked at it more closely than I have, and you're in there every day.

"If you want me to give her a call and remind her that you're the boss on personnel and restructuring, I'd be happy to do that."

"Not yet, Gordy. I can handle her for now. But I may need that when it comes to getting rid of some of her most top-level people and some of the most incompetent political ambassadors."

"And her, when and if."

"Right. For now, she's doing okay, but I'll need to put some closer reins on her soon."

"Indeed," Donne agreed.

Amy opened her briefcase and took out a thin manila folder, checked its contents and gave it to Donne.

"The first twenty pages there is a list of the people and positions I've eliminated so far, the next thirty is the next bunch to go, the next seven list the programs that were redundant and have now been or soon will be eliminated, and the final five list how the essential functions have been or will be redistributed at each step of the process."

Donne glanced through the folder and then put it in his inbox.

"I'll have to set aside some time to go over that more closely later today, but it sounds good. Keep at it, but be sure to get enough rest to stay sharp. She'll try to sabotage you whenever she can. And don't worry about reporting to me too often, just when you think you need to."

"No worry about that, Gordy. I know the rule: 'The amount of time spent reporting on a function is inversely proportional to the amount of time spent actually performing the function. Stasis is achieved when all of your time is spent making excuses for why nothing was done.'"

"Bravo, Amy; you've learned well."

"And how are you doing on finding candidates to be the new Secretary?"

"We're vetting about twenty people, experienced diplomats with minimal political ties. I should be able to get that down to the ten you asked for within another month at the latest."

"Good, good."

"Has Cody talked with you about our China plan?"

"Yes, he's got me up to speed on that, and I'm getting him as much info on that as I can, under the radar, of course."

"Great.

"Anything else?"

"Nope, that's it, Gordy ... at least officially. But Emily asked me to bring you some of my culinary specialty." She set the paper bag on Donne's desk.

"What's that, Amy?"

"Asparagus, artichoke, blueberry, broccoli, cauliflower, kale and tofu salad, with honey, chocolate and guacamole dressing."

-50-
Four Months Earlier

Saturday, August 13, 2011
12:20 p.m.
Bonita Beach, Florida

"That was delicious, Jake. Thank you," Pam said, wiping her mouth with a napkin, which she then crumpled and put in her beach bag.

"They are good," Jake agreed. "Geez, it's hot with no wind. Ready for some more water time?"

"You got it."

"Sea breeze should pick up in half an hour or so." He got out of his lounge unassisted and held out a hand, which Pam took and got up out of her chair. Noodles in hand, they headed to the Gulf.

"Vow, I luff your suit," a light female voice with a slight accent bubbled.

Pam said, "Thank you."

Jake said, "Hey, Dagi. Wie geht's?"

Dagi, a lovely, svelte strawberry blonde, said, "Danke, gut."

Pam said, "Sind Sie Deutsch?"

"Ja, ja. Und Sie?

"Nein, nein; Amerikanisch."

"Sie sprechen gut Deutsch."

"Danke, aber nicht so gut."

"Na, na, sehr gut."

"Sie können mich dutzen."

"Mich auch. Wo hast du Deutsch gelernt?"

"Vor vielen Jahren, wohnte ich drei Jahre in Hamburg."

"Ah. Und wie heisst du?"

"Pamela, oder Pam. Und du?"

"Dagmar, oder Dagi."

"Hallo, Dagi."

"Hallo, Pam." They shook hands.

"Hey, guys," Jake cut in. "Could we stick with English for the old fart?"

"Oh, sorry, Jake," Pam said. "Haven't spoken German in years."

Dagi said, "You speak it very well, good accent, too."

"Danke – oh, sorry; thank you, Dagi."

"Bitte – sorry; you're welcome."

"But, Jake, you spoke some German there."

"What, 'wie geht's'? 'How are you?' That's about all I know – oh, danke and bitte, and auf Wieder-see-ya-later, too."

Pam and Dagi both laughed and said, virtually in unison, "Oh, Jake."

"So do you work, Dagi?"

"Ja, ich bin eine Flugbegleiterin – ach, sorry, Jake. I am a flight attendant."

"She flies to Europe a lot," Jake said.

"Oh, cool. To Germany?"

"Ja, ja. Meistens München- – sorry – mostly Munich."

"Beautiful city."

"Ja, ja.. But I must run; Deirdre is waiting. Nice to meet you, Pam. Tschüss, Jake."

"Auf Wiederbye-bye."

"Tschüss, Dagi."

"Tschüss, Pam."

As Dagi walked away, Jake said, "You know, I love German food, but every time I eat any, half an hour later I'm hungry … for power."

Pam laughed.

"So, Pam, you're full of surprises. Any other languages?"

"Oh, a few."

"C'mon. Details, okay?"

"Okay; let's see. French, Italian, Russian, Japanese, Mandarin Chinese ... oh, Spanish, Portugese, a bit of Swahili, and I can get by in Arabic, but I still have a pretty thick American accent in that one. I think that's it."

"Wow! Really?"

"Gotcha. No, I'm pulling your leg, but only on the Swahili."

Jake laughed tentatively.

"Oh, sorry; I forgot. Also two dialects of Hindi."

"You're not pulling my leg again?"

"Nope."

"Wow. Definitely a Renaissance woman."

"Oh, Jake," Pam said, "you're embarrassing me."

"I don't mean to. I'm just continually impressed."

"Well, just to add to that, I was on the gymnastics team in the Montreal games."

"Really?"

"Really. But no medal; broke my ankle getting off the bus."

"Seriously?"

"Seriously. And for a 14-year-old, that was devastating."

"I'm sorry."

"Long time ago, lots of water under the bridge. Speaking of water, are we going in or are we just going to stand here and let it come to us?"

"Oh, we're going in." And they did.

<h1 style="text-align:center">-51-</h1>

Tuesday, December 20, 2011
11:45 a.m.
The White House, Basement
Washington, DC

In the cellblock, the four union bosses and their attorneys had been conferring for about an hour when they heard a heavy door clang open and two sets of footsteps approaching, one shuffling and one walking firmly. Then two figures appeared outside the bars, one up close and the other staying back four to five feet.

"He's th-th-the one who-who-who s-s-stole m-m-my ph-ph-phone. And he c-c-called m-m-me a re-re-retard. B-B-Bad m-m-man! No-no-no f-f-friend of J-J-Jimmy, no-no-no f-f-friend."

"Is that true, sir? Did you steal his phone?" said the heretofore silent guard who had been bringing their food since the beginning of their incarceration.

"I just borrowed it," Richard protested, holding the phone out to Jimmy. "Here, Jimmy. Thank you for letting me use it."

"So you do have his phone," the guard said, staring intently at Richard, but making no move to take the phone.

"He-He-He s-s-stole it, s-s-stole it. B-B-Bad m-m-man."

"I did not steal it. He loaned it to me."

"Did he say you could keep it overnight?"

"Well, he --"

"Don't say another word, Richard," Ms. Skinner cut in sharply. "Not another word."

The other attorneys looked at their clients and put their fingers to their lips. "Shhhh."

"Your name, ma'am?"

"I am Dawson Skinner, his attorney."

"Well, Ms. Skinner, your client has just lied to a federal officer in the course of his official duties, and that will add to his sentence as soon as Mr. Donne hears about it."

"What is your name and title, sir?"

"Bradley Deckerson, ma'am, middle initial F, for Franklin. Senior Guard, Federal Security Service, formerly with the US Secret Service."

"Well, sir, you may want to rethink your position. My client did not steal that phone; he borrowed it, as he stated."

"Did you ask for your phone back last night, Jimmy?"

"I d-d-did, I d-d-did."

"And did he give it back?"

"N-N-No, h-h-he d-d-did n-n-not. It's r-r-right th-th-there, in h-h-his h-h-hand. B-B-Bad m-m-man ."

"And did any of the other three attempt to give the phone back?"

"N-N-No."

"So we have conspiracy, as well."

The three male attorneys and their clients all began talking at the same time.

"All right, all right. I'll let the boss sort it out. But now give me the phone."

Richard looked at Ms. Skinner, who nodded, and he handed it out through the bars.

"You can continue your consultation. I'll have someone check back in another hour."

Mr. Creek spoke up. "We don't have any reception in here."

"That's correct; you don't."

The guard and Jimmy left, the heavy door slamming behind them.

-52-
Four Months Earlier

Saturday, August 13, 2011
12:35 p.m.
Bonita Beach, Florida

As they settled in on their noodles, Pam purred, "Ahhh, glorious."

"Bitte," Jake said. Pam chuckled.

After floating a while, Jake cleared his throat and said, "Pam?"

Pam opened her eyes and said, "Yeah?"

"I've been thinking, and I wonder ... wonder ..."

"Yeah, Jake?"

"Who ... ba-dum-dum-who ... who wrote the book of love? Oh, geez, sorry; couldn't resist."

Pam chuckled. "Well, that was about three and a half minutes."

"Maybe a bit longer, a new record. Sorry, really."

"So what were you wondering, Jake?"

"Okay; serious. I don't know if you've guessed, but you're not only the first person I've had a serious, intelligent conversation with about my little book, but you're the only one."

"The only one? What about the other people who suggested stuff in emails or here on the beach, the ones you interviewed?"

"That's different; I mean about the book itself, not just ideas from people's experience to go into it."

"Oh."

"And d'you know anything about neurolinguistic programming?"

"NLP? Yeah. We had to learn about that in the Service and ... and before."

"So you know how to spot a lie ... and a liar, from nonverbals and micro-gestures and micro-facial expressions."

"Some of ... well, most of the time, I guess."

"So does Donne. Me, too. And I've NLP'd you and I think I can trust you not to steal my work."

"You're right, Jake. Furthest thing from my mind. Cross my heart."

"I believe you, and I believed you earlier. So if you want ... and only if you want ... I'd like to let you read what I've written so far and maybe give me some feedback."

"I'd love to do that, Jake."

Jake looked closely at Pam as she said that, and then he said, "Maybe even collaborate. I like the ideas you've given me so far."

"What ideas?"

"Well, the new title, for one; I love that. And your idea that he needs a love life; the more I think about that, the more I think you may be right. And the more sure I am that I can't write it. So I think we can do something together on it. But only if you want to."

"Jake, I could kiss you right now; I'd love to."

"Well, that kissing part is nice, but let's hold off on that for now. I can give you my third backup CD, let you read it all and see what you think. But you have to promise not to let it get out to anybody else, for sure."

"Oh, I promise, Jake."

Jake looked closely at her as she said that and then said, "Okay. It's in my bag. We'll get it when we get out."

"Oh, I can hardly wait."

"Well, let's start with something now, okay?"

"Okay. What?"

"Just a word thing. I've got an Elvis impersonator singing off-key, and I want an adverb to go before 'off-key' in this phrase: 'belting out a ... blank ... off-key rendition of,' and all I've got in there now is 'significantly,' but I want some word that relates to how it impacts the ears of the listeners, and I've been stuck on that since last night, trying to fill that blank."

"Hmm. How about – no, that won't work. Wait a minute. You've got an Elvis impersonator in there?"

"Yeah. Maybe that'll make more sense after you've read it in context; it's just a bit of lightness in Donne's boring tax speech."

"Oh. Okay; it does make sense to wait. But I'll keep thinking about that till then, maybe something'll pop up."

"As the sea breeze is starting to. Good. That'll cool the air down and warm the water up a little bit."

"It doesn't actually cool the air down; it just feels cooler."

"True; okay. But the water actually warms up, because it blows the warmer surface water in. It can warm up maybe four degrees in an hour with a stiff blow."

"I guess a stiff blow could warm anything up."

Jake's eyes went wide and he reached out with one hand, grabbed Pam's wrist and pulled her sharply in toward him. With his other hand, he stopped a paddleboard that was heading toward where Pam's head had just been. The teen who'd been on it a moment before was flailing about in the water, the paddle still in his hand.

"You okay, Pam?"

"Yeah, fine. I didn't see that coming."

"Kid, you okay?"

The teen coughed up some water, but nodded.

"Your first day on the board?"

The boy nodded again, still coughing.

"Sorry," he spluttered.

"Until you get the hang of it, might be a good idea to stay further away from where folks are swimming, like way down that way."

"Toward the observatory house?"

"Maybe even past it, at least for the time being. And if I'm not being too intrusive, you'll balance better if you bend your knees a little more."

"Really? Thanks. I'll try that."

"Hope it helps. Meantime, why don't you just walk the board south a good ways and then try again?"

"Okay. Thanks." He grabbed the board and began carefully pushing it south through the crowds in the water.

"That was tactful, Jake. You didn't give him the ultimatum you gave that kid with the football in June."

"This kid was insecure; that one was an arrogant punk."

"He was, wasn't he?"

Jake just nodded. Pam leaned back on her noodle, closed her eyes and breathed deeply, again letting her feet float up.

"The water even smells delicious," she said.

"I think that's your perfume."

"I'm not wearing any."

"Ah, then it's you."

After a moment, Pam said, "Jake?"

"Pam?"

"Can you tell me about that gesture with Laurie? Is now a good time?"

"Good as any, I guess."

"Okay; I'm all ears."

"Not lying in the water that way, you're not."

Pam chuckled. "So tell me anyhow."

"Well, let's see. You know how there's a sort of ritualized habit in greetings? Like, 'G'morning. How are you?' or 'How ya doing?' and the ritual response is 'Fine'?"

"Yeah."

"Well, sometimes I like to shake things up, make people look at things maybe a little differently, maybe even ... and I know this is usually a long shot ... start thinking outside the ball."

"Don't you mean outside the box?"

"Ah, that's the conventional idiom, and that's still inside the box."

Pam raised an index finger and said, "Ah-ha. Got it. Good one," and smiled. She slid her finger down a bit and said, "One for Jake."

"Anyhow ... and this is a little awkward ... a couple times, but only with people I knew fairly well, when they asked 'How ya doing?' I'd answer with 'Mostly laid-back, mellow and ... hmm, maybe a little horny,' and I'd make that gesture with the thumb and index finger."

"You didn't! Really?"

"Yup, but only with totally safe people, like 75-year-old couples that I knew had at least a decent sense of humor and perspective.

And they usually chuckled or laughed out loud ... maybe just nervously, but they laughed."

"And you did that with Laurie?"

"No, of course not; with Laurie AND Jeff. And they got a BIG laugh out of it."

"And then she picked up the gesture?"

"Right, and sometimes greets me with that when she gets to the beach and is too far away to say hi. It's just light, not suggestive."

"And your response is three times as horny?"

"Just a joke, light."

"She is a cutie. You were never tempted?" Pam said, a slight edge in her voice.

"Thought and action are two separate things. Remember that movie, the one you copied at the Seafood Shack?"

"Yeah."

"Remember the line in there about every man wanting to nail every woman?"

"Yeah."

"Well, that's a built-in response, deep in our reptilian brain, but it's how we deal with that instinct that makes the difference, but only if we can recognize it for what it is before it overwhelms our judgment."

"Hmm" was all Pam could muster in response. Then "Okay."

"And a lot of males just can't or won't recognize it for what it is and deal with it directly. Which also makes for a lot of great jokes."

"So you haven't been tempted with Laurie?"

"Not that way. I respect her, and Jeff, too much. It's just light."

Pam looked at Jake closely as he said that.

"You're NLPing me, aren't you, Pam?"

"Yup. And I think you're telling the truth."

"Now, with the twins up there by the boardwalk ..."

"Oh, Jake."

"Gotcha. But only if I were thirty or thirty-five years younger."

Pam chuckled. "Okay; I get it, I get it. Okay."

"So we're cool?"

"Yup, Jake, we are." She held out her hand to Jake and he took it in his.

"Deal," he said.

"Done," she replied and smiled, as did Jake.

After a moment, Pam sighed, removed her hand from Jake's and said, "I think I'm ready to head home – if you're still okay with me reading your stuff. Yes?"

"Absolutely. Let's get you that CD."

"Thank you."

"But before we do, I wonder if you'd like to join me here in the morning to watch the sunrise ... since you're waking up early anyhow. It's a really nice time to be on the beach, but I don't often take the time to get here that early."

Pam looked closely at Jake, then said, "I think I'd like that. What time?"

"Maybe quarter to seven? Okay with you?"

"Perfect; I'll be here."

"Me, too."

They got out of the water, Jake dried his hands, got the CD from his bag, put it in a plastic supermarket bag and gave it to Pam. She put it in hers, wrapped a bright red, opaque sarong around her waist, picked up her stuff, gave Jake a peck on the cheek and headed out.

Jake lit a cigarette, took his noodles and went back in the water.

The Mimosa twins switched off their equipment and lay back on their towels, giggling a bit more than usual.

-53-

Thursday, December 29, 2011
8:30 a.m.
The White House
Washington, DC

Emily and four guards escorted seven slightly bedraggled men and one pristine woman into the Oval Office, where Donne, dressed as usual in his casual clothing, remained seated behind his desk.

"Lady, gentlemen, I've brought you up here this morning to find out if you've come to any conclusions during your stay with us."

"Our stay with you? You kept us locked up in there over the holidays, completely incommunicado with the outside. That is totally unacceptable," snapped the woman, glaring at Donne.

"Now, now, Ms. Skinner, you should know by now exactly why that occurred."

"Over a friggin' cell phone?"

"Theft, deception, exploiting the handicapped, lying to a federal officer in the course of his official duties, conspiracy. On those charges alone, I could keep you in a federal prison for several years. You've gotten off lightly."

"But you've also confiscated union funds and most of our personal assets."

"Absolutely, and deservedly so. You should never have tried to hide those funds so clumsily. There's another batch of conspiracy charges over those actions, as well, which we haven't even begun to address."

"You have no right to --"

"Lady, I have every right. I bought the country; I own it. I make the laws, I enforce the laws and I determine whether the laws are legitimate. If I wanted to be capricious, I have every right to be. If I wanted to ban purple houses, I could do that. If I wanted to lease the Capitol to an amusement park company and let them make it a tourist trap, I cou- – oh, Emily, could you take a note? 'Bungee jumping, Washington Monument.' Thanks.

"So you, madam, are in no position to tell me what rights I have or don't have.

"Now, I will ask you this again. Have you come to any serious conclusions during your time downstairs?"

Silence, eyes shifting and making occasional contact between and among the eight detainees, Donne quietly glancing from one to the next, occasionally to Emily and each of the four guards in the room, a very slight smile creeping to his mouth.

"Well?" He said after a long moment.

More silence.

"Okay. I understand. Let me give you a hint before you go back down there for another week or two – oh, by the way, you are each being billed a hundred dollars and twelve cents a day for room and board.

"Here's the hint. How have each of you managed to rip off your membership and the American taxpayers and consumers for your own personal gain? That's what you need to be thinking about and discussing as you spend your time down there.

"And, Ms. Skinner, I know you appreciate the fact that you have a separate but equal cell. No, don't say anything. I know.

"Emily, please escort these folks back down to the basement."

Emily and the four guards herded the eight out. As they were nearing the door, Donne said, "Too bad I can't wish y'all a Happy New Year."

-54-
Four Months Earlier

Sunday, August 14, 2011
3:16 a.m.
Bonita Springs, Florida

Jake slowly opened one eye and then the other, remaining stock still, stretching his muscles imperceptibly, loosening each group in turn, his hearing alert for any audible hint of what had awakened him, preparing himself for whatever instant response he might need to make to whatever awaited him anywhere in the house or yard or out on Hickory Boulevard.

Slowly, soundlessly, he reached under his pillow and carefully slid his handgun out, quietly clicking the safety off. Then he slowly turned his head to take in the locked inside door, the open sliders and the balcony beyond.

He saw nothing concerning, and all he could hear was the sound of surf in the Gulf rhythmically lapping at the shore and of palm fronds rustling in the gentle breeze coming off the water.

Then, in the far distance, he picked out a soft buzzing sound, which gradually resolved into the whup-whup of an approaching helicopter.

Slowly, Jake slid from the bed and duck-walked to the sliders and out onto the balcony, where he flattened himself and peered out to the Gulf between the vertical railing supports. He finally picked out the lights of the helo, far offshore, flying from north to south. He saw in the moonlight that it was light in color, maybe yellow, which told him it was probably a medical flight.

"Okay; no problem," he told himself and got to his feet, looking around the beach below, his front yard, his neighbors' yards, noticing that his southern neighbor still had not removed the tree that had been hit by lightning and blown down a month before.

A small dark figure crept out from below the trunk of the tree and crossed the beach in front of Jake's house, stopping at a marked turtle nest just north of the property line, one of the few that had survived the storm. It began digging into the nest, until Jake hissed at it and it ran off the beach.

"Damn raccoons," Jake muttered as he returned to his bed and stuck his gun back under the pillow, clicking the safety back on.

Earlier that day, after Pam had left the beach with his CD, he had spent a few more hours in the Gulf, alternating with three attempts to lie on his lounge on the beach for at least twenty minutes, but giving up after about seven and heading back to the water. He had a few nice chats and one fairly intelligent one with some people in the water, managing to avoid both Sonya and Ann Louise.

About four o'clock, as the thunderheads started building out from the Everglades, he stopped at Pop's and had a cup of wine with a few of the Beach Potatoes, who were quietly celebrating the 40th birthday of one of their members, a chubby and overly friendly woman whose name Jake quickly forgot, although it was one he'd never heard before, something like Bess or Tess or Jess ... or was it maybe Ness? Or Cassie, Elizabeth? Nope; it was gone, Quarterheimered.

Extricating himself from that potentially awkward situation, Jake walked back to his beach stuff, smoked a last cigarette, finished off his now-melted ice cream, packed up and headed home, running his now-habitual surveillance detection route through Bonita Shores, adding a quick spin through the parking lot of the condos across from the beach and out Forester before turning north on Hickory toward his house.

After unpacking his car, emptying and rinsing out his cooler, he went upstairs, showered and then settled in at his PC for another evening of staring at his screen, stretching, daydreaming and occasionally tapping a few paragraphs out on the keyboard, until he had managed to fill his daily quota of five pages.

He also cleared his inbox of thirty or so spam emails, replied to three of the six non-spam ones and sent out five of his own, only one with an attachment.

He did remember to move the Asperger's bit from the press conference to Donne's first speech, editing it so it fit better there, and about ten o'clock, he turned the PC off, coiling the power cord up and putting it back in the sideboard.

He made sure his security system was armed, grabbed his book on the Federal Reserve and headed up to bed, taking care to avoid the ninth step on the stairway. He read for about an hour, feeling his blood pressure spike twice in that time, and then fell into a deep and dreamless sleep which lasted until his 3:16 a.m. wakeup, after which he fell back to sleep until his alarm clock went off at five, the first time he'd used an alarm in over a year.

After a quick shower, shave and tiny breakfast to help digest his daily vitamins and aspirin, he packed his cooler and headed to the beach, again running an SDR through the condos from Forester and then through Bonita Shores, arriving at the entrance to the beach parking lot about 6:30.

-55-

Friday, January 6, 2012
10:57 p.m.
K St. NW and Connecticut Ave. NW
Washington, DC

The KSK triplets, Kathy, Stacy and Kristle, spotted the red pickup truck as it turned onto Connecticut and headed northwest, passing their SUV parked in front of the pharmacy. The number matched the one in their dossier, so they turned on their lights and pulled out into the heavy traffic, falling in about six car lengths behind their target.

"I hope the intel is right this time," Kristle said dejectedly. "We're running out of time."

"C'mon, worrywart," Stacy shot back laconically. "It's right. We got confirms from Loretta's people at the airport and Nancy's people at the car rental, and the GPS they stuck on his truck is working fine. It's him."

Kristle whined, "We had confirms in Glasgow and Bangkok and Melbourne, too. And none of those were him."

"Ssst," Kathy hissed. "You want to jinx it again? All those were from the Company, not our people."

"Keep your eyes on the road, Kathy. Don't want to get in another accident."

"You're never gonna let me live that down, are you, Stacy?"

"Nope."

"It wasn't my fault. First time in Rome, and those Italians are all crazy-ass drivers."

"And it was raining," Kristle interjected. "Hard. Reminded me of Seattle."

"So you adapt, take extra precautions, pay attention," Stacy said. "Don't you remember the training from Rona and Joel?"

"Of course I do. But that was after the accident."

"No, it wasn't; it was three months before, right after we did the job in Uganda."

"That was a bad one," Kristle said. "What a fat sonofabitch. How many bullets did it take to bring him down?"

"Fifteen," said Kathy. "Or was it seventeen?"

"Six of mine," Kristle said, "and five for you."

"Four for me," said Stacy. "But I got him in the eye and the – hey, where'd he go?"

"Not to worry; I've got him. He turned west on N. Here we go."

"Easy, Kath, easy. Keep it on all four, please?" Kristle cried.

"No problem, Krissy. See, not even a teeny squeal. And ... there he is."

"So six, five, four -- that's fifteen," Stacy said.

"Remember how he grabbed at his crotch after Stacy's first shot?" Kathy said, laughing. "He was so fat, he couldn't even find it."

"Wonder if his wife could," Stacy added, laughing harder than Kathy was.

"Eeewww," Kristle spewed. "Thanks for that image. I'll prolly have nightmares."

"Wives," Kathy said. "He had, what, thirty?"

"It's 'probably,' Krissy," Stacy growled, "You've got to put the B's in there."

"Yeah, yeah, I know; I just forget sometimes."

"You've done that since we were toddlers. Grow up."

"Look, Stace, we know you're the best shot, but who's the best of us with a knife?"

Stacy didn't respond.

"Poisons, chemicals, biologicals, nanos?"

No response.

"Garotte?"

Nothing.

"Unarmed, hand to hand?"

Silence.

"Defense rests. So don't bust my nonexistent balls over a silly little mispronounciation."

Stacy gritted her teeth at that one, but stayed quiet.

Kathy broke the silence. "Going right on 22nd. Uh-oh; only one car between us now. Time for the padiddle?"

Stacy said, "Let's hold off on that, wait till there's none between us and he makes a turn."

"Okay. What the – what street is that?"

"It looks like, ah, Newport Place on my map," Kristle answered. "Just one block long, back to 21st. And that's one way back south."

"He's doing an SDR. Damn," Stacy said. "Hit the padiddle switch just before we make the turn so he can't see the light go out."

"We're probably burned anyway," said Kristle. "Crap."

"Give me the EMP gun, Krissy."

"Here you go."

"Padiddle ... wait ... now."

"Switched off. Turning now."

"Crap! He's speeding up. We're burned."

"Hyperdrive, Kathy."

Kathy stepped on the gas and the SUV leapt forward, as the pickup had. But the SUV closed the gap; Stacy leaned out the window and fired just as the pickup reached the end of the street and started to turn not right, but left, the wrong way, onto 21st.

The electromagnetic pulse shut down all the electronics in the truck and the engine seized up, The truck tipped up on the two right tires, then flopped down on its right side, then on its roof, crashing into two cars parked on 21st. Its right front tire flew off and through the arched glass at the top of the front window of the gray brick house on 21st and got stuck there, hanging half in and half out.

"Well, so much for a soft kill," Kathy said.

"It's not even a kill," Kristle said. "Look."

"How did he survive that? And what the hell is he pulling out with him? Oh, shit; an RPG? Stace, I think this is yours."

"Got it."

She pulled out a silenced semi-auto pistol, aimed and fired just as the guy pointed the RPG at the SUV. The grenade exploded before the rocket could propel it out of the tube, blowing the entire cab of the truck, as well as the guy who was halfway out the passenger side window, into oblivion ... or at least into teeny tiny pieces.

Kathy smiled and said, "Great shot, Stacy; you hit the detonator. How did you do that?"

"Shit. I was aiming for his head."

"Well, maybe you'll have a second chance. It might come down somewhere along our exfil route."

"Could be."

Kristle asked, "Think we can make it look like a suicide?"

Stacy snorted. "If we had ten minutes or so. But we don't; we need to get out of here. Kill the taillights now, and once we're turning onto N, rotate the plates and kill the padiddle switch. Go, go."

"Okay, Stacy. Hang on back there, Krissy."

"Hanging on. Um ... you know, Stace, you won't get a second shot if it lands in the foilage."

Stacy gritted her teeth, rolled her eyes, but stayed silent.

Ten minutes later, they parked the SUV in the garage of a safe house near Logan Circle, called in to report their success, and settled in with Magda and Leah, the safe house caretakers, for a celebratory toast: "To the Egalitarian. May he rest in pieces."

-56-
Five Months Earlier

Sunday, August 14, 2011
6:30 a.m.
Bonita Beach, Florida

As Jake pulled into the Collier parking lot, he saw Charlotte, a middle-aged intellectual writer/editor, unloading from her car all the implements she used every day to feed and nurture the feral cats that lived in the brush between the lot and the beach.

"Hi, Jake. You're here early."

"I know, Charlotte. You, too. What's up?"

"Oh, I've got an appointment this morning at eight, so it's an early breakfast for my little friends here."

"An appointment on a Sunday?"

"Yes; it's the only chance I have to meet these clients."

"Well, good luck with that."

"Thanks, Jake. Have a good day."

"I will, Charlotte; thanks. You, too.

As he unloaded his stuff and headed to the beach, Jake heard Charlotte calling to 'her' cats. "Here, Andrea, Yasi, Casey. C'mon, Cori, Cocheta, Heidi, Tammy, Crystal, Diane, Dianne, Dianna, Dakota, Patrick, Susan, Courtney."

Two minutes after getting himself set up near the high water line, he saw Pam running onto the sand, carrying her beach stuff, an indecipherable expression on her face.

"Oh, Jake, I can't believe you did it," she panted.

"Did what? G'morning, Pam."

"You've just put yourself in the crosshairs again."

"What?"

In the elevated gazebo in front of the Lee County restrooms, Jill, one of the Mimosa twins, switched on her equipment. Carie, the other twin, hidden from view in the middle gazebo on the Collier side, also switched hers on.

"I told you not to touch that stuff, that it'd put you in danger, and now you've got 23 pages of it in there, all way too close to the real facts. Have you let anybody else see that?"

"What are you talking about?"

"The info that waitress gave you when we met over there," she said, pointing generally at the towers across the street, "the one I told you would put you in danger."

"Oh, that; yeah, I remember. I found a lot of stuff on the internet, and that led to lots more, and I just had to include it; it was so explosive and covered up."

"Well, it's a hornet's nest, and you have no idea what they could do to you just for knowing about it, much less putting it in the book."

"But it's all on the internet, I think. Some of it was awfully hard to find, but it's there. I did push some of the situations to add some pizzazz to the plot, but --"

"Jake, I don't know how you did it, but you were like 99 percent accurate."

"Really? Holy shit. I was just spicing it up. Damn."

"Has anybody else seen this? Anybody at all?"

"No, Pam, nobody; just you – well, I did send the stuttering stuff to a friend who's a speech therapist for some suggestions; that's it. Nobody else. Really."

"Well, you've got to take it out. If you leave it in and publish it, I guarantee you'll be dead within a month after that."

"Oh, Pam --"

Pam raised an index finger and shook it in Jake's face.

"No, Jake, I'm serious. Don't be naive; these people play for keeps. Don't forget, I've been on the inside, Secret Service and the CIA before that. Those people have long memories and they hold grudges over lifetimes."

"But --"

"No buts, Jake. Christ, I can't believe it. You don't seem all that suicidal, but you're setting yourself up in ways you can't even begin to comprehend. You like waving red flags in front of angry bulls?"

"How am I setting myself up, exactly?"

"Okay, okay. Let me catch my breath."

"Take your time. Want some water?"

"Got some right here, but thanks." She took a long swig from a bottle, then flipped open her beach chair and flopped into it, taking several deep, deep breaths.

"Okay? Better?"

"Just another minute. Geez, I still can't believe it." She pulled a towel from her bag and wiped her face, throat and shoulders, took several more deep breaths and moved her chair to face Jake, right beside his lounge, as close as she could get.

"Okay, Jake. First, you've got to keep this totally confidential."

"Okay. Promise."

"I mean it; it could be dangerous for both of us."

"I mean it, too; promise."

Pam dropped her voice to a near-whisper. "Okay. You know I was Secret Service."

"And CIA before that. I know."

"CIA's not relevant to this. But in the Service, I was on the PPD twice, once --"

"The what?"

"PPD, Presidential Protection Detail."

"Ah, okay."

"Once from '99 to '02, and again from '07 to '09."

"Wow. So Clinton to Bush and then Bush to Obama, right?"

"Right."

"Okay. Is that when you got shot?"

"No, no; that was '91, not relevant to this."

"Okay; sorry."

"Anyhow, I was assigned to the First Ladies both times."

"Wow. Bet you heard all kinds of stuff."

"Yes, I did. But I can't tell you anything about <u>what</u> I heard, other than to tell you that some of the stuff I heard in the last part of my second tour confirms what you've got in those 23 pages; I have no idea how you got it so right."

"Like I said, Pam, I was just taking what I got off the internet and spicing it up for a more dramatic oomph."

"Well, Jake, your oomph could get you killed."

"Geez."

"And maybe me, too, 'cause they know that I'm involved with you."

"Involved?"

"You know what I mean. I investigated you, I retired, I'm sitting here with you now. What would they think?"

"Christ, how paranoid are they?"

"Pretty paranoid. Think, Jake, think. Look at what you've got in those 23 pages, especially the last six or seven."

"Oh, about the --"

"Shhh, Jake. Don't even mention it. You never know who might be listening."

"Even here?"

"Even here."

"Geez, Pam; I didn't think. I had no idea that a little bit of fiction would put you in danger, too. I'll take those right out, tonight."

"Oh, thank you, Jake, thank you."

Pam leaned over and gave Jake an awkward hug and then kissed him on the mouth. Then she gasped and pulled away.

"Oh, Jake, I'm sorry." She blushed. "I'm so embarrassed."

"That's okay, Pam. No need to be. That was ... um ... nice."

"I was just so worried for you when I read that."

"And for yourself."

"That was later, much later, after I remembered what I'd heard."

"That's okay, Pam; it's gone."

"Good."

"Well, as soon as I get home. I'll write something around it. I can figure it out."

Pam pulled up her towel and wiped her eyes, although she tried to make it look as if she were wiping her whole face, and then her throat and shoulders. Jake lay back on his lounge, watching her, a smile playing its way across his mouth. After a moment, Pam glanced at him.

"What?"

"Again, you never fail to surprise and amaze me."

"Why, suh, whatevuh do you mean?" Pam asked, again dropping into her Southern accent. Then, without the accent, she immediately followed that with, "Actually, Jake, that feeling is mutual."

"Why, ma'am, whatevuh do you mean?" Jake asked, dropping into his own Southern accent.

"It's when I read your stuff, and from getting to know you and the brain behind all that."

"Oh, dear. I'm not sure you really want to know that. Sometimes it gets a little carried away; the filter goes bye-bye."

"The what? Filter?"

"Filter. That thing that we all learn to stick in there between our wacky old brain and the mouth, so we can fit in with society. But for me, I put it away when I get in front of the PC and let the craziness go through my fingertips into the keyboard and onto the screen."

"Ah."

"And sometimes it's tough for me to get it back and stick it in where it's supposed to be. It sorta goes bye-bye."

"I get it, I think."

"Sometimes I worry that maybe someday I won't be able to get it back, and then ... and then it's off to the loony bin for ol' Jake." He wiped his knuckles at the corners of his eyes.

"Oh, Jake," Pam said, "I don't think you need to worry about that. You seem to be able to put it back when you need to."

"For now, yeah. But down the road? I don't know. I just don't know."

"Oh, Jake," Pam said, reaching over and taking his hand in hers and holding it tightly. "We never know what the future will bring, do we?"

Jake squeezed her hand. "Thank you. You're right; we don't."

"Nobody does. So we just do --"

They finished the sentence together. "The best we can." Then they both laughed and looked into each other's eyes.

"Look, the sun's coming up, Pam," Jake said as the first gleam of its rays hit her and shone brightly on her face.

"Oh, cool. It's beautiful."

"Want to take a walk?"

"Sure. Will our stuff be safe?"

"Yup, no problem. Nobody's here."

"Let me just take my little bag along. And I'd feel a lot better if you brought your backup CD."

"Oh, I don't think – okay."

Jake pulled out his CD as Pam dug a smallish bag out of her beach bag and threw the strap over her shoulder.

"Ready, old man?" Pam asked, getting out of her chair.

"Ready, kid. I want to show you the Wacky Future house."

"The what house?"

"The Wacky Future house; that's what we call it. You'll see." Jake climbed off his lounge, with a quick assist from Pam and a subdued creaking from his knees.

As they walked south, arm in arm and then hand in hand as they adjusted their pace, Carie and Jill both turned off their equipment. Once Pam and Jake had gone a good ways, Carie sneaked out of the Collier gazebo and joined Jill up on the one in Lee County. They high-fived and then both of them wiped the corners of their eyes.

"This is gonna be good, Jillybean," Carie said, smiling.

"Nobody knows the future, Carie Berry," Jill said, also smiling.

"No, they don't," a deep, raspy female voice said in their earbuds. "But I can see farther into it than you two can."

"Don't you mean 'further,' Sharon?" said Carie.

"No, 'farther' is right," Jill interjected.

"Now, now, you two, don't be divisive,"

"Don't you mean divisive?" Jill said, chuckling.

"No, I mean divisive," Sharon snarled. "It's way too early in the morning. Why don't you go get a couple of Mimosas at Pop's? You've got time and I'll cover for you from up here."

"Now, that's a great idea," the twins responded. And they did just that.

-57-

Saturday, January 7, 2012
1:33 p.m. Local time
An obscure apartment on Via Tigre
Rome, Italy

The call came over his sat phone. "Gaetano here. Hold on." He hit the mute button and said, "Get dressed and be gone" to the blond Swedish beauty lying naked on the bed beside him, who looked at him quizzically until he translated his command into his native language, adding "You must never tell anyone about this. Do you understand?" The boy nodded, picked up his school uniform and began to put it on.

"No, not here; in there," Gaetano said, pointing to the bathroom. "And close the door while you clean yourself." The boy complied, slamming the door.

Looking out the window past the Villa Borghese to St. Peter's and the Vatican in the distance, he again hit the mute button.

"Speak." A brief pause. "WHAT? Dead? Minchia! Where? When? How?" He listened intently, his face betraying no emotion at all. And when he finally spoke, his voice was granite.

"An RPG? Anything to connect him back to us?" Another brief pause. "Good. Now, when will you have a replacement? We need it done by the original deadline." Another pause. "Then I will expect a full refund of the ten million." Another pause. "I don't care about his policy; he's dead. You will have that back to us by tomorrow. I will hold you personally responsible for that. Do you understand?" A longer pause. "Do you understand?" A shorter pause. "Good, and goodbye." He hung up and yelled at the bathroom door, "Out, now!"

-58-
Five Months Earlier

Sunday, August 14, 2011
9:55 a.m.
Bonita Beach, Florida

"I can see why you call that the Wacky Future house; that's quite a piece of architecture. Those three big holes in that flowing roof really give it a futuristic feel. And it looks like a fish from the side."

"Yup. I heard that the second floor floor is made of glass."

"Glass, really? That seems really ... um ... weird."

"Well, maybe it's so you can look down and see when dinner's ready."

"But can people look up, too?"

"I have no idea. Haven't been in there myself."

Pam leaned back on her noodle and let her feet float up again.

"Oh, I just remembered. Gratingly."

"What?"

"Gratingly. How's that for the word for the off-key Elvis guy?"

"Gratingly; hmm. Yeah, I think that'll work. Where'd you come up with that?"

"I don't know; it just popped up."

"Just now?"

"No, yesterday afternoon, as I was writing the love scene. But then I started reading your stuff and totally forgot it."

"You, Pam, forget? That's my shtick."

"Hey, it happens."

"I've got to write that down," he said and turned toward the shore.

"Don't worry, Jake, I'll remember."

"Promise?"

"Promise. Once I forget something and then remember it, especially in front of someone else, I almost always remember it better."

"Me, too. I think it's the negative feedback, like when I see someone I've met once or twice and have to ask for their name again, the embarrassment sorta locks it in better."

"That makes sense. Did you know that guidance systems on rockets work completely on negative feedback?"

"How's that?"

"It's like 'Oops, too far right, correct; too far left, correct; too far up, correct; too far down, correct,' and the rocket hits its target."

"Oh, I like that. Can I use that in the book?"

"Sure. It's not mine; it's just physics ... and rocket science." She smiled and Jake chuckled.

"That's right; I forgot."

"Ah. Hold out your hand." Jake did and she gently slapped his wrist. "There; negative feedback."

"Thanks, physics major. So did you work at NASA, too?"

"Just a couple of projects when I was in college; research stuff."

"So that's how the CIA found you and recruited you?"

Pam paused, looked around and up at the blue sky, then said, "Oh, what lovely weather," and then smiled at Jake, who smiled back.

"Got it. Can't blame a guy for trying."

Pam laughed, then glanced at the shore and back at Jake.

"Not too many people here, are there? And it's almost ten."

"It'll probably fill up a little more by noon, when the churches are all done."

"Ah. But there's those two girls again. You sure they're not pros?"

"The Mimosa twins? Naw, they're just beach bunnies."

"Mimosa twins?"

"Um, that's what I call 'em. Saw 'em drinking those at Pop's one morning."

"They look like pros to me."

"Naw – wait, you mean hookers?" Jake said, giving Pam his innocent, naive look.

Pam laughed. "Oh, Jake, no, no, no. Pros, spies, eyes, ears."

"Oh, surveillance." He looked up at the twins, who were tapping their feet on their towels as they listened to whatever music was coming through their earbuds.

"Naw, just cute little kids, kinda ditzy. I talked with them once."

"Remember their names?"

"Oh, geez, Pam. I did, once. Ah ... nope. Gone."

"Maybe you could introduce me to them sometime."

"Really?"

"Sure. Just for fun."

"Fun? I think you want to check them out."

"Got me there, Jake. Just to satisfy my suspicions. No rush."

"Okay; we can do that. But I'll bet you'll see they're just a couple of ditzy kids."

"Or ditzy chicks?"

Jake laughed. "Good one, Pam; that goes into the database."

"Thank you, thank you very much," Pam said; Jake laughed.

"I'll bet they get hit on a lot," Pam said.

"I'd guess so. The sniffers would go after them, for sure."

"Sniffers?"

"That's what I call 'em. The guys who come to the beach just to pick up girls."

"Ah. Lots of them around?"

"Eh, just like anywhere, I'd guess. Three that I can think of offhand; can't remember their names."

"Sniffers; hmm. That fits."

Suddenly, a burst of applause broke out. Pam, startled, looked over her shoulder to see where it was coming from.

"Ten o'clock; the AA meetings are letting out."

"Where?"

"You'll see 'em in a second. First gazebo down there."

"Oh, got it. I didn't see them arrive."

"Ah, that was while you went jogging after our walk. I hardly notice 'em anymore, other than the ten o'clock applause. Yup, here they come."

"Gee, Jake, look at the figure on her. Must be a 38 double D."

"Naw, she's really a 32B; she just has really good posture."

175

Pam cracked up. "Oh, Jake."

They watched the exodus of the AA people for a minute or two, and then Jake snapped his fingers.

"Pam, one serious question."

"Go for it, Jake."

"When I get rid of that section tonight --"

"Yeah."

"-- what do you think about the other part, Bush and Cheney's meeting with Donne?"

"That I don't know; I never heard anything about that. That reads more like fiction, anyhow."

"Damn. I meant it to sound realistic." Jake rubbed his forehead and ran his fingers through his hair.

"I probably should take that out, too. I don't want this to come off as anything even remotely partisan."

"That one probably can't put you in too much danger. But I can see what you mean about being nonpartisan."

"I'll look it over tonight, but I do think I'll need to take that out, too; keep things balanced."

"That one's up to you. But I can see what you mean about balancing it out."

"Yeah. By the way, were you there when that guy got shot in the knee on the White House lawn? I think his name was Pickett or Puckett, something like that."

"Oh, right. Ahh, it was Pickett, Robert Pickett, February of '01. No, Laura and my team were at the ranch in Crawford that day. I did know the officer that shot him, though."

"Just wondering. I think I read somewhere he got three years ... Pickett, I mean."

"I think that's right, something like that."

"Thanks."

"Bitte, and de nada," Pam said, smiling.

"Now you're just showing off," Jake replied, smiling more.

"Guilty as charged, Jake. Sorry," Pam fake-pouted.

"Nothing to be sorry about. I love it."

"Which reminds me. Are you ready to read my love scene?"

"Absolutely. Been looking forward to that all morning."

"Well, let's go, then. I printed it out for you."

"Lead on, MacDuff."

As they headed out of the water, Sharon's smoky voice came over the Mimosa twins' earbuds. "Now, don't you kids miss any of this. I want to hear every moan and groan, okay?"

The twins glanced subtly at each other and giggled. Jill replied, "Don't worry, you horny old hooker; we'll keep you plugged in."

Sharon laughed and said, "I don't make rugs. Over and out, you poor little virgins."

The twins giggled and settled in for the duration, still tapping their feet to the now-nonexistent music on their earbuds.

-59-

Monday, January 9, 2012
9:05 a.m. local time
The Reclining Buddha
Wat Pho Temple
Bangkok, Thailand

A youngish, pretty blonde woman using the name Missy sidled up to a short, heavy-set man waiting at the feet of the 46-meter-long gold-leafed statue and said, "He sure has big feet, doesn't he?"

The man replied with a leer, "You know what they say about men with big feet, don't you?"

"I do." She paused, then said, "They have to buy big shoes."

Recognition codes completed, the man said, "Okay, young lady, I'm here and I left the key next to the Buddha by the door."

"I know," she replied. "Our associate has already picked up the deposit and the target information from the locker."

"So we're all set?"

"Not quite. My principal always operates in the deep background, and the death always appears to be from either natural causes or an accident, or the body is never found. No women, no children, no innocents and minimal collateral damage. You understand?"

"I do. But for 20 million euros, we expect proof of death."

"He does not guarantee that. But you know that no one has ever been disappointed in his results."

"I will have to check with my principal on that."

"Go ahead. I'll wait right here. You have five minutes."

The man walked around to the front of the Buddha, and three minutes later, returned with an open cell phone. "He wants to talk to you."

"Not gonna happen. Tell him he accepts the terms or he loses his deposit."

The man spoke quietly into his phone, finally closed it and turned back to Missy, frowning.

"He accepts, but with objections."

"Tough. And he knows that his life is collateral for the final payment once the job is done, I trust?"

"He does."

"He understands we would have no problem taking out a lobbyist, even in the heart of DC, right?"

177

"He does."

"Even if he has a family."

"He understands."

"Now give me the email address and password for the account you set up."

The man handed her an envelope, which she put in her purse.

"And the instruction card that got you here."

The man handed over a 3x5 card, which also went in her purse.

"Your principal also understands that with the thin information on the target that you've provided, this may take a while?"

"He does, and he wishes he could give you more."

"My principal can work with what you've given him."

"Good."

"When the job is done, you'll find a message in the Drafts folder of the email account you provided, and the final payment will be due within 24 hours in the bank account that he will provide in that message. And under NO circumstances are you to send that message anywhere, but just change it with the single word 'Sent' in the body, NOT the subject line, and save it back in the Drafts folder."

"I understand."

"Once we have received the final payment, we will scrub that message and the account, which will let you know that we have finished and our arrangement is complete ... until the next time you need his services. Then you can contact us as you did this time."

"I understand."

"Any questions or concerns?"

After a pause, the man shrugged and said, "No."

"Good. The Andorran appreciates your business and thanks you for thinking of him. Now walk away ... no, no, casually."

Once he was out of earshot, she muttered to herself, "Geez; amateurs."

-60-
Five Months Earlier

Sunday, August 14, 2011
10:10 a.m.
Bonita Beach, Florida

"What' s so funny, Jake?"

Trying hard to control his laughter, Jake said, "Sorry, Pam. This is good, but that one word always gets me going."

"What word?"

"'Voluptuous.' Whenever I read or hear that, it takes me back to high school, when I misread it as 'volumptuous,' with an M in there,

178

and the whole class laughed at me. And then I had an image of a woman walking down the street and her chest bouncing along, going 'volump-volump, volump-volump.' It just cracks me up."

Pam laughed and said, "Volump-volump. Oh, god, Jake, that's – that's – I can't even think of a word for that."

"How about 'sophomoric' ... or 'juvenile' ... or just 'stupid'?"

"Yeah, but I was thinking more of ... of 'hysterical.'" Her laughter turned into cackling and snorting. "Volump-volump."

Up near the boardwalk, Jill and Carie started laughing, and quickly pulled out a cell phone and pretended to be looking at a photo or a video, focusing on it and completely avoiding looking anywhere near Pam and Jake. It didn't help them that Sharon's smoky guffaws came over their earbuds. "Volump-volump."

Pam pulled up a corner of her towel and wiped her eyes. "Oh, god, Jake, you got me going again." Then she laughed even harder. "Stevie ... Stevie ... Stevie Bruce. Oh, god." And off she went again.

Jake was the first to sort of get his laughter under control, but not at all successfully.

"Okay; serious. Let me get back into --"

"And what you did with him with Jennifer and ... oh, god, I'm gone ... Jennifer and ... and ... and Poopsie." And Pam truly was gone, to the point that she had to get her noodle and head into the Gulf, laughing all the way. Jake tried not to stare, but the white bikini she'd worn today, with the same gold-ring decorations as the black one, swayed so delightfully that he couldn't avoid it.

Finally, he tore his eyes away and looked back at the papers in his hand, still chuckling. Absently, he picked up a cigarette and lit it.

He had read only about halfway through the second page when Pam returned, having finally either controlled her laughter or let it drain itself away. She dropped the noodle and flopped back into her chair, looking at Jake expectantly.

"Wow, Pam, I had no idea that you could write so ... so ... so ... oh, what's the word? Graphically?"

Pam smiled. "You need two more syllables before that."

Jake looked at her blankly.

"Starting with a P."

"A P?" He puzzled on that for a moment, than said, "Oh, right. Right." He continued reading, with Pam watching him closely.

"Geez, Pam. 'Oh, my god, it's huge'? 'Throbbing'? 'Swollen'? 'Squeeze'? 'A tiny trickle of blood'? Pam, how could --"

"Just keep reading, Jake, and take that filter off."

"Okay, okay."

He turned his attention back to the pages. A moment later, he swallowed hard, then after reading a bit more, he gasped.

"Can a human body actually get into that --"

"Please, Jake, just keep reading."

"But I can't see how --"

"Please, Jake."

He shut up and kept reading. Another few moments and he looked up at Pam, who was still watching him intently.

"Feathers? Okay. But Neapolitan? Why Neapolitan?"

"'Variety is the spice of life,' right? Three flavors in one."

Jake shrugged, nodded and continued reading.

"Oh, my god!" He looked over at Pam, his eyes wider than the lenses on his sunglasses. "Where could you even get something like that?"

"Like what?" Pam asked; Jake pointed to the page.

"Oh, that? Lots of places; you just need to know where to go. And I know where to go."

"Ohhhh, okay."

"Or you might just want to make one of your own; gotta make sure it fits on exactly right. If you don't, it could cause blisters."

"Oh, god!!! I don't even want to think about that."

"Well, you wouldn't be the one getting the blisters."

"Like that makes me feel better?"

"Just keep reading, Jake. You've still got a ways to go."

"Okay." He continued, quietly.

Carie whispered to Jill. "What was that? Blisters?"

Sharon rasped over their earbuds, "I think I know what it is."

"Yeah? What?"

Sharon chuckled. "You're not old enough yet."

Jill whispered, "Oh, yes, we are. Tell us."

"Maybe later. Keep concentrating. Listen to his breathing."

Sure enough, Jake's breathing had gotten deeper and faster, and had he thought about it, he would have noticed that his blood pressure was rising, not dangerously, but definitely up to near normal.

"Geez, Pam, this --"

"You've still got the filter on, Jake. Set it aside, please." She smiled at him, gently running her tongue over the inside of her lower lip.

"I'm trying to." He looked back at the paper. "But it's hard – I mean difficult ... to concentrate out here in public."

"Don't worry about it, Jake; just keep reading. Please." Jake complied. Pam kept watching him. So did the twins. So did Sharon, but she had to use her scope and couldn't really get a good angle on his face.

"Oh, geez. Neapolitan again? Wow. 'Moist,' 'twitching,' 'writhing in ecstasy,' 'exposed,' 'volcanic eruption,' 'creamy'? Geez."

Pam smiled. "Almost done, Jake, almost done."

"I know, I know." He continued, his breathing getting even deeper and faster, then said, "Oh, my god," and let out a great sigh.

Then he folded the papers and handed them back to Pam, but she demurred.

"Keep it, Jake; I've got it on my PC."

"Okay." Jake put them in his bag, stubbed out his cigarette and picked up his noodles. "I've gotta get in the water."

"Me, too," Pam said, smiling to herself. The twins smiled at each other, and Sharon said, "Aw, shit; I'd thought he'd read the whole thing out loud," in their earbuds. "I was so ready for some volcanic erupting."

-61-

Monday, January 9, 2012
9:05 a.m. EST
Arlington, VA

An older yet stunning woman using the name Andreana sidled up to a rail-thin, very tall man waiting at the Tomb of the Unknown Soldier and said, "Do you know what war he fought in?"

The man replied, "His last one."

Andreana responded, "Actually, it was World War One."

"Okay, Andreana, if that's your real name" he said, "I'm here and I left the key in the pencil cactus pot next to the ticket counter outside the station."

"I know," she replied, ignoring his dig. "Our associate has already picked up the deposit and the target information from the locker."

"So we're all set?"

"Not quite. My principal always operates in the deep background, and the death always appears to be from either natural causes or an accident, or the body is never found. No women, no children, no innocents and minimal collateral damage. You understand?"

"I do. But for 20 million euros, we expect proof of death."

"He does not guarantee that. But you know that no one has ever been disappointed in his results."

"Then we must accept his terms."

"And your principal knows that his life is collateral for the final payment once the job is done, I trust?"

"He does."

"He understands we would have no problem taking out a televangelist, even in the heart of Houston, right?"

"He does."

"Even if he has a family."

"He understands."

"Now give me the email address and password for the account you set up, and the instruction card that got you here."

The man handed her an envelope and a 3x5 card, which she put in her purse.

"Your principal also understands that with the thin information on the target that you've provided, this may take a while?"

"He does, and he wishes he could give you more."

"My principal can work with what you've given him."

"Good."

"When the job is done, you'll find a message in the Drafts folder of the email account you provided, and the final payment will be due within 24 hours in the bank account that he will provide in that message. And under NO circumstances are you to send that message anywhere, but just change it with the single word 'Sent' in the body, NOT the subject line, and save it back in the Drafts folder."

"I understand."

"Once we have received the final payment, we will scrub that message and the account, which will let you know that we have finished and our arrangement is complete ... until the next time you need his services. Then you can contact us as you did this time."

"I understand."

"Any questions or concerns?"

"No."

"Good. The Reaper appreciates your business and thanks you for thinking of him. Now walk away." He did. "Good; at last, a professional."

-62-
Five Months Earlier

Sunday, August 14, 2011
10:35 a.m.
Bonita Beach, Florida

"That was an incredible scene, Pam, very visual, with strong images, almost photographic, just like you said. I liked it a lot."

"I'm glad, Jake. But?" Pam floated on her noodle, right in front of Jake, floating on his two, bicycling his legs under the water.

"But I can't see Donne getting tangled up in – oops; I mean involved in something that graphic. He just doesn't have any interest in sex ... at least as I've written him so far."

"Don't get me wrong. That may change, but I think his filters are pretty ingrained."

"Like most people's are."

"Yup, if you define 'most' as anything above 51 percent."

"In this case, I mean probably around 92 percent."

"92? How'd you come up with that number?"

"Uh, I just pulled it out of the air. It seemed about right. I mean, it could be 87 or 94, but somewhere in there. Why?"

"That's a number I've used for years."

"For what?"

"Stress reduction."

"What? How?"

"Stress reduction. I think that about 92 percent of most people's time is spent doing relatively routine, not emotionally charged, stuff, like laundry, sleeping, cooking, driving, all that kind of routine and boring stuff – well, not boring in the negative sense, just routine. So you don't have to worry much about that, and you can focus your energy on making the other eight percent as good as you can. I'd rather put energy into that small eight percent than the whole hundred. So it's a lot less stressful."

"So if --"

"OW!!!! What the hell?"

Jake swiveled to see who had cried out. He saw Christopher and Paige Davenport, an elderly couple who walked in the water every day, believing that the salt water was good for their arthritis. They were about eight feet from Jake and Pam.

"What is it, Chris?" Paige asked, worried.

"I just banged my toe on something down there. Christ, I knew we should have bought those water shoes."

"What did you bang it on?"

"I don't know. Can you hold these for a second?"

"Sure." He gave Paige his hat and sunglasses and ducked under the water, coming up a moment later with a large chunk of coral, about double the size of a football.

"Oh my god, it's huge, Chris."

"I'm gonna take this in to shore so nobody else gets hurt on it."

"Hey, Chris, I'm going in; I'll take it," said a female voice behind him.

"Oh, thanks --" Chris turned to see who it was "-- Sheila."

"No problem." She started toward the shore, coral in hand. "This'll look great in my garden; I'm doing a Neapolitan style with it. Thanks, Chris."

"No, thank you, Sheila."

She continued to shore, carrying her newfound treasure.

"So, Chris – what's wrong?"

"Sorry, Paige; it's throbbing, hurts like hell."

"Let me see it."

Chris lifted his right leg to the surface, where Paige held his foot and peered at his big toe.

"Oh, Chris, it's already swollen. And is that – yup, there's a tiny trickle of blood. Let me – oops."

"Ow."

"I'm sorry; my hand slipped. I'm sorry. Does it feel broken?"

"I don't think so. But I'm not sure I can keep my body in this position much longer."

"Oh, I'm sorry." She let his foot go and it sank back into the water; he sighed in relief.

"I think you'll need a bandage on that."

"Not if it's gonna squeeze it."

"No, but if we put it on carefully, it'll help."

"I used to have some in my fanny pack, but not now."

"I'll bet they have some up at the office. I'll go get one, okay?"

"The office is next to --"

"I know where to go. Be right back. Go in and dry it off as best you can, okay? Got something for the blood?"

"Yeah, I've got some tissues in my pack, I think."

"Hey, Chris," Jake said, "let me help you out. Where's your stuff?"

"Thanks, Jake. We're just up there." He pointed to a couple of chairs on the sand, a few dozen feet north of Jake and Pam's spot.

"Okay; let's go. Keep off that toe. I know how bad those can hurt."

By the time Paige got back with some bandages, Chris had managed to dry his foot almost completely, although it was still a bit moist in some places. Jake and Pam stood by, watching, ready to help if needed.

Paige carefully began applying the bandage to Chris' toe.

"Yow! Easy, easy."

"I'm sorry, Chris. I've got to put it on just right or you could get a blister. Hey, quit twitching, okay?"

"Sorry."

"There; all done. Feel okay, hon?"

"Well, I'm not writhing in ecstasy, but it does feel better."

Paige looked over at Jake and asked, "Where would something like that come from? How could it get exposed like that?"

Jake frowned and then said, "Maybe that storm we had last month. It dug out the sand here by the shore and built up the sand bar out there. Next storm, it'll probably reverse itself."

"So not a volcanic eruption or anything?"

Jake laughed. "I don't think there's ever been a volcanic eruption in the Gulf ... well, not since the Ice Age, at least."

Chris said, "Thanks for your help, Jake. I tell ya, being 83 can suck."

"No problem, Chris. Hope it heals soon. Take care. See ya later, Paige."

As Pam and Jake headed back to the water, Pam said, "They

184

seemed like a nice couple."

"Yup. I don't know 'em too well; I've only talked with 'em a few times."

"They seem very much in love."

"They do? Yeah, I guess so. Sorry. I was thinking if I could use them in the book somehow."

"Like how Donne could – oh, that reminds me. There's a typo in his first speech, when he legalizes gay marriage; you left the 'I' out, so it was 'marrage,' r-r-a-g-e."

"I meant to do that."

"You did? Why?"

"It's Donne's sop to the religious right, just so they can't bitch that he's legalizing gay marriage; same thing, all the same rights and all, but it's got that one tiny little semantic difference. So if they bring it up, he can argue that's not exactly the same."

"What do you mean, 'if' they bring it up? You're writing it."

"I'm not sure if it's worth writing out all the stuff I'd need to to get into and through that argument; I'm not sure yet how Donne would feel about me doing that, either. We don't always agree on every – I'm sorry; that sounds crazy. It's just how I do the writing sometimes."

Pam raised en eyebrow and said, "Really? What do you mean?"

"Well, remember that he's got two czars, one for anti-hubris and one for unintended consequences, Cissy and Cody."

"Right."

"Okay. So I play a sorta mental game with them and Donne. If I have a problem with some issue, I call the three of them up and ... now, this is the part that might sound a little crazy ... and stick them in a sort of boardroom, give them the issue and let them argue it out. This is just imaginary, okay?"

"Okay," Pam said, a bit hesitantly.

"And then I let them go back down into my subconscious and work it out, sometimes just overnight, sometimes as long as it takes. I mean, I gave them the Medicare/Medicaid challenge a couple of months after I first started this whole thing, and they hashed it around until this past May ... or maybe June ... before they popped the idea of the HSAs up into my conscious brain, just as I was waking up one morning.

"And then, if I'm quick enough, I'll grab my notebook and write out as much as I can remember, stick it with my other notes, and then finally write out either a speech, a question at a press conference or a discussion with somebody to get that out.

"Like that meeting he had with the guy from HHS-OIG, the guy going after Medicare fraudsters."

"Yeah, I remember that. Jim something, right?"

"Yeah. I don't remember his last name now. That was written

way before the HSA idea popped up."

"You know that HSAs have been around for a long time, right?"

"Yeah, and they fit with Donne's basic premise of returning power and choice to the individual, to the people. So he made them – I mean, I made them the cornerstone of his policy on Medicare.

"And Cody, of course, reminded Donne that whenever there's a chunk of money anywhere, somebody somewhere is going to be looking for some way to steal it. So he's always got to build in safeguards against that. But I don't want to get too overly arcane in writing the book; I mean, it's boring enough as it is."

"For some people, Jake. I find the whole idea fascinating."

"But you've been on the inside and you've got a pretty high IQ. Most people haven't been and don't."

"'Most people' being 51 percent or 92?"

Jake chuckled. "I don't know; somewhere between. Like Chris and Paige there. They're pretty typical of people their age, and I keep people like them in mind in figuring out what Donne might do and what the unintended consequences might be."

"And that's where Cissy and Cody come in and they all toss it around?"

"Right. For example, most retirees like them aren't getting any income at all on their savings, and for a long time there was a floor of five percent on money market funds and --"

"I remember that."

"So what happened to make that go away? I don't know. But if Donne, for example, were to mandate a five percent floor again, that would help them, but who would get hurt and what other ripple effects would there be? And how would that fit in with his basic principles? And who'd get pissed off enough to take out a contract for his assassination?"

"Why assassination?"

"So there's some drama and action in there. And he sticks to his guns, so negotiation and lobbying don't work, so they go extreme."

Pam thought about that for a moment and then said, "How about a really good betrayal? Wouldn't that add some drama?"

Jake winced and said, "Oh, Pam, you're getting ahead of me there."

"You've already got one of those? I didn't see it."

"Haven't written that part yet. And sorry, can't tell you ... at least for now."

Pam fake-pouted again. "Okay, Jake; guess I can live with that."

Jake said, "Sorry."

Pam leaned back on her noodle again and let her body float. "Ahhhhh. This feels so good. The water is a perfect temperature, maybe even a teeny bit too warm."

"I think the news said it was 88 degrees, but this does feel a little warmer, maybe 88 and a quarter – no, 88 and three-eighths. Last summer we had a whole week where it was 95; now, THAT was too warm, not even refreshing. But that was really unusual."

"How cold does the water get in the winter?"

"In the what?"

"The winter."

"What does that word mean?"

"Oh, Jake, c'mon; you know."

"Okay. Last February it got down to 58."

"58? Geez, that IS cold."

"When I lived in Boston – well, Cambridge, actually, when the Atlantic got up to 60, we thought that was great. Late August."

"And now?"

"Below 80 or 81, I only go in if I really gotta go ... in."

"Well, you sound spoiled, Mr. Devlin, suh."

"Yup, I am that ... and gloatingly so."

"Well, that's a new record."

"A new record? What new record?"

"I'm sure that was longer than three and a half minutes of you being serious."

"Oh, god," Jake said, slapping his forehead. "I am going crazy. I knew I shouldn't have eaten that tofu-salami-and-chocolate salad."

Pam chuckled. "Ah, he's baaaack."

"And he needs to get baaaack on shore and write some notes down before he forgets 'em."

"I'll join you; I could use some sun time."

"You've actually got a pretty good tan already."

"Just a start. Would you put some sunscreen on my back?"

"I'd be happy to ... hope it's not that greasy, oily stuff."

"Nope, this is the creamy kind."

"Okay, then. Let's go."

Jill and Carie looked at each other, smiled and said, almost simultaneously, "This may be good."

Sharon broke in with, "Damn well better be."

-63-

Wednesday, January 11, 2012
9:05 a.m. Local time
Lugano, Switzerland

An extremely obese woman using the name Michele sidled up to an equally obese man waiting at the Biblioteca Cantonale and said, "Do you know what 'Svizzera' means?"

The man replied, "'Sauna,' I believe."

187

Michele responded, "Actually, it's 'Switzerland.' 'Sauna' would be 'schvitz.'"

"Okay, um, Michele," he said, looking at a card in his hand, "I'm here and I left the key in the largest snowbank next to the ticket counter outside the train station."

"I know," she replied. "Our associate has already picked up the deposit and the target information from the locker."

"So we're all set?"

(The remainder of this conversation closely duplicated the ones between Missy, the Andorran's rep, and the lobbyist's rep in Bangkok, and between Andreana, the Reaper's rep, and the televangelist's rep in Arlington, Virginia, USA.

In this one, Michele represented The Linguist and the man represented a gaggle of environmentalists, tree-huggers and flower-fondlers from around the world; they reached precisely the same terms as the previous two.

The target was the same in all three.)

-64-

Wednesday, January 11, 2012
9:35 a.m. EST
The White House
Washington, DC

Emily escorted the four disheveled union bosses and their equally haggard-looking lawyers into the Oval Office, surrounded by both guards and Secret Service agents. Donne, looking bright-eyed and bushy-tailed in his crisp denim jeans and newly ironed tropical shirt, smiled at the seven men and one woman.

"Lady, gentlemen, today you are all free to go; you have served your sentences ... well, most of them; this is an early release. We need the space now."

Ms. Skinner was the first to speak. "Sir, we are going to object to this forced --"

"Object all you want, ma'am. File whatever kinds of suits you choose. But remember that in addition to owning the executive and legislative branches, I also own ... and am ... the judicial branch.

"Without getting too arcane ... and I know you lawyer types love to get into as much arcanity as you can ... any efforts you make will be immediately shot down, no matter what court you choose for your venue."

"We will be filing our objection with the World Court, Mr. Donne. Under international law, what you have done to us violates all levels of due process and constitutes human rights violations of the most serious --"

"Sit down and shut up, lady. Right there." He pointed to a chair.

She remained standing with her group.

"Okay, then. Emily, return this entire group to their cells for another two weeks. We'll squeeze the newbies into the other cells, and we'll have to find some more space somewhere for the overflow."

One of the agents said, "Mr. Donne, we have some additional cells in the basement of the EOB, Executive Office Building."

"Enough for these eight?"

"Yes, sir; room for three times that."

"And are those Level A accommodations?"

"No, sir; Level C, and some Level D."

"Well, I think that's appropriate for these folks.

"Emily, take them over to those cells, the Level D's, and begin them on the lower level diet, as well."

"Tofu plus, sir?"

Donne nodded.

"With pleasure, sir.

"Gentlemen, lady, follow me. Guards."

Once they had all left the Oval Office, Donne wriggled around in his shirt, crumpling it where he could reach, and rubbed his hands on his jeans, trying unsuccessfully to get rid of the creases.

Emily returned and said, "They're on their way; Tom and Lin will get them all settled in and get them their jumpsuits. I do like the paisley for the men and madras for the woman."

"Good, good. Now I guess it's time for the next batch. Are they ready?"

"Standing by, well guarded."

Donne sat back down, picked up some papers and said, "Showtime, Emily. Bring 'em in."

"Right away, Gordy," she replied, chuckling.

"Oh, Emily, no more starch in this stuff," Donne said, smiling.

"I'll tell Shawn." She smiled and nodded. "Here we go."

She returned a few minutes later, escorting nine men and eight women, accompanied by three guards and three Secret Service agents. Donne stayed seated behind his desk, inspecting each of the 17 new arrivals closely as the guards lined them up in three rows in front of his desk.

"Welcome, ladies and gentlemen," Donne began, smiling his brightest smile. "Before we begin, I'd like to remind you all of an old quote from a noted, but disreputable, figure from America's past, specifically the time of Prohibition.

"His name was Alphonse Capone, and the quote I'm referencing was this: 'You can get more with a smile --'" Donne paused for a good ten seconds -- "'and a gun --'" he paused again, for maybe two seconds – "'than you can with just a smile.' Now some history.

"My grandpappy was a Texas Ranger at a time when this Capone clown was thinking about expanding the reach of his Chicago mob into Texas.

"In the early '30s, Capone sent a bunch of his guys as a sort of advance party down to the Lone Star State, and they started raising all sorts of hell in one area up in the Panhandle, scaring the locals out of their wits and extorting protection money from the businesses in the area.

"Well, my grandpappy was part of a team that got sent up there to deal with these Chicago clowns and courteously invite them to go back up north and never return to Texas.

"But you know something? These mugs were not all that open to a courteous invitation, in spite of the fine smiles that all of the Rangers had on their faces. In fact, they responded with guns to the Rangers' smiles. That was the last mistake they made in Texas.

"Now, none of them died there on the scene, but they all scooted back north with at least a little bit of good ol' Texas lead somewhere in their anatomies, which made the scooting a little more painful than normal scooting would be.   And since it was February, also a little colder.

"A lot of that lead came from my grandpappy's trusty revolvers; he always carried four of them. He emptied 'em all in that little gunfight, smiling all the time. And he never got a scratch on him.

"While good ol' Al believed in a smile and a gun, the Rangers believed in a smile and <u>more</u> guns, more than the bad guys had.

"The rangers bandaged all the wounded, packed 'em up and sent 'em on their way, with one very clear message for that Capone dude, which was very simple.

"'Do not ever try to rip off the people of Texas, in any way, shape or form, or you will face the consequences.' What was not included in the message was that he and his team were the consequences. He felt that Mr. Capone was bright enough to infer that from the battered wounded bodies that greeted him when he met the train in Chicago.

"What those mugs told Capone is lost to history, but whatever it was, it was enough to convince the mobster to keep his operations out of the fine state of Texas.

"Now, my grandpappy may have embellished that story a wee bit here and there, but the moral of the story, and the reason I'm telling it to all of you, is that trying to rip off people brings with it serious consequences. In his case he was protecting the people of Texas, in my case, the people of the entire United States of America, especially in their roles as taxpayers, consumers, retirees and Medicare and Medicaid clients.

"And you 17 people have been ripping off the people I'm sworn to protect for years, you six with your over-priced mobility devices that you bill to Medicare and private insurance companies; you four with your reverse mortgages with hidden charges and outrageous interest rates; you five with your upcoding in your bills to Medicare and to private insurance companies; and you two with your over-priced and under-performing catheters and other so-called 'medical supplies' for diabetics and incontinents.

"Now, you 17 are only the first of hundreds of your ilk that we are tracking down and bringing in to face the consequences. And I am the cutting edge of those consequences.

"The first consequence is that, although you can expect due process, that due process is not necessarily a court process, but is the process as I define it, wearing the three hats that I wear as the owner of this country.

"And I find you all guilty of multiple ripoffs of the people of this country, including failure to report and pay your Al Capone tax in just the past two days, as well as since the first of this year. Your appeals of those convictions will fall on deaf ears ... mine, wearing my hat as the Supreme Court.

"As part of your punishment, I have confiscated all of your personal and business assets; you will keep your liabilities. Good luck with those.

"Additionally, you are all sentenced to ten years in federal prison, with no parole, no time off for good behavior, and no Club Fed environment. It'll be hard labor.

"No, no; no arguments ... unless you want to have another five years added for contempt.

"Guards, take these people down to the cellblock while we arrange for transport to the appropriate prisons. Keep them out of the Level A and B cells. Thank you.

"Ladies and gentlemen, I also thank you for your service, as we will be using you as widely-publicized examples for any others who have done what you have done and think they can continue to get away with it.

"Not that everybody in your businesses is crooked, by the way. But like lawyers, 99.9 percent of you give the rest a bad name.

"Enjoy your stay with us – oh, you will each be billed for room and board for the days you are here. Of course, with no assets left, I don't know how you'll pay for that, and frankly, I don't give a damn.

"Take them away, guards."

After the door had closed behind them, Donne said, "Cissy, Cody, c'mon in."

Another door opened and they entered, following Donne and Emily to the couches in the center of the office.

"Questions, problems, concerns? Cissy?"

"No, Gordy, I think you did just fine with that.'"

"Cody?"

"Well, Gordy, as we discussed, there'll be lots of backlash and lots of perps trying to move their assets out of your reach, as well as trying to churn up opposition to you personally."

"Anything else?"

"Nope, I think that's it. We discussed the other stuff before."

"Good. I hope they do try to move assets; makes it so easy to flag 'em, stop 'em and redirect 'em to the Treasury. And it makes it even easier to track the coding back to find out the originators, get 'em out of the woodwork, like cockroaches coming out when you turn the lights on.

"Which reminds me, Emily. Tony's all set to do his Jimmy routine for these folks. Spray for bugs about – let's see; it's almost ten now, so about noon. And then release the roaches about nine p.m."

"Okay, Gordy. Like Lisbon."

"You got it. And they'll all probably enjoy some of your oddball salads; I'll leave the choice on that up to you."

Emily smiled and replied, "I'll do my best." The other three all chuckled.

"Good, good.

"Cody, how are you doing on the China directive?"

"I'm still running the possible outcomes of that ... and there are tons of variables to consider ... but from my work so far, I think we'll need to hold off for a year or two, until our domestic economy is a good ways further into recovery."

"Cody, I think we need to put that in place in nine months to a year, max; narrow window there. But I agree we need to wait till our economy's stronger. I think we can do that in my time frame, though. We'll have to adjust that as the numbers start to come in. Keep at it."

"Sure will, Gordy."

"Cissy, any hubris problems with that?"

"Only on your public image and the backlash. Standing alone, no problems. I'll be sure the social media teams are prepping for that, as well as all the other stuff."

"Good, good.

"Emily, any other appointments today?"

"Nope, Gordy; I cleared your calendar. Tomorrow's full, though."

"Good, good.

"Okay, gang; that's it. Now I've got some work to do, so scamper away." They all did and Donne returned to his desk and his very full inbox, which he divided into his usual two piles in less than an hour and then lay down for a long-overdue and well-deserved nap. "Tofu plus; hope they enjoy it. And I hope there's a lot of starch in their jumpsuits."

-65-
Five Months Earlier

Sunday, August 14, 2011
11:15 a.m.
Bonita Beach, Florida

"Oh, this feels wonderful, Jake."

"Doesn't it, though? I'll tell you, I set a goal of twenty minutes, but usually I can only last maybe seven or eight."

"I think you lasted nearly twelve or thirteen. Bravo."

"Well, you made it easier."

"Oh, I didn't do all that much."

"It was enough. And we were interrupted."

"Now, if you can just lean back a little more, we can continue from where we left off."

"Like this? Or more?"

"Just a tiny bit more ... there; perfect. Okay for you?"

"Wonderful. Ahhhh. God, Jake, you're good."

"I'm kinda rusty; learned that move way back in college."

"Well, I'm loving it. I'll give you till the end of the year to stop.

"Just a teeny bit more to the right, okay?"

"Here?"

"Oh, yesssss, right there. Ahhh."

"The cream makes it awful slippery."

"That's okay. It still feels wonder- – oh, yes, yes, yes, right there."

"Like that?"

"Ahhhhhhhhhhhhhhhh!"

Jake smiled and continued his ministrations.

When they'd left the water twelve or thirteen minutes earlier, Jake made some notes, including the names Christopher and Paige, as he watched Pam spreading sunscreen on her arms, legs, stomach and shoulders, as well as a gentle dab to her face.

"Ready for the back?"

"Yup, if you would."

"Happy to, as long as I don't have to stand up."

"No problem. Last thing I want to do is make you stand up."

Pam moved to beside Jake's lounge, gave him the bottle and sat down in the sand, her back to him, as he sat up sideways.

"Ah, good brand, same as mine. But I only use a 15."

"For now, I think the 30 is better for me, at least until I catch up to you."

"I wouldn't hold my breath on that."

"You might be surprised. I tan pretty quickly."

"Quicklier than other blondes?"

Pam ran her fingers through her hair and laughed. "Sure."

After a moment, Jake said, "Geez, your shoulder muscles are kinda tense. Can you relax them a bit?"

Pam shrugged a couple of times, then let go. "Like that?"

"That's a little better. May I?"

"Sure."

As Jake finished smearing the sunscreen, he began gently massaging her shoulders. She sighed and let her head drop forward.

The Mimosa twins smiled and winked at each other. Norm and Janet, who had arrived an hour or so earlier, looked on, amused at the difference in Pam's demeanor now from two months earlier. Some of the Beach Potatoes got their cell phones and cameras out, the Beach Balls looked down their chubby noses in annoyance, but those of the Incontinentals who were still in their chairs, not using the facilities, were too far away to even notice.

"Ohhh, Jake, that feels soooo good."

He ran his fingers up her neck, gradually adding a little bit more pressure, seeking, finding.

"Let me know if it hurts. You've got some pretty tight knots up in here."

"Oh! You found that one."

"Sorry. Let me see if I can work it out."

"Okay," she mumbled, her chin down on her upper chest.

"This may hurt a little bit."

"Okay – ouch – no, don't worry; that's fine. Go ahea- – ahhh."

"Better?"

"I think so."

"A little pain, a little pleasure."

"That's life."

"But only in eight percent of it; 92 percent routine."

Pam laughed, but kept the laughter from moving her head.

"Well, this eight percent is pretty damned good."

"I'm glad."

Jake continued, the silence broken only by Pam's sighs and quiet moans.

But after a minute, Jake could feel Pam's neck tense up a bit.

"What?" he asked.

"Sorry. My brain kept going."

"Ah. What?"

"We didn't finish my notes on your stuff, and I remembered one thing."

"And that is?"

"I'm concerned about your having the Pope swearing."

"Oh. I debated that for a long time. Then I reminded myself that it's not the real Pope, he's fictional, so I think it's okay. And it fits with what they're plotting in that scene – I mean chapter."

"But you used his real name, sort of."

"Oh, the Bennie bit? No, he's Italian, not German, and his full first name is Benedetto, not Benedict. He's fictional."

"I don't know, Jake. That may be another red flag ... not just for Donne, but for you."

"What, you think the Church would come after me, too?"

"They're pretty powerful, always have been."

"I know that. I've read about the Inquisition, Galileo, and all the rest. Hell, I even read about Constantine and how he killed people who wouldn't accept the Nicene Creed ... allegedly. He was as bad as the radical Islamic terrorists today. I think one 'fuck' and three 'focus'-es in there aren't too far out of line. Hey, you're tensing up again."

"Sorry. But are you having him go after the Islamists, too?"

"Yup, but in a surgical way, a rifle, not a shotgun."

"Oh, geez."

"Hey, Pam, easy; quit fighting it. Relax, okay?"

"Sorry; I'll try."

"Ah, I've got it. Compartmentalize."

Pam laughed. "Your memory is getting better."

"I've been thinking a lot about that as I write, and whenever I've thought about you. Which has been a lot."

"Really?"

"Really, especially since yesterday. It's nice to see you relaxed."

"Well, you're sure helping on that front."

"Actually, I'm working on your back."

Pam laughed.

"Did you know you've got great shoulder blades?"

"What?"

"You've got great shoulder blades; they have a great shape and move really exotically."

"Exotically? I have exotic shoulder blades? That's a new one."

"Well, I like yours."

"Why, thank you, suh; ah do 'preciate that."

"Well, you deserve it. Now, try to relax, okay?"

"Okay. Sorry."

"Nothing to be sorry about."

This time, the silence was broken after a minute by a harsh, nasal voice.

"Hey, Jake, try this."

"What is it, Sonya? What do you want?"

"It's a cigar. I've been trying to tell you about them for weeks."

"Looks like a brown cigarette."

"Smokes just like one, too, and they're only a buck a pack, ten bucks a carton."

"Yeah? Where?"

"Over at B2B Liquors, in the green strip mall with the barber shop and print place. Try it; you might like it."

"Okay, I will."

"I'm sure you'll like it. That's a light, comes in a blue-and-white box. They also come in flavors, like strawberry, orange, peach --"

"Okay, Sonya, I'll try it later."

"I'm sure you'll like it. Let me know --"

"I'll try it, Sonya, promise."

"So who's this?"

"I'm Pamela."

"Hey, Pamela; I'm Sonya, and my husband, Herb, is up there."

"Oh."

"He's trying to solve Fermat's Last Theorem."

"Trying to solve what?" Jake asked.

"I thought Wiles solved that back in the '90s," Pam said.

A shocked look was the only response Sonya gave Pam, the first time Jake had ever seen her speechless.

"Well, Sonya, Pam and I were just heading back into the water. Thanks for the cigar and say hi to Herb for me."

"You know about Fermat?" Sonya said, moving closer to Pam.

"Yup. But Jake's right; it's getting too hot up here. Nice to meet you ... Sonya, was it?"

"Right.

"So, Jake --"

"Sonya, we've got to go. Thanks again."

"But --"

"I'll let you know how I like it. See ya."

"But, Jake --"

"Later, Sonya; I'll let you know. Promise."

"Want me to help you up, Jake?"

"Thanks, Pam. Wawa time. See ya, Sonya."

"Well, okay. Try it; you'll love it." She set the cigar on Jake's bag and headed back up to Herb and her chair.

"I see what you mean, Jake; she is kind of outspoken."

"Not by anybody I know."

Pam chuckled.

"We'll continue in the water, okay, Pam?"

"I'd love that, Jake, as long as your hands aren't too tired."

"Not at all, Pam, not at all."

Sharon's voice rasped through Jill and Carie's earbuds. "I'll bet you dollars to doughnuts they do it sometime today."

Jill said, "No bet; that's a f'sure."

Carie added, "Well, he better wake up and pick up on the cues."

Sharon said, "Her place or his?"

Jill said, "I'll put a buck on his."

"You're on, Jill. Carie?"

"A buck on his for me, too."

"Guess I'm in for two bucks on hers. And it's just three floors down, right under me. I'm gonna go put a bug in there."

Jill and Carie both said, "No, Sharon, no!"

"Hey, it's part of the mission; surveil and protect."

"We know, Sharon. And keep the principal in the dark."

"I still don't understand that part, CB. It'd be so much simpler if he knew."

"Ours not to question, kids, just follow the mission parameters."

"But we don't even know who the client is, and he's paying a fortune just for the three of us."

Sharon said, "It's obviously someone who wants to be sure his book gets published."

Carie said, "Or maybe someone who wants to know what he's writing before he gets it done. Remember, surveil before protect."

Jill said, "Somebody with lotsa bucks, that's f'sure. I wonder --"

Sharon said, "Speculate later. Meanwhile, I'll get that bug set."

"No, Sharon," said Carie. "You --"

"I can do it; Kal left all the equipment here."

Carie said, "Not in your skill set. I'll do it."

"Well, then get your butt up here quick and get it done; I'll get the stuff out for you. What do you think, audio only or both A and V?"

"Both, I think. Keep the options open."

"So get going, kiddo."

"On my way. Jill, hold down the fort, okay?"

"Holding."

Carie left and returned ten minutes later. "Done."

Jill said, "Cool."

Carie held up a thumb drive. "And I got that sex file off her PC."

Sharon rasped and Jill squealed, "Yippee!!"

-66-

Thursday, January 5, 2012
1:30 a.m. EST
New York, New York

In an Italian social club in the Bronx, the heads of five families were bemoaning the loss of nearly all their hit men, who had been dying of mostly natural causes or accidents over the past seven months or were simply missing.

The same sorrow and frustration was reflected in other mob enclaves in Chicago, Philadelphia, Detroit, Atlanta, St. Louis, Las Vegas, Boston, Providence, Atlantic City, Newark, Miami, Nashville,

Orlando, Dover, Albany, Burlington, Manchester, Indianapolis, Los Angeles, San Francisco, Seattle, Portland, Tacoma, Boise, Helena, Pierre, Phoenix, Denver, Fargo, Duluth, Milwaukee, Madison, Salt Lake City, Dallas, Scottsdale, Albuquerque, Houston, San Antonio, Minneapolis, Madison, Stevie Bruce, Hartford, Charleston, Berkeley, Worcester, Malden, Somerville, Lowell, Taunton, Sebring, Jonesboro, Palermo, Naples, Venice, Baghdad, Amman, Moscow, Cairo, Tokyo, Beijing, Mumbai, Jakarta, Sydney, as well as three other cities the author has forgotten, where each and every hit man on their payrolls had also died, most of natural causes or accidents, except for seven who had been blown to bits in explosions, two shot, one at close range and one from an extremely long distance, and one who had been smothered by the stomach of an elephant in a zoo in Oklahoma City; how he came to be in the elephant's domain and why the animal lay down on top of him remains a mystery to police to this day.

Bosses in the Russian mob, gathered in Brighton Beach, NY, had the same frustration and sorrow. The same was true of bosses in the Lithuanian, Luxembourgian, Estonian, Samoan, Fijian, Melbournian, Norwegian, Icelandic, Bolivian, Peruvian, Zimbabwean, Egyptian, Sudanese, Somalian, Mongolian, Kazakhstanian, Parisian, Berlinian, St. Petersburgian, Armenia, Turkmenistanian, Obsessivian, Scottish, Compulsivian, Irish, Torontoian, Vancouverian, Depressivian, Avian, Manician, Musician, Rastafarian, Ecuadorian, Guatemalan, Belizian, Zimbabwean, Repetitivian, Redundantarian, Indonesian, Japanese, Syrian, Antediluvian, Mexican, Spanian, Grecian, Zimbabwean, Belgian, Kievian, Munichian, Manichean, Einsteinian, Latvian, Colombian, Zimbabwean, Repetivian, Redundantarian, Darwinian, Sargassoian, Borneoian, Kegelian, Marshall Islandian, Violian, Bassoonian, French Hornian, Uralian, Carpathian, Galapagosian, Hungarian, Romanian, Czechoslovakian, Bosnia-Herzegovinian, Dusseldorfian, Trombonian, Trumpetarian and New Ulmian mobs.

In fact, other than the man with many names, only the tiny and mostly impotent Tubalian mob had a killer still alive, and she was stuck in the frozen Antarctic, where she had botched her most recent assignment, and was unable to return to her home island of Tuba.

-67-
Five Months Earlier

Sunday, August 14, 2011
11:20 a.m.
Bonita Beach, Florida

"The cream makes it a bit slippery."

"That's okay. It still feels wonder- – oh, yes, yes, yes, right there."

"Like that?"

"Ahhhhhhhhhhhhhhhh!"

Jake smiled and continued his ministrations.

Gradually, he could feel Pam's shoulder muscles relaxing and her neck beginning to loosen up, as well.

He put his hands under her ears, thumbs behind, palms in front, and very gently, very carefully, but firmly, twisted her head from side to side, back and forth, loosening the muscles in her neck, jiggling it very lightly on the top of her spine, finally letting it settle there, and then slowly removing his hands, sliding them down her neck, across her shoulders and back to rest on his noodles, a quiet smile on his face.

Pam leaned back on her noodle and let her feet and body float up.

"Mmmm.   Wake me up when it starts to snow; I'll just float here till then."

"That's a deal. I'll just float here and keep an eye on you."

"The way you just made me feel, you can keep more than that on me."

**This page left blank intentionally
(except for this note, of course).**

Well, that remark left Jake speechless for a whole page and a lot of lines. When he finally recovered his voice, he managed to squeak, "Th-that's nice, Pam."

Jill looked at Carie and said, "Oh, c'mon, Jake; wake up. She's all yours, but you'd better start listening to her signals. Remember your NLP training; geez." Carie smiled in response, then just nodded.

Sharon threw her two cents in. "C'mon, Jake. We didn't go to all the trouble of putting the bug in for you to not pick up on an open invitation. Get with it, old man. Quit being oblivious!"

Finally, Pam sighed and lowered her feet to the bottom and twirled to face Jake.

"Thank you, Jake; that was really great. You have magic hands."

"Any time, Pam."

Pam leaned back on her noodle and wrapped her legs around Jake's waist, pulling him closer to her.

Jake, once again perflutzed, felt his face flushing and was glad he was as tan as he was. But he couldn't find anything to say.

"I'm not making you uncomfortable, am I?" Pam said, smiling.

"You always surprise me, but ... but I can adjust."

Pam smiled even more and said, "I'm glad of that, Jake."

"Why, Mrs. Robertson-Brooks, are you trying to seduce me?"

"What do you think, Mr. Devlin?"

"Sure seems like that. But it's been a long time, so I'm not sure."

"Let me see if I can make it clearer for you, okay?"

"Okay."

She pulled him even closer and murmured, "Oh, that feels good."

"For me, too," Jake said, smiling.

"How about this?" Pam slid her legs down and intertwined them with Jake's, pulling him even closer and tighter to her, at least from their waists down, well under the water's rippling surface.

"Even better."

"I can tell. Mmmm."

"Wow, Pam. You are a total surprise."

"A pleasant one, I hope."

"Absolutely," Jake replied, as they locked eyes for a very long moment. Finally, Pam broke the silence.

"Let's go up to my condo ... if you want to."

"I'd like that."

Pam untwined her legs from Jake's and smiled as she turned to the shore.

Jake said, "Oh, wait a minute. I think I need to stay in the water a little longer." He smiled sheepishly.

Pam smiled knowingly. "Maybe if you thought about baseball or football?"

"Not much of a sports fan."

"Oh; too bad."

"In fact, in my whole life, I've only watched maybe a total of five or six innings of football."

"I'm not much of a spor- – wait a minute. Innings?" She saw Jake smiling and laughed out loud. "I guess that does get the point across."

"Only if people listen well; a lot of 'em just think I'm stupid."

"Which is fine with you, I'd guess."

"Yup; I --"

"Jake Devlin, I've got a bone to pick with you," a high, squeaky female voice intruded. Pam and Jake both laughed, as did Jill, Carie and Sharon. Jake turned around and saw the elderly leader of the Hat Squad glaring at him and, to a lesser extent, at Pam. He squelched his laughter as best he could.

"Yes, Alice? What is it?"

"I read the stuff you have online, and you need to take out all those F-words. It's disgusting and disgraceful."

Jill, Carie and Sharon laughed out loud; Pam covered her mouth.

Jake, biting his tongue, smiled at Alice and said, "Geez, Alice, I'm glad you read it, but those words help define Debbie's character."

"That may be, but those words are offensive, and I insist you take them all out."

"Alice, I would like to accommodate you, but they're important for the story. I'm sorry if you're offended by them, but they're staying in."

"And the N-word, too. You need to remove that."

"You know, Alice, on that one, I may do that; I've been debating that for a while."

"Well, do it, young man. Do it."

Jake held an index finger to the tip of his nose. "Tell you what, Alice, I'll change it so it reads 'N-word deleted' in parentheses."

"That's one," said Alice, not satisfied. "But you need to get rid of all the F-words, too."

"Sorry, Alice; those will stay in."

"Well, then I certainly will not be buying a copy, and none of my friends will, either."

"That's your choice, of course, Alice, if you're offended by it. I'm sorry you --"

"I'll write letters to the editor and put a warning in our community newsletter."

"Alice, you're free to do whatever you want to do. But I've got to run now; got an appointment."

"What kind of --"

"Frankly, Alice, that's none of your business."

"Why, of all the – you are a very rude young man."

"Sorry you feel that way, Alice, but I've got to run. Have a nice day."

He turned away, looked at Pam and worked very hard to keep

from bursting out in further laughter. Pam did the same thing, less successfully, and they headed for shore.

Jake said, "Well, at least I don't have to stay in the water any longer."

Pam smiled and said, "Maybe we'll have to send her a thank-you note."

"We may just have to do that. Maybe give her a commission."

"But now, Jake, let's go keep that appointment."

"Yes, ma'am, let's." They made it to shore, picked up their bags and headed off the beach to do just that.

"Hey, Norm, Janet, can you watch our stuff for a while?"

"Sure, Jake."

As they passed the Mimosa twins, Jake glanced at them and held two fingers to his eyes, then pointed them at his and Pam's stuff, questioningly. They nodded and he smiled and nodded back.

"Those ditzy chicks'll keep an eye on our stuff, too."

"Well, if they're pros, they'll be good at it."

"Oh, c'mon, Pam, they're just kids."

Out in the water, Alice had just gotten back to her coven – sorry, her group, and was talking and gesticulating angrily, pointing and glaring at Jake and Pam's receding figures.

-68-

Friday, January 13, 2012
9:00 a.m. EST
The White House
Washington, DC

Donne warmly greeted Admiral Dean Thomasson, Chairman, and the other members of the Joint Chiefs of Staff as they filed with military precision into the Oval Office and stood at attention in front of his desk. The Secretary of Defense, Leander G. Bentley, the Third, shambled in behind them and headed for the couches in the center of the room, settling his prodigious bulk into the nearest one.

"Good morning, gentlemen, and a very happy Friday the 13th, or if any of you are superstitious, happy Ides minus two of January – oh, at ease – no, more than at ease. Relax and let's sit down over there." He pointed to the couches, and they all filed over there, with Donne, Bentley and Thomasson sitting on one couch and the other three on the other.

"First of all, gentlemen, I want to congratulate you all on how well and with great restraint your troops have been dealing with the Occupy movement and the other protest movements that have been organized and financed by the radical left. Damage and injuries have been minimal, from the reports I've seen, and I understand your people have helped ensure that they have cleaned up their trash and repaired the damage they've caused, all under your supervision.

"And am I correct that your troops have had no problems with the Tea Party people, other than some of the radical far right-wingers and some left-wing plants?"

SecDef Bentley responded, "Correct." The others nodded.

"Good, good. Just keep on with the same procedures.

"Now, have you brought what I asked you for, Dean?"

Admiral Thomasson opened his briefcase, pulled out a thick sheaf of papers and set them on the coffee table in front of Donne and Bentley.

"There you are, sir --"

"Gordy, please."

"-- Gordy. That's the budget analysis we've prepared for you, with the three different percent reductions you asked for, 10, 25 and 40."

"Good, good, Dean. We'll go through it in detail and work with you to implement what we can without damaging our defense capabilities and our readiness."

"Well, si- – Gordy, the 40 percent would do just that."

"Of course it would. But that exercise helps us all to see what your priorities are over there at the Pentagon.

"The six of us will look that over in depth and come to some decisions together, and we'll bring some outside military advisers in to do their own analyses and give us their input.

"But how do you feel about no longer having politicians decide what you need?"

"That is the best thing you've done in this whole process, Gordy. I was getting sick of their meddling and ignorance. But mostly it made me sick to see them pushing pointless programs just for the sake of bringing the bacon back to their home districts or states. That was no way to run a professional military."

"How about that guy who thought Guam would tip over if the new Marines were added there?"

"I had to bite my tongue so hard that it bled while I was trying to answer his question and not laugh ... or shoot the SOB."

Everyone in the room laughed, remembering the scene.

Donne said, "I was watching it on the tube, so I didn't have to hold my laughter back. But it wasn't humorous laughter; it was ... I don't know the right word ... not nervous ... maybe contemptuous? Something like that."

"Sad laughter, Gordy?" Bentley suggested.

"Not quite, Lee, but that's in there, if there's no hope. I think it's more fear and anger and frustration."

Bentley said, "In any event, I'm relieved that we're all free of the idiots using us all for their political agendas. Now maybe we can actually make things work."

"And, Dean, you know we're going to have to overhaul your procurement processes? Way too much fraud, waste and abuse."

"Absolutely, Gordy. We've got over a hundred ongoing DIA investigations right now."

"Good, good; keep me apprised on all of that as things develop."

"Of course."

"And you've followed my guidance that reductions in force should first come in the upper bureaucratic levels, not at the operational level, right?"

Thomasson shifted in his seat, cleared his throat and said, "Well, Gordy, that's --"

"Now, now, Dean, don't you dare lie or deflect on that one."

"It's tough, sir; there'll be a lot of resistance and backlash on --"

"I know that, Dean. But if you don't get it done, I will, and I will be much tougher and carry a bigger axe than you will. But if we're really going to get down to a lean and mean military, the bloat has got to go. But without reducing our operational readiness. Got it?"

"Yes, sir."

"And don't try to snow me 'cause I'm new at this. Don't forget that DEI has been a big supplier to the Defense Department."

"And you've always come in under budget and ahead of schedule," SecDef added.

"Thanks, Lee, but I don't need the endorsement.

"Dean, guys, I will look over these papers and do my own analysis, along with staff, and I hope, for your sakes, that you have been very honest and deeply critical and analytical in this stuff," he said, patting the pile of papers. "I don't want to have you do it again in a cell downstairs.

"Okay. Any more questions, comments?"

Silence.

"Okay, guys. Dismissed."

Everybody, including the SecDef, left the office, as Donne picked up the sheaf of papers and began skimming through it, frowning and making wholesale redactions and writing many cryptic and nearly indecipherable notes in the margins.

Half an hour later, his intercom buzzed. "Yeah, Emily?"

"One of the guards just brought me an 18-page motion from that union lawyer, Ms. Skinner, objecting to the food, the jumpsuits and the general conditions in the cells, with a 23-page supporting brief, all handwritten. Do you want to see it?"

"No need. Just stamp it 'Denied,' sign it as Chief of Staff, make a copy and send it back down."

"Will do. Anything else you need, Gordy?"

"I'm all set – oh, could you have someone bring in a couple more of those donuts and another can of soda?"

"Oh, Gordy. How about --"

"No, no, no, Emily. Might as well give up on that. But I appreciate your concern. The donuts and soda'll be just fine."

"Can't blame a girl for trying."

"I never will, Emily."

He heard the intercom click off and went back to his papers.

-69-
Five Months Earlier

Sunday, August 14, 2011
1:55 p.m.
A seventh-floor condo
Bonita Beach, Florida

"Oh, god, Pam, again? You're insatiable."

Pam reared her head back, flinging her golden mane through the air, coming to rest against her glistening shoulders and back. She laughed, looking down into his eyes.

"I'm insatiable? Oh, Jake, you should talk."

"What? Me? Three times in ... what? ... two hours? I'm surprised I haven't died already."

"Oh, Jake, you have, three times, but it was just *la petite mort*."

"Just what?"

"The small death."

"None of them were very small, at least to me. I almost passed out that last time."

Pam laughed, "Me, too."

Jake said, "Can you imagine the headlines? 'Naked Couple Found Dead in Condo; Multiple Small Deaths Blamed.'"

Pam reared her head back and laughed again, her eyes sparkling. "I wonder if Sgt. Dooley would be the one to investigate." She giggled, and Jake chuckled.

"He's Collier; we're in Lee. So no."

"Oh, tough luck for him. He so wanted to see me naked. Remember?"

"Just that he was big and bald ... and that you backed him down pretty quickly."

Pam laughed. "I did, didn't I?" She stopped laughing and sighed. "Dealt with a lot of locals over the years, even back --"

She sighed again and rolled off of Jake and over onto her back, her eyes open, staring at the ceiling, her breathing shallow but regular. A long moment later, a frown wrinkled her brow, her eyes closed and a tiny tear oozed from her left eye, followed by another and then another.

Jake gently touched them with a fingertip, and Pam jerked up, her right hand curled into a fist, headed toward Jake's face. He grabbed it with his own hand, bent it down firmly but painlessly, and tenderly kissed it. Pam's eyes snapped open, flashed over to Jake's face and then focused.

"Oh, Jake, I'm sorry." She curled into his arms and shuddered, tears flowing freely down her cheeks and onto Jake's shoulder. They stayed that way, Pam cocooned, Jake enveloping and caressing her as she sobbed, for several minutes.

When her sobbing had finally faded away to nothing, Jake quietly and ever so gently whispered in her ear, "By the way, I faked that last one."

-70-

Monday, January 16, 2012
Various times
Various locations

In London, a woman using the name Dawn met with a man representing a group of oil traders and speculators, and following the pattern in the three previously noted meetings, a contract was reached for another 20 million euros for the Refudiator to take out the same target.

In Brooklyn, a woman using the name Amelia met with a man representing five families of organized crime figures, whose ranks of hit men had been decimated beyond repair, and following the pattern in the previously noted meetings, a contract was reached for another 20 million euros for the Deleter to take out the same target.

Over the next several weeks, an additional 14 contracts with the same terms and the same target were reached between these parties:

In Glasgow, a woman using the name Margaret, representing The Butcher, and a man representing a consortium of international drug companies (Big Pharma).

In Brighton Beach, a woman using the name Nevaeh, representing The Asp, and a man representing a group of Russian mobsters.

In Atlanta, a woman using the name Leandra, representing The Carnivore, and a man representing an anti-abortion group.

In Edinburgh, a woman using the name Rita, representing The Ocelot, and a man representing a group of political consultants.

In Detroit, a woman using the name Lexie, representing The Adder, and a man representing an American labor union.

Also in Detroit, a woman using the name Shandale, representing The Cobra, and a man representing two other American unions, who apparently had not coordinated with the one who'd hired The Adder.

In Tucson, a woman using the name Retha, representing The Subtractor, and a man representing a group supporting illegal immigration.

In Chicago, a woman using the name Dakota, representing The Decimator, and a man representing a group of ex-congressmen.

In Rome, a woman using the name Angie, representing The Hyena, and a man named Gaetano, whose clients he kept secret, but putting his own life on the line for the final payment.

In Boston, a woman using the name Azure, representing The Mongoose, and a man representing a group of health insurance companies.

In Mexico City, a woman using the name Robin, representing The Liquidator, and a man representing one of Mexico's drug cartels.

In Medellin, Colombia, a woman using the name Anna-Maria, representing The Separator, and a man representing two Colombian drug cartels.

In Buenos Aires, a woman using the name Charlie, representing The Gasser, and a man representing a group of aging ex-Nazis.

In Beijing, a woman using the name Peggy, representing The Gobbler, and a man representing the Chinese government.

In each case, a deposit of ten million euros was made into an account, and each of those deposits was transferred multiple times through multiple accounts, but all of them were finally consolidated and deposited into one account, which then held a total of 190 million euros. Another 190 million euros was due upon completion of the contract(s).

-71R-
Five Months Earlier

Sunday, August 14, 2011
2:05 p.m.
A seventh-floor condo
Bonita Beach, Florida

Pam's stomach quivered against Jake's, then shivered, then shook, and finally sent an almost volcanic eruption of uncontrollable laughter up and out through her quavering, creamy lips.

After a solid minute, when she was finally able to get it under some semblance of control, she used those creamy lips to give Jake the best kiss of the day, and said, "Thank you, Jake. I needed that."

Delicately wiping some residual tears from Pam's cheek, Jake said, "Better?"

Pam rolled over, pulled some tissues from the nightstand and blew her nose several times. Sniffling, she said, "Better. I'm sorry."

"Don't worry about it, okay? Take your time."

After some final blowing and sniffling, Pam tossed the tissues back onto the nightstand and cuddled up to Jake again. He caressed her neck and back softly, but stayed silent.

"Sometimes ..." She choked and snuggled deeper into Jake's neck and said, "Just hold me, please." He did, gently hugging her closer as she pulled herself even tighter to him, rolling her right leg over both of his.

A moment later, she giggled. "Feels like Stevie Bruce is ready to play again."

"I think he really likes Ginny May."

"And she likes him ... a lot."

Pam reached between the pillows and pressed a remote.

As Ravel's "Bolero" (the 17-minute version) began to play for the third time, Stevie Bruce and Ginny May began having a very deep and intimate conversation, which began slowly and gently, as many conversations do, then ebbed and flowed as they delved deeper and ever more intimately into each other's secret places and the hidden secrets to be found in them, gradually evolving into a more intense discussion, sliding in and out of many differing subjects, an assertion here, resistance there, an advance, a retreat, a moment of agreement, followed by a retrenchment, a further gentle assault, a quiet surrender, a re-engagement, a new discovery, an exploration leading to even more new discoveries, further and deeper exploration, a welcoming acceptance, a subtle shift of power and control, a slightly different angle of attack, an assertive envelopment of the argument, a brief pause to reflect on one's position, a slight adjustment, then a renewed depth of discussion, a momentary break in concentration, a sidetrack of introspection, a renewed focus on the main agenda, a slowly rising intensity, a shared moment of agreement again, a clever twist, a slightly increased acceleration, then building ever more rapidly and ever more intensely to a final volcanic eruption of complete, frenzied and simultaneous agreement, just as "Bolero" came to its crescendo.

"Oh, geez," Jake gasped, looking weakly up at Pam's contorted face, surrounded and partially obscured by a halo of damp blonde hair, as Pam alternately quivered and writhed, and then cried, "Oh ... my ... GOD!!!!!" and collapsed onto his chest.

Three floors above, that cry was echoed, albeit with some small bit of self-control, by a raspy, choking voice.

On the beach, the Mimosa twins pulled their earbuds out and

headed for the water for the fourth time that day. A few moments later, neck deep in the light chop, they each stifled similar cries.

Norm and Janet, who had each come to the same conclusion as to Jake and Pam's absence, smirked and nodded at each other.

Up on the seventh floor, Pam lifted her head and looked deeply into Jake's minimally open eyes.

"I don't think you faked it that time."

"I don't think I have the energy to fake anything. I'm completely wiped out." He exhaled and let his eyes close completely. "Geez."

"Thank you again, Jake. I really really needed that."

Jake mumbled, "Welcome."

Pam inhaled deeply, an inward gasp. "I'm really going to miss this."

Jake's eyes fluttered, but stayed closed, and he muttered, "Hm?"

"We just got to this point and I'm … I'm going to miss it."

Jake's eyes fluttered again, finally opening. "Whadya mean?"

Pam rolled off of Jake and onto her back beside him. Ginny May and Stevie Bruce reluctantly shared a quick goodbye kiss.

"I didn't know how to tell you, but now I have to. I accepted the offer from the private security firm."

"Um … congratulations?"

"Thanks. I start a month of orientation and screening a week from tomorrow. I really wasn't sure I wanted to take it, but I looked at my pension and everything, figured I'd have to do something sooner or later. So sooner it is."

"Not the forensic accounting place?"

"Nope; boring. And the same for going for my master's."

"So it's a good offer?"

"Oh, yeah.   Bodyguard work, some investigation, surveillance and undercover stuff. And they pay well."

"Really?"

"Yup; fifty thou a year draw just to be on call, then between a thousand and five thousand a day, plus expenses, when I take an assignment."

"Wow; fifty K just to be on call?"

"Yup."

"Wow. Definitely congratulations."

"Thanks, I think."

"Any more openings there?"

"You want to apply?"

"Hey, fifty K is fifty K."

"Oh, Jake, I don't know."

"My age?"

"Maybe; I don't know if they have an age limit. You could check their web site."

"Yeah? What is it?"

"Um ... Optimum dash Protection dot com, I think."

Jake smiled. "Really? Maybe I'll check that out sometime."

"I'm still ambivalent. But I had to go with the numbers."

"Well, I hope it works out for you. Really."

"But I will miss this town ... and you ... and ... this."

"That wasn't what got to you before, was it?"

"Oh, no, no. That was --" She paused and gazed up at the ceiling. "That was some old memories that just popped up. I'm sorry."

"Hey, Pam, no apology needed. Most people have memories that pop up from time to time."

"Most people haven't seen – I'm sorry." Her eyes welled up again.

"It's okay, Pam." Jake watched her, but stayed silent.

After another moment, still staring at the ceiling, Pam said, "This is just between us, Jake, okay?"

"Sure."

"I mean it, Jake. Just between us."

"Okay; absolutely. I promise."

"Okay. How can I --"

"I find just blurting it out works sometimes."

"Okay. I saw my husband get shot and die, right in front of me."

"Oh, geez."

"It was twenty years ago, but it still haunts me and pops up at all the wrong times. I'm sorry."

"Oh, Pam; I'm so sorry. I had no idea. I thought it was about that guy with Alzheimer's and your – oops; sorry. Sometimes blurting ain't the best idea. I'm sorry."

"No problem, Jake, really. That's something I love about you ... how you just say what's on your mind."

"Some of the time."

"Most, I think."

Jake shrugged. "Okay."

"And in a way, you're right. But it was mostly about that image of Zach getting --"

"Zach?"

"My husband. He was shot in the head, right in front of me; awful thing to see. Same op where I got this." She pointed to the scar on her left shoulder.

"Oh, geez. I'm sorry, Pam." He rolled onto his side and kissed her scar. She reached over and caressed his cheek.

"Thinking back about Dooley and all the locals I've had to – well, that triggered the memory again, and the loss was – was – and it was sort of the same with George and Marion, how she's lost him already."

"That was the couple at the ... um ... Seafood Shack?"

"Yup; and he looked a lot like my dad. So all the loss stuff just popped up and sort of overwhelmed me back then. Guess I was feeling pretty vulnerable. And just now ... well, obviously I was pretty emotional, and it overwhelmed me again." She turned her head and looked at Jake. "I'm sorry."

"Hey, Pam, it's okay. I've got some demons, too. I can relate, even if I can't totally get inside your head."

Pam glanced at Jake and then giggled.

"What? C'mon, Pam, what?"

"Stevie Bruce got pretty close a few minutes ago."

"Well, Ginny May sure helped. Where did you ever learn to do that?"

"Do what?" Pam asked, smiling innocently.

"You know. That thing you did right near the end."

"Now, now, Mr. Devlin, a girl has to have a few secrets."

"Okay, okay. But I'd bet you could make a fortune giving classes on that, never have to work again. Maybe sell franchises."

"But then it wouldn't be a secret. Naw, I think I'll keep that to myself – well, just between us."

"I like that. The world will never know what it's missing."

Pam put her finger to her lips. "Shhh."

Jake ran his thumb and index finger across his lips. "Zipped."

"Oh," Pam said, "what time is it?"

Jake looked over her to the clock on the oven. "I think that says 2:42."

"God, we've been here a long time. We probably should get back before people start to talk."

"I'm sure they already are. But who cares?"

"You know, you're right. Who cares?" She lifted her head a little, looked down and said, "Think he's ready for another round?"

"Oh, god, Pam, again? You ARE insatiable."

"I've got a lot more tricks up my ... sleeve, Jake."

"An-ti-ci-pa-ay-tion," Jake sang quietly, knowing it was gratingly off-key, then smiled and said, "So does Stevie Bruce. But next time."

"Mmmmm. Okay, okay. I'll wait. But if we're gonna head back over there, I've gotta take a quick shower. Can you scrub my back?"

"Sure; I'll give you a minute first."

He watched her exotic ... um ... shoulder blades as she rolled out of the bed and headed for the bathroom.

After the commode flushed, he joined her in the shower. A minute after that, he joined her in the shower.

-72-

Tuesday, January 17, 2012
8:47 a.m. EST
A network morning talk show

Back from commercial, the camera showed a single head shot of a lovely blonde anchor, looking about 27 years old and expertly coiffed and made up, but natural-looking. She smiled with expertly capped and very white teeth directly into the camera.

"Welcome back. I'm pleased to welcome our next guest, Wesley T. Farley, the new CEO of Donne Enterprises International, formerly COO under Gordon Donne.

"Thank you for being here, Mr. Farley."

The director cut to a two-shot, showing a handsome, tall, slim, forty-five-ish ebony-skinned male, casually dressed in stylish jeans and a short-sleeved knit shirt, seated on the couch with her.

"Call me Wes, Lindsey, and thanks for the invitation."

"Now, tell me, Wes, what was it like to work for Gordon Donne?"

"Well, Lindsey, it was never like working FOR him; it was always like working WITH him. We all knew he was the boss, the owner, and he could be very tough, but he had a way of making all of us feel like we were partners with him."

"Do you stay in touch now that he's bought the country?"

"Occasionally, maybe three times since December 9th."

"Can you tell us what you've talked about?"

"Sure, Lindsey. He's given me carte blanche to speak my mind with anybody. It's been a lot different with him not running the day-to-day operation of the company, so it's been mostly general stuff, like 'How's it going over there at the White House,' or 'Is Emily still trying to fix your diet,' or – I remember he asked 'How's Jean-Claude doing in Paris?'"

"And who is Jean-Claude?"

"He was the White House chef for the Obamas, and Gordy figured he'd be bored cooking for him, what with his simple diet, so he asked me to offer him the head chef job at one of our restaurants, and he accepted the one in Paris, his hometown, and so far he's very happy. Gordy kept the option to invite him back for any state dinners he might have to have ... and if I can, I'll say Gordy positively hates those kinds of things, all the diplomatic BS, as he calls it ... not using the initials, though."

Lindsey laughed politely. "Ah. We've heard he speaks his mind."

"That he does, Lindsey, that he does." He laughed, too.

"Do you have enough influence with him to get him to come on and talk to us?"

"Nope."

Lindsey, unprepared for such a short answer, stumbled on her own words, "Well, do – is there – do you know anybody who does?"

"Nope." Seeing her discomfort, Farley added, "If he wants to come on, he will; if not, he won't. He's the most independent ... and most ethical ... person I've ever had the pleasure of meeting anywhere in the world."

"Okay. Now, Wes, just how big is day?"

"We don't pronounce it like that, Lindsay; we just use the letters, D-E-I. But to answer your question, all told, worldwide we have about 1.4 million people working in our businesses, and we have about 2800 businesses within DEI. Those numbers fluctuate, since we are buying, building and selling businesses on almost a daily basis.

"Once we've done the turnaround and gotten a business on its feet and profitable, our goal changes to building the profit pool to the point where the employees of that business can buy it from us and run it themselves, with occasional consulting, if they want it."

"DEI is a private company, right?"

"Yes, it is. And the main reason we've remained private is so we don't have to focus as much on the short term to satisfy Wall Street each and every quarter, but can plan long-term strategies with and for each business in our portfolio, build a solid foundation for its growth and success.

"And what is Opus?"

"Again, we don't pronounce it that way. You're talking about the US division of Optimum Protection, the largest of our businesses and one that we'll never be looking to sell. We usually call it by its initials, just O-P-U-S, or sometimes 'Ahp-U-S.' O-P is our worldwide private security service, providing everything from light surveillance to home and business security installs, to bodyguards, undercover ops, analysis and recommendations, threat assessments, preemptive threat containment or removal and general security consulting.

"O-P has about 5,000 full-time employees, 107,000 part-time, and thousands of independent contractors we can use from time to time. The only place on earth we don't operate ... yet ... is Antarctica."

"That's a lot of people, Wes."

"Yes, it is."

"Can you stick around? We have to go to commercial."

"Sure, Lindsey, as long as you've got questions."

"Great. Folks, my interview with Wes Farley will continue after this short break. Stick around."

The screen went to a commercial for a prescription anxiety medication, followed by one for a prescription shortness-of-breath medication, another for car insurance, one for a scooter/wheelchair, one for an arthritis pill (prescription, of course) and one moderately entertaining one for a double-miles credit card.

-73-
Five Months Earlier

Sunday, August 14, 2011
3:15 p.m.
Bonita Beach, Florida

"They're coming," Sharon rasped over the twins' earbuds.

"What, again?" Jill said, giggling.

"No, they're coming our way," Carie said sharply.

"How is our way any different?" Jill shot back. Carie rolled her eyes, then put a finger to her lips. "Here they are."

"Nobody touched your stuff, Jake," Carie said as he and Pam walked out onto the sand. Jill snickered to herself and very quietly whispered, "Well, someone did." Up on the tenth floor, Sharon rasped out a laugh.

"Thanks, kids; appreciate it," Jake replied.

"Hey, guys. How was Marco?" Norm asked, while Janet focused on her sudoku, trying hard to hide her giggle.

"Marco?" Jake asked.

"We thought maybe you'd driven down to the island. You were gone long enough."

"Oh. No. But thanks for watching our stuff," Jake replied, smiling as innocent a smile as he could muster.

As Jake and Pam settled back into their lounge and chair, Janet whispered to Norm, "They smell like a spring day in Ireland."

Pam leaned in to Jake and said, "I forgot. You were going to let me see the first hundred directives. Did you remember to bring 'em?"

"Yup." He dug around in his beach bag for a moment and pulled out three or four stapled sheets of paper and gave them to Pam. "Here ya go. Enjoy."

Pam unfolded them and leaned back to read, while Jake lay back on his lounge, watching her.

Two minutes later, Pam said, "Jake, this one, Number 23, how does that --"

She looked more closely at Jake, whose eyes had closed and whose breathing was steady but light, a smile playing over his lips.

Pam smiled and whispered to herself, "Well, they do say there's a nap for that," and went back to the directives.

Five minutes later, a harsh, nasal voice intruded. "Hey, Jake, did you try that cigar yet?"

Pam looked up, eyes flashing angrily. "Shhhh." But too late.

Jake jerked on his lounge, reached behind his head and mumbled, "Wha?" but his eyes stayed closed. He rolled his head side to side, then settled back in.

"Did you try that cigar yet?"

Pam hissed, "Shhh. Can't you see he's sleeping?"

"Well, I was," he mumbled. "What d'ya want, Sonya?"

"Have you tried that cigar yet?"

"Not yet. I will."

"When?"

"After I wake up some more, okay?"

"Okay. That's a light. They also have flavors, like strawberry --"

"I know, Sonya; you told me before."

"-- cherry, peach --"

"I KNOW, Sonya; I know."

"And they're only ten bucks a carton --"

"Sonya, I get it. I know, I know. Blue-and-white carton. And I can get 'em at B2B. Got it. Got it."

"So when ya gonna try it? I know you'll like it."

"Okay, okay. I'll try it now. Where did I put it?"

"Right there." Sonya pointed at his bag.

He picked it up, pulled out his magnifying glass, lit it and took a puff. He immediately started coughing and stubbed it out in the sand, put it back on his bag.

"Too soon, Sonya. Later."

"But --"

"I said later. Got it?"

"But --"

"Got it?"

"Okay, okay; go tit." She glared at Pam and stalked back toward her chair.

"Well, back to the real world, Jake."

"Yeah. Geez."

"Sorry; I tried to stop her, but too late."

"Don't worry about it. Nobody's been able to stop her yet."

"I should have seen her coming. My situational awareness is already slipping."

"Oh, it'll come back when you get to O-N – orientation. Uh, I'm sure it's part of their training – in your case probably just a quick refresher and you'll be right back in top form."

"I hope so."

"I'm sure. Of course, you're in top form right now." He smiled.

"Why, suh, I thank you." She giggled and dropped her voice to a whisper. "So does Ginny May." She smiled broadly. And Jake smiled back.

"Not gonna touch that one right now, right here."

Pam fake-pouted. "Oh, well. Maybe later." Then she smiled. "We've got a week before I go."

Jake smiled. "Yup, we do. Ready for some water time?"

Pam smiled and said, "I love noodling with you."

Jake laughed. "Oh, Pam, you're so bad."

"I can be, but only when I want to."

"I know. Uh-oh. I really gotta get in the water." He picked up his noodles and foot-washing bag and headed in. Pam folded up the papers, put them in her bag and followed him in, giggling.

-74-

Tuesday, January 17, 2012
8:53 a.m. EST
A network morning talk show

"Welcome back. I'm talking with Wes Farley, the current CEO and former COO of Donne Enterprises International.

"Now, Wes, some in the press have noticed that Gordon Olin Donne's initials spell G-O-D. Does he think of himself as God?"

Farley roared with laughter. "Oh, god, Lindsey –" He looked up. "Oh; sorry, Gordy." He laughed even harder. "He's had to live with that his whole life, but he's gotten used to all the jokes and reactions that anybody's been able to come up with so far. And no, he does not think of himself as God, although ..."

Lindsey raised her eyebrows. "Although?"

"Well, he does apply the old Teddy Roosevelt line, 'Speak softly and carry a big stick,' and when he finds out something is going wrong anywhere in any of our businesses, he says, only half tongue in cheek, 'Don't make me come down there.' And if and when he does, people 'down there' do start to pray, especially those who know they haven't met our expectations."

"What happens to them?"

Wes looked at her, squinting his dark brown eyes. "You don't want to know, Lindsey – just kidding. Actually, it depends on what country the business is in. In some countries in the Mideast, we can cut off their hands ... or their heads."

"Oh, my god!"

"Gotcha, Lindsey." He gave her a twinkly-eyed smile.

"But we do have to deal with local laws and policies, so the remedies can range from mild reprimands to out-and-out termination, which we have done when the situation calls for that."

"Which leads me to this question, Wes. On balance, has Donne been a job creator or a job destroyer?"

"Both. But the records we keep, which I had updated before coming on this show, tell me that, as of last Friday, DEI has created 2,965,761 net jobs since 1985. And we've sold 3,789 businesses back to employees, at a P/E multiple of about ten, which seems pretty fair."

"Many people have looked at his directives and are accusing him of being terribly draconian. Is he?"

"Absolutely, but only if people abuse the freedom and flexibility he gives them or take advantage of weaker or more vulnerable people. The one thing he is not is an advocate of byzantine and labyrinthine over-regulation, micro-managing and nanny-statism."

"We've only got a minute left, Wes. Anything else you can tell us about Gordon Donne?"

"Well, I guess two things come to mind. First, his very top priority is customers; they always come first. And everybody in any of our businesses HAS to see their role as somehow serving that priority.

"The other is that he's terrific at delegating. He ensures that all of our people have the training, tools and authority to do the job right, ideally the first time, and he also makes sure they understand that they, each and every one, take full responsibility for their own success or failure in their role. Everyone is personally accountable."

"Any dark secrets?"

"Sure. Doesn't everybody have some?"

"I don't."

"Oh, c'mon, Lindsey. How about your affair with your produ- – sorry; never mind. Can we cut that?"

Lindsey, stunned, was silent.

"Lindsey, I'm so sorry." Then he looked off-camera and said, "I'm sorry. Can we cut that, please? Lindsey, I'm really sorry."

The screen went to a commercial for an online pet supplies provider, followed by others for a prescription allergy medication, a European car brand, a female hygiene product, a fiber-rich breakfast cereal, an online religious matching service, a Medicare supplement insurance plan, a prescription incontinence pill, two network situation comedies and the midseason premiere of a new reality competition show, "Naked Tycoons," in which a dozen billionaire CEOs are given a thousand dollars each, dropped in separate cities and compete to see who can not only survive, but start a business without access to their contacts or resources, using only their own wits and skills, and not their identity or reputation. After six months, the one whose new business is the most successful wins a million dollars from each of the other tycoons for his or her favorite charity.

Returning from the break, Lindsey's co-hosts, Rose and Tom, broke directly into an interview with a teenager from West Virginia who had taught his pet alligator to skydive. Lindsey's absence was not mentioned. That afternoon, Lindsey was fired.

Two days after that, she received a phone call from Wes Farley, who offered his abject apology and condolences for the loss of her job and suggested she keep her phone with her.

Later that same day, she received a phone call from a woman who identified herself as Emily, Gordon Donne's chief of staff, who invited her to the White House for what she called a "discussion," an invitation that Lindsey readily accepted.

A week after that, Lindsey returned to her network with a DVD of an exclusive one-hour interview with Gordon Donne and negotiated a return to her job at twice her previous salary. She also continued her affair with her producer, and married him six months later.

-75-
Five Months Earlier

Sunday, August 14, 2011
3:35 p.m.
Bonita Beach, Florida

"And that's why they call it the 'half-Dolly' house."

Pam laughed. "So if it had <u>two</u> observatories, it'd be a full Dolly?"

"You got it."

"And if it had three?"

"Oh, Pam, that'd just be weird." They both chuckled.

Jake leaned back on his noodles, looked over at the small crowd on the sand and in the water.

"Hey, Pam, how many people you think are here today?"

"Oh, I don't know. Maybe a hundred, hundred and ten."

"I was wondering, if all of them voted, how many of 'em – or maybe a percentage – would vote intelligently, with a clear idea of the actual issues, and what percentage would vote for mostly irrational and emotional reasons?"

"I'd think it'd be a small percentage for the first, much bigger for the second."

"Think the eight and 92 would work there, too?"

"Maybe; pretty close, at least. Just my opinion."

"And that 92 percent is probably half on one side of the sandbox, half on the other, and the spin doctors and poll dancers'll be going after some of them, but not so much the eight percent, for next year's election, mostly with negative campaign ads."

"I think it's gonna get really ugly," Pam said, frowning.

"Wonder which Republican will win their primary."

"Now, that race'll probably get really ugly, too."

They both lazed back on their noodles for a while, and then Jake lifted his head out of the water.

"Pam?"

"Yeah?"

"Looking at all those people again, how many would you guess have a life story that they would like to think is newsworthy?"

"All of them?"

"I'd go along with that. But how many of their stories actually <u>are</u> newsworthy?"

"I wouldn't know, Jake."

"Take a guess."

"Okay – oh, ah-ha. About eight percent?"

"Good guess. So eight out of a hundred, almost nine out of a hundred and ten."

"Right."

"So, Pam, as we look at all those people on the beach, to us, 92 percent of them are just objects, and as any of them look back at us, we're part of <u>their</u> 92 percent ... at least until they get to know us ... and vice versa. And then instead of objects, they're subjects, people we know something about.

"Remember that woman who was running and kicking like a showgirl and soccering that little ball on the beach this morning?"

"Dorothy, right? She seemed nice. Good figure, too."

"She's the one who taught me that martial arts move. She teaches at a place over in the hardware plaza. Her hubby has a sign company.

"And there's a guy named Joe who gives me a stock market report every weekday morning; gets it from his radio."

"I haven't met him, have I?"

"Nope; just weekdays. Maybe tomorrow, if the weather holds."

"And then there's Dave, an older guy who walks the beach and hunts for shark's teeth. Finds a lot of 'em, too, some days; but some days, nada. All of them used to be in my 92 percent, but now they're in the eight; I know them ... to varying degrees.

"And there, Pam. See that woman power-walking, the one in the orange T-shirt and funny-looking white shorts?"

"The short one, thin, with a craggy kind of face?"

"That's the one. Her name is Marlene and she used to be a comedy writer for Milton Berle or George Burns or somebody like that, and she won a worldwide competition in the '70s in playwriting. Now, that's newsworthy, right?"

"Yeah, I guess so."

"So she just moved out of the 92 percent and into the eight."

"Yeah. She sounds like somebody I, and probably a lot of other folks, could have a great time talking with. Bet she has a lot of super stories to tell."

"And I'd bet you have a lot of great stories you could tell, too."

"Oh, Jake, you have no idea."

Jake looked past Pam, eyes widening slightly.

"Uh-oh. Lightning."

"What? Where?"

"Down there toward Naples. Looks like the summer storms are

building in earlier than usual today."

Pam swiveled on her noodle and looked south. "Wow, those are dark, and they came up fast."

"Oh, not so fast. They usually build up over the Glades in the afternoon, but the seabreeze keeps them away until maybe 4:30 or 5:00, but then they move west and drench the beach. It's like the weather forecast for the whole summer could be one tape that they show every day, over and over."

"That would save a weatherman's salary."

Just then, a loud clap of thunder rolled through.

"Okay, about 25 seconds, so five miles. We're okay for a bit. But I think we oughta get outa the water."

When they got back to their chairs, Jake happened to look up and see Sonya and Herb. She was pointing to Jake's bag and pretending to hold a cigarette to her mouth. Jake waved and nodded.

"I think I'll try that little cigar Sonya gave me, keep her from coming down and blabbing again."

Pam glanced up at Sonya and said, "Yeah, good idea."

Jake lit it with his magnifying glass and took a light, careful puff.

"Hmm; not too bad, actually." He took another puff and inhaled. "Yeah, not bad. Want to try it?"

Pam said, "Sure; okay." She took a puff and inhaled. "You're right. Not bad at all. And ten bucks a carton?"

"That's what she said. Over there at B2B Liquors."

"I may give them a try."

"Me, too." Jake turned, caught Sonya's eye and gave her an okay sign. Sonya, to Jake's relief, just gave him a thumbs up, and then she and Herb started packing up their stuff.

"Whew," Jake sighed. Pam chuckled.

"So do we need to rush?"

"Not really. I usually wait until the clouds cover the sun. That might be another ten, twenty minutes. But I think we can finish this and then make a slow and easy exit."

Pam took another puff and handed the cigar back to Jake. "I think that's enough for me. Go ahead and finish it, if you want."

"Okay."

"Want to come back up to my condo?"

Jake, taking another puff, began coughing, but managed to smile and say, "I do like the Bolero."

"Me, too. Maybe we can try 'Hall of the Mountain King' after that."

When Jake finished the cigar, they packed up their stuff, Jake put his in his car and he and Pam walked over to her condo.

An hour later, having discovered that the 'Mountain King' was less than three minutes long, they went back to the Bolero, the full 17-minute one, and used that as background to their two encores, not counting a final Bolero-free one in Pam's shower, both of them laughing a lot and humming the "Mountain King" slightly off-key.

Jake delicately extricated himself, ran through the rain to his car, still in the beach lot, and went home to write, but within ten minutes of locking the door behind him, the sound of heavy rain and his own exhaustion lulled him off into a deep yet dream-filled sleep, with the strains of the Bolero ebbing and flowing through his subconscious.

Back in her condo, Pam scanned Jake's list of directives into her PC and then settled in to study them and make some notes.

-76-

Sunday, August 14, 2011
11:30 p.m. local time
Cyberspace

The Suppressor checked one of his multiple email accounts and found two messages, one sent Friday evening and one sent on Saturday morning. He opened the earlier one.

"Sir or Madam, We have received the files you sent and after reviewing them, we have concerns, as we're sure you anticipated. As to your request for confirmation of the allegations in the 18-page file Rep.pdf, we decline to confirm any of the blatant falsehoods therein.

"However, we would appreciate your efforts to keep that file from being published, and while your requested consideration is far from reasonable, we will accede to that request. Please advise as to the method of payment you prefer.

"As to the 16-page Dem.pdf file, we believe that to be one the American public deserves to read at the earliest opportunity, and we urge you to have the author include it in its entirety."

The Suppressor smiled and opened the one from Saturday.

"Got the file Dem.pdf you sent us unsolicited. You get no confirm from us, and we want to know who the author of this libelous screed is before we even begin to consider your ridiculous request for what you called 'consideration' to keep that out, with no evidence that you are even able to do that.

"On the other hand, we believe that the file Rep.pdf is absolutely accurate and factual and deserves immediate publication.

"Let us know immediately who the author of Dem.pdf is and we will proceed from there."

The Suppressor laughed aloud and closed both emails, put his PC to sleep, poured himself a glass of very expensive wine and lay back in his recliner, savoring the moment. "The game's afoot."

An hour later, he awoke his PC and began drafting a reply to the Friday email.

"You are correct that we anticipated your having concerns, and we have no preference as to whether you confirm or deny the contents of Rep.pdf or, for that matter, Dem.pdf.

"However, we have received new information from members of the opposing side; therefore, we must adjust our discussion.

"They have offered us 25K to keep Rep.pdf in, which is 15K more than our original suggestion to you to keep it out. They have also offered 25K to keep Dem.pdf out. Thus a total offer of 50K.

"Please advise as soon as possible how you would like to proceed in light of this new information."

He saved that to his drafts folder and began a second email.

"First, there is NO WAY we are going to disclose the identity of the author, and we frankly don't care whether you confirm (or deny, as we anticipated you would) the accuracy of Dem.pdf, nor do we care about your opinion of Rep.pdf, which we also anticipated.

"However, we have received new information from members of the opposing side; therefore, we must adjust our discussion.

"They have offered us 30K to keep Dem.pdf in, which is 20K more than our original suggestion to you. They have also offered 30K to keep Rep.pdf out. Thus a total offer of 60K.

"If you want to match or exceed that offer, let us know. Else we will accept theirs in the next week."

He sent both through the anonymous mail server he used for that email address, turned off the PC as he usually did, drained and rinsed out his wine glass and headed to bed.

-77R-

Sunday, August 14, 2011
7:55 p.m.
A tenth-floor condo
Bonita Beach, Florida

"Well, kids, that first round was like all first ones are, awkward and fumbling and full of fire and passion. It had all the delicacy and technique of two high-schoolers in the back seat at a drive-in."

"At a what?"

"Oh, right; before your time. Used to be places where you could watch a movie in your car."

"On your phone? DVD player?"

"No, no, no. There was a big screen out in a field, and lots of cars would drive in, park, pull a speaker off a pole, hang it on the inside of the window, go get some popcorn and pop at a concession stand and then watch the movie after it got dark enough."

"That's stupid."

"Look, Jill, it was a long time ago, probably before you were even a glimmer in your father's eye. When were you kids born, anyhow?"

"1982," the twins said simultaneously.

"That explains a lot."

"What's pop?" Jill asked.

"Soda, tonic, soft drink; 'fizzy drink' in England."

"Ah, okay. Pop; hmm."

"Anyhow, I didn't see any teachable moments in that one. Too bad it's black and white and sorta grainy."

"I noticed a few things."

"Okay, Carie. What?"

"Well, first, that ring clasp in front on her top was pretty cool. She just popped it open and the whole top opened. And when she said, 'Say hello to your new friends, Mitzy and Bitzy,' that was great."

"She sure couldn't have named them Itsy and Bitsy, could she, CB?"

"That's f'sure, JB."

"And I noticed she's starting to get some tan lines."

"Yeah, she is, kid."

"Hey, Sharon, did you see how I handled that sniffer that was bugging us last week?"

"Nope; missed that."

"Well, this one was named ... Tim, or Lou, or maybe Tom, I think, about 50, kind of a paunch, shaved head, gold chains, all the usual shit. And he was giving us the typical crappy pickup lines and schmoozing as much as he could, full of stupid, juvenile double entendre and raised eyebrows, and Carie and I were sorta letting him think he was getting somewhere. Right, Carie?"

"Yeah," Carie replied, chuckling at the memory.

"Anyhow, he asked if I was as tan all over as I was on the skin he could see, leering at me. I told him no, my skin was a lot whiter. And he told me to prove it. I know he wanted me to pull out or fold back the top of my bikini, and he just wanted a better glance at more of my boob."

"So what did you do?"

"I took my watch off ... and told him to get lost."

All three of them laughed.

"Nice move, kid."

"Thank you, Auntie Master."

"That would be 'Auntie Mistress' to you, kid," Sharon replied, still chuckling.

Carie continued, "I also thought the quick-release rings on the sides of her bottom were pretty cool, too. Just one flick and gonzo."

"Even in black and white, I could tell she's not a natural blonde," Jill added. "But her boobs looked real."

"I don't know, Jillybean; they were way too perfect."

"Perky, not floppy, like Sharon's are. Unga and Bunga."

"Hey, wait a minute, Grasshopper," Sharon hissed, but then chuckled. "No, I know. Mine were a lot perkier in the seventies."

"Had to be, for you to have been such a star."

"Well, not a star, but I made a good living with 'em."

"Not just with those. I've seen some of your films."

"Oh, god, I hate those now. Totally plot-free, and nobody in them had even the faintest idea who Stanislavski was. And I was a lot thinner back then, too."

"That you were, Sharon, that you were, by what?   80, 90 pounds?"

"Now, now, Grasshopper; show some respect for your elders."

"Okay, okay; sorry … Elder Auntie Mistress," Jill said and bowed, smiling. "But I loved your screen name. Fannie Woodcock. Totally loved it."

"Hey, kid, I always liked those birds."

Carie cut in with, "He's got a very white butt."

"But great tan lines, Carie Berry."

"I don't like tan lines at all; I like an all-over tan. I can't wait to get back to Europe, where they're not as prudish as these damn Yanks."

"Don't sweat it, Carie; our contract's up next June. But I do like it on the beach down here."

"Except for the sniffers."

"Oh, even them. They remind me how stupid men can be; they're so easy to lead on and manipulate."

"Got to admit, Jill, you're really good at that.   Most of 'em never know what hit 'em," Carie said, giggling.

"Y'got that right, Carie Berry. High five." They did that, then Jill added, "And you remember that one guy, the chubby one with all the tattoos?"

"The Schmoozerator?"

"Yeah. Bald, 40s, hairdresser; you thought he was gay."

"Right."

"Kept bringing the ugliest women here and doing 'em right there in the water. Moved away a few months ago. John, Jim … Jeff?"

"I think it was Jeff, JB, but I'm not sure. We could probably go back and find the videos, if Sharon hasn't sent 'em in already."

"They're gone, kids. Weekly pouches."

"That's good. I don't think JB could handle watching that again."

"Got that right, CB. Ewww."

Jill and Carie laughed, then Sharon cut in.

"Ah. Kids, did you notice how quickly she rolled him over and got on top?"

"Good for her," Jill said. "It was what, maybe a minute in?"

"Quick enough that we hardly saw how hard he was working," Carie added.

"If he was at all."

"Oh, meow, Jillybean. Meow. Pull those claws back in."

"Okay; sorry, EAM."

"EAM?"

"Elder Auntie Mistress."

"Oh, okay.

"And did you notice, no protection?"

Carie said, "I'd bet they talked all that stuff out on the way over from the beach. They do seem to be pretty bright, both of 'em."

Jill added, "I'll bet she took the lead on that."

"I don't know. They both seemed to be leading each other."

"Oh, no, Carie Berry. She was definitely doing the leading. She was in charge all the way."

"Think about it, Jillybean. The sunscreen, the massage. He knew exactly what he was doing and where he wanted things to go."

"No, no, no. She was seducing him all the way. Her idea to write the sex scene; he'd never even thought about that."

"Oh, that reminds me, Sharon. Can you print this out?" She held up a thumb drive.

"Sure. Just take a minute."

"And could you send the signal to that big TV in the corner before we go to the next round? It's kinda hard to squinch around this little screen on your PC."

"Can do. Another minute."

-78-

Thursday, August 18, 2011
10:30 p.m.
Cyberspace

The Suppressor checked his email account and found two more emails, one sent on Tuesday, the other sent that morning. He poured himself a glass of his very expensive wine and opened the first one.

"Sir or madam, We have received your email and now have some additional concerns.

"Firstly, we are highly concerned that the Rep.pdf file is in the hands of our opponents. It could be terribly damaging to our interests should they use it in their usual partisan and underhanded manner.

"Secondly, we are concerned that your mercenary-like actions show us that you have no conscience to which we may appeal, that you, in point of fact, are either socio- or psychopathic, and that that reduces to nearly zero our ability to trust that you will keep your end of any bargain we may strike.

"Thirdly and finally, despite having analyzed the multiple possibilities we find in those two concerns, we must bow to your terms and consider the fact that both parties have copies of the other's damaging file, thus assuring MAD (mutual assured destruction) if both are released.

"With that in mind, we are hereby changing our offer to a flat 40K to keep the Rep.pdf file out, and another 40K to keep the Dem.pdf file IN. Take it or leave it, sir or madam."

He laughed and opened the other email, and was not at all surprised by what it said.

"Look here, punk, we're not sure just what game you think you're playing, but you're in the big leagues now and way out of your depth.

"Tell us who the author of Dem.pdf is and we won't come after you ... for now.

"As for your extortionate demands, stick 'em up your ass."

The Suppressor laughed harder. "Perfect. So predictable."

Then he put the PC to sleep, poured another glass of wine and leaned back in his recliner. Within ten minutes, the wine helped put him to sleep.

An hour and a half later, he woke with a start, then slowly and painfully unwound himself from the cramped position in which he had fallen asleep, stretched his arms, legs and especially his badly kinked lower back, then awoke his PC and prepared his replies.

To the first, he wrote, "This will acknowledge your offer of 40 plus 40. However, be advised that the other side has offered 50 and 50. I will await your response."

To the second, "Now, now, now, ad hominem attacks tend not to work with us. I would suggest that you avoid them in the future and get someone who is not still in high school to write your future responses.

"Please review the attached seven-page file, Dem2.pdf (which has not been provided to your opponents ... as yet) and consider your options. As of this moment, the other side has offered 60K to keep Rep.pdf out and another 60K to keep Dem.pdf in. Should I accept their offer, I will advise the author to give them Dem2.pdf at no additional cost.

"I will await and expect a more courteous response from you."

He sent both, backed up his work, then powered down the PC, drained and rinsed out his wine glass, took a couple of OTC painkillers and a sleeping tablet and went to bed.

-79R-

Sunday, August 14, 2011
8:15 p.m.
A tenth-floor condo
Bonita Beach, Florida

"Sonofabitch. That explains it. When they went at it the second time, they were playing out the scene she wrote, feathers and the Bolero and all. Geez."

"Well, you were watching it, Sharon; we only had audio and your comments. Let's see it."

"But I didn't have what she wrote. Okay, Jill. Here goes."

"They're just lying there."

"Oops; this is just a while after the first round. Let me --"

"No, no, no, wait; let it play. What's she doing now?"

"Oh, right; I forgot about that. She's doing a Suzanne."

"A what?"

"A Suzanne. See how she's just using her tongue, not her whole mouth, and just in that one spot, back a ways from the end, on the underside?"

"Yeah."

"That's really the only sensitive spot on the whole thing."

"Yeah, we know that. But why's that called a Suzanne?"

"Well, back in the seventies, we had fluffers on the set, and they complained a lot about neck pain after a long night's work. Then one of my co-stars came up with the tongue-only idea, and she taught it to the whole staff, and bingo, no more neck pain. Her name was Suzanne, and she wanted credit for the idea."

"And did she get credit?"

"Mostly in the Valley; don't know about elsewhere."

"Didn't I hear somewhere about some fluffers union suing the maker of those little pills for putting them out of work?"

"Oh, Grasshopper, that was a hoax some friends of mine put together way back when. One crazy, but legit-sounding, press release that no one realized was a joke, and it got some good distribution. We laughed our guts out over that. You can still probably find it on the internet."

"Cool, EAM."

"Ready to fast-forward? Good; here goes."

"Go ahead – wait. Wasn't there a line in her scene that went 'Oh, my god, it's huge'?"

"Yup, Jillybean, right here, before 'throbbing' and 'swollen.'"

"Well, from what I just saw, that line won't fly. It's just average."

"But she didn't know that when she was writing the scene, did she, JB?"

"Oh, right. Never mind."

"Okay, kids; coming up on it now."

"Hey. Where'd he get the feathers?"

"I think I saw a big vase in the corner with a bunch of 'em in it when I was in there planting the bug, JB."

"Okay; she's got a remote and there goes the Bolero. Now I <u>know</u> she was planning this."

"Maybe, JB, maybe."

"Okay, kids, enough blah-blah. Here we go."

"Wait, wait. Didn't the massage part start with her suit on? Yup, right here on the first page."

"Hey, Grasshopper, don't expect them to follow the fictional scene she wrote exactly; this is reality, and they can improvise."

"Okay, okay, EAS. Boy, his butt really <u>is</u> white."

"But look how gentle and tender he is with her back, and he's always leaving one hand in contact when he takes the other away for a new stroke up her spine, JB."

"He does know what he's doing, kids. That's from the seventies, too. Erotic massage."

"Wow. That must feel great."

"Listen to her moan. She's not faking that, CB."

"I thought she was faking it that first time, JB."

"Could be, but that was only ... what? ... five or six minutes from start to finish?"

"Four minutes, 28 seconds on the counter, kids."

"Not much foreplay there, was there?"

"Nope, but she was leading him on pretty fast."

"Leading him in, you mean, CB," Jill said, laughing.

"Reminds me, kids. Do you know what redneck foreplay is?"

"Nope," they said in unison.

In her best raspy, smoky, accented voice, Sharon said, "'Git in the truck, bitch.'" They all laughed.

"And now her neck ... so gentle, but firm. Strong."

"Look how he's doing her arm ... and her hand. Wow, each finger separately? Geez."

"You'd never know from looking at him on the beach, wouldya?"

"And now the other one. Ohhhh."

"Careful, JB; don't get carried away. Still a long way to go on this one."

"Okay. I'm just imagining being where she is."

"Well, you're not there."

"Oh, geez, look at that. He's not gonna do what I think he's gonna do, is he?"

"No, he's just moving back to massage her thighs."

"Good. I'd hate it if he did do dat."

"Lotta that back in the day, kids. And it did hurt. Never again."

"Me, neither, f'sure."

"Nor me. Yuck."

"Oh, she likes that, doesn't she?"

"Oh, yeah, CB. And look at that, not a gram of cellulite or cottage cheese anywhere on her."

"And now her calves, one hand on each."

"Ankles."

"Feet. Oh, look, he's doing each toe. Ohhhh; nice."

"Ease up, JB."

"Okay, okay, CB."

"Now watch this close, kids."

"Oh, geez, how can she bend like that?"

"She was a gymnast, remember, JB?"

"Oh, ri- – wait, she's fifty, isn't she?"

"Yup. But she's obviously kept herself in great shape."

"And flexibility. I could never twist my back like that."

"Now that's a kiss! And upside down? Wow!!!"

"Got that right, CB."

"Wait, wait, Sharon. Back it up. How did she get rolled over like that? I must have blinked. Oh, I see. Wow; really limber. Thanks."

"And he's heading for – wait, what'd she say?"

"She said, 'Not yet, Jake. Feathers first, okay?'"

"Sorry; the Bolero was getting a little louder there."

"Yeah, but they're still on track. Watch and wait, kids."

"Okay, okay."

"Yeah, but – oh, there he goes."

"What kind of a feather is that? Peacock?"

"Looks like it, JB."

"Oh, he's got one in the other hand, too."

"That looks like an ostrich feather to me."

"Starting on her shoulders; cool. She likes that; look at her face."

"And the outside of her arms, slowly, teasingly, gently."

"'Light as a whisper,' I think she said yesterday."

"I think you're right, JB."

"And now on the inside, coming back up. Oh, geez, I'd love for a guy to do that to me."

"Hmf. Like one of those sniffers? Maybe Tim or Tom or whatever his name was?"

"Ewwww. No way. He'd just go right for my boobs. Yuck."

"Well, Jake isn't going there. He's working her sides – oh, she's ticklish. Listen to that giggle. Wow."

"That's not just a giggle, CB; it's like a cackle – oh, she snorted!"

"You do that, too, JB."

"I do not -- okay, okay, I do. But you're more ticklish than me."

230

"No, I'm not."

"Yes, you are."

"Am not."

"Am."

"Hey, kids, you want me to pause this so you can argue?"

"No, no," the twins said.

"Okay. Watch."

Carie whispered, "It would be 'more ticklish than I.'"

"No, I'm not."

"No, I mean – oh, never mind."

"Now, kids, right there. See what he's doing?"

"Wow. Look at her abs ripple."

"She's laughing, JB. But they are taut."

"Hey, kids, look at what <u>he's</u> doing, not stroking, but sort of lightly tapping, all over her stomach and sides."

"But not her boobs."

"Right; he sure knows how to tease. And now watch this."

"Sliding down the outside of her hips, down to her legs, still on the outside."

"Can you zoom in, Sharon?"

"Nope; sorry, Carie. What you see is what you get. Now watch what he does when he gets to her feet, kids."

"Geez; he is <u>really</u> playing with her."

"And she's really ticklish there."

"Ohhh, she's loving that, CB. Look at her wriggle and writhe."

"'Cause he's coming back up on the inside."

"Oh, almost – no, no, no! So close, and he slides back up to her belly. And – oh, geez – up between 'em??? What the fuck? Can't he see she's –"

"Shhh, JB. I can't hear."

"Okay, okay. Her throat, chin, cheeks – wait a minute. Ears? He's doing her ears???? Jesus."

"She's smiling, JB. Can't you see she's loving that? Look close."

"Okay, okay. Ah, now to her eyelids ... and down the sides of her nose to her mouth. That's better." Jill smacked her lips. "Ah, now he's lingering there. Mmm."

"Okay, Jill, here you go."

"Ahh."

"Happier now?"

"Well, he finally got to Mitzy and Bitsy. Wait, wait, he's just circling 'em, not going for home. That's got to be driving her crazy."

"Remember, Jill, she wrote it and he's just following along."

"Okay, okay. But I gotta tell ya, mine are getting hard."

"So are hers, JB."

"Really? I can't tell."

"Look for the shadows."

"The – oh. Ah, okay. Got it. Thanks, CB."

"No problem, JB. Listen to her moan."

"Yup, driving her crazy."

"Can you turn the volume up a bit, Sharon?"

"Sure. Better?"

"Maybe a little more?"

"How's that?"

"Great; thanks. Boy, the music is getting even a little louder, and has the tempo picked up a bit?"

"Just a little bit, Carie. Hang in there."

"Oh, there he goes, at long last! Both left and right. Bravo!!!"

"I wonder if the feathers feel different."

"Oh, yeah, they do."

"Really, Sharon?"

"Yup. But the best was the marabou, if I remember the name right. Been nearly 40 years."

"Never heard of it."

"Remember Mae West's feather boas, the ones she flung around her shoulders?"

"Who's Mae West?" asked Jill.

"Oh, JB. She was a sexy movie star of the '30s or '40s."

"Right, Carie. Remember the boas?"

"I think so. Kinda soft and fluffy?"

"Right. Those were the greatest. These aren't anywhere near as soft, I don't think."

"They sure seem to be doing the job."

"Yes, they do, JB."

"Oh, he's dropped them and he's going in himself, starting with Mitzy ... or is that Bitsy? Cool. And look at her writhing. She's either absolutely in ecstasy or she's a great faker."

"I'd bet – no, I guess I'm 50/50 on that one. Sharon?"

"Faking it, definitely."

"You think so, really?"

"Yup. Been there, done that. I can tell."

"Oh, no, Sharon, don't spoil it."

"Sorry, Jill. It is what it is."

"No, no, no; I don't believe you."

"Watch and see, kid; watch and see."

"Damn, Sharon. I missed the other one, and now he's heading downtown."

"Wait, Jill, wait ... ah, there. Surprise!!"

"What? She's pulling him up and in? WTF? What's the matter with her? No thigh squeezing on his ears? Shit."

"Looks like she's ready, ready ... oh, yeah, JB, definitely ready."

"And they're off, kids. Listen to the music; starting to build to the crescendo. In ... ah ... five minutes from ... now. And from here on," it's pretty much a repeat of the first time, with her winding up on top again ... and faking it."

"Fast forward, Sharon, and let's see if she's faking the end."

"Okay, kid. You'll see." She checked a note card next to her PC and then held down a key on her keyboard, and the video sped to half a minute before the end, the two figures on the screen bouncing and squirming at triple speed.

"Okay, Jill. Now watch ... and listen ... closely."

"Okay. Shhhh."

After a moment, as Pam's moans and siren-like cries, ending in a loud "Oh ... my ... GOD," and then a quiet moan from Jake echoed from the speakers through the condo, Jill exclaimed, "No, no, no; not faking it, no way."

"Way, kid. Remember, old age and treachery beat youth and inexperience every time."

"Yeah, so?"

"So I need a smoke break now. Anybody want to join me on the balcony?"

-80-

Monday, August 22, 2011
12:40 p.m.
Cyberspace

The Suppressor powered up his PC, checked his email account and found four emails, three from one side. He opened the earliest one, sent the prior Friday afternoon.

"Dear Sir or Madam, After careful consideration of all factors involved, we have come to a decision.

"We will now offer you 75K to keep Rep.pdf out and another 60K to keep Dem.pdf in. Please advise as to method of payment and date of publication."

He smiled and opened the first of the three from the other side, sent Saturday at 7:43 p.m.

"Fuck you, asshole. If I want to use ad homi- --" and it ended. The second one had been sent six minutes later.

"Please be advised that the intern with whom you have been communicating has been fired, and senior members of the Committee will be dealing with you from now on.

"We have only just now begun to review the two files you sent and the correspondence prior to this. We will respond further within 24 hours. Please make no decisions before you hear from us."

He laughed out loud and opened their third email, sent on Sunday at 6:46 p.m.

"Please be advised that we have now reviewed the two files you sent and the previous correspondence with our intern.

"While we deny absolutely that any grain of truth is contained in Dem.pdf and Dem2.pdf, we hereby offer you 100K to keep the content of those files out of the book and 80K to keep Rep.pdf in. We can go no higher than that. Please advise.

"And again, we apologize for our intern's attitude."

The Suppressor laughed out loud again. "Okay, getting there."

He immediately composed a reply to the earlier email.

"Your offer of 75/60 is acknowledged. The other side has just offered 90/90. Please respond with your final and best offer by 6 p.m. EDT Wednesday, 8/24. I'll decide on Thursday, 8/25."

He did not respond to the other email, but simply turned off the PC and headed immediately to bed.

He replied to the other party the following night, at 10:45 p.m.

"Your explanation and apology for your intern's behavior is accepted.

"I acknowledge your offer of 100/80. The other side has offered 90/90, essentially a tie, so I will allow one more round of bidding. Please submit your final and best offer by 6 p.m. EDT tomorrow. I will decide which offer to accept on Thursday, 8/25."

Another glass of wine, a relaxing few minutes in the recliner, glass rinsed and off to bed.

-81R-

Sunday, August 14, 2011
8:52 p.m.
A tenth-floor condo
Bonita Beach, Florida

"Where'd you find the popcorn, kid?"

"Up in that cabinet over the fridge, way in the back."

"Didn't know that was there. I'll keep that in mind for another time. Thanks. Good initiative, too."

"Got any ... what was it? ... pop?"

"Should be some cans in the fridge, behind the bucket of chicken."

"Okay. Ah, good. Want one?"

"Sure."

"Carie?"

"Any diet in there?"

"Yup."

"One of those, then. Thanks, Jillybean."

"All set, kids? This one does have some teachable moments."

"Ready," said Jill.

"Go for it," Carie added.

"Okay. Here goes." Sharon tapped a key on the PC, and the video came to life on the big TV, with the Bolero playing.

At that moment, Ned and Joan McDowell, a retired 75-ish couple from Point Pleasant, New Jersey, had just returned to their ninth-floor condo, directly below Sharon's, from a delicious, but long and almost unbearably tedious, dinner at Ray's, a high-end restaurant in the Boulevard, an upscale shopping center near West Terry and US 41 in the northern central part of Bonita.

"Christ, Joan, those people are the most obnoxious couple I've ever met. 'I'm Ole Jorgenson, O-N, and this is my wife, Esmeralda Jorgensen, E-N; she wanted to keep her maiden name. Ha-ha-ha.' Why do we keep spending time with them, anyhow?"

"I just can't say no to her, I guess. She did go to school with my sister up in Ohio. Take your pill, Ned."

"Okay. Well, you need to learn to say no."

"Okay, kids, now they're just getting started," said Sharon, in the condo above.

"They're just playing kissyface and caressing, and geez, they look tired."

"He does, that's for sure. How long after the second round was this?"

"Hmm. Looks like ... 1:07 minus 12:31 ... 26 – no, 36 minutes."

"And how much of a break between the first and second ones?"

"Um. 12:13 minus 11:51 ... uh ... 24 minutes."

"Well, no wonder. She's not giving him time to recharge. And at his age, he would need a lot longer than a guy in his twenties, I'd think."

"Like at least an hour or two, CB."

"Maybe not that long, JB, but a lot more than he had today."

"Wait, wait. What just happened?"

"She asked him to take out his dentures, see what kissing him without 'em would feel like."

"Ewww."

"Watch, JB. She's doing fine with it."

"You know, I remember hearing that part on the beach."

"And you said, 'Ewww' then, too, JB."

"That I did. It's just too weird. Ewww."

"Hey, Joan, can you bring me a beer? Our show's about to start."

"No."

"What do you mean, no?"

"I'm practicing."

"I didn't mean to me. I meant to Esmeralda."

"Oh, okay. Just a minute."

"Hey, Sharon, where'd he go?"

"Hang in there, Jill. Wait and watch."

"Oh, geez, is that what I think it is?"

"Yup, probably straight from the freezer."

"Oh, this could get sloppy, CB."

"Want some chips with the beer, Ned?"

"Please. Geez, what's wrong with the TV?"

"What's the matter?"

"I don't know; some kind of interference."

"Are you on the right channel?"

"I think so. Let me just click – holy Jesus!!!"

"What?"

"Did you leave one of our videos in the player?"

"I don't – no, I'm sure I didn't. Here's your --"

"Well, this is – take a look."

"Well, that's a new one. I don't think it's from our collection. At least, I don't remember it."

"She looks familiar somehow. Recognize her?"

"Maybe she was the one in 'Texans Hold 'n Poke Her'?"

"Could be, but I can't be sure."

"Oh, what's he doing now?"

"Ah, Sharon, here comes the Neapolitan."

"You're gonna love this part, kids. And there you go, one small two-finger dollop on the right --"

"That's Mitzy, right?"

"Right; Mitzy, right.

"-- lick it off teasingly, then on the left –"

"Bitsy."

"-- same thing, still teasing."

"She's sure not tired."

"Ohhh, that's got to be cold, CB! He'd better be careful or he could poke his eye out on one of those."

"Oh, Ned, let's try that sometime."

"Okay. But definitely not with the Jorgenson/sens."

"Of course not. They'd complain about the flavor and the texture."

"Maybe with Norm and Janet. They're fun."

"Yeah, they sure are. I think we're with them next week."

"No, they're with Dave and Pat; guess we've got Ken and Marsha."

"Oh, they're no fun. We'll save it for Norm and Janet."

"What flavor is that, hon?"

"I can't tell; the picture's too grainy. Can you fix it, Ned?"

"Okay, kid; time for your favorite. He's heading downtown now."

"Oh, goodie; it'sth high time."

"What's with the lisp, JB?"

"What lisp?"

"Happy now, kid?"

"She obviously is. There's that flexibility again – oh, no, no, don't bend your knee like that! Damn. Sharon, we need more cameras."

"Sorry, kid; that's the only one I've got."

"Shit."

"Can't get it any clearer, Joan; sorry."

"Well, at least I get the idea."

"Gives me a few ideas, too."

"Did you take your pill, Ned?"

"Yes, hon."

"What'd she say, Sharon?"

"I couldn't hear, kid; the music's picking up again. Want me to back it up?"

"Yeah."

"Okay; hang on."

"What the heck is going on there, Ned?"

"It's rewinding. What the hell?"

"That's good, Sharon; right there."

"Nope, still couldn't make it out."

"Oh well; that's okay."

"Ah, it's playing again, Joan."

"Oh, good. What did she say?"

"Sorry; I didn't catch it, hon."

"Oh, well; we'll see what we'll see. That music is familiar, isn't it, Ned?"

"Yeah; can't place it, though."

"Oh, geez, CB, that's a big dollop. And look, she's pulling him up and in again. Oh, that's got to be cold on him now, too. Wonder what that would do to a guy."

"Shrinkage, kids, shrinkage."

"Joan, I don't think I'd want to do that bit."

"That's okay, Ned; I can understand."

"Well, Sharon, from the look on her face and the way she's writhing again, it doesn't seem like that's a problem for her."

"I'll say it again, kids; she's faking it."

"No way, Sharon."

"Absolutely, she is."

"And there she goes, rolling him over again. Aaaand once again, she's on top," Carie said.

"Oh, not only shrinkage, but I'll bet there's gonna be leakage."

Giggling, Jill added, "I'll bet she's glad they're using Neapolitan and not Rocky Road or Butter Pecan. That'd hurt."

"Gee, Ned, if we try that, I'll have to get the rubber sheets out again."

"Whatever you want, hon."

"And now, kids, we're getting into the home stretch. Hear the

Bolero? Coming to the end."

"And so are they, perfect timing," Jill moaned.

"Oh ... my ... GODDDD!!!" shrieked Pam as she collapsed onto Jake's chest again.

"Ohhh," groaned Jake.

"Wow," said Ned.

"Hmmm," Joan murmured.

"Yee-hah," cried Jill, heading for the bathroom.

"Cool," Carie added, reaching for the printed pages of the scene Pam had written.

"Okay. Time for another smoke break," Sharon said, clicking a key on the keyboard. "Definitely faking it."

"Turn off the TV and grab some ice cream while I change the sheets, Ned."

"Will do, hon. Oh, hon, want to try the harness again?"

"Nope; I got dizzy hanging upside down in that. And it chafed and gave me blisters. Let's just try it with the ice cream."

"Okay, hon."

-82-

Sunday, August 21, 2011
7:37 p.m.
International Airport
Fort Myers, Florida

After a week in which Jake and Pam had watched five sunrises together and spent hours and hours both in the water and on the sand; a week in which the Bolero had been played in Pam's condo a total of 37 times; a week in which they had exchanged 22 sensual, erotic massages; a week in which Jake got very little actual writing done, but had lots of new notes; a week in which the energy expended and the ice cream consumed balanced out, so that he neither gained nor lost any weight; a week in which the Mimosa twins and Sharon had found 147 teachable moments in the replays, of which seven involved squeeze bottles of chocolate and strawberry ice cream topping; and a week in which Ned and Joan had exhausted both themselves and Ned's supply of little pills, Pam and Jake were sitting in his car in the cell phone parking lot.

"You're sure you want me to just drop you off outside?"

"Please, Jake, okay? I have enough trouble with goodbyes in private. But in public? No, thanks. Please?"

"Okay, sure, Pam. But it's not a goodbye, it's 'See ya in a month,' the 18th, right? And you'll be all oriented and screened."

"I'm sure gonna miss you, Jake."

"And I'll miss you, Pam. But you're a pro. What was that word you used? Compartmentalize? You'll do just fine."

"Oh, I'm not worried about that, Jake; I know I'll do okay there. I just know I'm gonna miss you ... and SB."

"SB?"

"Stevie Bruce."

"Ah."

"I'm looking forward to getting reacquainted with you both when I get back."

"And I with you and Ginny May."

"Jake, do you think we have ..."

"Oh, Pam, you said goodbye to him three times on the drive over here, and that was only maybe twenty minutes."

"But Ginny May didn't."

"Ah. I'm sorry, Pam. Hard to do anything while I'm driving."

"But now we're parked and I've got lots of time before my flight."

"Yes, you do. But not here; this is too open and every car has a driver in it."

"How about the short-term garage?"

"Probably got cameras in there."

"Let's go look. Maybe we can find a spot between two vans or SUVs. And it is dusk. We can figure it out."

"Okay."

Twenty minutes later, Stevie Bruce and Ginny May having had their deeply moving (in fact, very deeply moving) and fond farewell, Jake pulled his car up to the terminal entrance, where Pam gave him an equally deeply moving goodbye kiss and got out and walked with an only slightly bowlegged gait toward the terminal doors, followed by a skycap carrying her two bags, whose eyes had no difficulty staying focused on his client ... or at least on one part of her body.

Just before she passed through the doors, she turned, waved and blew a kiss at Jake, which he returned.

As the doors closed behind her, he wiped a small tear from his left eye and pulled away from the terminal.

On his way home, he stopped at a fast food drive-thru and got a cheeseburger and fries, but noticed that their apple pies, which had been two for a buck previously, now were 69 cents each.

Quickly doing the math, he murmured, "That's 38 percent inflation in, what, a couple of months? Geez."

As he exited from I-75 onto Bonita Beach Road, he noticed a dark SUV with only one headlight a couple cars behind him. From perhaps an excess of caution, he turned right on Imperial Parkway, then left on Dean Street, and he saw that the cyclopean SUV followed him, staying a good ways back, no cars between them.

He took the Matheson-Terry-Pine Avenue route and pulled into the public library parking lot, up to the dropoff box, where he

239

dropped an empty book-sized tissue box in, and pulled back out onto West Terry. The SUV was nowhere to be seen.

Slightly relieved, but still cautious, Jake took a right onto West Terry, not noticing a dark SUV idling on the corner of Lavinka and West Terry that turned on its single headlight, then the other one, and pulled out from Lavinka, keeping a healthy distance between itself and Jake's car.

When Jake got to US41, instead of a left, he took a right and headed north. The double-headlit SUV followed discreetly, blending in with the light traffic.

When Jake reached the intersection with Old 41, he turned left and pulled into the shopping center, swinging into the lot for the Scottish Pub, parked for a moment, carefully checking everything around him, and then pulled back out, finally turning south on US41, not seeing the SUV following him, a quarter mile behind. The driver of the SUV chuckled. "You may be good, but I'm better."

When he reached Bonita Beach Road, he turned right, did an SDR through Bonita Shores, then headed home, with one final precaution: he drove past his house, then turned into the parking lot of Big Mike's Seafood Grill, across from Access 10, where he turned off his lights, pulled back out to where he could see the northbound traffic on Hickory Boulevard and watched for ten minutes.

Several cars and trucks passed, but none aroused Jake's suspicions, so he turned on his lights and headed south, turning his lights off a hundred yards north of where he pulled quickly into his driveway and into his garage, closing the door as soon as he cleared it. Only once the door was completely closed and light-proofed did he turn on the inside light.

He failed to notice a dark SUV with two working headlights that passed his house heading slowly northbound. The driver looked left at Jake's house, but continued north, smiling.

Inside, Jake reached the first floor and headed to his study, where he booted up his PC and settled in with his cheeseburger, fries and a can of soda from his refrigerator. He checked his email and found several messages, but one caught his attention.

"Well, well, well," Jake said after a cursory read, "my first death threat." He created a folder named "Death Threats," and moved that message into it, smiling to himself.

He replied to five messages needing answers, then closed down the PC, finished off his burger, fries and soda, put the PC power cord back in the sideboard and headed up to bed, remembering at the last moment to avoid the ninth step. Humming his new theme song, he showered and climbed into bed, falling immediately into a deep and dream-filled sleep.

-83-

Thursday, August 25, 2011
11:30 p.m.
Cyberspace

The Suppressor opened two emails, each sent the previous afternoon.

The first read: "Our final and best offer is 100K to keep Rep.pdf out and another 100K to keep Dem.pdf in. Please advise as to method of payment and date of publication."

The other read: "Our final and best offer is 150K to keep Dem.pdf and Dem2.pdf out and 125K to keep Rep.pdf in. We hope that is sufficient to win the bidding. Let us know ASAP and we will make the payments immediately."

He smiled and wrote two replies, each accepting the offer and providing a wire transfer account number, a different one for each, as well as a request for email notice once the transfers had been made.

Those email notices were received the following day, but the Suppressor also received notices from one of his banks that $200K had been received and from another that $275K had been deposited.

He moved those funds electronically through three other banks, consolidating them into one account in Singapore, where an associate converted them into bearer bonds. He then walked two blocks and deposited the bonds, less his 10K commission, in yet another bank, from which The Suppressor electronically moved them through five more banks, after which they finally landed in an account in the Cayman Islands, bringing the total in that account to a little over 58 million dollars. That whole process took three hours.

He waited five days and then sent two emails, each reading: "Funds received; both files will be kept out. No refunds will be given for the one you wanted kept in. Sue if you want, but both files will then come out. Publication date is December 15, 2011. Thank you both for playing. Sincerely, The – no, you don't need to know that."

To one of them, he added a postscript, "Tell James his imitation of an intern sucked big time. ;-))"

He closed that email account and scrubbed all traces of it from his PC and the anonymous mail servers he'd used. He then backed up his work, turned off the PC, poured a huge glass of wine and settled back into his recliner. Half an hour later, he drained and rinsed the glass and headed up to bed.

A week later, anonymous donations of $155K each were received by private micro-loan programs in Appalachia, New Mexico and India.

Friday, February 3, 2012
8:30 p.m.
The Oval Office
Washington, DC
via a 24-hour news channel

Gordon Donne faced the camera from behind his desk, this time in a plain beige short-sleeved polo shirt, a somber look on his face.

"Ladies and gentlemen, my fellow citizens, good evening. I have three announcements to make tonight.

"First, today's jobs report for January was encouraging, with a net gain of 422,000 jobs, even with the offset of 146,000 job losses in the federal government; that means the private sector added nearly 570,000 jobs in the month. Bravo! And the job losses in the federal government will continue for several more months as we trim the bloat. I would note here that only the very lowest-level workers will be eligible for unemployment benefits.

"Second, as you may remember, in my first speech to you two months ago, and in my first press conference, I told you that my administration would be going after wrongdoers of both parties, as well as lobbyists and other beneficiaries of the immoral, unethical and corrupt actions of the politicians. Tonight I'm announcing a part of that process, and seven directives that go into the details will be posted on our web site by ten o'clock tonight. Here's the gist.

"We know that most, if not all, of our representatives and senators gorged themselves, their families and cronies at the public trough, mainly through the so-called 'earmarks' that they sneaked into must-pass bills, and the so-called Senate Ethics Committee ruled that if an earmark benefited just <u>one</u> other person, it passed muster; a similar ruling came out of the House Ethics Committee. That sort of self-exoneration is and was appalling, but now it will no longer suffice to cover up and justify the out-and-out theft of taxpayer monies.

"So we will be going back and not only clawing back the proceeds of those actions, but also levying fines on each and every single participant in them. That includes, but is not limited to, representatives and senators, staff members, campaign donors and bundlers, lobbyists, spin doctors, family members, cronies and anyone else who benefited or who traded their vote in some back-door deal.

"In order to facilitate that process, I've eliminated all statutes of limitation on that kind of corruption, part, but only in part, using the RICO statutes; we will go back as far as we can or have to. The

242

Congressional Record and other sources have given us all the info we've needed to ferret out and document all the instances that are relevant, going back several decades.

"We have now compiled a fairly exhaustive list of people who fall into that category, but we will not be releasing it either to the public or to people who are on it. We're going to see if people on the list have enough of a conscience to realize that their behavior was corrupt and will do the right thing by coming forward now.

"Those individuals have sixty days from today to 'fess up and tell our staff what they did and how much they and their associates profited from what they did. Those who do come forward within that time will have to repay the Treasury the amount of corrupt proceeds they received, either directly or indirectly. That also includes any increases in the value of property they owned that rose in value due to that kind of corruption.

"Additionally, they will be subject to a fine of up to fifty percent of their assets ... not their net worth; they will keep their liabilities ... and they will not be eligible to declare bankruptcy.

"For those who do not voluntarily come forward and/or try to hide assets, in violation of Directives 213 through 217, we will find you, and the fine will then be up to one hundred percent of your assets; again, you will still be subject to your liabilities and ineligible for bankruptcy. And there could be serious prison time, as well.

"Now, if someone comes forward who is NOT on our list, and disgorges their corrupt proceeds, there will be no fine; we will not be confiscating any of their other assets. Word to the wise, okay?

"I will also ask all investigative journalists right now to continue their efforts at unearthing corruption, current or historical, and we will look seriously at their discoveries and continue to add to our list.

"All the details will be posted by ten o'clock tonight, in Directives 421 to 427.

"My final announcement is actually more just a quick reminder. The national sales tax goes into effect in about eight weeks, on April 1st, and any business that has not prepared to collect and transmit that should go to our web site, _____.gov, and download the instructions and the software we've provided there. It's free and works with all hardware and software platforms.

"And for consumers, if I were in your shoes, I would seriously think about stocking up on whatever staples you can between now and the end of March. Another word to the wise.

"That's it for tonight, so I'll wish you all a good evening and a very enjoyable weekend ... well, other than those of you who might be on our list and may have a few well-deserved nightmares. Good night."

Once he was sure the camera was off, Donne smiled and said to himself, "Oppressing the oppressors; on our way."

-85R-
Five Months Earlier

Sunday, August 28, 2011
11:03 a.m.
Bonita Beach, Florida

"Hey, Sharon, got your ears on?"

"I do, kid. What's up?"

"Grab your scope and take a look at that couple in the water down there to the south of us, maybe 80 meters – sorry; a little less than 90 yards, just out from the fifth gazebo."

"Hey, meters are fine with me, Jill. But which couple?"

"The guy has a big straw hat on, and she's got gray hair, cataract sunglasses, no hat."

"Got 'em. Think they're a threat?"

"No, no threat. I'm just wondering if you can tell if they're doing what it looks like they're doing from down here."

"Okay. Let me just swing the – oh, geez, gotta move the tripod for that angle; the doorframe's in the way. Okay. Swing, focus ... ah, got 'em. Oh, geez; they've gotta be pushing 80, and they're playing heavy duty kissyface out there."

"That's them. Are they --"

"Yup, I think they are. Lemme – oh, geez, I think he's got his suit on his arm, right under the water. It's around her back and – oh, geez, look at her face. She's – wait a minute. Yup, she's done. Okay, there he goes."

"Ewww, ick."

"Hey, kid, respect your elders."

"Ewww. Sorry, EAM."

"Hey, they're not that much older than I am, kiddo. Well, maybe ten yea- – wait a minute. Oh, geez." Sharon guffawed.

"What, what?"

"His suit ... it ... it ... sorry, kiddo. His suit slipped off his arm and he's thrashing around looking for it. But he's going the wrong way; it's behind him, and the waves are taking it further away. Oh, geez." She exploded into gales of laughter. "Poor guy. Now what?"

Carie spoke for the first time. "Jill, why don't you go down there and get it? Sharon could spot for you."

"Ewww, not me."

"No, I can't; it's gone. I can't see it anymore. The waves are too -- oh, wait; there it – nope, that wasn't it. It's gone. Poor guy." Her laughter kept her from saying anything more.

"Now, now, EAM; respect your elders."

"Oh, geez. He – wait. What's – oh. She's come on shore and – oh, she's getting one of their towels and – oh, okay. Boy, that's gonna be one heavy towel, all wet like that."

"What's going on?"

"He's got the towel around him now, Carie, and he's – yup, out of the water. Geez, that thing is dripping a lot of – oh, she's wringing it out."

"And here come some walkers. What are they making of all that?"

"Wait a minute, kid; I've got to – oh, they look – I guess they haven't noti- – wait; she's saying something to him, he just looked over, and they're both snickering. Okay; they've gone by, coming your way."

"Don't say it, JB; bite your tongue."

"Okay, okay, CB. Bitten."

"She's done wringing and they're heading your way."

"I hope he's wrapped it well, EAM. Hate to see that fall off. Some things people just shouldn't see."

"Hey, kid, someday you'll be that old."

"Not in this line of work."

"Sssst," hissed Carie.

"What? Suddenly you're superstitious?"

"No; here they come. Don't be obvious."

"But --"

"No, no, no; bite your tongue."

"Geez, CB, it's already bleeding."

"Look at me, JB, look at me. And look serious."

"Okay, okay. Okay?"

"Okay. They're on the boardwalk."

"Coming your way, Sharon. Now you can bite your tongue."

"Not a problem for me, kid."

A few minutes later, Sharon said, "Oh, geez; looks like they're heading for my building. Hang on."

Another few minutes passed, and then Sharon said, "Hey, kids, it seems they're in the unit right under mine. Lemme – yup, the water trail leads from the elevator right to their door."

"That explains those noises we heard that night we were up there with you."

"Ewwww."

-86-

Monday, February 6, 2012
8:30 a.m.
The Oval Office
Washington, DC

Emily escorted John Kelly, his Treasury Secretary, and Eugene Brynn, the Director of the Mint, into the office, where Donne waved them to the couches and sat across from them.

"John, Gene, thanks for coming over. How are we doing on Project Newpaper?"

"We're on track to meet your deadline. Production is well ahead of schedule, but with the confidentiality issues, we've had to take some extraordinary precautions that have slowed distribution a bit, especially overseas."

"Okay, Gene; thanks.

"What's the challenge with the distribution, John?"

"We've been having some difficulty claiming that all those huge crates are actually diplomatic pouches in some countries."

"Isn't Amy over at State greasing the skids well enough?"

"Oh, she's doing fine, Gordy. But there's still some pushback from some of the ambassadors who were appointed by the previous Secretary. I'm even afraid some of them will leak the plan."

"Get me a list of them, John, and I'll make sure they know that they'll be in deep shit if any of them do anything that even remotely threatens the secrecy of the project."

"I've got that right here, Gordy." Kelly pulled a thin plastic binder from his briefcase and set it on the table.

"Great, John; I can always count on you to be ahead of the game. By the way, forget the binders from now on, okay? A staple is fine for my purposes. I don't need a lot of presentation value."

"Will do, Gordy. And I'll spread the word through the whole Department."

"Good, good. Emily, are you there?"

Emily's voice came over the intercom. "Right here, boss."

"Put an email in the queue to get rid of the binders and other presentation stuff, okay? For wide distribution. No reorders, okay?"

"Will do."

"Thanks, doll.

"Oh, funny, boss."

"Better than 'mom,' huh?"

"Okay, okay. Over and out."

Donne chuckled and said, "Thanks, Emily.

"Is the Air Force help with distribution working out, John?"

"They're doing fine, Gordy. And the CIA has agents riding herd on each shipment, even though nobody knows the contents."

"Any other concerns about leaks, John?"

"Always. Something this big is bound to leak somewhere."

"Any concerns in your shop, Gene?"

"Well, obviously, Mr. Donne --"

"C'mon, Gene. I know you're a holdover, but you and I have been working on this project long enough that you can call me Gordy."

"I'll try to remember that, Mr. – I mean Gordy."

"Anyhow, with three shifts at all locations running at full tilt, lots of the workers have an idea of what's going on, but with the oversight Secretary Kelly has provided, I think they're all absolutely clear that their loose lips would cause them big problems personally, so so far, I think we're okay."

"Good, good. I'll rely on both of you to keep it that way."

John and Gene both nodded.

"And if you run into any more problems with distribution, John, let me know and I'll do what I can to smooth them out, okay?"

"Will do, Gordy."

"And, Gene, be sure to let me know immediately if and when you run into any problems, any at all, okay?"

"Yes, sir – Gordy."

"Good, good. Thanks for coming. Oh, if either of you are into grassy veggie foods, just tell Emily on your way out that I've donated whatever she's prepped for me to you."

"I heard that, boss."

"I know you did, mom."

"Thanks, guys."

The three of them rose, shook hands and left Donne alone with his overflowing inbox, which he emptied within two hours and took a well-deserved and long-overdue nap.

-87-
Five Months Earlier

Sunday, August 28, 2011
11:24 a.m.
Bonita Beach, Florida

"Hey, kids, guess what I just saw."

"No, idea, EAM."

"There's a swim suit floating right in front of you two."

"So?"

"I got an idea. Can one of you go get it?"

"Ewwww. Not me. CB?"

247

"Oh, okay, JB. I'll go. Where is it, Sharon?"

"Right in front of you – no, a little to your left."

"I don't see it."

"A little more, right in the surf there."

"Oh, okay; got it. Got it. Now what?"

"Bring it up here."

"Ewwww."

"Quiet, Jill. Carie, be sure to wring it out first, okay?"

"Will – oh, shit; it's got skid marks."

"Double ewww."

"Just wring it out and bring it up here ... please."

"Okay. Be right up."

Ten minutes later, Carie rejoined Jill on the beach, giggling.

"What?"

"Oh, this is gonna be good."

"If it's got you giggling, it must be good."

"Just wait."

Ten minutes later, Sharon said, "All set; listen well, kids."

At that moment, inside the ninth-floor condo, Joan said, "Ned, is that somebody knocking?"

"I think so, hon. I'll get it ... nobody there. Oh, what's this? My swim suit? And a note? 'I hope you're proud of yourselves. At your age, you should be. We saw what you did and thought you would like this back. Sorry, we didn't have a chance to wash it properly. By the way, bravo.' It's not signed. Who --"

"Well, come back in and close the door. The breeze is melting the ice cream." The door slammed.

"How'd ya like that, kids?" Sharon said, pulling a tiny mike up over the railing in the atrium.

"Not as good as I expected, Sharon," Carie replied.

"Ewwwww."

-88-

Friday, February 10, 2012
8:47 a.m. EST
A network morning talk show

Back from commercial, Lindsey smiled directly into the camera.

"Welcome back. I'm Lindsey Framingham, and I had the chance last month to do an exclusive interview with Gordon Donne, the man who, two months ago today, bought this country and has instituted hundreds of new policies.

"Here's a quick clip."

The screen cut to a shot of Lindsey and Gordon Donne, clad in his usual jeans and tropical shirt, facing each other on chairs in the Oval Office.

"Mr. Donne," Lindsey began, "to get right down to brass tacks, why did you buy the country?"

"Well, somebody had to do something, Lindsey, before the entire country imploded economically and socially. It was crying out for an adult, maybe any adult, to come in and just take charge, get it off its fat, complacent, lazy butt, clean up the corruption and get back to the business of growth and optimism. And I happened to be --"

"We'll be running the whole interview on this show on Friday, March 16th. Be sure to mark that on your calendar. But now, back to Rose and her guest, the sister of a woman who now claims that she had not really understood what the difference between breast augmentation surgery and breast incrementation surgery actually was when she had the latter performed."

This promo and clip ran ten times a day for the next week.

-89-
Six Months Earlier

Sunday, September 4, 2011
6:08 p.m.
Bonita Beach, Florida

Jake lay in a reclining lounge on his balcony, protected by the overhanging roof from the rain sprizzling down on this windless late afternoon. Looking out onto the quiet Gulf, he sipped from a glass of white zin and longed for a little cigar. But it was nine days since he'd smoked the last of the carton he'd bought the day after Pam had flown out of his life for a month, and he'd vowed to quit completely by the end of August. So far, he'd been able to keep that vow, but on more than one occasion, he'd been seriously tempted to cheat, and this was one of the strongest temptations he'd had.

He picked up his non-spiral notebook and tablet from the table beside him and began organizing the notes he'd made since Pam had left, humming his new theme song as he typed:

"China-India war? Pakistan – Arab?

"UN – out? Rent on UN property in NYC?

"World Trade Org/World Court – out?

"Basel – out?

"Kyoto?

"Educat – Tchr evals – NYC rubb rooms

"Insurance fraud – medical auto life

"Dr./hospital fraud, upcoding

"Dan's joke: Egomaniac/Communist/Muslim.   "Welcome, Mr. President." NO

"12/22/12 – National Oops Day?

"Carrots/Sticks – S need enforce, C w/quals -- save from cons

"all $$$$ lumps – crooks after 'em – HSAs, Roths, etc Protect

"Rating agencies

"Seniors – CD's low. 5% again? Unint Cons? Punish savers, lure debt/borrowers, then raise rates, default – conspiracies?

"FDA – 510K – licensing (fees too high); Japs refuse – med devs

"Canada/Eur model for FDA?

"Lease out NIH/FDA/CDC labs?

"University research grants?

"CPSC ?

"Cong. White Caucus – uproar if

"Pendulum – too far L, too far R, settle down – good?

"Grilled gecko – ick

"HS pep rallies – poli conventions

"Boston vs. NY fans – how bright? D's vs. R's

"Down With Donne"

"Jet packs, flying cars? ~~No~~ Maybe

"National Lottery ???

"Surcharge – Vanity/Specialty plates ??

"Fed Reserve audit ??

"Tax havens/evade - confront or maybe <u>co-opt</u>

"Randi – Indi - cute couple – Puerto Rico

"Joy – Jodi – Sarah/Sara

"displaced aggression

"dashed his balder

"Bolero CD?

"PLA's – Project Labor Agreements – unions – right to work

"Israel/Pal/Arab/Iran

"FDR – undistributed profits tax – NO way

"nude beaches ??

"Internet gambling – legalize and tax?

"Sales tax – 6% 5 4 3 18 ???

"Past the talking points

"Political response – straight response vs. blah-blah

"Statute of limitations – RICO – Congress? Sov Imm – gone?

"Tree > Bush > sucks arrrghhhh, etc. Wendi – Myrtle Bch

"pay to play

"Acts of God insurance – prove God exists before payout :-)

"Obesity

"Turmoil in your life does not warrant an emergency response in mine – from me" ??

"power-hungry demagogues - JJ/AS shakedowns ?

"gullible dupes – useful idiots (Lenin) - most voters ??

"greedy moochers/misers vs

"Section 8 subsidies

"better class of gold-diggers after me for my $$$ - recession

"towel-shaking – sand/wind – thanks for doing that carefully

"Obama college transcripts – suppressed – why?

"Strawberry Twins?? Daiquiri? Pink Alexander – no.

"Opal/Ruby – black jewel thieves ?? Hmm

"Cayley – 7ish, cutie Mom? Jane, Jean, Joan?

"Alert the Watchers

"Stuxnet ?? leak for poli purposes, destructive to policy

"Sam and Christine – captain LEO ret

"Ron/Eileen – judge

"Classified stuff – hmm – how?

"Laura – Houston C/R JJ- NoCaro ??

"Martha Smith – NZ, sub tchr Denv

"zero sum – slice of pie vs. bigger pie !!!!!

"MWBE – Minority/Women Biz Enterprise – law 20% extra cost

"Compliance costs

"Karen – Austria - ??? Who? QH'd that.

"Aff Action – cash cow for JJ/AS/attys

"Tortie/Veronica (Ronnie)

"Statehood – PR/Guam/USVI/ etc. ????

"NZ model – 1984 – driv lic good till age 75, no renewal, no fees

"Your mission? Overlap wit other Miss's? Cost/Benefit? Staff? Essential or --- need/want; ego/budget "Mine's bigger than yours."

"National DrivLic, good in all states, $500 for lifetime – ID card??

"cui bono – cui malo (who benefits, who's harmed?) CrimLaw

"nanny state – ick

"Agencies: trans, indianaff,TSA,NASA,ArmyCorpEng/etc

"GSA – natl parks (rent?), real estate (sell, lease?) etc.

"Rent out soldiers/equip ???

"Lacey/Rachel/Evie baby/mom/aunt OK

"RockyMtn Oysters

"sewing/sowing/sosoing

"balloon under sand – dangerous – punk AH's" fr. Ann Louise

"Jeff/Shari – Toledo OK

"Alan – London - "Could he fix my country next?" Hmm. ???

"self-indulgent navel-gazers"

"Zachary - "If I can spell it, you can say it – NOT Zach!!!!"

"Enviros – front for anti-capitalists = anti-business = anti-Amer

"Creative idea/sols, not more $$$ just thrown

"flatten midlevel bureaus – fewer layers ??

"FAA/airlines/electron devs safe?"

As he typed that last one, the wind picked up and the rain began to blow onto his balcony, so he packed everything up and headed inside, closing the sliders behind him, and began humming his new theme song again.

He stacked and fluffed the pillows on his bed, sat down, leaned back and, with just a few notes to go, continued:

"Close mil bases overseas which? $$ saved?

"Charge 'em for keeping bases there?

"Arab Spring?

"Russia?

"China – subsidies, curncy manip, h. rights, prison labor, cheap products to US. Power/backlash – war?

"Immigrants – legal/illegal – quotas, visas, college, engineers, India/Asia

"Andorra – mob? :-)

"Free market princ for honest, good people; regs nded for crooks

"OSHA 42-in safety railings 41.5? $500 fine. Stuck, checklists, micro, stupid

"FDA – 30% higher prices delays, egos

"TSA – union – gone.

"Top Ten reasons why I procrastinate:

10.

"Energy Dept. gone or reduced; new mission: Yes, not No

"Ed Dept – same – more charter schools, less admin in publics

"EPA – same, mostly gone.

"Dodd-Frank – how, why – most gone

"Obamacare – mostly gone. Pre-exist, 26-yrs, infant pre-ex YES

"I'm going to talk to the adults in the room now."

"No more pandering to the children; no more nanny state !!!!

And with that, he'd finished the notes, so he closed his tablet and headed downstairs. He got the PC cord out, plugged it in and booted the PC up, nuking a pot roast sandwich while waiting. Taking that and a can of soda back into his study, he sat down, copied the notes from his tablet to the PC, then checked his email and found one from Pam there. He hurriedly opened it.

"Hi, Jake. Hope you and SB are doing okay, Miss you (both :-)) a LOT. Hope you're getting mucho writing done; I'm looking forward to reading a lot when I get back (two weeks!!! Yippee!!). VERY busy here; only allowed communication tonight and next Sunday eve, and can't say much about the courses, other than that they're tougher and more advanced than the Farm was; but that was a long time ago. I'm doing fine with it all. But I have to remember to compartmentalize a lot. Really missing you (both) a LOTTTT. Love, Pam ... and GM :-)"

Jake heaved a deep sigh of relief and smiled happily, leaning back in his chair, savoring Pam's words and the deeper meanings hidden within them, the ones meant only for his eyes.

Finally deciphering all the meanings, he leaned forward and wrote a carefully crafted reply, trusting that Pam would not only get his words, but also the hidden meanings he'd buried in there.

"Hey, Pam ... and GM. Missing you ... both ... a lot here, too, and M&B, too. I'm so glad you're doing well with the O&S stuff, and I'm trying to keep your idea of compartmentalizing in mind here, but it's hard(SCR)er for me, without your experience; new to me. Not much actual writing since you've been gone, kind of an emptiness filling the void (oxymoronic, but true). A few notes and a very few interesting conversations with a few of the eight percenters, and lots of not-so-interesting ones with a whole bunch of the 92 percenters. Looking forward to the 18th ... a LOTTTTTT, too. Love backatcha, Jake/SB"

He looked it over closely, thought back to all of his time with Pam and added, just in case: "PS. SCR = Sorry, Couldn't Resist," then hit SEND.

Jake leaned back, closed his eyes, stretched his back and arms, began humming the Bolero again, and checked the rest of his emails. He found seven that needed replies, sent those, then sent three new ones, each with an attachment, and then settled in to do some real writing, for the first time since Pam had walked slightly awkwardly through the airport terminal doors two weeks before.

He was pleased to notice that he hadn't coughed at all that day.

-90-

Friday, February 17, 2012
8:47 a.m. EST
A network morning talk show

After a solid week of promos for Donne's interview, using the same question, Lindsey smiled at the camera after a commercial.

"Welcome back. I'm Lindsey Framingham, and I've now got another clip from my exclusive interview with Gordon Donne, the man we all now call boss."

The screen cut to the same shot of Lindsey and Gordon Donne on the chairs in the Oval Office that was used in the first promo series.

"Mr. Donne," Lindsey began, "is the rumor true that you had an affair with a porn star?"

"Absolutely, Lindsay, I'm proud to say. Of course, I didn't know she was a star at the time. I mean, I was only 20 years old. I met her at a party celebrating the sale of my algorithm, and she – well, she was after some of my new money. And she succeeded; that she did." Donne smiled. "I smile at the memory. First, best and only sex I ever had. Her screen name was Fannie --"

The screen cut to a medium closeup of Lindsey in the studio.

"If you want to find out the last name of Gordon Donne's one and only love ... or maybe just lust? ... we'll be running the whole interview on this show on Friday, March 16th. Be sure to mark that on your calendar. But now, back to Rene and her guest, the Montana woman who holds the world record for pencil eraser collecting. We'll find out just how many erasers she has ... and why. Rene?"

-91-
Six Months Earlier

Sunday, September 18, 2011
8:28 p.m.
International Airport
Fort Myers, Florida

Jake saw Pam as soon as she emerged from the terminal doors. She was striding confidently, wearing a loose light blue T-shirt and, for the first time since they'd met, a skirt, knee-length and dark blue. A skycap followed with her three bags on a dolly, his eyes focused on her solidly swiveling derriere.

Jake pulled the van up to her and opened the side door for the skycap and the passenger door for Pam. She gave the skycap a ten, slid the side door closed and climbed into the passenger seat, immediately leaning across the console and giving Jake a deep, long-lasting, tongue-twisting, denture-dislodging kiss.

She was letting her hand slide down his belly when a sharp tap on the driver's side window caused her to look up into the impatient face of a Port Authority police officer, who gestured with his flashlight for them to move along.

"Short-term parking garage, Jake, now," Pam ordered, then added, much more gently, "please?"

Jake, as he pulled away from the curb, smiled and said, "I'd like that, Pam. And welcome home."

Pam, still leaning over the console, nuzzled Jake's throat and slid her hand up his leg, letting it come to rest still on his thigh, but stretching an index finger up to caress Stevie Bruce through Jake's bermuda shorts. Naturally enough, Stevie Bruce responded to her light touch.

Jake hurried into the garage and found a space between a large white SUV and a heavy-duty green pickup truck, put the transmission in Park, turned the ignition off and fumbled to unlock his seat belt as Pam pulled him onto the mattress in the back of the van. Then it was Pam's turn to fumble, even though she had gone commando since just before picking up her bags.

Finally Stevie Bruce and Ginny May had their long-anticipated, warm and initially gentle reunion.

"Woh," Pam exclaimed, and then giggled. "Maybe I need to start calling him Steven Bruce now."

"What? Why?"

"He seems to have grown up a little bit. And no, it's not my imagination."

"Really? You're not just trying to flatter me now?"

"Nope, Jake; promise. He's bigger. I can feel it." Ginny May gave Stevie Bruce a gentle squeeze, then another and another; Stevie Bruce responded.

"Yup, definitely a bit bigger."

"Oh. I quit smoking; maybe that's part of it, more blood flow."

"You did? Bravo. So did I."

"Really? Cool. Congratulations."

Then they both let SB and GM take over and continue their ecstatic, sometimes frenetic, reunion.

Mitzy and Bitsy also enjoyed a reunion with various parts of Jake's anatomy.

As Pam collapsed once again onto Jake's chest with a stifled cry, and Jake joined her with his quiet moan, Pam quivered and murmured, "That was a loverly welcome home, Jake, just loverly."

"I'm glad," Jake managed to mumble.

After several long moments of heavy breathing, Jake was able to mumble, "So we both quit smoking. Wow."

"Yup; sometimes, with some of the stuff they had us doing, I got a little short of breath. So I quit."

"Wow, it was that tough?"

"Oh, yeah. But let's save that for later. Right now, I just want to snuggle and feel you in and around me."

And that's what they did, for another half hour, planes taking off and landing overhead.

When they finally got onto I-75 heading south, Pam asked, "Where'd you get the van, Jake? And with a mattress in back?"

"It's a new mattress."

"Not anymore, it isn't," Pam said, giggling.

"A friend loaned it to me; he owns a chain of mattress stores."

"Nice to have a friend like that."

"Oh, yeah."

"Nice ride."

"It's got heavy-duty suspension."

"I wasn't talking about that. Nicest ride I've had in a month."

Jake looked over at Pam and saw her smiling. He chuckled and then got serious.

"So, Pam, how was it? Only whatever you can tell me. Looks like you're even more sculpted, maybe lost a couple pounds."

"About five, actually. It was tough, but really good. And they gave me an okay to tell you a lot ... not everything, but a lot."

"You told them about me?"
"Yup. And they may be giving you a call; they were impressed when I told them about your moves."
"My moves? What moves?"
"How quick you were, like with that football and the Dunn guy."
"What football? Oh, right. But those were both just lucky."
"No, no, Jake; you've had some training."
"Just that little bit from Dorothy."
"More than that, I think."
"Nah, just that."
"Okay," Pam said, still skeptical.
"So what can you tell me? Where was it, anyhow?"
"I don't know."
"You don't know?"
"I really don't. I know it was a private island somewhere in the Caribbean, but I don't know exactly where. It was a big island, nothing but water all around. I got there by private jet from Miami, where I met my mentor/trainers, Rona and Joel, ex-Mossad."
"Israeli? Really?"
"Yup. Tough, but totally supportive. They refreshed me on Krav Maga."
"On what?"
"Krav Maga; it's a form of hand-to-hand combat."
"Hmm."
"Very aggressive; and they're experts. We really hit it off right from the start, and it only got better after that."
"That's great."
"Let's see. Oh, one of the first things I had to do was give a pint of blood, so they'll have mine on hand if I ever get injured. They took another pint just before I left, and I need to give another pint every two months from now on."
"It's that dangerous? Geez."
"Of course, Jake; it's bodyguarding."
"Geez."
"But what's really cool is the assignments. They post them, in general terms, on a web site, with the per diem, the general location and type of protectee, and I log in with my nickname and password ... I can't tell you those ... and if I want to take the job, I just check the 'Yes' box. I don't know how they decide who gets it, but if I do, I'll be contacted and go off and do it."
"And if you don't want to?"
"I just log out; that's it. I just need to work at least 50 days a year to cover the 50K draw at a thousand a day. But if the jobs pay more, fewer days. Plus any more I want to work."
"Oh; I guess that makes sense.
"So what else can you tell me?"

"There was a lot of training, seminars and field work. We had a guy, Levi, from Moscow, worked with the ballet there, probably ex-KGB, and he taught us a lot of new stuff on changing your walk, your gait and posture when you're undercover.

"Then there was this one guy named Robert – not sure where he's from – who taught us disguises, wigs, costumes, makeup, even how to do fake teeth over our own. Lots more cutting-edge stuff. He looked kinda familiar to me, but he was in disguise, and told us so.

"Then there was Mauricio, ex-Nicaraguan secret police --"

"What?"

"You heard me. But it's ex. He's a pretty cool guy, taught a quick course on camouflage."

"What? You're going to guard somebody dressed as a tree?"

"Oh, Jake," Pam said, laughing, then put a serious face on and said, "If the guy's in a forest, absolutely." Then she chuckled. "It could happen. Like the one about the two Irish guys who walked out of a pub."

"Yeah, I love that one."

"Anyhow, the segment I liked the most was threat assessment and the psychology of assassination. We'd role play both sides, trying to figure out how to get through to the target, and the other team would try to counter that. And then we'd switch sides and run the exercise again. That took me back to my early days in the Company."

"Wow. You were okay with that?"

"With what?"

"Playing assassin?"

"Yeah; it's what we've got to protect against. We even had a quick course on sniping; sometimes we've got to be preemptive, just like in the Service, take out the bad guy before he makes his move."

"Geez. No, I can understand that."

"And the woman who taught that was superb, named Sharon. And I felt sometimes like she knew me, that she was looking right through me, that I couldn't get away with any BS with her."

"Hmm."

"And a pretty young woman named Kirbey led a good seminar on tactical and foreign weaponry.

"Let's see. Dick and Jane ... really ... covered what they called 'aqua-surveillance,' all kinds of under- and over-water audio stuff, on and from boats, subs, even jet skis.

"Then ... let's see ... ah. Another couple, Coco and Nobo, led --"

"Who?"

"Coco and Nobo; nicknames, I think. They did a basic seminar on forensic accounting; old stuff for me, but a good basic overview.

"And a guy named Dayne gave a fascinating seminar on some very cool new photographic and video techniques and technologies.

"John and Dot did a quick seminar on adapting to local cultures, trying to fit in as a local, if you're physically compatible.

"Roger and Toula ... now, there was a cute couple ... did a whole morning on false flag ops."

"False flag ops?" Jake asked.

"When you do something that can be attributed to an enemy, or an infiltration op, like Hoover's COINTELPRO."

"Oh, I read about that; infiltrating the antiwar movement back in the '70s."

"And lots of other groups, too.

"Then another couple, Dick and Mary .. again, really ... did an intro to covert surveillance. Some VERY cool equipment that I never even knew existed. Can't tell you more about that, though."

"You gonna plant a bug on me?"

"Oh, Jake, of course not – hmm. That would be fun. Maybe we could post some of that online."

"There's enough of that out there already."

"But I'm thinking <u>we're</u> not out there."

"And I'm glad we're not. I like things between us staying between us."

"Like Vegas?"

"You know what I mean, Pam."

"Yeah, I do. Okay.

"Let's see ... oh, a couple of really cute girls, Shauna and Bridget, taught a quick course on ... well, it was on honey trapping."

"Really? Your expertise."

"C'mon, Jake. You should know by now that I wasn't doing that to you ... at least not for any ulterior purpose."

"I know; just pulling your leg a little. Gotcha."

Pam started to say something smart in response to that, but bit her tongue. "Ouch."

"What's wrong?"

"I just bit my tongue."

"Want me to kiss it and make it better?"

"When we get home, absolutely; and I'll kiss a lot of other parts of you."

"Whee!"

"I actually probably could have taught that course a bit better, but they did a good job. One nice idea they had was 'Use what you got.'"

"Ah; nice phrase."

"I'll let you use what I've got if you let me use what you've got."

"Once we get back to your place, I'll take you up on that, in a big way."

"Now that you've quit smoking, I expect nothing less." She smiled; so did Jake.

"Let's see. Then there was Kathy, with a Y, who taught us evasive and anti-ambush driving. Young, but amazingly effective. By the way, you know we've picked up a tail, right?"

"The white convertible?"

"You got it."

"Been with us since we left the garage. I'm getting used to it."

"The convertible?"

"No, being followed."

"Really? How long has that been going on?"

"I don't know. I guess I first noticed it just after I met you."

"Oh, geez, Jake. Have they tried anything?"

"Nope, just following; I've lost them a few times, running those – what did you call 'em?"

"Oh. SDR's, surveillance detection routes, you mean?"

"Right; that's it."

"And they broke off after you did those?"

"I think so, far as I could tell."

"Well, once they know you're onto them, that's what they'd do, and then probably swap out vehicles until you catch them again.

"Tell you what. Why don't we just go straight to the condo, no SDR, see what they do? Okay?"

"Okay. I can do that."

-92-

Friday, February 24, 2012
8:47 a.m. EST
A network morning talk show

After another week of promos for Donne's interview, using the first and second questions, Lindsey smiled at the camera after a commercial break.

"Welcome back. I'm Lindsey Framingham, and I've now got a third clip from my exclusive interview with Gordon Donne, the man we all now call boss."

The screen cut to the same shot of Lindsey and Gordon Donne on the chairs in the Oval Office that was used in the first two promos.

"Mr. Donne," Lindsey began, "without elections, aren't we all subject to taxation without representation?"

"If you look at it one way, yes. But I think that whole idea went out the window decades ago, with the corruption that envelops the whole election process, and the special interests that have controlled that process. So what I've done has --"

The screen cut to a medium closeup of Lindsey in the studio.

"If you want to see the rest of his answer, we'll be running the whole interview on this show on Friday, March 16th. Be sure to mark that on your calendar. But now, back to Bob and Rene and their guest, a shrimp fisherman who's started a 'Save the Mosquitoes' nonprofit. Bob, just how crazy is this guy?"

This clip was added into the rotation with the first two promos and the three clips played ten times each each day until March 16th.

-93-
Six Months Earlier

Sunday, September 18, 2011
9:25 p.m.
Bonita Springs, Florida

Jake pulled into the lot at Pam's condo and watched as the white convertible, which had stayed with them, but far behind, often out of sight, passed on by and headed up Hickory Boulevard.

"Whew," Jake sighed. "As usual."

"So it looks like you're not a target, just a surveillee."

"A what?"

"Surveillee, the subject of surveillance."

"But who are they? And why are they watching me?"

"I don't know, Jake. But let's get inside. We can leave the luggage here."

"No, no, they're gone. Let's get the luggage, too. We should be okay for now."

"Well, if ... okay."

Six minutes later, snug on a couch inside Pam's condo, they both breathed a sigh of relief, as Sharon's recording equipment three floors above turned itself on and alerted Sharon that it was running.

"Okay, Jake, let's try to sort this out. You first noticed them about the time you and I met, right?"

"Right; before you got me all paranoid that afternoon at the Seabreeze, I wasn't looking for anything like that."

"So it could have been going on before that."

"Could have."

"That wasn't a question, Jake; I was just talking to myself."

"Oh, okay."

"I do that sometimes."

"Don't we all? Oh, did I say that out loud?"

"Yes, Jake, you did."

"Oh. Sorry."

"So here's what I think. I think you've been way too free about giving that link to the JakeDevlin.com site out, and somehow it got to the people who set up the surveillance. Now, they may be friendly to you or they may be hostile, but if they were hostile, I'd think they'd

260

have made a move on you by now.

"Since they haven't, I'd guess it's either friendlies or maybe it's what you most suspected when we first met, that maybe they're from some publisher looking to keep tabs on you before you get the book done, maybe steal your ideas."

"But after you investigated me, that changed for me, 'cause you made me paranoid that someone in government, like your ex-boss, might still be coming after me. And all over a stupid little novel."

"Hey, Jake, you can't expect everybody to be rational. You have no idea what big egos some people in government, especially the political ones, can have, and how irrational and stupid they can behave as a result. And they have very long memories and can carry irrational grudges for a long time. And you've got to admit, there are parts of your novel that'll piss political types off ... a lot."

"Yeah, but I can't help that; he IS anti-political, and that's a big part of the whole basis for the book."

"I know, I know, Jake, and I know it's important to you, and I do want to help, in any way I can, but I think you need to be a whole lot more careful about discussing it with just anybody. You never know who might pass it on to the wrong person."

"Oh, geez; hmm – ah; Wendi. I think I have an idea of how that might have happened."

"Yeah?"

"There's Wendi, this woman I knew up in Myrtle Beach who was a total Obamabot, and I emailed her a link when I had Donne's speech done."

"Uh-oh."

"Yup. She emailed back and told me in no uncertain terms that she did NOT like my dissing her 'kid.' That's what she called him. She could well have passed that along to some higherup Dems."

"And she was a fanatic?"

"Oh, god, yes. But I think it was more anti-Republican and that her kid filled the bill for her when he made his appearance. I mean, before any of us had ever heard of him, she would do things like ... if someone pointed out a pretty tree, she'd say, 'Tree? Reminds me of Bush, arrrrgggghhhhh,' and go off on a passionate anti-Bush rant. And she had a whole coterie of libs with similar feelings, and they'd reinforce, coddle and support each other."

"I know how that works, on both sides. Like pep rallies in high school."

"Yeah. Or sports fans as so-called adults, like Boston fans versus New York fans."

"I wonder if that's how it got to my ex-boss's bosses."

"From Wendi? Don't know; could be."

"But I don't remember how it got to me, and that was way before it got to them."

"And then there was Frank, an equally passionate Republibot, and he could have done the same thing on the other side. And all I wanted to do was get some feedback on some specific things in Donne's policies."

"Red flags in front of angry bulls, Jake; both sides. I sure hope whoever is tailing you is a friendly and can also protect you."

"Oh, geez, oh, geez. Back to paranoia."

"Paranoia is what keeps us alive, in our business; that's what we used to say in the Agency. Jake, I gotta tell ya, I'm still looking over my shoulder, 'cause I made some pretty dangerous enemies back in the eighties, and they do have long memories. Believe me, I speak from experience." She shuddered and stroked the scar on her shoulder. After a beat, Jake reached over and stroked her hand, then took it in his.

"I believe you, Pam, and I'm ... I'm ... I don't know ... what do I – what do we do now?"

"We wait, and watch, and see what happens, keep our eyes open and stay cool, very cool. But you should stop giving every Tom, Dick and Harry the link to the web site."

"I can do that, I think."

"Geez, Jake, your shoulders are really tight. How about you try to compartmentalize all that stuff and go lie down and I'll give you a massage?"

"That sounds great, Pam; thanks."

"Just put the tailing stuff in a little box in a back corner of your brain and take several deep breaths ... and take your clothes off."

Jake smiled for the first time since they had gotten to the condo and complied. Pam, also in her birthday suit, got to work on Jake's shoulders and back.

Ten minutes later, with Jake's back and shoulders feeling as relaxed as a plate of spaghetti (cooked, of course), Pam did a final feather-light tour of his back, arms and legs and then rolled off of him and stood up.

"Okay, Jake, now roll over, take out your teeth and keep your eyes closed, okay?"

"Okay," Jake mumbled and did as she asked.

A minute later, as Jake gasped and squirmed, Stevie Bruce was the ecstatic recipient of a Neapolitan Suzanne, and a few minutes later, of a Neapolitan Ginny May, the latter accompanied by the Bolero.

Seventeen minutes after that, Pam's "Oh, my GODD" was louder and much longer than usual, followed immediately by yet another ... and another ... and another ... and another, and then she collapsed onto Jake's chest, breathless and gasping.

When she finally caught her breath, she whispered, "Oh, Jake, I love it that you quit smoking. Did you quit again between the airport and here? My god!!!"

Jake, also breathless and gasping, managed to mumble, "I guess it was good for you, too."

Pam started with a giggle, then a chuckle, then a full-out laugh, to the point that she started snorting again. She rolled onto her back, pulling him over on top of her, Stevie Bruce and Ginny May still in their joyful but now relaxed communion.

"I so missed this, Jake. I love having you in and on and around me."

"Me, too, Pam. Who'da thunk it?" Jake nuzzled her throat and ear, until Pam turned her head and began what turned into a solid half hour of mouth-to-mouth resuscitation, cuddling and snuggling, with Stevie Bruce and Ginny May alternately throbbing and squeezing, until Stevie Bruce appeared to be fully resuscitated, at which point Pam hit the remote and the Bolero played once again.

Three floors up, Sharon's voice rasped, "Good for you, Jakey baby, good for you." Then she headed to the balcony for a smoke.

One floor below Pam's condo, Michael and Janice McGilligan, 80-ish snowbirds from Indiana, had just returned from a bingo game at their church and were setting their walkers beside the bed as they slowly clambered in.

"Do you hear that, Janice?" Michael asked. "Remember when we used to make love to it?"

"That was fifty years ago, you old fart. Twenty years ago, you couldn't even last as long as the 'Hall of the Mountain King,' and now you probably can't last as long as a thirty-second commercial jingle."

"Ah, go to sleep, you old bitch."

"You too, sweetie."

They air-kissed and were sound asleep in minutes.

Twenty-six minutes later, as Jake lay breathless and sweating and Pam lay breathless and glistening, a little box opened in the corner of Jake's brain and sent a message, which Jake tried but failed to keep from exiting his mouth.

"I guess this would be a bad time to mention the death threats."

-94-

Friday, March 2, 2012
8:47 a.m. EST
A network morning talk show

After another solid week of promos for Donne's interview, using the first three questions and answers, Lindsey smiled at the camera after a commercial break.

"Welcome back. I'm Lindsey Framingham, and I've now got another clip from my exclusive interview with Gordon Donne, the man we all now call boss."

The screen cut to the same shot of Lindsey and Gordon Donne on the chairs in the Oval Office that was used in the first promo series.

"Mr. Donne," Lindsey began, "on your foreign policy, what style do you intend to use?"

"Well, Lindsey, I'm not a wuss like your last president and I'm certainly not a cowboy like the one before him. I intend to be flexible, since every foreign issue is full of its own nuance. But generally, as you've seen, I tend to be strong, but thoughtful. For example, when Iran -- "

The screen cut to a medium closeup of Lindsey in the studio.

"If you want to find out what Iran did and how Donne reacted, we'll be running the whole interview on this show on Friday, March 16th. Be sure to mark that on your calendar. But now, back to Rose and Tom and their guest, the brother of a 57-year-old bodybuilder who told people he had the body of a 22-year-old, which proved true when the Toledo Police came and took her corpse out of his freezer.

"Rose, Tom, take it away. Oh, oops." She giggled and blushed as the camera cut to a three-shot of Rose and Tom and their guest.

-95-
Six Months Earlier

Sunday, September 18, 2011
11:05 p.m.
Bonita Springs, Florida

"What death threats, Jake? When? How many?"

"There've been sixtee- – no, seventeen of 'em, I think. All anonymous emails, from untraceable email servers. The first one came in just after I dropped you at the airport last month. Then they sort of trickled in, with a few big spurts here and there, and I found the last one just before I left to pick you up tonight; it was sent this afternoon."

"Oh, geez, Jake. Were any of them credible?"

"Maybe four, five; most of 'em were just rants, with a 'you should die' kind of thing in there."

"But the others? Specifics? Reasons? Methods?"

"Reasons, yes; specifics or methods, not really, at least as I remember them."

"You saved them, right?"

"Of course. You want to see 'em?"

"Absolutely. You know that was a big part of what I did in the Service, threat assessment, judging credibility and profiling and tracking down the senders."

"I figured that, but I didn't know for sure."

"Yup; four years out of my twenty."

"You want to see 'em?"

"Do any of them have an immediate timeframe?"

"No; all just sorta general."

"Can we look at them tomorrow?"

"Oh, of course. I didn't bring them along. I just wanted this to be a big welcome home night for you."

"It sure has been, Jake, even bigger than I could ever have hoped for." She giggled and then yawned. "I'm sorry, Jake."

Jake chuckled, too. "Oh, Pam, that's okay. And I'm sorry for even bringing it up; it just sorta popped out."

Pam giggled even more.

"What? What'd I say?"

Pam, laughing even harder, said, "Think about it, Jake."

Perplexed, Jake did, and then finally chuckled. "Oh, Pam."

"Bravo, Jake."

Then, again entangled in and around each other, they drifted off into a long, deep sleep.

As the sun rose, the Bolero played ... and so did they.

-96-

Friday, March 9, 2012
8:47 a.m. EST
A network morning talk show

After another solid week of promos for Donne's interview, using four questions, Lindsey smiled at the camera after a commercial break.

"Welcome back. I'm Lindsey Framingham, and I've now got another clip from my exclusive interview with Gordon Donne, the man we all now call boss."

The screen cut to the same shot of Lindsey and Gordon Donne on the chairs in the Oval Office.

"Mr. Donne," Lindsey began, "some people are still confused about your fix for Social Security. Can you clear that up for them?"

"Sure, Lindsey. First, we eliminate the cap on earnings subject to the tax, we include investment income and capital gains, we drop the rate to five percent, and we exclude the first 20,000 dollars from that tax. Then --"

The screen cut to a medium closeup of Lindsey in the studio.

"If you want to find out more on that, we'll be running the whole interview on this show next week, on Friday, March 16th. Be sure to mark that on your calendar. But now, back to Rene and her guest, the mother of the eight-year-old girl who was arrested by Dallas police for operating an unlicensed business by charging neighborhood kids a quarter each for rides in her back yard on her imported Egyptian camel. Rene, what's the deal with that?"

-97-
Five Months Earlier

Monday, October 10, 2011
10:55 p.m.
Cyberspace

The Instigator finished editing the latest in his series of emails, added the appropriate attachment, leaned back in his chair and hit SEND.

This email, similar to the others, read as follows:

"Dear Sir/Madam(s):

"This is to advise you that the enclosed document will be included in a forthcoming publication, and will be delivered simultaneously to law enforcement authorities and to the press, not only in your country of residence, but around the world.

"Nothing you can do can stop this process, but I can. I can also solve the problem for you ... permanently. However, since there is great personal risk and danger involved for me and/or whichever of my associates actually performs the action, it will be costly for you. In fact, the price is a non-negotiable 20 million euros, ten million as a nonrefundable deposit, the balance due upon completion.

"I am sure, once you have perused the attached document, you will see that that is a minor cost for you compared to the damage that publication and distribution of that information could do to your organization and/or to you and your associates personally.

"While this email address is untraceable (and I suggest strongly that you make no effort to try; you will regret the result), you may reply to it. I am in no rush for your decision, but the date of publication is coming upon us very quickly, and that should inform and hasten your deliberations.

"Please be advised that the attached document includes some documents which the United States has classified, some up to the level of Top Secret/NOFORN, but I have redacted any information which could in any way reveal the identities of confidential informants or foreign assets who may have contributed information contained therein. However, that information is currently in my possession, and once your current problem has been solved to our mutual satisfaction, we may (I emphasize MAY) be willing to provide those identities to you in the future, at a price to be negotiated at that time.

"Once I have received your reply, I will provide you with contact information and the process you will use to deliver the deposit and finalize the contract. Take your time.

"Sincerely, The – no, you don't need to know that."

After sending the email, the Instigator shut down his PC, took his glass of very expensive wine to his recliner, switched on the hi-def TV and settled in to watch the local news and weather. Once the sports segment began, he turned the TV off, sipped the last of his wine, rinsed the glass and headed up to bed.

-98-

Tuesday, March 13, 2012
1:30 p.m.
The White House
Washington, DC
via a 24-hour news channel

Gordon Donne strode into the Press Room and directly to the podium, dressed casually, as usual.

"My fellow Americans, members of the press, it's a pleasure to meet with you all again.

"I'm sure you all know that February's jobs report, released on the 2nd, showed even better job growth than January had. We had a net gain of 613,000 jobs, even with the offset of 153,000 job losses in the federal government; that means the private sector added about 766,000 jobs in the month. Bravo!

"Now, two reminders. First, the new national sales tax begins in about two weeks, so if you want to stock up on things before that goes into effect, now's the time. Word to the wise.

"The other reminder has to do with the announcement I made last month of the corrupt proceeds clawback program. The deadline for taking advantage of the reduced penalties is April 3rd, about two weeks from today, and compliance has been, as we expected, only minimal. So if you have even the remotest idea that you might be on our list, you've got only two weeks before we start coming after you with the big penalties. Another word to the wise, okay?

"And a big thank you and keep at it for all the investigative journalists whose ongoing efforts at unearthing corruption, current or historical, have helped us expand that list. Keep at it, guys and gals, okay? And thanks in advance for all your help.

"Now, I'd like to read you a letter we received last week from a young girl in Topeka, Kansas. And here it is for you to follow along if you want to." Donne pressed his tablet and a handwritten letter on yellow lined paper appeared on the TV screen on the wall.

"'Dear Mr. Donne,' she begins, 'My name is Melinda Galt (no relation; my mom made me put that in, I don't know why) and I am twelve years old. I live in Topeka, Kansas, with my mom; my dad left us when I was four or five, I think. My mom has a pretty good job at a company that makes a lot of plastic things for furniture.

"When I was eight, she opened a checking account for me, with her being the bank and using some checks and a check register (my mom helped me with that word) from an account she had closed.

"'Each week, when she gave me my allowance, she would give me a quarter of it in real cash money, and I could do whatever I wanted to with that. The other three quarters she put in the checking account and told me that that was for me to save for things I might want to buy later on.

"When I opened my lemonade stand, we did the same thing with the money I earned from that; a fourth to me, three-fourths into the checking account. Sometimes I spent my share right away, but sometimes I gave some of it back to Mom to put in the account.

"When I was nine, I used some of that money to buy a bike I wanted, and now I'm saving to buy a motorcycle when I get my driver's license.

"'I think I learned a lot from doing this with my mom, and I think you should make everybody in the whole country do that so their kids learn about saving money for later and only spending part of it now.

"'I keep hearing on the news and in current events programs at school that my country has a big problem with a debt of some kind. So I'm putting a check for ten dollars in with this letter to do a little bit to help with that. I know it's not much, but I wanted to do something to help.

"'Sincerely, Melinda Galt.'

"And here's the check she enclosed." Donne held up a check, covering the magnetic codes with his index finger.

"Melinda, if you're watching, first of all I want to thank you for sending your letter. It was inspiring to me to hear from you. I will be sending your check back to you, though, in part because we can't deposit it because the account is closed, and in part, the bigger part, because I want you to keep your money and keep saving for that motorcycle you want; maybe you can use that ten dollars to help pay for a safety helmet, okay?

"And, Melinda, I would love to order everybody to do for their kids what your mom did for you, but I can't do that. I can, however, put on my bully pulpit hat and encourage everybody to follow Melinda's mom's example and teach your kids about personal finance as soon as they're able to understand the idea.

"What I CAN order ... and I've done it with Directive Number 514, which I signed this morning ... is that all schools include a module on personal finance in the sixth, eighth, tenth and twelfth grades. We've got free age-appropriate sample modules, with rubrics and tons of supporting materials, on our _____.gov web site; just click the link for 'Education,' then the one for 'Personal Finance' in the list on that page, and you can view or download those modules. They're set up for teachers of any subject to use and understand, so you won't need to hire special teachers to implement them. Parents, you're welcome to get those, as well; again, free.

"Melinda, I'm going to be sending you your check and a special thank-you letter later today, and I wish you all the best in your life, and I hope you drive your motorcycle safely when you get it. And give your mom a big bravo and a thank-you hug for me, okay?

"Okay; let's start with the questions. Who's first? Sandra?"

"Sandra _____, from _____. My question is this. What was the last name of the porn star you had the affair with?"

"Sorry, Sandra, that's an answer that you'll see when Lindsey airs our exclusive interview. I won't take the wind out of her sails on that. Watch her show this Friday morning and you'll find out. Yes?"

"Heavan _____, _____. Mr. Donne, when you dispatched Army and Marine units to help out with the tornado damage in Kentucky and Indiana, why didn't you just have the governors call up their National Guard units?"

"Well, Heavan, in good part, it was because we were already paying the soldiers, no matter what they were doing. And it just seemed to be a good use of that resource to use them. All we really had to pay extra was for fuel to transport them there. Everything else was already being paid for anyhow, so that was the only extra cost. It just made sense to me to do it that way. Okay. Yes?

"Crystal _____, _____. We understand that you're considering deprivatizing prisons. Is that true and could you expand on that?

"Yes, Crystal, that is under – well, it's more than under consideration; it's gonna be another done deal. The privatization experiment has been a total failure, filled with corruption and inefficiency, and we're going to fix that and turn it totally around.

"Additionally, we're in the process of revising the antiquated sentencing guidelines and separating offenses that require some kind of incarceration from those that don't. Violent offenders and others who pose a danger to society will continue to be kept in jail or prison, but non-prison sentences for non-violent offenders will be available to judges in the federal courts, at least, and we will be encouraging individual states to follow our example. We will no longer tolerate prisons becoming schools for crime for non-violent offenders, nor making them prey for the violent ones.

"We will also be applying a Latin principle, the opposite of cui bono, who benefits, which is cui malo, who is harmed, and running our entire federal criminal code through that filter, with punishments rising in proportion to the degree of harm.

"And we will look carefully at the issue of rehabilitation. Yes?"

"Honey _____, _____. Mr. Donne, have you developed a plan for dealing with the student loan bubble?"

"Honey, that is a very tough problem, and it goes back many decades. Like insurance or any form of subsidy, in fact, any kind of third party payment, one of the side effects, the unintended consequences, if you will, is that the price of whatever is subsidized goes up out of all proportion. That's simple economics and human psychology. Think about it.

"We have seen college tuitions rise, we have seen hospital costs rise, we have seen doctors' bills rise, we have seen auto repair costs rise, we have seen home repair costs rise, all significantly above the average rate of inflation for things that are not subsidized. The people are sensible enough, as individuals and en masse, to resist the inevitable and ongoing desire of producers to raise their prices, which is no different from an individual in a job hoping for a raise; same principle, same psychology. It's called pricing power, and when the government negotiators are either beholden to the other side or downright corrupt or just plain wusses, that gets out of hand.

"Let me be very clear. I and my people are NOT wusses, and we will be renegotiating all kinds of third-party payment processes where the government is involved, and we will reduce the pricing power of providers of all kinds, including student loans and the colleges that benefit from those. Okay. Yes?"

"Bill _____, _____. Mr. Donne, many people are unclear on your foreign policy and feel you have been mostly focused on the domestic economy. Can you clarify that for us?"

"Sorry, Bill. That's another issue that I covered extensively with Lindsey, so watch her show this Friday, and if you still have any questions after that, I'll be happy to go into more detail. But as I said in the clip she's been running, I am neither a cowboy nor a wuss. Strong but thoughtful; that's my underlying principle. Okay. Yes?"

"Maude _____, _____. Mr. Donne, there is a lot of pushback from nonprofits about your 50 percent tax on them. How are you planning to deal with that, and is your policy open to change?"

"Let me answer your second part first. No, my policy is not subject to change; it will continue precisely as I stated it in my first speech to the country.

"As to how I plan to deal with the pushback, there are a couple of ways. First, we plan to deal with noncompliance head-on, just as we have dealt with and will deal with noncompliance with our corrupt proceeds clawback program: with strength that some may consider harsh. Too bad.

"Second, with mathematics. As our tax credit has already begun to push money toward nonprofits, directly from the individual and/or corporate taxpayer, without any of the overhead of going through the byzantine and labyrinthine maze of the government, which reduces the value of taxpayers' money by nearly 80 percent ... or has up until now, the nonprofits who are supported by some portion of American taxpayers will wind up with more money than under the previous setup. Run the numbers yourselves and see what results you reach.

"Again, I'll reemphasize the point I've made over and over again, in my underlying principles across all segments of this country, it's up to the PEOPLE, not only as to what breakfast cereals they choose to buy, and thus which cereals succeed or fail, but as to which nonprofits they choose to support, and thus which ones will succeed and which ones will fail. Okay. Yes?"

"Gemma ____, ____. Mr. Donne, the stagehands union has been particularly negative in reacting to your position on unions, so that many Broadway shows have gone dark as of this past weekend. Do you have any plans to deal with that?"

"Yes, Gemma, I do. This morning, I issued a directive ordering them to immediately return to work, with big penalties, especially for the union bosses, for noncompliance. That is Directive Number 523, I believe it was. I've also ordered members of the military to observe and oversee each and every production that uses members of that union or any associated union, and to ensure that any attempts at sabotage or any other noncompliant behaviors fail or are severely punished.

"Additionally, I have ordered the FBI to --"

At that moment, a rumble of voices and loud footsteps was heard in the hall outside the press room, followed by shouts, screams and gunshots. The press corps ducked for cover and the guards and Secret Service agents in the room surrounded Donne and rushed him to and out through the hidden second door.

The first door, the main door, then burst open, with Marines backing in, firing their machine guns at an approaching horde of zombies, who kept coming and coming through the door, arms extended, shuffling along in spite of repeated bullets striking them in their torsos, their heads, arms and legs. They overwhelmed the Marines, chewing on their necks, arms, legs, and torsos, blood spurting and flowing freely across the floor, drenching the walls and furniture. Then they made their way inexorably toward the cowering, screaming members of the press corps, as ...

-99-
Five Months Earlier

Saturday, October 15, 2011
10:25 a.m.
Bonita Beach, Florida

"Zombies, Jake? ZOMBIES!!!?? You put zombies in the freakin' White House? What the hell is that?" Pam fairly shrieked at Jake, waving the pages in front of him, as best she could from her chair at the foot of his three-way lounge. Jake just smiled at her.

"You're kidding, right? Tell me you're kidding." Jake just kept smiling, his eyes twinkling behind his sunglasses.

"You're joking, right? You're joking. Yup, you're joking. Okay, you got me."

"I got you, babe," Jake warbled, off-key, as Pam began giggling, then chuckling, then chortling. Jake joined in.

"Why else do you think I'd give you the printed pages instead of the CD I usually do? I just wanted to give you a laugh ... and watch."

"You <u>are</u> going to take that out, right?"

"Of course, Pam; I put it in just for you. I'll take it out of the final draft. Of course, the zombie lobby would probably be offended by --"

"Oh, c'mon, Jake --"

"What's this about zombies?" an alto male voice squeaked.

"Nothing, Ron, nothing," Jake said, not bothering to turn around to see the speaker.

"Nothing? Sounded funny," Ron said as he came around Jake's lounge and looked at Pam with what he fantasized as his "come hither" look.

"So what's a gorgeous babe like you doing with a schlub like this?"

Pam looked up at him, pulled her sunglasses slightly down her nose and said, "I'm sorry. Are you talking to me?"

"Yeah."

"Oh. I thought you might be talking to your wife." She looked at Jake and winked. Jake nodded and smiled. Ron just kept on, not getting it at all.

"No, Jenny's up there. And Jake, she sent these for you." He held out a plastic bag with some chocolate brownies in it. Jake took it, looked over at Jenny and made a "thank you" gesture. She smiled and shrugged in her "I'm sorry" gesture.

"Well, that buys you a minute, Ron," Jake said, putting the bag in his cooler.

"So you gonna tell me who this pretty woman is or not?"

"Pam, this is Ron, and that's his wife, Jenny, up there; she loves to bake and she's terrific at it."

Pam turned and waved at Jenny, a pretty white-blonde-haired woman, who smiled and waved back.

"So, Jake, you gonna put me in your book?"

"Not sure yet, Ron – wait, I may have a job for you, in the White House."

"I think I'd make a great Secretary of Defense. You know, I was in Vietnam."

"I know, Ron; you've talked about that as long as I've known you. Not sure if SecDef is a good fit. But I'll think about it."

"Cool. Have you seen Ned and Joan?"

"I think they got in last week."

"Ken and Marsha?"

"Haven't seen 'em yet."

"Norm and Janet?"

"I think they're on a cruise this week."

"Dave and Pat?"

"Who?"

"Dave and Pat, from New Jersey; they sit over near the stairs when they're here."

"Can't place 'em; don't know."

"We got in on Thursday."

"Good for you."

"Had to unpack and get all settled in or we woulda gotten to the beach yesterday."

"Ah, well. The beach survived."

"Yeah, we had to get the A/C cleaned, and Jenny wanted to get some baking done. Too bad the rest of the gang isn't here. I can't eat all that stuff." He patted his beer belly.

"I'm sure you'll find something to do with it."

"Excuse me, Jake, Ron. I'm going to go talk with Jenny," Pam cut in.

"Okay," Jake said. Pam got up and walked up toward Ron's wife, who was sitting about ten feet west of the Mimosa twins, who shifted one of their beach bags slightly. Ron's eyes followed Pam's swiveling bright red bikini bottom, then reverted to Jake when Pam sat down in Ron's chair.

"How about Paul and Evelyn? Have they come down yet?"

"Haven't seen 'em."

"George? Will? Lucy? Bill? Peggy? Barbara 1? Barbara 2?"

"Nope, nope, yup, nope, nope, nope and nope. Okay, Ron, time's up. Into the water for me. Have a nice day." Jake got up, grabbed his bag and noodles and headed to the Gulf. A few minutes later, Pam joined him with her noodle, wrapping her legs lightly around his, running the tops of her feet up and down his shins.

"She seems nice, and she really loves baking. But he is kind of an arrogant jerk."

"Oh, he's tolerable, especially with Jenny's brownies to balance him off."

"What was that about the brownies buying him a minute?"

"I set that up last winter. Told him the only reason I tolerated him was because of Jenny's baking."

"To his face?"

"Yep. But with a laugh, and after a lot of setting him up to be able to take it. You know, that guy thing of calling each other names."

"Oh, yeah. Clever."

"No big deal. He's also an Obamabot, so I tease him on that, too."

"Oh, I'd like to see that sometime."

"I'll make sure you're here next time I do that."

"Cool."

"Not too bad; it's about 82 degrees, according to the TV."

"What?"

"Weren't you talking about the water temp?"

"Oh, no, Jake; I was – oh, you got me." She chuckled.

"Yup, gotcha. Probably another month of noodleable water ... for me, at least."

"How cold does it get in the winter?"

"Lowest I've seen was 58 degrees. Last February. When I was up in Boston, we thought that was warm."

"Ooooo; I don't know. Sounds cold to me."

"Tourists and snowbirds, especially the Canadians and Germans, go in and think it's fine."

"I think I'll have to try it then."

"Oh, I got an email from Marti and Dave; they're having their boat parade party in December and we're invited."

"Marti and Dave?"

"Fishbuster Charters. Remember that T-shirt you had on at – wherever it was we met when --"

"Oh, right; I liked the name. What day in December?"

"I think it's the 17th, a Saturday."

"Uh-oh. I think I have a thing with O-P around that time."

"Oh. On the 17th?"

"I'm not sure; I wrote it on my calendar. It may be that week, or it may be a week earlier. I'll check."

"I hope it is; you'll like Marti ... and Dave, too. Nice, genuine people."

"Do you like to fish?"

"Me? Nah."

"Me neither. But some folks love it."

"To each his own."

"Or her own."

"Right.

"So what's going on with O-P?"

"I don't know if I can talk about it."

"Oh, okay. No problem."

"Uh-oh; behind you, Jake."

"Have you accepted Jaysus as your lord and savior?" a female voice intoned from behind Jake as he swiveled on his noodles in response to Pam's alert.

"Excuse me?" he asked.

"Have you accepted Jaysus as your lord and savior?" she asked again, more pointedly.

"Ma'am, if we have, that is our personal business," Pam said over Jake's shoulder, "and we prefer to keep it to ourselves."

"But if you don't, you will go straight to --"

"Ma'am," Pam interrupted, "while I respect your right to your own opinion, I hope that you will show the same respect to my choice not to hear it."

"But --"

"Ma'am," Pam said in her commanding tone, "please find someone else to talk to ... now."

Shaken, the woman backed away in the waist-deep water and took her boogie board with her as she looked for another mark.

Jake bit his tongue until the woman was out of earshot.

"Wow, Pam, that was very cool."

"Learned that a long time ago, in a place far, far away. 1994 or '95, Nashville, Tennessee. I was undercover there, got a lot of that kind of stuff. Had to develop a response of some sort."

"Ah. You know, I may have to use that, if that's okay?

"For Donne? Sure."

"You know, I have one, too, but I've never had the guts to try it."

"And?"

"Well, if someone came up and said, 'Have you accepted Jesus,' I'd say, if I had the guts, 'Accepted? Hell, I pay him and his cousins Joe-zay and Joo-awn twenty bucks a month to cut my lawn.'"

"Oh, Jake," Pam said, laughing, "that <u>would</u> take guts."

"Hell, I'd probably get another death threat."

"Maybe two of 'em."

"Oh, right; could be two. Geez. Oh, thanks for getting O-P to help with those. Helped set my mind at ease ... a bit, at least."

"They were happy to do it; they do that sort of research every day, and even a bit better than the Service did when I was in that division."

"Got a few more of those last night."

"Really? Same kind or more serious?"

"Same kind, just ranting. I'm not too worried about those. Just those four or five in the original bunch."

"Stay paranoid, my friend."

"Oh, Pam, believe me, I am. Wish I knew how to do it better."

"Maybe I can show you some stuff."

"I like it when you show me your stuff."

"Oh, geez, set you up again," Pam said, chuckling.

"How about we try some of Jenny's brownies?"

"Sounds good," Pam said.

As they headed toward the shore, they noticed the Jaysus woman talking with Sonya, the Blabberator.

"Oh, I'd love to be a fly on the wall for that one," Jake said.

"Oh, yeah," Pam said, chuckling.

"Y'know, Pam, one thing I never understood about religion is why people have to put human characteristics on their god figures."

Pam thought a moment and then said, "Anthropomorphism? My guess? Because people need to have a daddy figure or a mommy figure to be dependent on, so they don't ever have to take personal responsibility for their lives, just live kind of like perpetual toddlers."

"Hmm," Jake said. "That makes some sense."

"And then the hierarchy can get people to give them stuff --"

"Like money."

"-- like money, to feed their dependency needs."

"Hmm. Or votes."

As they got settled and started in on Jenny's brownies, Jake said, "You're not gonna repeat that fake orgasm thing for these, are you?"

"Oh, I never fake it with you, Jake. No, I promise. But these are really scrumptious."

"They do sorta balance Ron off, don't they?"

"Oh, yeah; definitely worth a minute of jerkdom. Mmmmm."

Jake and Pam both caught Jenny's eye and gave her okay and thumbs-up signs, as well as big smiles, parts of which had brownie bits covering a few teeth. Ron was squeaking at some stranger and didn't see.

A moment later, Pam said, "Jake, you promise you'll take the zombie stuff out, right?"

"Promise."

-100-

Tuesday, March 13, 2012
1:53 p.m.
The White House
via a 24-hour news channel

"Additionally, I have ordered the FBI to detain all the bosses of the stagehands union and any other associated unions and bring them here to DC. They will be here shortly, I'm told, and I will be reading them the riot act and ensuring that the lights will be back on on Broadway tomorrow afternoon. They are in direct violation of Directives 27 and 33, the no-strike and no-encourage-to-strike directives. Okay. Yes?

"Alicia _____, _____. Mr. Donne, with your ban on outdoor smoking bans, are you not encouraging people to smoke and do harm to themselves and others with secondhand smoke?

"No, Alicia, I am not. What I am doing with that is removing oppressive and over-reaching behavioral control regulations by local and state regulators who seem to be overly power-hungry. What they can do and I would support is encourage people to quit when and if they want to, through education, information and persuasion, but not to bring the heavy hand of government down on their behavior and criminalizing it or subjecting it to civil penalties, such as fines.

"Let me parallel that with the abortion issue. If the churches want to prohibit their members from having abortions, I have no problem with that, nor with them evangelizing and trying to get people to convert to their point of view. However, again, their beliefs have no place in creating public policy for others who do not share their belief system.

"In fact, as of yesterday, I have ordered all jurisdictions that have fined anyone for outdoor smoking, ever, to refund whatever fines they have collected, and, in addition, to double that refund for the inconvenience and harm done to the victims of these petty little power-hungry bureaucrats."

Donne looked at the camera directly. "So if you were ever fined or punished for smoking outdoors, you are entitled to a refund of double whatever you paid, no matter how it's characterized, be it as court costs, the fine itself or any other costs, including lost work time, bond fees, et cetera, et cetera. Okay. Yes?

"Alyssa _____, ___ --"

"Hold on a second, please. Alyssa?"

"Yes, Mr. Donne?"

"And Alicia?"

"Alicia, yes, Mr. Donne."

"Are you related to each other?"

"No, Mr. Donne," said Alyssa.

"No, sir," said Alicia.

"Okay; just wanted to check on that. Go ahead, Alyssa."

"Thank you, Mr. Donne.

"Alyssa, _____, _____. You have fired a lot of federal employees in the past three months. Do you expect to keep on doing that?"

"Absolutely, Alyssa. We are going through every department, every agency, every nook and cranny, and every day we find new pointless paper-pushing positions to eliminate. I would expect that you'll see about 150,000 job losses in those positions each month for the next several months. So people who are 4P'ers, in Pointless Paper-Pushing Positions, be prepared to get your pink slips." Okay. Yes?"

"Robin ____, ____. Mr. Donne, we have only seen you either in the Oval Office or this room. Do you leave the White House at all?"

"Actually, Robin, no, I haven't left this building since I bought the country, for three main reasons.

"First, I've got an awful lot of work to do, and I'm sort of a happy workaholic, other than those previously scheduled state dinners that I have to do; luckily, I've only had to do two of them so far, and I plan to do only three more this year. I'm not big on ceremony and fake diplomacy, and foreign leaders are starting to get the message on that. I'm a brass tacks kind of guy, and I can get more done with ten minutes of heavy thinking and two direct phone calls than with twenty big get-togethers.

"B, I don't need a lot of entertainment and distraction, and I don't need a lot of back-slapping, hand-shaking, Mr. Happy kind of stuff, and I think the people are comfortable with me looking out for them from right here.

"And 3, my security people, including the Secret Service, tell me that, although the people in general are genuinely supportive of my policies, the power guys that have been displaced or disgraced are still pretty pissed off at me for pulling the rug out from under their dirty greedy games, so many of them are apparently gunning for me, figuratively and literally, and my people have strongly suggested that I stay here to make it easier for them to do their job of protecting me. And for the time being, I will defer to their judgment.

"By the way, all these assassination plots are pretty stupid, since even if I die, my policies and directives live on. I've got a good team behind me, ready to take over and make sure they continue to be implemented. So the usual rational reasons for assassination, stopping something from happening or getting a block to something happening out of the way, won't apply. Irrational reasons, like revenge, of course --"

Donne paused, pressed his ear and appeared to be listening to something possibly coming through an invisible earpiece.

"Okay. Time for one more. Yes?"

"Susan ____, ____. Mr. Donne, are you an atheist?"

"Susan, I have no problem with you or anybody asking that question, but it is one that I will not answer. My religious beliefs, if I have any, are my personal business, and whatever they may be, they have absolutely nothing to do with how I set public policy. That would be pretty hypocritical of me if they did, wouldn't it, now?

"Okay, gang, that's it for today. I've got to go get the lights on Broadway shining again. Thanks for coming, all."

The news channel returned to the talking heads as Donne left the press room.

When Donne passed Emily's desk on his way to the Oval Office, he said, "Could you get John Kelly over at Treasury and Al Johnson at the Fed on the phone for me, Em?"

"Sure, Gordy."

"And when those Broadway union guys get here, have the FBI hold them in the vans outside for a good couple of hours and then bring them in."

"Will do, Gordy."

"Thanks, doll."

"C'mon, Gordy."

"Okay, okay. Mom."

"Be careful or I'll sneak some tofu into your cheeseburgers."

"Yes, Mom."

He headed on into the Oval Office, chuckling, leaving Emily also chuckling.

-101-
Two Months Earlier

Saturday, December 17, 2011
5:27 p.m.
Bonita Springs, Florida

"Great party, Marti."

"Thanks, Pam. And thanks for bringing the deviled eggs; they're delicious. Never had 'em with peanut butter mixed in before. And thanks for pronouncing my name right; most people say it like it ends in a Y."

"Jake told me about that and coached me. But if I screw it up, please accept my apology in advance."

"No problem. I'm just glad you were able to make it and I was able to meet you at last. Jake wasn't sure about your schedule."

"I got it cleared; this seemed important to him. And I'm glad I was able to make it, too. It's nice to finally meet you; I've heard a lot about you and Captain Dave. He's really a native Floridian?"

"Yup, born and raised in Fort Myers, just up the road."

"And he does fishing charters?"

"Yup. Best native guide around, but I'm a little biased."

"Hey, Marti, the first boat's coming!"

"On our way, Dave," Marti replied, as she and Pam finished filling their plates and headed out to the deck, where the whole gang was gathered at the railing, watching the first decorated boat heading up the Imperial River, a Santa and six elves waving to the shore, with "Jingle Bells" playing over a loudspeaker.

"Cool," Pam said, as the gang on the deck waved and hollered back at the boat. "Ringside seats."

"Yup," Marti said and nodded. Then she looked over at Jake, who was sitting with an older man at a table, and whispered to Pam, "I think you two make a great couple."

"Thanks, Marti; I do, too," Pam whispered back.

"Hey, girls, no whispering," the man with Jake said, slurring his words slightly. "Come on over and join us."

"Oh, Paul, behave yourself," a woman's voice came from behind Marti and Pam.

"You, too, Gayle; come on over and join us. Jake's gonna put us in his book."

"You two go ahead; I've gotta play hostess," Marti said. "Hey, Jake, you doin' okay on your limeade?"

"Just fine, Marti; thanks."

Jake got up and pulled out a chair for Pam; Gayle sat down next to Paul.

"So, Jake, what's this about?"

"He's gonna put us in his book."

"I'm asking Jake."

"Just your first names; I'm putting friends' names in the book when I can, rather than just making 'em up. And I've got just the scene in mind for you two."

"Go on, tell her, Jake. Gayle, you're gonna love this."

"Okay. It's Donne's first press conference, and there's this 40-ish family, three kids, driving to the beach, Bonita Beach, and the dad has his tablet, 'cause he wants to watch it. And that's how it leads into the press conference. I made up some names for the parents, but if you two are okay with it, I can swap those out easily and stick yours in."

"I'm fine with that, Gayle. What d'ya say?"

Gayle thought for a while, then said, "Oh, what the heck? Okay by me."

"Cool," Jake said. "Let me make a note, so I don't forget."

"Jake, you never forget anything," Marti said, as she brought a platter of chicken wings, a shrimp ring, a plate of Pam's deviled eggs and a big bowl of meat balls and her homemade sauce to the table.

"Sorry," said Jake, looking up at Marti, "what's your name again, waitress? And could we get some more of that great tofu casserole the chef made? Thanks." He turned to Paul. "So, Paul, when you --"

"Oh, Jake," Marti said, laughing, as she slapped him lightly on the shoulder and he smiled back at her. Pam chuckled.

"So, Jake, how's the book coming?" Gayle asked. "Still coming out this month?"

"Nope," Jake said. "I ran into a snag with some assho- – excuse me – some idiot lawyers."

"What happened?" Paul asked.

"I got a letter in October claiming I was using a trademark without permission and to cease and desist. So I had to do a bunch of research on that, and figured I'd lose if I fought it. So I went back and took out all the references that used brand names, and that ticked me off and slowed me down a lot.

"And then I got another one in early November from another lawyer who said I couldn't use fat, gay Representative from Massachusetts' name with his masseur, so I had to change that to 'fat, gay Representative from Massachusetts,' and that only added to my anger and the delay."

"Lawyers can be such assholes," Paul said angrily. "I had to deal with whole gangs of 'em before I sold the agency, and even afterwards. I remember one time --"

"So, Pam," Gayle cut in, "how did you and Jake meet?" Pam and Jake glanced at each other and chuckled. Marti joined in.

"Did I say something funny?" Gayle asked perplexedly.

"No, no, Gayle," Pam said. "It's just – just --"

"You wouldn't believe it," Marti said. "I didn't when Jake told me."

Pam looked at Jake and said, "Go ahead, Jake. You tell it."

"You sure, Pam?" Pam nodded and smiled. "Okay.

"Well, there was this big gorilla head that popped out of the Gulf while Pam was interrogating me --"

"Wait. What?" Paul mumbled.

Marti cut in. "You remember. I sent you the link to the stories in the paper last summer. Remember?"

"Oh, that was YOU?" Gayle exclaimed. "YOU'RE the Secret Service agent?"

"Was," said Pam. "I've retired."

"I thought you looked familiar," Paul said. "We saw some videos online. You know you've got over a million hits?"

Pam and Jake exchanged another glance and giggled.

"No, not that kind of videos," Gayle said. "The ones with the bullets flying and people screaming."

"Now, THAT's a story," Paul said. "You guys oughta write that one up."

"Maybe once I get the Donne one done," Jake said.

"Hey, Jake, I was in advertising; I know what I'm talking about," Paul pressed. "That's a story I could sell easy. Think about it."

"Okay," Jake said, "I will, Paul."

"What do you think, Pam?" Paul continued.

"I'd have some concerns, Paul," she answered, blushing slightly. "I'm not sure the Service would be too happy. But I'll think about it, too, and we'll talk it over. Okay, Jake?"

"Uh, yeah, okay."

"You do that, guys," Paul said, "and let me know. I could help a lot with that." He took another deviled egg and popped it in in one piece, rolled his eyes in delight.

"I think that's a great idea," Marti added.

"So do I," Captain Dave added, having heard the tail end of the conversation.

"Okay, okay; we'll think about it. Promise," Jake said.

"Marti, these eggs are great. Can you give Gayle the recipe?"

"Not mine, Paul. Pam brought 'em."

"Not only stunning, but a good cook. Great." Pam blushed.

Jake asked, "Oh, Paul, where was your agency? I've forgotten."

"Philly."

"Right, right. I'll move it to, uh, maybe Chicago for the book, okay?"

"Works for me. Okay with you, Cakes?"

"Fine," Gayle replied.

"Cakes?" Jake asked, looking up from his notebook.

"Pet name," Paul replied. Gayle blushed. Jake made a note.

After a few moments of awkward silence, Jake said, "Another thing that held me up was that things keep coming up that I want to stick in there, like the Super Committee's announcement last month."

"What Super Committee?" Gayle asked.

"The one that got set up by Congress last August, to come up with a bipartisan plan for deficit reduction by November 23rd. They made an announcement that they couldn't come up with anything on the 21st, and nothing came of that, other than more crappy political grandstanding."

"As usual," Paul grunted. "Idiots." Another few moments of silence followed.

"Hey, maybe you guys can help me with something," Jake said. "I'm thinking of having my guy suggest moving the government from Washington to some small town somewhere, and I was thinking of Bonita. Any other ideas? Anybody?"

"Hmm," Gayle said, "we just got back from a trip to Oklahoma to see Ray, our grandson; he's a bull rider, competes all over. Maybe – Paul, what was the name of that place with the great diner?"

"Ahhhmmm, Lenox?"

"No, no, that was the name of the diner."

"Best hamburger I ever had."

"And the cherry limeade was delish, too," Gayle continued. "But what was the name of the town?"

"Oh, wait. Ahhh, Valentine?"

"No, Paul; that was something about the type of building, I think."

"Ah, Enid," Paul said, snapping his fingers.

"That's it; Enid, Oklahoma."

"Great burgers."

"You said that, Paul."

"Hey, Jake, Ray told us one about the two cowboys sitting around the campfire after their first day working together. Heard it?"

"Oh, no, Paul; don't tell that one."

"Aw, Cakes, it's funny."

"It may be, but I've heard it so many --"

"Nope, haven't heard it," Jake said. "Pam?"

"New to me."

"Okay, so they're talking about all kinds of stuff, sports, politics, nothing about art or religion, and finally they get talking about sex. And one says, 'I just like the missionary position.' And the other guy says, 'Nah, boring. I like the rodeo position.' 'Rodeo position? What's that?'

"'Well, ya git both of ya buck nekkid, git 'er down on the bed or floor on all fours, get in from behind and then reach around and grab her tits and say, 'Wow, these feel jus' like your sister's,' and see if you can hang on for eight seconds.'" Paul laughed loudly, Jake and Pam joined in, more quietly, Marti chuckled and Gayle blushed.

"I'm driving us home, Paul. You're drunk."

"Naw, Cakes, I'm fine."

"I've got the keys. I'm driving."

As Paul and Gayle continued their discussion, Pam leaned over and whispered to Jake, "Let's try that tonight."

Jake paused for a beat, smiled and whispered back, "What? Sit around a campfire and talk?"

Pam slapped him lightly on the forearm and said, "Oh, Jake," and laughed.

"Gotcha."

"Nope, that doesn't count."

"What'd I miss?" Paul asked.

"Nothing, Paul, nothing," Jake said. "Hey, that's a pretty cool boat," and they all turned to watch the rest of the parade, emptying their plates of Marti's delicious home-cooked cuisine and Pam's eggs.

After the parade, Gayle drove Paul home, and Pam and Jake, in her new sixth-floor condo, experimented with the Rodeo position, which they found fairly silly, then with Boarding the Stagecoach (awkward, but tolerable), both versions of the Synchronized Duck Walk (impossible to maintain, and they quacked up over both) and finally the Two-Leg Intertwined Pogo Stick (painful, both before and after they lost their balance; luckily, no bones were broken in the fall).

Then, ready for a return to some degree of normalcy, they swapped sensual massages, which led to another deeply intimate, but this time comfortably horizontal, encounter between Stevie Bruce and Ginny May, after which Jake and Pam finally fell into an exhausted, deep sleep in each other's arms.

As the sun rose, the Bolero played again ... twice.

-102-

Tuesday, March 13, 2012
2:09 p.m.
The Oval Office
Washington, DC

"Thanks, Emily. Got it.

"Hey, John, Al, good morning ... And backatcha ... Okay, I've got two issues – three, actually ... first, John, how are you doing on getting that IPO set up on Yellowstone? Right, non-voting shares, restricted sales, no dividend, institutional ownership only, minimum amount a million bucks. I've got the social media folks working on a subtle, stealthy dog-and-pony show. Rumors, denials, the whole schmeer ... yup, I think right around the Fourth should be a good time. Good. Keep me posted, okay? Good.

"Al, when John announces the 50-year bond auction for next month, I want to see you and your people sending out some quiet rumors that you're very interested in those instruments ... no, no, no, I'm not expecting you to buy them all ... or even any of them. I want you and John both to punch up demand for those, especially with the Chinese. I want to see them buying as close to all of that entire issue as we can get them to. I've asked Wes to push some rumors out through his teams, as well ... well, of course. He's a solid partner in this whole process. I want them to think that they've got to bid for the whole 600 billion in order to get any, and I can't have any leaks that will lead back here. I mean, they'll probably figure some of it out, but they can't let themselves lose too much face by not participating. And then we'll have them right where we want them, if all goes well.

"Good, Al, good. John, everything clear with you on that? Yup, scarcity, scarcity, scarcity. But do it subtly, below the radar. Get it going as if it came from the primary dealers who are drooling to get a piece of it. Right, just like we did it back at DEI with the Venezuelans.

"Right, John. Al, you got it all clear? Great. Okay. See ya."

As soon as he hung up, Emily buzzed him. "Gordy, I've got the mayor of New York City holding for you."

"I'll take it.

"Good afternoon, Your Honor. It's your dime; go ahead ... yeah, I'm meeting with them soon and we should get it done by the end of the day ... yeah, they should be all back up and running tomorrow ... well, I'm happy if you're happy ... what? ... no, I won't; you're stuck on that one ... well, it was a stupid move in the first place ... nope, double refunds, immediately ... wait, slow down ... too bad; live with it ... don't make me come up there ... that's better. Now, I've heard some rumors about you wanting to ban large soft drinks. What the hell is that about?"

Donne listened patiently, asking a few clarification questions, and then said, "Absolutely not. That's way too much nanny statism ... well, get over it ... that's my policy. Now, if I'm gonna get the theaters open up there, I've got to go. Have a good day ... if you want to."

Donne hung up the phone and turned to his overflowing inbox, which he emptied in less than half an hour. He noticed that the approved pile was now larger than the disapproved one, and both were smaller than usual. He smiled and said to himself, "Ah, they're learning."

Then he took a nap before meeting with the boys from Broadway. As he drifted off, he murmured, "Let there be light," and chuckled.

-103-
One Month Earlier

Wednesday, February 15, 2012
1:23 p.m.
Bonita Beach, Florida

"No, no, no, Jake. Put it there first, <u>then</u> do that and then back <u>there</u> next."

"You sure of that, Pam?"

"Absolutely. And we need to keep our voices down; too many people might hear."

"Hey, it's season; they're always close," but Jake dropped his voice to a near-whisper. "Okay, I can do it that way. But then I'll need to tweak this over here."

"Oh, yes, yes. But if that's too tricky, we can try it the other way."

"No, no, Pam, I think it's great; in fact, it feels just right."

"I'm glad you like it, Jake."

"And then just stick it in there?"

"Only if it really feels right to you."

"Hmmm. Yeah, it does."

"Really, really feels right?"

"Oh, yeah. Really."

"But if you change your mind, that's okay with me."

"I'm glad you're so flexible, Pam."

"One of my many great features," she said, giggling. Jake chuckled.

"One of many I love."

"Why, thank yuh, suh," Pam drawled. "Ah do so appreciate your lovin'."

"It ain't hard, ma'am."

"Okay. Anything else you want to stick in there?"

"I don't think so; it feels a little too long already."

"Better a little too long than too short."

"Yeah, I know. But if it gets really long, then it doesn't work right."

"How about this? Split it in two and put it in front and behind?"

"Split it? How would we do that?"

"Right down the middle. Let me see. Ah, right here. Does that feel okay to you?"

"Oh, there? When the screaming starts? Or should we keep the gunshots in the first part? I could tweak that a little bit and then pick it up with the gorilla head deflating after something from the Donne timeline. What d'ya think?"

"Wait, wait. Isn't that when Jennifer gets back to Poopsie after the Occupiers and the paint on her coat?"

"Oh, right. Let me see. Ah, yes, there it ... yeah, that works for me. Gunshots, screaming, Occupiers, paint, Poopsie, gorilla head."

"Cool," Pam said, chuckling. "I like it."

"Oh, geez. That was the scariest day of my life, bullets flying all around. I really thought I was gonna die. I still get nightmares."

"Really? You've never had them when you've stayed over."

"Guess I have other things on my mind on those nights."

"But when you do wake up in the middle of ..."

"Oh, yeah; or when you wake me up ..."

"Mmmm. Yeah. I love it when --"

"Ohh, that's hot," a squeaky alto voice intruded.

"Yeah, and it's dry, too, Ron," Jake said flatly, not moving his head at all. Pam looked over Jake's shoulder and saw Ron, dripping wet after a quick dip in the Gulf.

"The news said it was 61 degrees, I think," she said.

"Right; it's hot," Ron squeaked. "Like you."

"Oh, put it to rest, Ron," Pam said.

"So you got a part for me in the book yet, Jake?"

"Matter of fact, Ron, I do."

"Secretary of Defense?"

"Nah, sorry. Pam and I talked it over and we've got a very special part for you. Right, Pam?"

"Oh. Right, Jake."

"It's a very, very special part," Jake said.

"So tell me."

"Okay. First, you've got no lines."

"No lines?"

"Nope. When we first see you, you're dead."

"Dead?"

"And gay."

"WHAT??? Gay?" Ron said, his face turning a deep red-brown.

"And you're a transsexual."

"No."

"Yup. And you've got AIDS."

"Nooo!" His throat tendons started to throb.

"And you're a dwarf. Tried out for that pest control commercial, but you didn't get it."

"Shit, Jake."

"And you're a Republican."

"You son of a --" His fists clenched.

"And a member of the Tea Party."

"What? You can't do that." He shook a fist at Jake.

"Well, maybe, just maybe, if you get Jenny to make us some more brownies, I could leave it at dead and gay."

"Now, now, Jake," Pam cut in, "that sounds like a bribe."

"Naw, just letting him do some lobbying."

"Ah," Pam said, laughing and glancing up at Jenny, who was smiling back and laughing quietly.

"Oh, I'd also have to leave you as a Republican."

"No, no, Jake. I'll talk to Jenny. How many to take that part out?"

"The Republican part?"

"Yeah."

"Oh, probably a couple dozen might do it. No, make it four."

Before Ron could turn around and see Jenny, she flashed Pam an okay sign, then a thumbs up, smiling. As Ron turned, she buried her nose in her book, trying unsuccessfully to stifle her laughter.

"Of course, you'll always be an asshole," Jake said, only slightly under his breath.

"I heard that," Ron squeaked as he walked away. Ken and Marsha, Ned and Joan, both Barbaras, Bill, Peggy, George, Will, Lucy, Rosemary, Patrick, Norm and Janet, Paul and Evelyn and a couple of strangers within earshot all laughed. Ron glared at them all and plopped down into his chair next to Jenny, sulking. The Mimosa twins focused on a cell phone, trying to justify their giggles.

"That was a little cruel, Jake," Pam whispered.

"Just that guy thing, remember?" Jake whispered back. "He calls me a schlub, I call him an asshole, and Jenny gets complimented on the baking she loves to do. Balance."

"Her brownies are delicious."

"And they freeze well."

"You freeze 'em?"

"Of course. If I ate 'em all, my belly would look like his."

"Ewww."

"Hey, that's my word," Jill whispered to Carie. "Maybe she's got us bugged?"

"Shhh," Carie whispered.

"So, Jake," Pam said, "what's next?"

"I think my shoulders need a break. We've been at this for a couple hours. How're you doing?"

"I could use a break, too. Massage swap?"

"Sounds good."

"Let's go."

"We'll watch your stuff," Norm and Janet said in unison as Pam and Jake got up.

"Get ready, Sharon," Jill whisper-giggled into her beach bag.

-104-

Tuesday, March 13, 2012
4:35 p.m.
The Oval Office
Washington, DC

Emily and six Secret Service agents and four of Donne's private guards escorted five handcuffed union bosses from the Broadway theater industry into the Oval Office.

Donne looked up at them all, his mouth full of cheeseburger, and waved them to a point in front of his desk. He left them standing there, fidgeting, while he slowly finished his meal, took a final sip of his soda, carefully wiped his mouth with a paper napkin and leaned back in his chair.

"I understand some of you are mob-connected," he began. "So I think it's best to keep you all restrained while we have our little chat. Keep a close eye on them all, guys." The guards all nodded.

"Now, boys, it's come to my attention that your members have gone on strike and that Broadway has gone dark. That violates my no-strike directive and my no-encouraging-strikes directives.

"So my question is this. What do you have to say for yourselves before I find you guilty and sentence you?"

"I want to speak to a lawyer," one of the bosses said.

"Me, too," said another, and the other three concurred.

"Well, kids, that ain't gonna happen. Your due process rights are only what I decide they'll be, and for you they do not include lawyers.

"Now I'll ask it again. What do you have to say for yourselves?"

All five remained silent.

"Well, boys, that makes things pretty simple.

"I've gone over the contracts you have with all the producers, and they are the most appalling, disgusting, restrictive and downright criminal contracts I've ever had the pain of reading.

288

"Not only that, but you have all been abusing your members for decades, skimming money from their dues for your own personal lifestyles and your mob bosses, sending more money to national lobbying groups and requiring your members to buy overpriced health and life insurance from companies you control. And that's just the tip of the iceberg.

"I find you all guilty of violating the two directives I mentioned before, and in addition to a prison sentence starting right now in the cellblock in our basement and continuing for ten years in a federal prison with no amenities and only minimal sustenance, for which you will be billed, I am also confiscating everything each of you owns or controls, leaving you and your families destitute. I am also clawing back any and all payments you have made to other cronies or mob bosses over the last twenty years.

"Emily, do we have room for these five downstairs?"

"Afraid not, Mr. Donne. Those cells are all full. We do have some empty cells in the EOB, but they are the D level cells."

"Well, guys, those'll have to – oh, wait. Emily, are those four other union bosses and their attorneys still over there?"

"Yes, they are, Mr. Donne."

"Oh, dear, I completely forgot about them. It's been ... what? ... three months, I think. Can you have them brought up here?"

"Now, Mr. Donne?"

"Yes, Emily; right now."

"And these gentlemen?"

"Hold them somewhere until those others get here."

"Yes, sir."

-105-

Tuesday, March 13, 2012
12:35 p.m.
Bonita Beach, Florida

The Mimosa twins, Jill and Carie, finally got fed up with the five drunken spring breakers who'd sat too close to them and had been leering at them and making lewd comments about them for the past half hour. The twins knew they were beautiful and looked younger than their real age (30), but these 19-year-olds' behavior had finally crossed the line when they started goading the biggest one. He lurched over to Jill and slurred, "Hey, babe, wanna suck my dick?" His buddies all laughed.

"Excuse me?" Jill asked, removing one of her earbuds, glancing at Carie and nodding; Carie nodded back, imperceptibly.

"I said, 'Wanna suck my dick?'" the kid slurred again, leaning closer and stretching his hand out toward her chest.

Jill snapped her arm out and gripped his hand, twisting it into a *kote gaeshi* wrist lock. The boy's eyes widened and he tried to squirm out of her grasp, but she just gripped tighter and twisted more, and he started writhing in pain, falling to his knees on the sand next to her towel. Carie kept a wary eye on the other four, shaking her head and raising an index finger at them.

"Now, sonny, I want to make sure I understand exactly what you said. What was it again?"

"Ow, ow, ow, let go!"

"No, no, I'm not sure that was it." She squeezed tighter.

"Oh, Christ! Let go!"

"Was that what he said, Carie Berry?"

"I don't think so, Jillybean. Doesn't sound anything like what he said."

"I agree. Sonny boy, we agree that that's not what you said. I'll give you a second chance. What was it you said, precisely?"

"Ow, ow, ow!"

"Ding, ding, ding. Wrong answer. One last chance before I break your fingers. What. Was. It. You. Said. Precisely?"

"Okay, okay. I asked you if you'd suck my dick."

"Close, but no cigar. Precisely?"

"Ow, ow. Okay. I think I said, 'Wanna suck my dick?'"

"And just before that?"

"I don't remember. Ow!"

"Try."

"Umm ... ow, ow. I don't remember."

"I believe he said, 'Hey, babe' to start it off, JB."

"Why, thank you, CB; I do believe you are correct."

"I do believe I am, JB."

"So, sonny boy, is my sister correct?"

"Yeah, yeah, I guess so. I don't remember. Ow, geez."

"So you agree that what you said, precisely, was 'Hey, babe, wanna suck my dick?'"

"I guess so ... ow. Okay, okay. I agree."

"Now, sonny, by what stretch of your insipid little imagination do you believe that that is in any way, shape or form respectful to me?"

"I -- I guess not."

"Ding, ding, ding; not responsive. I'll rephrase the question. Did that question show any respect at all to me ... or to women in general?"

"Uh -- ow. No, no."

"No what?"

"No, it did not show respect."

"Well, at long last, some awareness. Now I have a few more questions for you. And I expect a prompt and totally truthful answer; otherwise, I'll twist harder and that'll feel like this."

"Yee-oww!"

"First, what's your name?"

"Jerry."

"Last name?"

"Hagopian."

"And how do you spell that, Jerry?"

"H-a-g-o-p-i-a-n."

"Okay; Jerry Hagopian.

"And where do you go to school, Jerry Hagopian?"

He named a well-known university in New Jersey.

"Which campus?"

"Camden."

"And how old are you?"

"19."

"Very good, Jerry. Now I'm going to ask you a compound question, and that may be tougher for you. What year are you in and what is your major?"

"I'm a sophomore, marketing."

"Well, well, well. Maybe you're not as stupid as your behavior would indicate. Or maybe you are precisely that stupid. What is your GPA?"

"Oh, geez. Um, 2.1."

"Two point one? Maybe you ARE that stupid. Are you from New Jersey? Were you born there?"

"Yeah, yeah."

"And your buddies here are also from New Jersey?"

"Yeah, yeah."

"All of them?"

"Yeah."

"And you probably think you're pretty tough guys and your shit don't stink, right?"

"No, no ... owww ... well, okay, okay. Yeah."

"And you also probably think any girl would be happy to, as you say, suck your dick, right?"

"Okay. Right."

"Well, you can learn some things pretty fast, at least. Now, do you see those two signs just north of us there, one brown, one blue?"

"Yeah."

"Can you read what the bottom one says? Oh, can you read?"

"Yeah, I can read. It says 'Entering Lee County.'"

"And you are going back north when?"

"Sunday."

"I want you to listen very closely to what I am about to tell you. If I see you OR any of your buddies south of that sign at any point between now and then, you will find out precisely what your tiny little

291

dick and your testicles taste like, and you will also probably bleed out in less than half an hour ... and your body will NEVER be found. Do you understand what I just told you?"

"Um, yeah."

"And will you all stay north of that sign ... no, stay away from this entire beach until you head home?"

"I ... ow ... okay, okay."

"Say it."

"I will stay north of that sign ... away from this whole beach."

"And your buddies will, as well. I'm holding you responsible for them, too; you will suffer if they break my rule. Do you understand?"

"Yeah."

"What is it you understand ... precisely?"

"I will suffer if my buddies break your rule."

"Very good, Jerry Hagopian.

"Now all you guys, listen up. You have seen how I have humiliated and frightened your buddy Jerry here, right?" The buddies all nodded.

"When I let him go, he's going to try to compensate for that, and you will probably hear him saying lots of stuff, blustering and full of himself, lots of bravado. He'll probably even call me a bitch, or worse, and he'll need to do that for the sake of his little ego, and you all need to be very gentle with him until he figures out that his behavior and attitude toward women is completely unacceptable.

"In fact, Jerry Hagopian, I believe that your college has an introductory course in Women and Gender Studies, and you will take that course as soon as you can register for it. Perhaps that will teach you to have some respect for women, which you have obviously not learned to have up to now. Do you understand?"

"I ... ow ... okay."

"That course number is ... let me see ... WS 988, colon, 201, and you WILL register and take it, AND get at least a B in it."

"How do you ... ow!"

"When you DO get home, I will be sending someone to watch you and, if necessary, have a further little chat with you on the subject of gender and respect. She will be as firm as I am, possibly even firmer, and you will do precisely what she tells you to do, especially about fixing your attitude. She may also have to have a talk with your father, Harry, at his clothing store, with your mother, Naomi, and even with your sisters, Harriet and Stephanie."

"Wait, wait. How do you ... yeeoww!"

"I have access to lots of information; you don't need to know how. Just know that you can't hide from me and my allies. You will be watched and you will never know who may be with us. If you remember nothing else after you sober up, you will remember that. Now get your buddies and your stuff and get your pathetic little dicks and asses out of here. And don't let me ever see you again."

A moment later, Carie leaned in to Jill and said, "Amazing how fast some people can move when they're motivated, huh?"

"Uh-huh. And you know, CB, I almost had some fun with that. And, Sharon, thanks for the research."

Sharon's raspy female voice came thru her earbud. "No problem, kid; that's part of what I'm here for."

"And, Carie Berry, you know what really annoys me?"

"What, Jillybean?"

"Assholes like that are allowed to vote."

Down by the waterline, Jake caught Pam's eye and said, "Wonder what that was all about."

"I don't know, couldn't hear, but she sure took charge, didn't she?"

"Oh, yeah. Guess the ditzy chicks aren't all that ditzy."

"Told you they were pros."

"Don't think I'll take the other side of that bet."

Pam held her index finger and thumb slightly apart and let Jake, but no one else, see it. Jake nodded and held his own digits a good bit further apart. Pam nodded and they both got up.

"We'll watch your stuff," Norm and Janet said in unison.

"Get ready, Sharon," Jill whisper-giggled into her beach bag.

-106-

Tuesday, March 13, 2012
4:55 p.m.
The Oval Office
Washington, DC

The five Broadway union bosses were standing and fidgeting in front of Donne's desk when Emily and five more Secret Service agents and three private guards escorted Ms. Skinner and her three associates and their four clients in, all eight handcuffed.

Shockingly thin and disheveled, the men unshaven, but all belligerently resistant, they stood as stolidly as they could to either side of the Broadway guys, whose faces showed their dismay at the appearance of, but solidarity with, their union cronies. Donne let them stew in their own juices for a long three minutes as he looked intently through a stack of papers on his desk. Finally, glancing up, he spoke.

"Well, boys and girl, now we come down to the nitty-gritty. I do hope you're all ready; I don't think it will be pretty."

Ms. Skinner wavered a bit and Donne said, "Ms. Skinner, you look a bit faint. There's a chair behind you. Sit down, if you like."

293

"I'll stay standing, Mr. Donne."

"Your choice. But feel free to sit if and when you want to.

"Now, excluding the lawyers, there are nine of you who are facing a serious choice. Four of you have already made the wrong one, and five of you have indicated you want to make that same choice. I think you should take a close look at your four buddies and think very carefully about what the choices you make in a few moments will mean to your individual futures. Take a close look, and note that their condition is only the beginning. It's only been three months. Study them closely and think. I'll give you a few moments."

Donne looked back down at the papers he'd been studying and continued to read them and make occasional notes on a separate notepad.

After what seemed an eternity to everyone in the room but Donne, he looked up and said, "Ms. Skinner, you're looking even more faint. Please sit." She reluctantly complied, but maintained as hostile an expression as she could muster.

"Good, good; I hope you start feeling better soon. All that tofu does have an effect, doesn't it?

"Now, you Broadway boys, I have found you guilty and passed sentence on you and your families and cronies. Now, I don't do this often … in fact, this is a first for me … but I'm going to give you a chance to convince me to set those findings and those sentences aside. So take a moment, gather your thoughts and when you're ready, go ahead."

After a few moments of silence, Donne added, "I'm sure you were talking amongst yourselves in the other room, so why don't you pick one of you and just spit it out? Let me know when you're ready." He went back to the papers on his desk, ignoring everyone in the room.

The Broadway guys fidgeted, looked at each other and the other union bosses and their attorneys, gathered together and whispered to each other for a few minutes. Then the head of the stagehands union cleared his throat.

"Mr. Donne?"

Donne held up an index finger, wrote another note on his pad, made a mark on the papers in his hand, put them in his outbox and then looked up.

"Yes?"

"We … we …"

"You need to use the facilities?"

"N-n-no, sir."

"Well, then, spit it out, man. Don't waste my time."

"We can –" he looked at his cronies for confirmation; they nodded. "We will get our people back to work tomorrow."

Ms. Skinner spoke from her chair. "No, no, you --"

But she was cut off as a plexiglass-encased half-wheel snapped from the floor in front of the chair, rotating over and around her and the chair, encasing her completely. After a moment, she began beating on the plastic in front and on both sides, with no effect. Donne ignored her and continued as if nothing had happened.

"For the matinees?"

"Uh ... yes, sir. For the matinees." His cronies nodded, glancing at Ms. Skinner in her cage, yelling soundlessly.

"Well, that's a step in the right direction. And how about the losses the producers have sustained and refunds to ticket holders for the dark nights?"

"Uh --"

"You do understand that you are the cause of those losses, of course?"

"I --"

"And you and your members should take responsibility for them, wouldn't you agree?"

"Uh --"

"A simple yes or no will suffice."

"Uh ... yes, sir."

"Good, good. I will expect to see your unions making full restitution for all of that. Too bad you can't use your strike funds, the ones I froze in December.

"Now, what do you need to do to get your people back to work?"

"Uh, a few phone calls."

"Emily, would you give them back their phones?"

"Yes, sir."

She beckoned to one of the guards, who brought a box over, from which each union boss took his phone after being unhandcuffed.

"Make the calls, gentlemen. They will be recorded. I'll wait."

He went back to his papers, ignoring them as they each began to comply.

After a few moments, Emily spoke up. "Mr. Donne?"

"Yes, Emily?"

"You may want to do something about her."

"About – oh." He looked over at Ms. Skinner, who was now gasping for breath and beating weakly on the glass of her cage. Donne reached under his desk and a nozzle extended itself from the side of Ms. Skinner's chair, releasing a spurt of pale blue smoke.

"Ooops," Donne said and moved his hand again. The smoke was blown away from the nozzle, and Ms. Skinner began to breathe a bit better, but still gasping. After a few moments, her breathing returned to normal and the belligerent look returned to her face. Donne returned his attention to the papers on his desk.

A few moments later, the head of the stagehands union spoke up. "All set, Mr. Donne." Donne held up an index finger, finished with the set of papers in front of him, carefully placed them in his outbox and looked up.

"Good, good; a step in the right direction.

"Now, as to restitution, I've got the totals here." He picked up a stack of papers from his desk and held them up. "I will leave it up to you five to determine how to split those costs, but I expect to see those funds transferred by the close of business tomorrow."

"I'm not sure we can --"

"I am absolutely certain that you can ... and will. If not, I will impose a fine equivalent to the total of these totals for each day you fail to comply. Each day. Do you understand?"

"I – ah ... yes, sir." He looked to the others, who all nodded sullenly.

"And since you are the one person who spoke up, I will hold you personally responsible for the performance of your buddies here. Do you understand that?

"But I --"

"I didn't ask for an objection. I asked if you understood. Do you understand?"

"Yes, sir," was the sullen reply.

"Good, good. Another step in the right direction.

"I have not yet decided whether to set aside the sentences I imposed earlier, but I will suspend them temporarily, and I will be watching very closely to see how well you all ... all ... comply with my orders and directives.

"I have ordered several members of the military to oversee your members' activities at each theater, and I expect you to make sure none of your members does anything less than his or her very best at their jobs, for each and every performance. Do you understand that?"

"Uh, yes, sir."

"Good, good.

"I will also be sending a representative to facilitate good-faith negotiations between you and the producers for new and fair contracts. He or she will act with my full authority and will have absolute veto power over any parts of any proposal that seem to him or her to be out of line. He or she may also simply impose contract terms that make sense to him or her. Do you understand that?"

"Yes, sir."

"Do you also understand that another strike is not an option in your negotiating tactics?"

"Uh --"

"Do NOT waste my time. Do you understand? No strikes?"

"Yes, sir."

"Good.

"Finally, do you understand that if you do encourage a strike, directly or indirectly, I will immediately rescind my suspension of your sentences?"

"Uh --"

Donne waved an index finger once.

"Yes, sir."

"Emily, see these gentlemen out, give them each a DVD of our time together, at our expense, and get them transport back to New York, at their expense, or let them arrange their own, if they prefer."

"Yes, sir.

"Gentlemen?"

The five were escorted out, leaving Donne and the four attorneys and their clients alone with the agents and guards. Donne went back to his papers until Emily returned a few moments later.

"All taken care of, Mr. Donne."

"Good, good.

"Now, gentlemen and ... oh." He reached under his desk and the plexiglass cage rotated back under the floor, leaving Ms. Skinner breathing room air again. She climbed quickly out of the chair, her chest heaving, and headed toward Donne's desk, fists clenched.

"You – you --" she spluttered.

-107-

Thursday, March 15, 2012
11:43 a.m.
Bonita Beach, Florida

"Oh, geez, not yet for me," Pam spluttered.

"At least you gave it a try, and almost all the way in," Jake replied.

"I don't know how you can stand it."

"It's not that bad, Pam. Plus, I made the resolution, and I always stick to my resolutions."

"Really?"

"Absolutely. Back when I was a teenager, I made one to never eat broccoli, asparagus, brussels sprouts, cauliflower, turnips, kale and a bunch of other stuff like that ... oh, and tofu ... and I've stuck to that one for nearly fifty years."

"Really?"

"Yup. And I've done the same with this one; only missed twice, and that's because the rains came in early, about 10:30."

"Well, that's forgivable, I guess," she said, wrapping herself in her towel and shivering in her chair.

"Yup. And it's getting a little warmer now, so it's not as bad as a month ago."

"What'd I hear? 71 degrees?"

"That's about right."

"But why did you make that resolution in the first place?"

"I don't know; it was a pretty stupid ass one. But later on, I came up with three justifications."

"Yeah?"

"Or maybe rationalizations.

"First, the salt water's good for my aging shoulder joints."

"Okay."

"Second, the showers don't feel quite as cold after being in the Gulf."

"Yeah."

"And back in January and February, when the water was ten degrees colder, I was shivering so much I'm sure I was losing at least a pound a minute."

Pam chuckled. So did the Mimosa twins, but quietly; Sharon's raspy roar echoed in their earbuds.

"So every day?"

"If I come to the beach, yeah, up to my neck. Oh, I skipped the couple weeks after I got those stitches last summer; doctor's orders."

"Forgivable."

"Right."

"The ones on your shoulder have healed up pretty well; just a small scar."

"Matches the one on your left shoulder."

"Symmetry."

"Mirror images."

Pam sighed. "I love it when they rub together."

"So do I, ma'am," Jake drawled, smiling.

"Let's do that again soon, Tex."

"Tex?"

"When you drawl, it sounds like Texas."

"And yours is like a fine Southern belle, maybe Georgia or South Carolina."

"Like Myrtle Beach?"

"Well, MB is more of a tourist town, so lotsa mixed accents there. But Savannah, now, you'd fit right in."

"Why, I thank you ver' much fo' that, suh."

"Yore quat welcome, Belle."

"Belle? Hmm. I like that." She pulled her towel away and lay back, soaking up the sun. "Oh, that feels a lot better. I do love the sun."

"That's two of us. I'll bet you missed it a lot on that London job."

"Oh, yeah, but that was January, and only a week."

"And it was a little chilly here that week. I think I only got to the beach three days."

"Wow. Did you have withdrawal pains?"

"If they'd been in a row, I probably would have."

"I'd love to be as addicted as you are."

"You're getting there."

"I love the summer here."

"Yup. Warmer water, no crowds."

"Like now. What'd you guess, a thousand people today?"

Jake sat up and looked around. "Maybe; I can't count crowds well."

"Used to do that all the time in the Service. If you like, I'll show you how."

"Nah, I'll leave that to you; you're the expert. It is really crowded, though. And not just on the beach."

"At least we were able to get into Pineapple Pete's, with that great bay view, for Marti's birthday party."

"Well, her sister reserved the tables in the chickee."

"It was nice to see her and Dave again. And Paul and Gayle, too."

"Yeah. And did you see his smile when I told him we took his suggestion?"

"Yeah, he fairly beamed."

"I don't think I coulda even started that without your help. We've definitely got to find a way to give you some credit."

"No, no, Jake, no need."

"Oh, c'mon, at least think about it. We could change your name."

"Okay, Jake; I'll think about it."

"Ready to get back at it?"

"Back at it? That was five hours ago. But I'm ready."

"Oh, no, not that; the book."

"Oh," Pam fake-pouted. "Sure; let me get my notes."

"Okay."

Pam reached into her beach bag, pulled out a couple sheets of paper and looked them over for a moment.

"Okay.

"On the currency swap, are you going granular or macro on that?"

"A little bit of both, I think. Got him doing an announcement and then going into details with some of the players, with dialogue. But when I get into how people react around the world, I think macro'll work better.

"I'm also thinking about trying to squeeze in something that ties in to Bonita, just for fun, and what I'm thinking of is maybe putting in something about the Bali Hai."

"Bali Hai? What's that?"

"It's an old resort over on Old 41, was a health spa back in the Twenties, built around the spring that gave Bonita its name. I think Al Capone spent some time there in the thirties, and I was thinking maybe I could put something in about him burying some money on the grounds and never coming back for it. But if people started digging for it there and maybe even found it, it'd be worthless."

"Oh, I like that. Futility."

"I'll show you the place next time we're out and about. Maybe some rainy morning we can pop up to Cafe Mesureé for breakfast or brunch; it's on Wilson Street, right behind the little grocery store there on Old 41, and Bali Hai is on the way there."

"Think we can get in? In season?"

"We probably won't have much of a wait if we time it ri- --"

"Hey, Jake."

"Oh, hey, Birgitte. How's it going?"

"Great. Hi, Pam."

"Hi, Birgitte."

"Jake, if you can, swing around and watch this."

"What's going on?"

Birgitte looked at her watch as Jake sat up and looked toward where she was pointing. Pam swiveled her chair, as well.

"Wait, wait. Okay. 10, 9, 8, 7, 6, 5, 4, 3, 2, 1. Hmm. Our watches must be off. Any second now."

"What are we waiting for?"

"Ah, there he goes." She pointed to her husband, Karsten, who was looking at his watch and then stood up and pressed a button on a boom box.

"One for the money," he blared out, singing with the background music from the boombox.

"Two for the show," some other people sang as they, too, stood up.

"Three to get ready," even more people joined in, and they all started dancing toward and around Karsten, breaking into a fairly well choreographed and mostly on-key rendition of "Blue Suede Shoes."

"Oh, Jake, a flash mob," Pam said, quietly joining in the singing, but not the dancing, staying in her chair.

"Not bad, not bad at all," Jake replied, and started to hum along.

"He's good, isn't he, Jake?"

"Yes, he is, Birgitte."

"He got the whole thing going with the Hysterical Society."

"The Gator Day people?" Pam asked.

"Yup," Birgitte replied.

"Cool."

When the mob finished with that one, they segued into "You Ain't Nothin' But a Hound Dog," then "Jailhouse Rock," finishing with "Love Me Tender," bowing to a noisy round of applause, hoots and hollers, and then all the singers slowly blended back into the crowd, back into their chairs and onto their towels, people near them starting to chat with them, smiling and laughing.   Even the

Incontinentals got involved.

"Cool," Pam said, finished applauding.

"Look, Pam. See what's happening?"

"What?" She looked around at the crowds. "Oh, yeah."

"Not a bad icebreaker."

"Cool."

"I'm getting to like the Hysterical Society more and more."

"Me, too." Pam swiveled her chair back to facing Jake and held her index finger and thumb an inch or so apart.

"Sooo, big Amellican sodier boy, you wan' ruv me tenda? Cheepy, cheepy, velly nicey-nicey."

"Oh, god, Pam, Vietnamese, too?"

"Velly nicey-nicey, make Stevie Blucie velly happy." She held her finger/thumb gesture out again. Jake returned the gesture and laughed.

"Whatever happened to my dear Belle?"

"Oh, Ah'm in heah, too. But yuh'll hafta dig deep ta find me."

"I can do that. What are we waiting for? Let's go."

"We'll watch your stuff," Norm and Janet said, again in unison, and Jill whisper-giggled into her beach bag, "Here we go again."

Sharon's raspy voice came back over her earbuds. "Oh, joy."

-108-

Tuesday, March 13, 2012
5:19 p.m.
The Oval Office
Washington, DC

Ms. Skinner climbed quickly out of the chair, her chest heaving, and headed toward Donne's desk, fists clenched.

"You – you --" she spluttered.

She got no more than three feet from the chair before two guards grabbed her arms and restrained her, while she struggled and cursed Donne.

Donne sat placidly behind his desk, looking directly at her with a mixture of curiosity and bemusement.

"Now, now, Ms. Skinner, I'd suggest that you settle down and let us have a nice quiet chat ... unless you'd prefer more time in your chair and cage."

"You have no right to restrain me in that ... that ... that ..."

"I call it the Madonna cage, Ms. Skinner, and I have every right to restrain you or anybody whose behavior, attitude or verbalization calls for it ... totally at my discretion. You are a guest in my house, however you choose to interpret that.

"Now, are you prepared to have a reasonable conversation about your client's behavior and his future ... and your own?"

Deflated but still belligerent, Ms. Skinner only nodded.

"Good.

"Now I am going to speak directly and solely to your client and the other three clients, and you will remain silent ... or go back in the cage. Do you understand that?"

Ms. Skinner, arms crossed over her still-substantial stomach, nodded.

"I need a verbal response for the record."

"Yeah."

"A clear verbal response."

"Yes, I understand."

"Good.

"Now, gentlemen, you heard what I told the five guys who just left this office. Did you understand everything I told them?"

The four union bosses all nodded. Donne pointed to his mouth, and the four all responded, "Yes, sir."

"Good.

"Everything I told them applies to you and your memberships, other than military oversight ... for now; I reserve the right to call them in if and when I deem it appropriate. Do you understand that?"

"Yes, sir," the four said simultaneously. Ms. Skinner turned away and walked over to her fellow attorneys. Donne glanced at her only briefly, then back to the four union guys.

"I am imposing and temporarily suspending the same punishment I did on them on all four of you, as of this moment. And I will put this in language the four of you can definitely understand. Do. Not. Fuck. This. Up. Got it?"

All four again said, "Yes, sir."

"Good.

"Now, Ms. Skinner, do you have anything to say?"

"I object to --"

"Overruled.

"Anything else?"

"You can't --"

"All right, Ms. Skinner. I see we're going to get nowhere. You are hereby disbarred in each and every state in which you are licensed ... permanently. That punishment is NOT suspended, but takes effect immediately, right now.

"Additionally, all of your assets ... again, not your liabilities; you keep those ... are hereby forfeited to the United States Treasury. I will not incarcerate you, but I reserve the right to do so at any time I deem appropriate.

"Emily, have these people escorted back to their cells to gather their belongings, give each of them a DVD of both this and the previous discussion, at our expense, and then have them escorted out to the street and their freedom."

"Yes, Mr. Donne.

"Gentlemen, ma'am, follow me."

The nine left the room, escorted by both Secret Service agents and guards. As they left, Donne returned to his inbox.

Ten minutes later, Emily returned and said, "All set, Gordy."

"Thanks, Em. By the way, did it look like I actually forgot she was in the cage?"

"Oh, yeah; you pulled that off really well."

"And the oops on the blue vapor?"

"Same; looked like you really meant it."

"Good. Thanks."

"And the Madonna cage worked perfectly."

"Come a long way with that since Vienna, hasn't it?"

"Absolutely, Gordy."

"Well, I think it's ready for market."

"Want me to let Wes know?"

"Sure."

"Ready for some dinner?"

"Yup; surprise me, but my style, not yours."

Emily frowned, but said, "Okay, boss."

-109-

April 8, 2012 (Easter Sunday)
7:36 a.m.
Bonita Beach, Florida

Another lovely spring day in Bonita, 73 degrees, clear skies, and now, the annual sunrise service held by a local church was in full swing, having begun at seven a.m. Nearly three hundred were in attendance, most sitting on beach chairs or blankets, some standing in the back, closer to the water. A few of the more curious morning walkers stopped to watch what was going on, but many just passed on by, keeping up their pace, from shuffling to jogging to sprinting.

George and Marion Herman had driven from their riverfront mansion to enjoy the service; they were sitting in beach chairs about in the middle of the crowd, having arrived ten minutes before the service began. George had his hearing aids turned down, and he was a bit groggy, this being two hours before his usual waking-up time.

Jake and Pam had arrived about 7:10, setting up in their usual spot on the high tide line, a bit south of the periphery of the church crowd, and had gone for their southerly morning walk. They chatted

303

briefly with two middle-aged fishermen, one of whom was calling out, "Here, fishies, here, fishies," and laughing with his buddy.

Neither of them had had any luck yet, although one told Jake that he'd caught a four-foot sand shark a couple of years ago from the same spot. His buddy, standing behind him, shook his head and held his hands about two feet apart.

A little further south, near their usual turnaround point, they noticed a teenager fishing near a small red skiff, which he'd pulled onshore; he was standing knee-deep in the water. As he got closer, Pam saw his T-shirt, which said, "How Come They Call It Season If We Cain't Shoot 'Em?" Laughing quietly, she pointed it out to Jake.

Chuckling, he called out, "Hey, I like your T-shirt." The teen made no response. Jake tried again, "Catch anything?"

The teen, scowling, turned and said, "Naw, nuthin' yet," and faced back to the Gulf.

Jake shrugged, said, "Well, good luck," then, under his breath, "Punk," and he and Pam headed back north, hand in hand.

At they passed the gazebos, the Mimosa twins turned on their equipment.

When Pam and Jake got to about ten feet from their stuff, Jake a bit winded and looking forward to horizontalizing himself, they suddenly saw a giant bright red-orange devil's head popping up from the water, perhaps 30 feet from the shoreline, and a loud, deep voice roaring, "Jesus was gay! You're all going to Hell! Jesus was gay! You're all going to Hell!" repeatedly.

All the folks on shore for the service looked at the apparition, shocked. Some screamed, beach chairs were overturned, and a few injuries, none serious, occurred as people were trampled in a rush for the parking lots. Marion stood next to George, protecting him from the onrushing crowd; George, oblivious to the surrounding rush, asked Marion, "Jesus was gay? Who knew?" Marion said, "No, George, it's just a prank," and continued to hold off the crowd. The roaring voice continued from the water.

The pastor, recovering slowly from his own shock and outrage, finally grabbed the mike and pled for the crowd to calm down and return to their chairs. "Folks, it's just a balloon! Come back! Just a balloon!!!!"

A few people in the crowd, realizing it was an inflatable, began to snicker, but the true believers were outraged, along with their pastor, and they started yelling for someone to turn off the noise. Two of the younger men in the crowd, who were wearing swim suits, swam out and searched for a way to disconnect the speaker.

Meanwhile, Jake glanced south and saw the teenaged fisherman looking north and giggling. Jake grabbed his binoculars and focused on him and his little red boat. He saw a small metallic box in the teen's hand, and as he refocused on the teen's boat, the teen tossed all his gear in and took off. But before he got turned fully away, Jake got his registration number and wrote it down and handed it to Pam.

Pam pulled out her cell phone and called 911. The operator had already received several calls, but Pam asked to speak to Sergeant Dooley, telling the operator that she might have the boat registration number of a possible suspect, and that the boat was heading south toward Naples. The 911 operator took the information and said she'd pass it on to Dooley and to the marine division.

Finally, the two men in the water managed to disconnect the speaker and the service continued, until the arrival of Sgt. Dooley and four Collier deputies, as well as two Lee County deputies and their sergeant. But the devil's head stayed inflated.

As the Lee and Collier sergeants conferred, they concluded that while most of the servicegoers were sitting in Lee County, about a third of them were in Collier, the devil's head was in the littoral waters of Collier County and the suspect had been in Collier. So, after a bit of ego competition, they agreed that Collier would be primary and the Lee deputies would assist with the witnesses north of the county line.

Sgt. Dooley headed over to Pam and Jake, scrutinized Pam and said, "You?"

"Hello, Sergeant," Pam said, smiling.

Dooley just hissed. "Okay, you two, what the hell happened here this time?"

Jake smiled and said, "As to this inflatable event, of course?"

"Of course," Dooley said, glancing suspiciously at Pam.

Just then, his radio squawked, and he was informed that the marine division had stopped the red skiff and was bringing it and the teenager back for identification; they said they also retrieved a metal box that the teen had thrown overboard, but which stayed afloat long enough for them to scoop it out of the Gulf.

Pam and Jake both gave statements, as did the pastor and scores of people at the service. Several people also provided cell phone videos. The teen was arrested and taken to the Collier County Jail. A trailer was brought in and the skiff removed from the scene.

The pastor fought hard for the teen to be charged with a hate crime, but his lawyer successfully argued that there was a fine line between mischievous and malicious, and the US Attorney declined to press those charges.

A federal investigation of the gorilla head incident, which the teen admitted, placed the blame for the shooting part on an albino Marine private named Murphy overreacting. The fairness of that investigation surprised everybody involved, including the teen and his lawyer. No federal charges were filed. Sgt. Ron Danuski's death had previously been ruled an accident, and no charges were filed against Norm or Janet.

The teen ultimately pled guilty to state misdemeanor charges of disturbing the peace, two counts, one for each inflatable, and spent sixty days in juvenile detention.

Seven years later, he was hired by a major New York-based department store as a designer of balloons for their Thanksgiving Day parades.

-110-

Friday, April 27, 2012
8:30 p.m.
The Oval Office
Washington, DC
via a 24-hour news channel

Gordon Donne smiled at the camera from behind his desk, his colorful red-blue-and-green tropical shirt contrasting with the bland curtains in the background. A stack of papers about six inches tall sat in front of him, and he drummed his fingers on them as he began.

"Good evening, ladies and gentlemen, fellow citizens; tonight I've got five announcements." He slid the papers to one side and tapped them.

"First, these papers summarize the current results of our corrupt proceeds clawback efforts, which I announced in February and which are ongoing. So far, we have recovered nearly five billion in direct clawbacks and over eleven billion in confiscated assets from over four thousand individuals and corporations, including five ex-Presidents, four ex-VPs, nearly eleven hundred ex-Congressmen, and over five hundred senior ex-military officers. We have posted a searchable list of all of these people on the _____.gov web site.

"Of those, only approximately ten percent came forward on their own, which is about what we expected. Of the other ninety percent, approximately twenty percent have begun or will soon begin serving prison terms ranging from several months to several years. There have also been seventeen suicides of people on the list, and we are investigating six other suspicious deaths, which have been classified as homicides by the medical examiners involved.

"We still have several hundred individuals and corporations to go, with more being added every day, thanks to ongoing journalistic investigations. Bravo, guys and gals. Keep up the good work.

"Second, GDP growth for the first quarter came in at 3.2 percent in today's report, slightly above our projections, probably due in good part to raised dividend payments to shareholders and in part to more folks stocking up ahead of the national sales tax than we had expected. So we will not be surprised if second-quarter GDP growth backs off a bit, although the February and March job reports both showed net gains of over half a million jobs, even with the offsets of over a hundred thousand job losses in the federal government each month. That's brought the unemployment rate down to 7.4 percent. Still a long way to go to get to my goal of four percent, but overall, the recovery seems to be progressing well.

"Third, our health insurance reforms appear to be popular, but it's still early. Allowing companies to operate nationwide and to offer multiple choices, from bare-bones to comprehensive policies, and to provide ala carte rider selections, along with the expanded health savings accounts, all are getting upwards of 75 percent approval ratings in the latest polls. And our requirement that all medical providers post their prices prominently in their offices, in print and on their web sites, which helps consumers to make more informed choices when they can, also gets positive approval, above eighty percent, in the same polls. So we're encouraged on that front, as well. There's still much more to do there, of course.

"Fourth, as for the protests, demonstrations and occasional riots, we are making good progress on containing and redirecting those. My policy of holding organizers and instigators personally liable for any damages and requiring participants to repair those damages, under supervision of military personnel, has begun to have some positive results. I don't have any statistics on this yet, but I've gotten anecdotal reports that many demonstrators have moved into apprenticeship programs in carpentry, plumbing, electrical and glass repair and are preparing for good jobs in those fields.

"Finally ... and this is going to require a lot of explanation, which you'll find in Directives 558 to 573 by ten p.m. tonight ... as of the end of June, the one-hundred-dollar and fifty-dollar bills will no longer be legal tender; they will be replaced by brand new bills in those two denominations, which will be legal tender as of ... well, right now.

"We've been printing them up since late December, so we should have enough available. Here's what they look like."

Donne held up two bills and flipped them front and back for the camera, which zoomed in for closeups.

"Both bills have multiple anti-counterfeiting features embedded, as well as embossed numbers, so the blind can distinguish them."

Donne set them aside and the camera zoomed back out.

"Individuals will be able to exchange the old bills for new ones at their local banks all around the world, beginning tomorrow morning, and can continue that until June 30th. There will be a limit of one thousand dollars per person per day, and thumbprints or other biometric identification will be required.

"Businesses will be able to exchange old for new up to their average daily deposits, and will have an extra week in July to make the swap, since they will be accepting old bills up through the end of

June. Again, thumbprints or other bio ID required.

"After that, any of the old bills in anybody's possession might make good kindling for a fire, because they will have zero value ... well, some collectors might give you a few cents apiece for them ... or, if you have lots of them in bundles, you might add some water and glue and use them for building walls. I don't believe they have any nutritional value, so I wouldn't suggest eating them ... unless you don't care about nutrition, which many of you apparently don't.

"I guess that's all for – oh, one more thing. I want to thank the 38 billionaires who've joined me in donating at least a billion dollars to help with the deficit, and the more than five thousand millionaires who've donated at least a million dollars each, for another five billion bucks. And I'll continue to extend that invitation to any others at our wealth level to do the same.

"Now I do believe that's it for tonight, so I'll wish all of you a good evening and a great weekend. Good night."

* * * * * *

As soon as the camera was off, Donne stepped from behind his desk and joined the other people sitting on the couches in the middle of the Oval Office.

"Okay, folks, are all our surveillance assets in place and ready?"

The directors of the Secret Service, CIA, DEA, FBI, NSA, IRS and Homeland Security all nodded.

"Good, good. And our military backup teams are also in place?"

Martin Dean, director of the Defense Intelligence Agency (DIA), said, "Locked and loaded, Gordy."

"And we've coordinated with the governments we can trust?"

Eileen Tavestory, the new but experienced Secretary of State, looked around the room, nodded and said, "Yes, other than Pakistan, North Korea, Iran, Syria, Egypt, Venezuela, Cuba, Mexico, China, Russia, Libya and some others."

"Great. So as soon as any of these bozos start to move their dollars, your teams will move in and either confiscate or burn their caches or just surveil and report, depending on their assigned targets and priorities.

"Grant, Dave, your teams in Mexico and Colombia are prepped for heavy resistance?"

The directors of the CIA and DEA both nodded.

"And, Grant, you know that your legit agents will be able to convert their safe house stashes for the rest of the year, right?"

"Right, Gordy. As for the rogues, too damned bad."

"Good. Any questions?"

The director of the DIA spoke up. "We're fully authorized for deadly force if needed?"

"Absolutely, General, especially with the drug cartel assholes, the arms runners and the human traffickers. And we are more interested in intelligence than in prosecution when it comes to any prisoners."

"Any other questions?"

Nobody else responded.

"Okay. Operation Dragon Scramble is a go. Keep me posted."

As everyone stood to depart, Donne touched the Director of the Secret Service on the shoulder and said, "Pamela, hang back a second, would you?"

"Sure."

Once the door had closed, Donne waved the Director to the couches, where she settled her substantial bulk onto one while Donne took a seat on the opposite one, picking up the clipboard and setting it beside him.

"Two things I wanted to discuss with you, Pamela. First, it's been three months since I promoted you into Mark's slot when he retired. Any problems settling in?"

"Well, sir, I've been in the Service for 35 years, and worked pretty closely with Mark the last five, so it hasn't been too difficult so far."

"Good, good. No problems with the security team I brought with me?"

"Well, a few of the agents are a bit disgruntled at playing second fiddle."

"In a major way?"

"No, just the usual ego stuff; I can handle it."

"Good. Now, the other thing is this: I've been hearing about a few agents on advance teams last year breaking protocol and letting hookers into their rooms with sensitive materials in plain view. That was before I took over, but it's apparently an ongoing concern."

"Yes, sir; it's a cultural thing, going on since the mid-90s, but only with a small minority of the male agents. I hadn't been able to push to change that until you promoted me, but now that I've been investigating, I've fired seven agents so far, with fourteen more on suspension, and they'll most likely be gone soon, too."

"Good."

"But it cost me one of my top investigators, CIA experience, science and accounting, also did some honey-trapping in the '80s. She took retirement as soon as she turned 50, after a really nasty conflict with her boss last summer down in Florida, and now she's working with a private security company. I've tried to get her to come back, but she says she's very happy where she is."

"What company is that?"

"Uh ... oh, it's Optimum Protection. Is that – yeah, that's it, O-P."

"That's a DEI company; no wonder she's happy there."

"Oh. Can you help get her back?"

"Sorry, Pamela; I don't mess with people's choices. And I'm not in charge or even involved over there anymore, as you know; conflict of interest."

"I understand, sir. Just thought I'd give it a shot."

"No problem; no need to be anything but forthright with me."

"Her boss was one of the seven I just fired, and good riddance. Still a ways to go with the investigation, though."

"Anything I can do to help you with that?"

"I don't think so, sir, at least for now. I've got a pretty solid handle on it."

"Good, Pamela, very good. If you need anything, just call."

"Thank you, sir; I will."

"And, Pamela, you can call me Gordy, okay?"

"Okay, Gordy. Thanks again." She pushed a loose strand of gray hair away from her eyes, struggled to get up from the couch, accepting a helpful hand from Donne, and slowly made her way to the door. As she reached for the handle, Donne said, "Oh, Pamela, one question."

"Yes, sir – I mean Gordy?"

"What was that agent's name, the one at O-P? No promises, just curious."

"Pamela Robertson-Brooks."

"Could you send her file over? Especially anything about that conflict with her boss."

"I'll do that as soon as I get back to my office," Pamela said, smiling broadly. "You should have it in ten minutes, max."

"Appreciate it. Good lu- – wait a minute. Did you say 'Robertson-Brooks?'"

"Yes, si- – Gordy."

"Was she the one who was married to the Beige Man, the CIA guy who was killed in '90 or '91? Uh, Zach? Zach Robertson?"

"That's her, and yes, that was him."

"Oh. He was a legend. I met him once. So nondescript, he could fit in anywhere, almost invisible."

"That he was. She was shot in the same op that got him killed and came to us right after she recovered."

"They had her doing honey traps all through the '80s, right?"

"Right; codename 'Pepper.' But when she came to us, we paid for her to get an MBA, forensic accounting, and she was top-notch. She also rotated into the presidential protection detail twice, overlapping Clinton to Bush and then Bush to Obama. Best I ever worked with."

"Hmm. I do want to see her file. Thanks."

"Okay. Ten minutes and you'll have it." She headed out.

Once the door closed, Donne returned to his desk, picked up a paper from his inbox, then set it down and buzzed the intercom.

"Emily, could you have the kitchen send up my usual, please?"

"Sure, Gordy. Uh, can I suggest --"

Donne chuckled. "No, no, Emily, I'm just fine with the grilled ham and cheese. Save your mothering for your grandkids and your hubby, okay?"

"Okay, boss."

"Maybe someday I'll try something different, but – oh, remind me to call Jean-Claude tomorrow. I want to see how he's enjoying Paris and see if he can come back for that state dinner in July."

"Will do, Gordy. Mid-afternoon his time?"

"Probably about two; the restaurant should be quiet then."

"Got it; in your calendar for eight a.m."

"Thanks. And Pamela will be sending a file over soon. Can you get it in here as soon as it shows up?"

"Will do. She told me about that when she left."

"Thanks, Emily." Donne clicked off and went back to the papers in his inbox, finished them up in just over an hour, then, with Pamela's file in hand, headed over to the Residence, where he settled in for a much-needed good night's sleep.

-111-

Sunday, May 6, 2012
9:17 a.m.
Bonita Beach, Florida

The Mimosa twins began their day strolling north and south from their usual spot on the beach, near the boardwalk from the Collier County parking lot, Jill going south, Carie north. Jill glanced into the gazebo with the AA meeting and saw that all seemed to be going normally there. She walked to the southernmost gazebo and turned back north, scanning the slowly growing crowd, ignoring the men ogling her young, lush body. As she neared the boardwalk, her sister's voice came over her earbuds.

"Jillybean, got a possible situation up here near Pop's, by the volleyball net. A young couple just set down a beach bag and turned back north, where they came from. It may be nothing, but they're acting a little hinky, so I'm gonna follow them. You got your tool kit with you?"

Jill replied "Rodger Dodger, Carie Berry. I'll check out the bag."

"Yup. It's the yellow one right by the post."

"I see you. Got it. Be there in a sec."

"Okay. Keep me posted."

"Will do." Jill meandered up to the bag, opened it, lifted up a corner of a folded beach towel and looked inside.

"Oh, geez, it's a bomb, all right; C4 and ball bearings, with a timer set for noon and a backup cell phone detonator."

"Can you defuse it?"

"Of course. But I've got to sort it out. Blue, red, green, black ... hmm. I don't see any booby traps, at least. Amateur hour, looks like. Okay. Here goes." Jill pulled the blue and red wires together, then the green and black ones separately, pulled out a pair of wire cutters, then a second pair, held her breath and simultaneously cut all four wires. The timer stopped and Jill exhaled.

"Got it. Gonna pull all the detonators out now. Done. Think we can use some C4 sometime?"

"Oh, yeah, Jillybean. Take it all back to the van."

"Will do. Uh-oh. Some of the locals are watching, and a couple are pointing cell phones at me."

"Got your floppy hat down, Jillybean?"

"Oh, yeah, CB, all the way down. Casual, casual. Okay, I think I'm clear, but my cover may be blown. What are your guys doing now?"

"Just coming up on Access 2. Can't tell if they're parked in there yet."

"I'll head up your way in the van, back you up."

"Good. Ah, not Access 2; they're going on. Maybe they're not in one of the accesses; maybe they're in one of the McMansions. You might want to put some speed on."

"Will do." Jill walked nonchalantly back to where they had dropped their own towels, picked those up and jogged out to the Collier lot, climbed into their van, got it started and headed out.

"Okay, Carie Berry, on my way."

"We're coming up on Access 3."

"Damn; the light's red. But there's a car ahead ... ah, here we go."

"Okay. Just passing Access 3."

"Just starting the curve onto Hickory ... okay, passing Pop's."

"Good ... hold on ... okay, they're angling up toward Access 4. Maybe 50 yards to go. I'm about 30 yards behind 'em."

"Just passing Access 3. Silencer on, taser charged."

"Mine, too."

"Descriptions?"

"Mid-twenties, maybe younger. He's about five-eight, medium weight, short dark hair, clean-shaven, I think, red and black striped jams; she's maybe five-three, heavy, long dark hair, black scarf, dark brown one-piece, yellow skirt, small red over-the-shoulder bag."

"Got it. How you wanna play it?"

"Barcelona?"

"Naw. How about London?"

"Sounds good. But I don't want to spook them or get burned. Can you get there before they do?"

"I think so. Ah, here's the flag."

"They're about twenty yards from the boardwalk. Great timing, Jillybean."

"Oops. There may be another one, 50-ish, skinny, full beard, just standing on the boardwalk, looking your way. He's a little hinky, too."

"Can you take him out of play?"

"Sure, no problem. Okay, outa the van now, and it's blocking this end of the boardwalk."

"They've seen him, JB ... and ... yup, a quick wave. He's with 'em, not a local."

"Anybody else around?"

"Just some locals coming south at the shoreline. So not London. How about Joberg?"

"Okay. I'll hold off till they meet up."

"Good. I'll be right there once you've contained them. Silencer on, taser charged."

"Okay ... ah, here they come. Excuse me! Are you leaving?" Carie could hear muffled voices in the background, then "Hold it right there; hands up. HANDS UP! DROP THE PHONE! DROP IT!!"

"On my way, JB."

"I SAID DROP IT!!! Aw, shit. Okay. I've tased him, CB, covering the other two. But he pushed a button and the phone in the van is ringing."

"Boy, he IS twitching, huh?"

"Oh, yeah – CB, look out! She's --"

"No, girlie, don't even THINK about it! Oh, fuck."

"Geez, CB, she's twitching even more than he is."

"Now, buddy, that's both of our tasers. So if you fuck around, a gunshot is a LOT more painful. Jillybean, can you get the door, get the flex ties and tape ready? And gag him. Good. Now keep him covered while I ... well, well, well, a little handgun in her bag, looks like a tunnel gun; haven't seen one of those in a looonnngg time. Okay, buddy, now you and I are gonna get your girlfriend into the van. No, you WILL touch her ... NOW! Heave ho. Geez, she shoulda gone to Fatties Anonymous. Okay. JB, keep him covered while I flex-tie and gag her."

"On your knees, raghead. And quit crying. Geez."

"Okay. Now the old guy, buddy. I said NOW! What are you, a germophobe?"

"Maybe he thinks he's Howie whatsisname, CB."

"Well, Howie, here's my offer. You pick up his feet and I won't have my sister shoot you. Deal or no deal? Which one? That's better. Heave ho. Geez, JB, I coulda done this by myself; he's nothin' but skin and bones. Good."

"Back on your knees, Howie. Or is it Kamil? Abdul? Zafir? Rashad?"

"All set, JB. Now, buddy, hands behind your back. Good. Now get over there and sit down on the mattress, feet together. Good.

Now roll over on your side, bend your knees back up. Good. This may hurt a teeny weeny bit. Just don't wiggle around; you might dislocate your shoulders."

"Hogtied 'em all, CB?"

"Yup. And I got some car keys from the old guy."

"Umm ... probably fit that old green sedan, rusty. Yup. Guess we oughta take it along."

"I'll drive the van; you follow, okay?"

"Sure. I'll check the trunk first. Let me get my gloves on."

"Cool. Where'd you put the chloroform, JB?"

"Glove compartment. And the C4 is on the front passenger floor, the electronic stuff in my bag. Holy shit! I think we've got a couple hundred pounds of C4 here, detonators and wires and phones separate. And I saw a laptop on the passenger seat. Jensen'll love that."

"I think he's going by Johnson this week."

"And next week it'll probably be Jacobsen. Sometimes dealing with the Company can be a royal pain in the butt."

"Hang on a second, JB. Deep breath, Howie. Good boy ... okay, they're all out now, Jillybean."

"Rodger Dodger, Carie Berry. Ready to head out? Oh, geez, this shitbox needs a tuneup."

"When we're done, it'll need a lot more than a tuneup. And off we go."

"Right behind you, CB."

An hour later, Jill picked up an encrypted satellite phone and dialed. "Authentication 4873645. Hi, Amber. We need a helo exfil with a medic and a driver. No, we're fine. East end of Bonita Beach Road, in the woods on the south side ... yup; we'll come out in a white van when we hear you. Two plus three, one kneecapped ... he put up a bit of resistance ... plus two heavy duffels. So not Phyllis with the the Phlying Phantom, Little PP; it's too small. Can you send Mike with the big one, the Woodcock? Soon as possible. Thanks.

"And you can call Johnson ... Kaiser? Really? Geez ... call Kaiser and tell him we'll drop the three to him in Andorra, usual spot. We've got some good intel, a laptop, encrypted, two low-level and one mid-level AQs; his boys can wring 'em dry. We'll brief him after we've crossed the Pond. One of the jets available? Good. And we'll need to rotate out; we may have been burned by some locals. I think Wayne and Linda would be good, if they're avai- – oh, too bad. Tokyo? Well, Justin and Lindsay, then? Great. They'll probably fit in better than we did, anyhow. And we'll need a full cleanout at the condo. Great; thanks. Oh, you'll love this. Guess whose picture the AQs had on their beach towel? Yup, but how'd you know that? Really; hmm. And there's intel woven into 'em? Okay; we'll take special care of that. Guess that's it. ETA? Fifteen? Okay. Out."

Half an hour later, Lee County deputies and firefighters, responding to a report of heavy smoke at the east end of Bonita Beach Road, discovered a green 1997 sedan with a yellow beach bag holding some ball bearings, two bricks of C4, detonators, a timer and a cell phone on the passenger seat parked behind a bush on the south side of the road and a pile of green brush burning in the center of the concrete turnaround; the fire was easily contained.

Forensic analysis of the C4, detonators, timer and cell phone (and fingerprints on the timer and cell phone) matched evidence recovered at bombings on Miami Beach and Fire Island, both at noon on the same day, which claimed 19 lives and caused over 150 serious injuries and for which Al Qaeda claimed responsibility.

Other than the prints, it also matched evidence found by counterterrorism squads in seven foiled plots to bomb other East Coast beaches on the same date and time, roughly a year after the death of Osama bin Laden. 23 AQs were taken into custody, not counting the Mimosa twins' three, whose further interrogation led directly to the takedown of sixteen AQ networks in the US, Europe and the Mideast, and indirectly to the elimination of 27 other networks over the next eight months.

Two days after the Mimosa twins had dropped off their three AQs, Amber called to let them know they had each been given a bonus of a hundred thousand euros, as well as a month of free use of a fully-crewed 39-meter yacht moored in St. Tropez, well stocked with their favorite beverage and all provisions, which they enjoyed to the fullest, all the while reacquiring their all-over tans and doing some successful beach-sniffing with lots of French and Italian man-boys, some of whom, to the twins' dismay, engaged in false advertising, stuffing a potato into their tight-fitting swim trunks, except for one Italian guy, Pasquale, who put his in the back. "Ewww," said Jill, when she saw that.

All in all, Jill and Carie were glad they'd requested that the freezers be stocked with lots of Neapolitan ice cream and that they'd brought a good collection of feathers and chocolate and strawberry syrup along.

Monday, May 7, 2012
8:12 a.m.
Bonita Beach, Florida

Justin and Lindsay pulled their hybrid into the Collier County lot, having just bought an annual parking sticker at Veterans Community Park, unloaded their beach towels, chairs and bags and headed out to the beach. They set up just about where the Mimosa twins had sat for the previous several months, plugged in their earbuds and began alternately reading and people-watching while chair-dancing in time with the whisper-soft music in their ears, the recording equipment in their bags ready for Jake and Pam's arrival.

"Welcome aboard, kids," a voice in their earbuds rasped. "Nice to be working with you again."

"Hi, Sharon. Been what, eight, nine years?" Justin replied.

"About that. Have fun, but keep your eyes and ears open."

-112-

Monday, May 7, 2012
8:30 a.m.
The Oval Office
Washington, DC

Gordon Olin Donne paced in front of his desk, glaring at everyone in the room. He stopped in front of the CIA director, who was sitting in the Madonna chair.

"Grant, how the hell did all those AQs get their bombs built and in position?"

"Sir, I --"

"And on our BEACHES!"

"Sir, the --"

"20 dead, 150 injured."

Donne punched his right fist into his left palm, then took a deep breath, reached out and touched Grant's shoulder.

"Sorry, Grant. I've been up all night, sorting through all the info coming in minute-by-minute about this shit."

Olivia Meredith Gwynn, the FBI director, said, "Gordy, if I may?"

"Go ahead, Mere."

"Grant's people and mine were tracking hundreds of AQ cells, and even though three of them got through, we stopped seven others that were on their way to other beaches, and we're already getting good intel from the scores of AQs we took into custody."

"And, Mere, you're going along with my intel-over-prosecution priorities?"

"Yes, Gordy; no problem with that."

"All right." Donne took another deep breath and began pacing again.

"Now, let's focus. What happened with the one on Miami Beach?"

Grant spoke up. "We had those guys under tight surveillance, following them with an eight-car detail, DD877 on their car --"

John Kelly, the Treasury Secretary, asked, "DD877?"

"Sorry. GPS tracker.

"We had cars ahead and behind on the MacArthur Causeway, but when they got to Fifth, they ran an SDR, so we had to do a swapout, and we lost visual on them momentarily. The DD877 went stationary on Collins, so we ran a car past them, and they were gone, probably in a new vehicle. The bomb must have been in the new car, 'cause they did not have it when they left Miami, and they planted it in Ocean Beach Park and disappeared.

"But they screwed up and drove back to their original car, and we nabbed the three of them there, plus the new driver, put them in the interrogation van and drove around the area. Three of them kept their mouths shut, but one got a little hinky around the park, so we pulled him out of the van and walked him in there with two of our agents, and he went willingly enough, even pointed to where the bomb was and led our agents toward it. But he timed it so that as they got within about twenty feet, the bomb went off, killing him and one of the agents and severely injuring the other one; he'll live, but he probably won't ever walk again. We got them all out of there before the locals showed up, so no exposure there.

"The bomb went off at noon. Twelve dead, about eighty injured. We still haven't got all the casualty reports in.

"We've got the other three, including the new driver, prepped for rendition, I think to Andorra, and the forensics guys are going over their cars with a fine-toothed comb. We'll break them and go up their line as far as we can."

"Shit. One SDR and they're gone," Donne muttered.

"Do we know where the bomb came from?"

"No, sir, not yet. But we will, I guarantee you that. And we'll find the builder and the rest of the guys who passed it to the guys we got. We'll get 'em all to Andorra and break 'em."

"And the one on Fire Island?"

"Same thing, but no other vehicle or driver. Tight surveillance, no bomb in the car, SDR, DD877 went stationary, lost us, picked up the bomb somewhere, planted it, went back to their car and we got them and the vehicle. That one went off at noon, too, and they cheered and praised Allah when we heard the blast. They're going to Andorra, too."

"Okay.

"And what happened in that little town in Florida?"

"Bonita Springs. A couple of OPUS operatives –"

"OP-U-S."

"Sorry; OP-U-S.

"A couple of their operatives stumbled onto the bomb there, got the perps, did a quick interrogation and exfil, left the bomb and their car for the locals, and gave us a quick headsup. They're on their way to Andorra with the perps ... one's been kneecapped ... and we'll have a full briefing from them there and then break the buggers.

"The bomb is now in our custody, and it matches some of the

pieces we've recovered from the other two. We'll know more as the forensics guys dig deeper into that and the car. The locals are out of the loop."

Gwynn asked, "What were they doing in ... what was it again? ... something Springs?"

"Right, Bonita Springs.

"As I understand it, they were on a private surveillance job, and just got suspicious and took action."

Donne asked, "Did you have that cell on your radar?"

"No, sir. We just got lucky on that one. Very lucky."

Kelly, the Treasury Secretary, asked, "What's OP-U-S?"

Donne said, "It's a DEI company, one of our – their biggest and best. Private security, high-end, the US division."

Grant added, "We've done a lot of work with them. Absolutely the best. And the DD877 comes from DEI, too."

Donne said, "Do you have any 878s?"

"The ones with audio?"

"Right."

"Yes, but not enough of 'em."

"I'll call Wes, have him get you another thousand of those, at cost and – no, I'll do it on my personal tab."

Kelly said, "Your tab, sir?"

"Sure. No need to have the government pay for those."

Kelly and Grant both said, "Thank you, sir."

"Well, one of those would maybe have given you an idea that the Miami guys had gotten out of their car.

"And I think you may want to develop some additional tailing strategies for high-value targets, some kind of counter-SDR tactics."

"We'll work on that, Gordy."

"Cody, if you're not too overwhelmed with the China plan, could you get together with Grant and throw in your two cents, too?"

"Sure, Gordy. I've already got a couple of ideas."

"Good, good. Okay.

"Anything else I need to know right now?"

Silence.

"Okay, gang. Thank you all. Keep me posted. And mea culpa for my outburst earlier; I've usually got that stuff in better control.

"Emily, if anyone here wants a DVD, let 'em have one."

"Will do, Gordy."

"Gentlemen, ma'am, I'll show you out."

Once they left, Donne ran his fingers through his thinning fringe, rubbed his face and leaned back in his chair, breathing deeply for a good five minutes, his eyes closed, his body, other than his chest and diaphragm, absolutely still.

About noon, after his televised speech, which both consoled and fired up the American public, he finally found an hour to catch up on his lost sleep. Rejuvenated, he dug back into the papers in his inbox, finding fewer to be denied than to be approved, and fewer of both.

-113-

Saturday, May 12, 2012
8:13 a.m.
Bonita Beach, Florida

"I hope they're all right. It's been at least a week."

"I'm sure they are, Pam. Probably just took a cruise or something, maybe visiting their parents."

"It's odd. I was so suspicious of 'em and now I sorta miss 'em."

"They sure boosted the EC to AEP ratio on the beach."

"The what?"

"EC to AEP ratio. Eye candy to antique elephant parade. They're nowhere near as cute as you are gorgeous, but you gotta admit, they're definitely eye candy."

"God, I haven't heard that in years."

"Well, you know, Pam, I'm no spring chicken. I'm so old, I don't even remember what hormones ..." Jake paused.

"Are? Do?"

"... sound like."

Pam puzzled a moment and then laughed. "Oh, good one. I'll give you a refresher on those later."

"Oh, I'd like that."

"So would I."

"And I'm just figuring out that YOLO thing."

"Oh, You Only Live Once, you mean?"

"Right. Sorta like a redneck's last words, but for the kids."

"Redneck's last words?"

"Yeah. 'Hold my beer and watch this.'"

"You're in rare form this morning."

"That's what she said."

"She was me, and that was about an hour ago."

"Well, the rare form seems to be ongoing. You, my love, have a lasting effect on me."

"Why, thank yuh, suh."

"Yes, indeedy, Belle."

"Okay. Ready to get back to the book?"

"I guess so. My brain is running weird today, though."

"So what else is new?"

"Why, thank yuh, ma'am."

"Okay, Tex."

"All right. What do you have now?"

319

"Well, I think we need to set a cutoff date for the beach and the political story, 'cause that just keeps going on and on."

"Well, with Donne, most of that political shit doesn't happen, like the primaries and both parties playing chicken, and all the talking heads and books coming out on both sides, just criticizing the other team."

"I know, I know. But I mean, do you want to get this actually out at some point? If you do, we've – I mean you've got to decide when to cut it off."

"But things keep coming up, like those bombs over in Miami and up in New York last Sunday."

"God, those were horrible."

"I'd like to figure a way to get those in somehow."

"That may be too close, too emotional."

"But on beaches? That's outrageous."

"I know, I know. But we – I mean you do need to come up with a cutoff date, a deadline, if you ever want to get this thing out."

"Well, how about right after the Olympics ... or maybe after the conventions?"

"The Dems and Pubs, you mean?"

"Yeah. I mean, I've done most of the natural disasters that have come up since December, and Donne's handled those as best he could, and now it's looking like there's gonna be a drought this summer, from what I've seen on the news.

"And then there's all that foreign stuff, like with Israel and Iran, Syria, Afghanistan, Iraq and on and on."

"Sure you want to keep all that stuff in?"

"You know, I'm not. I'm still rolling back and forth between the two stories, the fiction of Donne and the reality of us and the beach and current events. It's tricky, for me, at least."

"You know, as I bounce back and forth, I've gotten used to the two timelines; I think you could probably do away with the 'Six Months Earlier' and that kind of stuff. I'd think readers should be able to follow those time shifts pretty easily by now."

"Hmm; maybe I could get rid of those – no, I'll leave them in for the first parts, then drop 'em. How's that?"

"Works for me.

"On the natural disasters, I think you showed how he does stuff with the tornadoes in Kentucky and Indiana in ... what ... March?"

"I think so, but I don't remember how I --"

"I think it was just a question in a press conference. I think."

"Oh, right, right. Yeah, that was it. I guess I'm just more focused on the economic stuff with Donne, trying to figure out how that all works out over time."

"And the assassination plots."

"Of course. And I'm getting a little more scared, I guess; still a few more death threats in my inbox. I think you were right; I was way too loose in giving out the link."

"Well, that's blood under the bridge, Jake. We'll deal with those like we did with that first batch last fall."

"Okay. So where are we now?"

"Well, I have some news. My ex-boss was one of the agents fired over that hooker scandal in Colombia last month."

"Really? Raunchy Randy?"

"You remember his nickname?"

"Kinda stuck in my head. So how do you feel about that?"

"Deserved what he got. 'Nuff said."

"I think I put something in about him somewhere, maybe ... oh, right. It's in the bit after the currency announcement, when Donne talks with you – I mean you as the Secret Service director."

"Have I seen that? I don't remember it."

"Uh ... not yet. Still got some cleaning up to do."

"Okay. I'll look forward to seeing it. I hope you made me – I mean her ugly."

"Well, sort of; I think I just dropped a hint or two, nothing major."

"Speaking of ugly, I'd love it if you could put something in about the primaries; those are sure getting nasty."

"Oh, just wait till the general after the conventions. I'll bet ugly and nasty won't begin to describe that one."

"The one in '10 was pretty bad ... and '08 was awful."

"Oh, yeah. And you were on the inside for that."

"Yup, both Bush and Obama. I wish I could tell you about all the crap that went on in there with both of 'em."

"Oh, yeah; I'd love to hear about that. But I understand."

"But with no more elections under Donne, no more primaries, either."

"Right; he's non-partisan."

"Oh, I think he's beyond that, far beyond it. He's anti-partisan."

"Oh, nice word."

"Lots more accurate that either non- or bi-."

"Oh, I did like how you slipped that stuff in about the GSA's 800 thousand dollars wasted in Vegas."

"That's exactly the kind of stuff that pisses Donne off ... and me and most taxpayers, too."

"Me, too. Gave every federal employee a black eye."

"And gave every taxpayer an emptier wallet."

"So true."

"And then that whole thing with that retailer allegedly bribing officials in Mexico to expand down there. And those corrupt idiots in Congress are making all kinds of self-righteous, pious BS over that. Geez."

"I've got a note about that here. And then there's that order to install handicap lifts at every public swimming pool in the country."

"Right; I saw that. Wasn't there one hotel that had installed one eight years ago and used it fifteen times … or was it fifteen years ago and used it eight times? One of the two. And now they want to make every public pool install one. More regulatory stupidity.

"Takes me back to the Gulf oil spill, when the regulators kept the skimmers from doing <u>anything</u> because they couldn't meet the 99 percent pure water output standard. I mean, if they managed to get rid of 75 or 80 percent, that's better than doing nothing. Idiots. Just made it worse.

"I swear, the more research I do, the angrier I get. It all just gets more and more corrupt; it's ubiquitous. And that's just the stuff I can find as a plain ol' citizen and taxpayer."

"Easy, Jake. Your blood pressure's going up."

"Yeah; it might be even up to normal. Damn."

"Let's get into the water for a while."

"Good idea; that'll help."

As they headed into the Gulf, with only a quick yelp, Pam said, "Nice that the water's up to 82."

"Noodleable at last. A long winter."

Pam surveyed the shoreline. "It's a lot quieter now, too, isn't it?"

"Yup. May and September, the quietest months. In fact, Deb closes her hot dog stand for all of September, waiting for the Return of the Snowbirds." He made that last bit sound like a movie title.

"They say tourists and snowbirds are like women; can't live with 'em, can't live without 'em."

"That's not you, Pam; that's for sure. You are the most patient, tolerant, thoughtful and smartest woman I've ever known."

"You left out sexy, Sexy."

"Oh, with you, Pam, that's a given. It's like saying, 'Oh, there's air in the atmosphere.'"

"Why, suh, y'all say the nahcest thangs."

"Geez, Belle, that thar had a bit of a Texas twang at th' end."

"Guess I'm picking up more and more stuff from you, Tex."

"And I from you, m'dear."

Justin leaned over to Lindsay and whispered, "I think we got some good stuff in there."

Lindsay whispered back, "Oh, yeah. The client should be very happy with that."

"But what's with the Belle and Tex stuff?"

Sharon's rasp came over their earbuds, "They're falling in love, kids. Geez. Can't you tell? That's when the nicknames start."

"But we've been together for a dozen years and we don't have nicknames," Lindsay whined.

"Then you're not really in love yet. Work it out. But not now; keep your eyes and ears open."

Friday, January 3, 2013
8:30 p.m.
The Oval Office
The White House
via a 24-hour news channel

Gordon Donne, dressed in his usual casual clothing, his fringe of hair a bit thinner and grayer, his face paler, smiled into the camera.

"Good evening, my fellow Americans, and Happy New Year.

"It's been a little over a year since I've been doing my best to serve you and this country. In my mind, it's been a pretty good year, and it seems we're well on our way to full recovery. Tonight, I can only give you a brief overview, but I know everyone watching has seen what has been going on for themselves, and you'll all have your own experience to rely on much more than whatever I tell you.

"First, of course, I want to talk about the economy. Last year, 2012, working together, we got the unemployment rate down to 6.7 percent, as we heard this morning, and put more than six million people back to work and paying taxes. We don't have the final GDP numbers yet, but based on the first three quarters' reports and an educated guesstimate on the fourth, it's looking like we'll be coming in at just over three and a half percent growth for the year, pretty much in line with my expectations and a good first-year start on getting to my goal of ten percent annual growth within eight years. Congratulations!

"Now, I want to warn everyone that what I am about to say is not at all in my usual character. But to the one economist who had the low line on that spaghetti chart I showed you all a year ago, the one that started with the Gulf Coast and hurricanes and morphed into an economic projection graph, to you, Paul, I just have to go out on a limb and say, 'Nah-nah-nah-nah-naah-nah.' Sorry, gang; I just had to do that, couldn't resist.

"But, seriously, folks, I'm quite pleased with how well you all have been doing with the taxes and rules the way I set them up a year ago.

"Now, I know we've had our share of tragedies and disasters this past year, like the tornadoes in Kentucky and Indiana, the drought in the Midwest, the May 6th bombings in Miami and New York, Tropical Storm Debby, Hurricanes Isaac and Valerie, not to mention all the problems at our Mideast embassies on September 11th and after that.

"I know the government's responses to the natural disasters could never have been sufficient; we're just not that good at fighting Mother Nature. But I believe that the actions we took, in conjunction with the private sector, alleviated much of the damage and pain those events caused. We can never resurrect the dead, but we can honor them as we live our lives to the highest and best levels we can. And those injured in the bombings and the hurricanes all seem to be well on their way to recovery, again with the help of mostly the private sector.

"I'm pleased to report that the European Union has joined the US in fixing its currency to oil and thus fixed to ours. So have Britain and Switzerland. Too bad, forex traders. China, of course, has continued to manipulate its currency, but I have a feeling that they'll soon learn the error of their ways on that front. I'm also pleased to report ... well, probably more just remind you ... that the price of gasoline here has stabilized at about $2.25 a gallon. And I'll also tell you that once certain goals I have set are met, we will be reducing and ultimately totally eliminating the federal gasoline tax, which should drop that down to closer to, maybe even below, two bucks a gallon.

"I'm also pleased to report that millions of our citizens, mostly seniors, have invested over 800 billion dollars in the USA Sovereign Wealth Fund, the proceeds of which have been invested in some infrastructure repair and new construction, private equity and other investments, using similar strategies to those I used at my hedge fund. Most of those investments are updated weekly on our web site, _____.gov; click on the "Sovereign Wealth Fund" link to get to that list. Less than 30 percent of our investors have chosen the annual withdrawal option, so we have more capital to invest over the long term and they will get the higher returns."

Donne pulled out a handkerchief and rubbed his shiny forehead, scalp, face and neck.

"As for worker-employer relations, now that the union bosses are no longer exploiting their members, for the most part, and employers have learned the wisdom of profit-sharing, we have a much greater level of cooperation, worker satisfaction and shared goals. We still have a long way to go on eradicating those bosses and their almost hypnotic hold on their members, but we are making progress there.

"On the Medicare and health insurance fronts, I'm also pleased with the responses to our new alternative programs. Millions of you have signed up, and I'm sure you'll be much happier with the results and your outcomes. And I'd like to give some credit to Sam and Eileen Kriatofskial of Sandwich, Illinois, and to Ron and Christine Florescuiello of Kanasaugua, Iowa, for their suggestion of adding a medical errors registry accessible by the public and a compensatory damages board to handle medical malpractice claims expeditiously and fairly, with no lawyers involved, with a few very limited exceptions.

"Speaking of lawyers, I'm also pleased to announce that tens of thousands of them have left the profession and gone into productive careers in the real world. And our courts' backlogs have been reduced by up to 90 percent in some civil sessions.

"On the criminal and law enforcement side, our prison population has been reduced with alternative sentencing for nonviolent offenders, and the deprivatization of federal prisons, which was completed in early October, has shown huge benefits, not only in higher wages for guards and administrative staff, but in an overall reduction of nearly 31 percent in our incarceration budget.

"The changes in court rules and the rules of evidence that went into effect last February have also expedited both civil and criminal trials, and the reduction of many grounds for appeal has reduced that long-abused lawyer-enrichment process, without damaging the rights of any parties, criminal or civil, plaintiff or defendant.

"I've also dismissed over 1.7 million frivolous lawsuits, with prejudice, and sanctioned the lawyers who filed them. Over 200,000 attorneys have also been penalized for egregious delaying tactics, overbilling or any of several other types of malfeasance. Nearly 50,000 of them have also been criminally prosecuted and/or had their law licenses permanently and involuntarily revoked.

"On the Al Capone tax, I will only say this. It has more than met my own expectations and far surpassed the expectations of even the most vocal supporters and surprised the hell out of its critics. Along with the improvement of the economy, it has contributed, I believe, to the 23 percent reduction in crime rates across the whole country. It has certainly helped us to cut down on Medicare, Medicaid and insurance fraud in general, and the drug cartels. We've got 'em on the run, folks.

"In terms of foreign affairs, possibly the decision that has caused the most controversy and backlash has been the one I made to drop out of and stop contributing financially to the United Nations, along with dropping out of the World Trade Organization and the World Court. The UN people are also pretty pissed off about my decision to start charging them rent on their building in New York. The confrontations and controversies have not been settled yet, but I'm standing firm on all of those decisions.

"Of course, my decision to sever diplomatic relations with and end foreign aid to the 47 countries I have done that with has come under constant criticism and threats. Again, I am standing firm on all those decisions. If any of those countries want to restore those relations, they each know what they have to do. As to the aid we've provided to them in the past, sorry, that won't happen again for decades, if ever. We've learned just how big a sucker this country's government has been in the past, and that wussiness and gullibility is gone, over, done with. Words to the wise. Got it?"

Donne pulled out the handkerchief and rubbed his head again.

"Domestically, my prioritizing of people and business over all the cutesy little animals that the anti-capitalists and anti-business folks have used as excuses for sabotaging our growth has shown what to me are great results. In over three hundred cases, I have given the tree-huggers and flower-fondlers thirty days each to relocate the tiny little spiders, owls, turtles, snails, bats and all the rest of their straws before the project they're protesting resumes, and in exactly two dozen of those, the protestors have complied and construction has continued. In all the rest, those enviro-wingnuts have sought other excuses to stop the projects, at least until they were exposed as the anti-business anarchists, saboteurs and radical anti-Americans they are, and I have incarcerated them or confiscated all of their and their organizations' assets ... NOT their liabilities, as is my policy. It does appear that most of them have learned their lesson, because we have only had to deal with 23 of those kinds of protests in the last four months.

"On a more local level, my directive ordering federal, state and local governments to eliminate all their rules, regulations, ordinances or any similar orders banning soap and/or shampoos from outdoor showers went into effect in October, and other than unscientific objections, primarily from uninformed petty bureaucrats and those same enviro-wingnuts, the public is unequivocally in support. Now, if someone can do some serious scientific studies ... NOT junk science, but real, unbiased studies that show some demonstrable negative consequences, I may ... and I emphasize MAY ... take those under advisement. But meanwhile, I trust our beaches will smell better.

"Along that line, during this past year, my staff and I have been going through all of the EPA's regulations and eliminating those that make no sense and/or have insufficient unbiased scientific evidence behind them. After a year, we're only about halfway through that morass, and we've completely eliminated 92 percent of what we've gotten to, and seriously loosened 92 percent of the other eight percent. We streamlined our process as we went along, and I'd bet we'll be done in less than another three months."

Donne pulled out his handkerchief and rubbed his entire head again, took a deep breath and continued.

"Meanwhile, of course, as I announced in my very first speech to you, all EPA enforcement actions have been suspended, and we will be going back through penalties that have been assessed over the past ten years and determining where refunds need to be made. Wait one. That may not have been in my speech, but it was in one of the first 25 directives I signed. Sorry; this has been a bit of an overwhelming year, and I do get confused from time to time.

"We've also suspended all enforcement actions under the ADA, FCC, OSHA, and a lot of other agencies too numerous to list here. Check those out on the web site. Same for the Endangered Species

Act, which has been so abused ever since it was enacted."

Donne pulled out his handkerchief and wiped his head again.

"As for education, we have received gots of lood feedback – I mean lots of good feedback from both schools and parents about our personal finance module, and we've added amother nodule – I mean another module for the fifth grade, and we will have moo tore for the neventh and sinth cades groming out --"

Donne gasped for breath, pulled his handkerchief out again, but then clutched at his throat, massaging it, gasped again, then once more choked, gasped again and collapsed facedown on the desk, a small trickle of blood dripping from his nose.

As Emily, three Secret Service agents and two of Donne's private guards ran into the shot, the screen went to black.

-115-

Saturday, June 30, 2012
11:22 a.m.
Bonita Beach, Florida

"Hey, Sharon. Take a look at this. I thought Pam was in France on a job."

"She is," Sharon rasped back. "Till Monday, I think she said."

"Well, isn't that her coming down the beach?"

"Can't see her yet, Justin. The building's in the way. Oh, wait – let me get the scope. Ah. Nope, not her, but it could be her twin."

"She's a knockout."

"Hey, Justin!"

"Well, she is, Lindsay. And look at how she walks."

"Flouncing, strutting ... whore."

"Cool it, you two. Eyes and ears open."

"Hey, Jake!"

"Wha- --JJ? Is that – how are you?"

"Just great. Still sexy as hell."

"That you are. Haven't seen you in ... what? ... two years?"

"Yup. Just here for a month again."

"Cool. Still doing the fundraising gig?"

"Oh, yeah. They can't get enough of me up there. I'm hitting up Fortune 500 CEOs now."

"Good for you. Where was that again? Raleigh?"

"Greenville."

"Oh, right; Greenville."

"Still going with that builder guy?"

"Nope; that's done, over a year now. I'm on the loose."

"I'll alert the media. 'All males now in imminent danger.'"

327

JJ dramatically unwound her beach wrap, revealing a tight, very well-proportioned figure in a stunning teeny-weeny green bikini, with gold rings on both sides of the bottom and another in the cleavage. She spun around and wiggled her butt, showing Jake a golden heart embroidered on the back.

"Like it?"

"Yeah. You know, I've heard of women wearing their hearts on their sleeves, but --"

"But not on their gorgeous asses, huh?" She wiggled it some more, glancing over her shoulder and giving Jake a winning smile.

"Oh, Christ," Lindsay whispered to Justin. "Who the hell does she think she is?"

"Now, now, Lin, back it down. We're just observing."

"Well, JJ, I have to admit, you've got one of the nicest butts this beach has seen in a while."

"You've always had great taste and discernment, Jake Devlin."

"That I have, JJ."

"So what's up with you? Did you ever get that book idea going?"

"Yeah, I did. I sent you the link, didn't I?"

"Yeah, but I only glanced at it."

"Well, I'm almost --"

"Lotsa sex in there, right?"

"Oh, not much; it's mostly political and some spy kinda stuff."

"Oh, pooh. You've got to put a lot of sex in. I could be a model for you, give you some pointers." She flounced closer to him, leaned down and gave him a big kiss on the mouth, ran her hand down his chest, then stood back up and pulled her sunglasses down and batted her dazzling blue eyes at him. "Or you could give me one."

Perflutzed but amused, Jake laughed. "Oh, JJ, you'll never change, will you?"

"Not in the slightest. I do love me and I do love life."

"Truer words were never spoken."

"So you gonna invite me to sit or am I gonna have to sashay around here in front of you for the whole damn day?"

"I'm sorry. Sure, plant your gorgeous ass anywhere you want."

JJ picked up the beach chair she'd dropped, flipped it open and slithered into it, threw her arms up in the air, sighed and exclaimed, "Ah, Bonita, I'm back. Feast your eyes!"

Jake laughed. Lindsay hissed, Justin stifled a chuckle and, behind the scope, Sharon rolled her eyes.

"You want me to take her out, don't you, Lindsay?"

"Oh, please do, Sharon, please do."

"Sorry, kid; you're on your own."

"I could claim she was a threat."

"Unless she's got a gun in that bag of hers, that won't fly. She sure doesn't have one in that suit. So just cool it and observe."

"Damn."

"So can I be in your book, Jake?"

"I think you already are, JJ. You're an Under-Secretary in the Treasury, in charge of --"

"No, Jake, no. I don't want to be under any secretary; it's got to be at least a vice-president, and he's got to be phenomenally rich and handsome and have a really, really, <u>really</u> big --"

"Okay; not an --"

"-- yacht."

"Okay; not an Under-Secretary. I'll make you a Deputy Secretary in Charge of Jewelry."

"Oooh, oooh, perfect! I love it. Jewelry! Count me in. And I'm really gorgeous and sexy, right? Lots and lots of sex with the President, maybe?"

"Nope, there is no President."

"What?"

"There is no President, no Congress, no Supreme Court. My guy fired 'em all and took over."

"Well, okay. I'll have lots of sex with him. Is he gorgeous?"

"Oh, not really; he's kind of a --"

"Well, shoot, Jake, y'gotta have a good-looking President."

"Sorry; he's not."

"So have you seen Laura? The cute girl from Houston you introduced me to? Retired from – oh, I forget."

"Court reporting. Y'know, I don't think so, not since then. Or maybe I've QH'd it."

"You've whatted it?"

"Oh, sorry; QH – Quarterheimered it, forgot."

"How about Joy?"

"Joy?"

"Cute, short blonde hair, maybe 30ish, mom named Betty."

"Oh, Joy. Right. Yeah, she's around, I think. Saw her maybe a couple weeks ago."

"We had such fun cruising around together, blowing guys' minds away."

"Just their minds?"

"Oh, Jake, you raunchy old coot."

"Sorry, couldn't help it. I know you too well."

"Well, it was mostly their minds. Joy and Laura were sorta chicken."

"Oh, you poor thing, stuck with a couple of wallflowers."

"I didn't say that, Jake. They were just <u>sorta</u> chicken. I got 'em outa their shells within three days, and they made great wingmen."

"Wingwomen, don't you mean?"

"Oh, Jakey, Jakey. Picky, picky, picky."

"Hey, JJ, you know I'm CDO."

"CDO?"

"Yeah, like OCD, but with the letters in the correct alphabetical order." He emphasized the last three words individually.

"What's OCD?"

"Oh, geez, JJ. Obsessive-compulsive disorder."

"Oh. Anyhow, we all had a great time. Wish I'd gotten their emails, coulda kept in touch."

"Ah, well. If wishes were --"

"So how's your love life?"

"Great."

"So you got a girlfriend?"

"A little more than that."

"What? You married?"

"No, no, just really close."

"Is she gorgeous?"

"Yup."

"More than me?"

"Different. I'd give you both a ten."

"Not a ten and a half?"

"Oh, it goes higher? Okay, sure."

"Smart?"

"Absolutely."

"Slutty?"

"Now, now, JJ --"

"Okay, okay. Sexy?"

"I'd have to give that a yes."

"More than me?"

"Different. But then, with you, I don't really know, do I?"

"Your loss."

"Ah, well."

"So where is she?"

"Ah ... Europe somewhere."

"What? Europe? Where?"

"I'm not sure today. She's traveling."

"Really? Without you? Oh, you poor dear. Maybe we --"

"Nah, she's working."

"Working? So what does she do?"

"Uh ... security consulting."

"Oh. So what else is new down here?"

"Not much; just the usual placid, calm retirees' paradise."

"It is calm, that's f'sure. Shuffleboard and golf. What was that you said, something about the average age?"

"Oh. Ah, 'Average age, average temperature, same number.'"

"Right, right." She laughed. "Hope I can remember that."

"Oh, I'm sure you can do whatever you set out to do, JJ."

"You are so right, Jakey.

"Oh, there's Mike. I'm gonna go toy with his emotions for a while. Nice to see you again, Jake. I'll be around. See ya. Hey, Mikey!!!"

"Have fun, JJ," Jake said aloud, and after she'd picked up her stuff and sashayed away, he said to himself, "Good luck, Mike," and then, "Whew."

He took several deep breaths, picked up his non-spiral notebook and wrote, "JJ back -- how to use her ?? Laura and --" he rubbed his temple with his pen -- "Joy?" Then he picked up his noodles and foot-washing bag, tucked the bag in his waistband and headed for the water.

Norm and Janet, on their own noodles in the water and full of curiosity, watched Jake approach and noodled over to intercept and interrogate him.

Lindsay raged silently as Justin's eyes followed JJ's swaying, flouncing, gorgeous bottom, and Sharon said, only to herself, not over the earbuds, "Well, Jake, you made it through that one. Bravo."

-116-

Friday, March 8, 2013
11:30 a.m.
The White House
Washington, DC
via a 24-hour news channel

Gordon Donne, his fringe of hair a good deal thinner and grayer and his gaunt face the grimmest that the nation had yet seen, but still dressed in his casual clothes, glared at the camera from behind his desk in the Oval Office.

"My fellow citizens, I am now fully recovered and rejuvenated after the collapse from exhaustion that you witnessed in January, and I'm fully capable of continuing to serve the people of the United States to the best of my ability.

"Today, I have an extremely serious announcement to make.

"As you may have heard on the news, this morning, at about one a.m. Eastern time, the People's Republic of China, without provocation, began an air assault and ground invasion of India. I have been in communication with both parties and have expressed the United States' outrage at China's behavior and have assured the Prime Minister of India that, up to and including active military involvement, the United States will stand with his country, our ally.

"Therefore, I have issued several new directives, for immediate implementation. We will have these on the web site _____.gov within half an hour, so everyone can study them.

"For a brief overview, I have immediately imposed an embargo on the importation of any goods or materials into this country that come, directly or indirectly, from China. Ships currently in our harbors, regardless of their country of registration, that contain or have unloaded anything of Chinese origin are immediately sequestered, and no Chinese goods will be allowed into this country. Any ships with manifests showing Chinese goods will not be allowed to dock.

"Second, all Chinese holdings of US Treasury bonds, notes or bills are hereby sequestered and may not be traded or redeemed, and all interest payments on those instruments have been halted. We have not made a decision as of yet ... and I emphasize 'yet' ... as to whether we will declare those instruments null and void, worthless; that decision will be made after we have evaluated China's response to our diplomatic efforts. We do have all of the CUSIPs of those instruments, and any attempt by the Chinese government to move, transfer, sell or liquidate any of them in any way will result in my declaring those particular instruments worthless.

"Third, I have ordered CentPac to bolster our naval and air force presence in the South China Sea and surrounding areas, without reducing our readiness in the rest of the Pacific.

"Fourth, using our naval and air force presence, I here and now declare a complete embargo on all goods and materials, including oil, from whatever source, going into China.

"Fifth, I have, effective immediately, frozen all Chinese assets, of whatever nature, in the United States or its possessions.

"Sixth, an immediate evacuation of all American citizens within China is ordered, including embassy personnel, who will remain until all civilian citizens have been safely evacuated.

"Seventh, all financial transactions of any form between China and any other party are hereby frozen, including electronic, cash or any other store of value.

"Eighth, anyone traveling on a Chinese passport is hereby placed on our No-Fly list and is subject to refusal of entry at our borders.

"Ninth, any ... and I emphasize 'any' ... actions by China against citizens or any interests of the United States will be considered an act of war against this country and will be dealt with swiftly and with overwhelming force, strategically and carefully targeted.

"I have summoned the Chinese ambassador to the White House this afternoon and will be laying all of this out in great detail face-to-face in this no-BS, no-ego zone. I will be watching his responses very carefully and using those to inform any additional decisions I make.

"With that, I wish all of you watching this as good a day as you can possibly have."

Once the camera was off, Donne got up from his desk and shambled over to the assembled men and women at and around the couches in the center of the room. He pulled a chair up to them and awkwardly seated himself in it.

"First, Cody, I know this came on unexpectedly and sooner than we had anticipated, but have you looked into more of the unintended consequences of these decisions?"

"Yes, I have, but still not all. I will have a full spreadsheet for you by this afternoon, including an analysis of the Chinese ambassador's probable responses, to help inform your discussion with him."

"Good, good, Cody.

"Cissy? Hubris?"

"No problems, Gordy. Strong, straightforward and clear. Use of 'I' and 'we' was perfectly balanced."

"Thanks, Cissy.

"Eileen? State?"

"We've been getting lots of cables from our ambassadors all around the world, asking for guidance and giving us reports on local reactions to China's aggression. After what you just told the world, I think they'll all have the guidance they wanted, but I'll deal with the ones that are still concerned or need clarification."

"Good, good. Tell them all to be sure to stand strong, stay the course; it's going to get very rocky for a good time. If you need any further info or guidance from me, feel free to ask for it. Rosemary will be happy to help. Good.

"Grant? CIA?"

"Our operatives have been and will be reporting as close to real time as they can, and we'll be collating and passing the info along as quickly as we can, as well. This is going to get very hairy very quickly. It's looking like Pakistan and the whole Arab world is going to come into the fray soon, and India may or may not be able to fend them all off."

"Good, good, Grant. Keep me posted.

"Lee, Defense?"

"CentPac has begun moving much of the Pacific fleet into the South China Sea, and we have gone from DEFCON 5 to DEFCON 3. Do you want the details on the ship movements?"

"No need, Lee. I just need the macro view for now. If we go to DEFCON 2, then we can get more granular."

"Okay, Gordy."

"Good, good. Anything else, gang?"

"I think we're all set," Eileen said.

"CIA is okay," from Grant.

"Ready," said the SecDef.

"Good, good. Everybody, stay alert and keep me posted. I've got your live feeds coming in and I'll stay on top of this. Thank you all."

When everyone had left, Rosemary, his new chief of staff, hurried over to Donne and helped him out of the chair and to one of the couches, where he lay down, coughing and wheezing.

"Thanks, Ro. Could you grab my tablet off the desk, please? I need to see those feeds. And a soda, too."

"Sure, Gordy."

She brought the tablet and positioned it on the coffee table so that he could see it and handed him the can of soda.

"Thanks, Ro." He took a long, big gulp from the can, set it on the table, sighed deeply, lay back and closed his eyes. "Ahhh, much better."

"I know this is a bad time, Gor, but you need to get some rest. It's been over two days."

"I know, Ro, I know, but I can't afford it now."

She put her hand on his forehead and said, "You're burning up, Gordy. I don't think it's all out of your system yet."

"It's been two months, Ro; it should be all gone by now, shouldn't it?"

"She screwed up the dosage, so there was more to start with."

"Yeah, you're right; maybe there is some still running around in there." He patted his stomach, winced and then coughed. "Oops."

"Still painful?"

"Yeah. But it's getting better."

"I'll be right back."

"Okay."

She left for a moment and returned with a damp washcloth, which she gently placed across his forehead and scalp.

"Oh, that's good, Ro. Thank you."

"I don't know why you didn't just stick her in a cold, dark cell somewhere."

"She meant well, in her own mind."

"I hope she doesn't go after Wes."

"No; he'll be fine. She's got no reason to go after him."

"He actually likes that stuff?"

"Yeah. No accounting for taste."

"I've never tasted it."

"Neither have I, even though I've eaten it ... twice."

Rosemary chuckled.

"Sorry; that was kind of a tasteless joke."

Rosemary's chuckle turned into a laugh.

"I am worried about you, Gor."

"It'll work its way through, Ro, really."

"She's doing okay back at DEI?"

"That's what Wes tells me. She's in the nutritional R&D division, probably be taking the helm of it in a couple of years."

"Happy as a vegan on a bean farm, I hear."

"Or as a – ah, crap; I got nothing. You win that round, Ro."

They both chuckled. He dug a new hundred-dollar bill out of his shirt pocket and gave it to her.

"I thank you very much, Gordy."

"No problem at all, Ro."

"I know."

Then the red phone rang.

-117-
Six Months Earlier

Tuesday, July 2, 2012
12:27 p.m.
Bonita Beach, Florida

"So she poisoned him? That seems pretty extreme."

"Right. But she just wanted to scare him a little, get him to think his diet was a problem, so he'd start eating healthier."

"Don't you mean healthilier? Or maybe healthierly?"

"God, you do have a photographic memory, Pam."

"Just part of the package, Jake."

"A package I do love."

"Me, too – I mean same backatcha."

"Geez, you almost sounded like JJ there for a second."

"She sounds like a character. I'm looking forward to meeting her."

"Well, it should be soon; she said she'd be here this afternoon."

"Except for the rhythm, that was maybe a B poem."

"What?"

"You rhymed."

"I did? Didn't mean to."

"You do that sometimes."

"If you say so."

"Anyhow, so that takes care of Emily. What about Lindsey's interview? Did that get aired?"

"Yeah, but I'm sure not gonna try to write that whole thing and expect people to read it. I'll just do a lookback on that somewhere."

"Okay; that makes sense."

"What do you think about the China war, Pam?"

"Depends how granular you want to get with that. I mean, that could be a whole book on its own. I think macro is probably better on that."

"Like another lookback?"

"That's how I'd do it. Like you did with the hurricanes."

"Oh, right; what were – oh, right. Isaac and Valerie. Yeah, I could do it that way, like stick it in his next State of the Country speech."

"Right, like just a quick comment. But how'd you come up with the names Isaac and Valerie?"

"Looked at the list of 2012 names, and after Debby, last month, I just sorta looked at the calendar and figured maybe we'd get to Isaac by late August and Valerie maybe late October. Didn't want to pin them down to dates or anything, just general, that they happened."

"Oh. And have you decided how the China war went?"

"Not yet; still hmming on that."

"Ah."

"Heads up, Sharon," Justin whispered.

"The bitch is coming," Lindsay added.

"I'm ready, kids," Sharon rasped.

"Jake Devlin, you sonofabitch!" a strident female voice yelled.

"Your wish is about to come true, Pam," Jake sotto voced, as Pam turned in her chair to see her almost-twin, wearing a bright red bikini, striding angrily from the boardwalk toward her and Jake. No flouncing was visible; neither was any sashaying, wiggling or swiveling.

"Shoot her, Sharon, shoot her," Lindsay hissed.

"Not yet, kid. Chill out," Sharon rasped back.

"You're gonna tax nonprofits? What the fuck is that?"

"Hi, JJ. Pam, this is JJ. JJ, Pam."

"Nice to meet you, JJ."

"Hi. So what's this with taxing my charity?"

"Hey, JJ, it's just fiction."

"I don't care. People might actually read it and get an idea."

"Who knows? But look, the charitable tax credit should offset that."

"The what?"

"Oh, you missed that? He sets up a 50 percent tax credit for charitable contributions."

"I did miss that. I got bored with all his numbers and shit, just skimmed the rest. But that nonprofits tax caught my eye."

"Go back and find that; I think you'll see it should balance out. And if it were real, it would also give you another selling point for the CEOs."

"But --"

"Go back and read it," Jake said more sharply (sharplier?). "But for now, give my girlfriend here a nicer hello, okay?"

Deflated, but only slightly, JJ looked at Pam and said, "Sorry. Hello. What was your name again?"

"Pamela."

"Hi, Pamela," she said, holding out her hand. Pam shook it, all the while examining JJ closely from behind her sunglasses.

"But you can call me Pam."

"Okay. Pam."

"You know, JJ, you're just about as pretty as Jake said you were."

JJ immediately perked up. "You think so? Thank you ... Pam."

"From up here, I can hardly tell them apart," Sharon said.

"Two knockouts," Justin whispered. Lindsay fumed.

"Looks like you don't have to do much work to stay that way, right, JJ?"

"Ah, a little here and there, just touchup," JJ said, running her fingers through her long blonde tresses.

"So, Pam, how do you know my old buddy, Jake?"

"Long story, JJ, but we met about a year ago."

"Is he any good in bed?"

"Hey, if you two are just gonna do girl talk, I'll leave you to it."

"No, no, no, Jake. Stick around; this'll be fun," Pam said, reaching out to pat his shin.

"So, JJ, how do you know Jake?"

"Oh, I was down here a couple summers ago, setting up a fashion show for my charity, and I just bumped into him here."

"Your charity? Do you own it?"

"Oh, no; it's a big nationwide thing; I'm a senior fundraiser, hitting on CEOs of big, really big companies."

"I'd bet you're good at it."

"Phenomenal, actually. I raised over 28 million last year, 18 so far this year, on my way to 40."

"Wow. That's impressive."

"Oh, yeah; I'm the top producer. They love me."

"Salary or commission?"

"Both."

"Cool. Not a bad way to earn a living."

"I love it. I get to meet some of the most interesting men."

"And rich, too, I'd bet."

"Of course; they're CEOs."

Pam smiled at Jake and said, "Are they any good in bed?"

"Some of them – oh, I shouldn't say, should I?"

"Not unless you want 'em in Jake's book."

JJ looked at Jake, "You wouldn't, would you?"

Jake smiled. "You might want to keep some stuff to yourself, JJ." He reached into his cooler, got his water bottle and took a long swig.

"So what did you do before the fundraising gig?" Pam asked.

"Dancer."

"Really? What type? Exotic?"

"No, no, no. Flamenco."

"Really?"

"Really. Twelve years; I was terrific, made a ton of money."

"Cool. Ever had a *ménage à trois*?"

Jake spat some water out, then spluttered, "Pam!"

Justin gasped, Lindsay fumed. Sharon rasped, "Uh-oh; I may need more cameras." Norm and Janet's ears perked up.

"Gee, I – oh, I'd better keep that to myself," JJ said, glancing at Jake.

"Ah, well," Pam said, giving Jake a quick, hidden smirk. "Nothing ventured, nothing gained.

"So, JJ, you travel a lot?"

"Oh, yeah. All over the country, all the time."

"Europe?"

"Nope, never been."

"Mexico, Latin America?"

"Nope."

"Canada?"

"Once, nine, ten years ago."

"What part of Canada?"

"Montreal."

"Did you like it there?"

"It was great. I was putting on a charity fashion show up there for a sister charity."

"Get to see much of the city?"

"Not really; I was stuck in the hotel most of the time."

"Too bad; it's a great city."

"Oh."

"So you've never had a three-way?"

"Just twi- – oh." She looked at Jake. "Oops."

"Two guys or two girls?"

"Gir- – oh, oops."

"Oh, goodie." Pam smiled at Jake.

Sharon rasped, "Definitely wish I had more cameras." Justin, now breathing heavily, looked at Lindsay, whose scowl threatened to freeze permanently. Norm and Janet were now only pretending to work on their puzzles.

"What d'ya think, Jake?" Pam asked. "Want to give it a try? We're nearly twins, after all."

JJ interrupted, "I don't know, Pam; I'm not sure I --"

"Oh, c'mon, JJ. You know you --"

"Okay, give it up, girls. You almost had me there, but no gotcha. Good try, though."

Stunned to the point of perflutzity, Pam and JJ could only stare at Jake. Jake grinned at them both.

"Ah, shit," Sharon rasped.

Justin, "Damn."

Lindsay stared at Justin and hissed, "Pig."

Norm and Janet leaned further towards the trio.

"Of course, if you two really want to --"

"Heads up, Sharon. This guy looks a little hinky," Justin said.

"Which guy?" Sharon asked. "Oh, shit!"

Pam finally said, "What gave it away?"

"Well, first, you both have the same --"

JJ and Pam simultaneously yelled, "Gun!!!!!!"

Jake saw it out of the corner of his eye, snapped his leg up and kicked the gunman's right wrist, then grabbed his left hand in a *kote gaeshi* wrist lock, while JJ reached out and pulled the gun from his right hand just after he pulled the trigger, the bullet flying into the air and ultimately landing harmlessly in the bay behind the guardhouse at the entrance to the Collier parking lot; it was found three years later embedded in the shell of a sea turtle caught near Marco Island.

The gunman screamed as Jake put more pressure on his wrist and fingers, forcing him to his knees and then onto his face in the sand, where Jake sat on his back while Pam got some flex-ties from her bag and tied him with those, and JJ expertly added another set around his ankles.

"Nice move, Jake," Pam said.

"Pizza cake," Jake replied, breathing heavily.

Justin said, "Did you get that, Sharon?"

"Yup," Sharon replied. "Seen and recorded. But shit; we were too slow."

"Luckily, they were fast enough," he replied.

"All three of them," Sharon said. "Hmm."

The man on the PVC lounge, having seen the whole event unfold, pulled his right hand out from under his lounge, scratched his right temple and then went back to reading Pirandello's "Enrico IV."

Pam took out her cell phone and dialed 911. Within minutes, Sergeant Dooley and six deputies arrived and, after ascertaining what had happened, took the gunman into custody, applied first aid to his broken left fingers and right wrist, and whisked him away in a cruiser.

After taking statements from Pam, JJ, Jake and many other people on the beach, as well as reviewing six cell phone videos, a charge of attempted murder was filed against the gunman, who, further investigation revealed, was a pro-life fanatic with a lengthy criminal record, mostly assault and battery, as well as a history of bipolar disorder, who was enraged that Devlin had written that Donne had legalized abortion. He'd heard about Jake's web site from a girlfriend who'd gotten the link directly from Jake the previous year. He pled guilty and was sentenced to 25 years to life. Two months into his sentence, he died after being shanked by a pro-choice nutjob in the prison laundry.

At three o'clock, after they had given their statements, Jake looked at Pam and JJ, smiled broadly and said, "Now, about that three-way ..."

Friday, January 2, 2015
8:30 p.m.
The Oval Office
The White House
via a 24-hour news channel

Gordon Donne, dressed in his usual casual clothing, his fringe of hair a good deal thinner and grayer, smiled into the camera. His complexion and demeanor gave a picture of general good health.

"Good evening, my fellow Americans, and Happy New Year.

"It's been a little over three years now that I've been working for y'all, and I have some generally good news to report.

"First, as usual, on the economy, I'm pleased to tell you that GDP grew at about 5.5 percent last year; I say "about," because the final figures aren't in as yet, but the first three quarters grew at that rate or better, and the fourth quarter, even without China in the global economy, should have come in at or above that average.

"So, since that met my goal of five percent growth a year ahead of my projection, I'm reducing income tax brackets for individuals by one percent for this year, 2015. New withholding software for all platforms is available on our web site, _____.gov, and we urge all employers to download and install that as quickly as possible.

"I've also eliminated the partisan surcharges, again for this year and all future years, and I've cut the minimum tax in half, from $720 a year to $360.

"The country reached a record revenue of 4.3 trillion dollars last year, and our budget for this year is only 3.1 trillion, down to 17 percent of GDP, so we've started paying down our debt. It's down to 15.3 trillion dollars, and it's looking like we'll have it down to ten trillion in another three years or sooner. When we get there, I'll consider another tax cut for individuals.

"For businesses, the rates will stay the same, and we've found that the US is turning into a tax haven of its own, simply because we no longer have the highest business tax rates in the world; we have close to the lowest. We have found that tax avoidance and evasion by businesses has gone way down from 2011 and before, and CEOs tell me again and again that this country is the best place in the world to locate and do business.

"The unemployment rate, as you all heard this morning, is now down to 5.9 percent, and we added over nine million jobs last year. So we're making good progress on that front.

"Our Sovereign Wealth Fund now has over two trillion dollars under management and has made an 18.3 percent return over the last

340

two years. That fund has financed thousands of infrastructure repair and construction projects, mostly roads and bridges, and since fewer than 15 percent of our investors have chosen the annual payout option, we've still got lots of capital to invest. I'd give that a grade of about a B plus; it's good, but it can do better.

"The Medicare, Medicaid and Social Security fixes we put in place in 2012 have made all of those programs solvent through 2085, so I'm very pleased there. And the Al Capone tax has rendered fraud in all of those virtually nonexistent. We continue our vigilant monitoring, of course.

"The environment continues to be healthy, and the regulatory agencies that still exist are efficient, non-invasive and cooperative with the 92 percent of businesses that still maintain their A rating, and tough, micromanaging and invasive with the eight percent with the dreaded B rating, which they keep for a minimum of two years from when they receive it. 3,012 businesses have gotten their A back.

"On the energy front, we have achieved 85 percent independence, with nuclear now generating most of our electrical energy needs, along with coal, natural gas and a minimal contribution from solar and wind farms, and a tiny bit from bioenergy sources.

"As you all probably know, nearly every country has joined us in fixing their currencies to oil, and here in the US, after we eliminated the federal tax on gasoline, that price is down to under two bucks a gallon, and our refining companies and the oil companies themselves are still showing record profits and distributing them in dividends.

"On the education front, the high school dropout rate nationwide is down to six percent, with pockets here and there where it is higher. But by giving school districts greater flexibility to address their local issues, and not just throwing money at them, I expect those pockets to bring their dropout rate down to or below the national average. We are now actually graduating high schoolers who know how to read, write and plan their personal finances, and who are eager for higher education, be it college, trade school or one of the thousands of apprenticeship programs the private sector has implemented.

"As for defense, our military is the strongest, leanest and meanest in the world, but ever since the China-India-Arab war, in which we intervened with insurmountable power, we have only had to utilize it minimally.

"Our steadfast support of the right of Israel to exist and prosper, while criticized vehemently both here at home and in the Arab world, has ensured our Israeli friends' continued existence and cooperative contributions to the American economy, especially in technology.

"Obviously, our support of Israel before, during and after their coordinated attack on and complete decimation of Iran's nuclear facilities was instrumental in the regime change in that country. Of course, the new regime is no less hostile to this country, but they have given up their nuclear ambitions and know that we hold the leaders completely accountable for the actions of their people, especially after the China war, so they have been a good deal more docile than the previous leaders. I doubt we'll reopen diplomatic relations with them for several years, but if and when they come to the table with serious and verifiable options that align with American interests, we may ... and I emphasize may ... consider that.

"Of course, we maintain a strong presence on the homeland security front and have had no terrorist attacks since May of 2013, in the midst of the China war, and that was contained to one bomb in a sparsely populated area. I congratulate everyone in our intelligence community for their hard work and ongoing success.

"I'm going to end with that and let you all know that you can find more information about the state of the country on our web site, _____.gov.

"So I'll now simply wish you all a very happy and prosperous 2015 and say good night."

-119-

Monday, July 16, 2012
11:49 p.m.
Cyberspace

The Instigator reviewed his emails for the first time in several weeks, then checked the balance in the account, which was now exactly 190 million euros plus a relatively small amount of interest. He debated for a moment about perhaps instigating some more contracts, but finally decided against it, satisfied that nineteen contracts were plenty ... for now.

"Pizza cake," he said quietly. "I can run this all again in a year or two."

Smiling to himself, he turned off the PC, settled back in his recliner, sighed, stretched and finished off the last of his expensive wine, then rinsed the glass and headed up to bed, where he slept soundly, deeply and dreamlessly through the night, awakening refreshed and fully restored at a little past nine a.m. local time. He opened the shutters and looked out at the expansive, virtually limitless view from his windows.

"Ah, another gorgeous day. Hope the locals are enjoying it."

-120-

Friday, January 3, 2020
8:30 p.m.
The Oval Office
The White House
via a 24-hour news channel

Gordon Donne, dressed in his usual casual clothing, his fringe of hair even thinner and grayer, smiled into the camera. At age 60, he looked to be the picture of health for his age.

"Good evening, my fellow Americans, and Happy New Year.

"It's been a little over eight years now that I've been working for you, and, as usual, I have some good news to report.

"Tonight, I'm going to limit myself to the economy, and I'm very pleased to tell you that GDP grew at about 11.5 percent last year, beating my goal of ten percent within eight years; I say "about," because, as usual, the final figures aren't in as yet, but the first three quarters grew at that rate or better, and the fourth quarter will have come in at or above that rate.

"Our revenue hit 6.8 trillion dollars last year, and our budget for this year is only 3.3 trillion, down to 13 percent of GDP, so we're doing great on paying off our debt. It's down to 8.8 trillion dollars, and it's looking like we'll have it down to four trillion in another four years, possibly only three.

"Unemployment is now at 4.8 percent. I expect it to come down to an even four percent by the end of this first quarter of 2020, and back down to what we call the "full employment" level, just over three percent, by the end of this year. Below that, there's pressure that can lead to inflation above our acceptable rate of one percent per year, which we have maintained for the past five years.

"I'm going to end with that and let you all know that you can find more information about the state of the country on our web site, _____.gov.

"So I'll now simply wish you all a very happy and prosperous 2020. Good night, all."

Wednesday, September 12, 2012
11:49 a.m.
Bonita Beach, Florida

Pam nudged Jake's calf under the water and said, "Ready for some sun time, Jake?"

"Getting cold?" Sonya asked.

"Not at all; this is perfect. What's the water temp?"

"86, I heard," Jake said. "But I'm ready for some sun, too. See y'all."

He and Pam headed to shore, leaving Sonya, Ann Louise and a third woman, Sandy, continuing to bitch about the county's removal of the showers on the stairs leading up to the restrooms and its banning of soap and shampoo in the relocated ones. Phrases like "No public input, petty damned bureaucrats, user-unfriendly parks and rec department, no scientific tests after 18 years of soap use, fuckin' paranoid risk manager" and "Let's have a soap-in, a big one," echoed across the water.

Once settled in, Jake said, "Sorry about that, Pam. What was it you were saying before all that?"

"I forge- – oh, right. What do you think about Romney picking Ryan for VP?"

"Eh. But if I were writing that story, the team I'd put on that side would maybe be Gingrich and Jesse Ventura; that would make for some great debates. And Ventura would offset Gingrich's religiosity, at least a bit. That would be more fun than what's really coming."

"Already here."

"Oh, yeah. This is probably the worst, most vicious, negative campaign I've ever witnessed. And it's only gonna get worse."

"On both sides."

"Got that right, Pam. You know, with all that crap about Romney's tax returns, I'd think he should just say he'd be happy to release all of those if Obama would release all his college transcripts and records, even --"

"Oh, Jake, shhhhh! Don't even think about that, and for god's sake don't write anything about it."

"What? Why?"

"Red flags, angry bulls. That is NOT a rock you want to poke around under. Remember, I was there."

"Oh, right. Geez, is it that big a deal?"

"From what I overheard and the millions he and his supporters put into suppressing those, I'd say it sure is. Leave it alone."

"Okay. But it would be a good counter- --"

"No, Jake, please, not another word."

"Okay, okay. But I do like the idea of Gingrich and Ventura."

"That's fine; ain't gonna happen."

"Right; but it'd make for great debates. Substantive, not just 'He's a bastard,' 'No, he's a bastard,' on and on.

"Another big problem is that most of the voters are either emotionally locked in on one side or the other or totally ignorant of the real issues and are easily manipulated.

"You know, I read a study a couple days ago – this happened right after the conventions, mind you – where people were either shown photos of or given descriptions of several people and asked to identify them, and 92 percent could identify the lady singer who'd worn the meat dress, but only 8 percent could identify the Treasury Secretary. The Chairman of the Federal Reserve got 13 percent, and a bunch of sports figures I couldn't identify got between 43 and 64 percent.

"And nearly 40 percent couldn't even identify the governor of their own state, and that's with BOTH the photo and the description.

"These are the people who elect the leaders of the Free World. Geez."

"That's a pretty sad commentary on our culture, Jake."

"In a lot of ways, it's a pretty sad culture, isn't it?"

"I'm afraid you're right."

After a momentary pause, Jake said, "By the way, Pam, I made that up."

"Made what up?"

"The study."

"No."

"Gotcha."

Pam slapped Jake's shin, but lightly, said, "You sonofabitch," and then laughed. "Yes, you did; got me good with that one. But it was so believable."

"That's what I do. Remember my three-and-a-half-minute limit on being serious."

"Well, you lasted longer than that with those three bitching about the showers and the soap."

"My tongue was bleeding a lot through that. But then I don't use the showers all that much."

"I can tell."

"What?" Jake raised his arm and sniffed.

"Gotcha."

"That you did, you daughterofabitch." He laughed, but he sniffed again.

"Oh, Jake, I've got an idea for the name you asked me for."

"Sorry?"

"The name. What do you think about this? Bonnie Springs."

"Oh, your pen – hmm. Bonnie Springs? Let me – yeah, I like it."

"Oh, goodie."

"Let's use it. In fact, you've been so much help on this, I probably should really give you top billing."

"No, no, no, Jake; it's your work. I'd even like it better if you put it in parentheses or a smaller font or something."

"Really? Like ... oh, maybe 'with Bonnie Springs'?"

"Works for me."

"Hmm. Yeah, I like it. Okay."

"Cool. Deal."

"Done." Jake leaned forward and they shook hands, holding them a bit longer than normal, then finally lay back.

"You are one amazing woman, Pamela Brooks."

"I know. You have great taste and discernment, Jacob Devlin." She ran her fingers through her blonde tresses, smiling at Jake.

Jake, off-key, sang quietly, "Getting to know you, getting to know all about you ..." but then broke off and said, "Well, not all."

"But purdy neah all, Tex," Pam drawled.

"Workin' on it awl, Belle," Jake drawled back.

Justin whispered into his beach bag, "Hey, Sharon, nicknames again; bet they're getting ready for a condo visit."

Sharon's raspy voice came over his earbud. "No bet; nothin' better'n a nooner."

Justin leaned over and whispered in Lindsay's ear. "How about one for us sometime soon? Like next time it rains."

Lindsay whispered back. "Ain't gonna happen, you pig."

"I heard all that," Sharon said. "Eyes and ears open, kids."

"So when did you first figure it out about JJ?"

"When I saw the two of you together. But when I first met you, the very first time, I'm glad I had a cookie in my mouth; if I hadn't heard you say you were Pamela93, I would have blurted out, 'Hi, JJ.' You are very much alike. But that cookie gave me time to look more closely and pick out the differences. And I knew her real name was Judy."

"So, on the three-way?"

"I figured you were colluding and pulling my leg ... again. But it was fun."

"Oh, Jake, I don't pull your leg that much."

"Well, you --"

"But as for Stevie Bru- – oh, shit."

"What?"

"Ron."

"Hey, schlub, am I still dead and gay?"

"Yes, you are, asshole."

"Well, then no need for these cupcakes Jenny baked."

"Sorry, Ron. Still dead and gay ... and an asshole."

"But you're not a Tea Party Republican or a dwarf," Pam threw in.

"Oh, right. Okay. Here ya go. So am I gonna get a free copy of your book?"

"You're a Democrat, aren't you, Ron?"

"Yup."

"Thought so, and nope."

"Thank you, Jenny," Pam called over to her, smiling and giving her a "thank you" nod as Jake put the cupcakes in his cooler.

"Or do you want one now, Pam?"

"Naw, I'm fine. Maybe we can get a hot dog."

"Good ide- – oh, wait. Deb's not here; it's September."

"Oh, right. Ah, well. Then I guess I will have one."

"Okay." Jake got the cupcakes back out and Pam took one. Jake debated a moment, but then he too pulled one out. Ron went back and sat with his wife, sulking.

"Mmmmm. Oh, oh, ohhhhh. That's positively orgas- – oh, shit."

"What?"

"Behind you." Pam swallowed quickly and moved the cupcake to her left hand.

"What? Ron again?"

"Who the fuck is that?" Sharon's raspy voice asked over the twins' earbuds.

"Just a homeless bum," Justin said. "Scraggly beard, dirty clothes, probably drunk, stumbling and stagg- --"

"Heads up, kids. Something hinky about him."

"Be cool, Jake. This is gonna be troublesome."

"I'm cool."

"What the hell are you doing here, Randy?"

Obviously drunk, slurring his words, the man spat out, "You bitch, you bitch! You ruined my fuckin' life! And now you're sitting here with this fuckin' trainer – traitor. What the fuck? What the --"

"Randy, you're drunk, and I didn't ruin your life. You did. It was your op that --"

"And you, you fuck," Randy slurred, turning to face Jake, "you're the cause of this all. You bastard. You fuckin' her?"

"I don't think that's any of your --"

"Don't you say a word, you fuck. I'm --"

"Gun!!" Pam yelled.

The poetic way to describe what happened next would be to say that Randy's head simply exploded in a red mist, but that would in no way do justice to the absolutely gruesome reality of what happened when a .50-caliber bullet entered Randy's head right at his hairline, with a downward trajectory, just as four .45s hit his chest from in front of him and two .44s struck his gun hand and then his temple from his left, all within two seconds.

Yes, his head did explode, but with the impact of bullets of those calibers, bits of skin, hair and skull flew back, sideways and even a bit forward, while his eyeballs fell intact, one on the sand and one in the Gulf, both of which were immediately spirited away and swallowed by two scavenging seagulls.

His brain also spattered over the sand and water, mixed with his flesh, bone and blood; seventeen migrating bull sharks over a mile offshore detected the scent and started their journeys to the source.

Randy's gun hand disintegrated, adding more blood, flesh and bone to the mix on the sand and in the water. The gun itself, with an index finger still in the trigger guard, was knocked twelve and a half feet south, landing about a yard from Norm and Janet, who had been focused on their puzzles until the gunfire erupted.

The bullets to his chest knocked him four and a half feet back, blood spurting from the four wounds, until his heart stopped and his body lay, nearly headless, half in the water and half on the sand, the red pool staining the sand and spreading five feet or more from Randy's empty neck, then being shifted north toward Pop's by the mild swell and the small breakers coming in on the gentle seabreeze.

Then the screaming and running began.

"What?" Justin yelled into his beach bag as he put his .45 back in and Lindsay did the same with hers.

"Get your ass up here, Justin, and help me down with the fuckin' bags and the rifle, now! Oh, shit; get the bug in her condo on your way up, too.

"Lindsay, grab all your stuff, get out of there in the mess, get the van and meet us behind the building. You'll need to come in off Forester up by Pop's; they're resurfacing the other end. And while you're coming, tell Amber we need a quick exfil, from the east end of Bonita Beach Road, and to send the big Woodcock. Tell Mike we'll need a driver to get rid of the van, too."

"Got it," Justin yelled.

"Go tit," Lindsay said.

The man on the PVC lounge put his .44 back in the holster under his lounge, straightened the fringe, and calmly went back to his book, a cleverly written thing with two choices for the reader at the end of each chapter, leading to multiple possible stories and outcomes.

Pam and Jake sat stunned and silent, but only for a moment.

"Are you okay, Pam?"

"I'm fine," she said, wiping blood and flesh and brain from her legs and chair, dropping the cupcake in the sand. "Shit. That was a delicious cupcake, too. Are you okay?"

"A little shook up, but okay. Gonna have to clean this lounge up, though, and wash the towel. Where did those shots come from?"

"Two from that guy on the PVC lounge behind you. The others, I don't know. Goddamn Randy."

"Your ex-boss."

"Now doubly ex, I guess." She lifted her head, listening to the approaching sirens. "And here come the locals."

Sure enough, within minutes, Sergeant Dooley and nine Collier deputies and six Lee deputies forced their way through the running, screaming mob all the way down to the body.

"Again, you two. Why is it whenever there's gunfire on my beach, you two are involved?"

"I take it that's a rhetorical question, Sarge," Jake said.

"So what the hell happened here, Jake Devlin?" the sergeant hissed. "And there's no inflatable this time."

One of his deputies was talking to the man on the PVC lounge, who casually pulled out a leather wallet, opened it and displayed it to the deputy, who damn near poked his own eye out as he almost saluted.

"Sarge, you'd better come over here ... now," he yelled.

It wasn't until three o'clock, after statements were taken, cell phone videos were reviewed and what remained of Randy had been removed, that Pam and Jake were able to get to her condo for their nooner -- actually nooners, accompanied, of course, by the Bolero.

-122-

Friday, January 7, 2028
8:30 p.m.
The Oval Office
The White House
via a 24-hour news channel

Gordon Donne, dressed in his usual casual clothing, his fringe of hair even thinner and grayer, smiled into the camera. He looked to be the picture of health for his age, now 68.

"Good evening, my fellow Americans, and Happy New Year.

"It's been a little over sixteen years now that I've been working for you, and again I have good news to report.

"First, on GDP, our growth has backed off a little bit, as we should expect as the economy has matured. We only grew by 12 percent last year, down from the peak of 15 percent in 2025. Not bad, not bad at all, in my opinion.

"Our revenue hit 9.4 trillion dollars last year, and our budget for this year is only 4.3 trillion, down to nine percent of GDP, so we're doing great on paying off our debt. It's down to 1.8 trillion dollars, and it's looking like we'll have it down to an even one trillion by the end of this quarter.

"Unemployment is now at 2.8 percent, slightly under the 'full employment' level, just over three percent. So we're concerned that inflation might be above our one percent acceptable rate, but only slightly, in the near future.

"You have given us tremendously positive feedback on the work and jobs that have been funded through our Sovereign Wealth Fund, and with that fund now topping five trillion dollars in capital, we are able to expand our funding and the returns to our investors, mostly seniors, by a factor of 1.8 this year. So you seniors will have almost twice as much spending money this year as you did in 2027 ... well, for those of you who chose the annual withdrawal option for this year. And don't forget, that option is available to all of you at any time, so feel free, okay?

"I'm going to end with that and let you all know that you can find more information about the state of the country on our web site, _____.gov.

"So I'll now simply wish you all a very happy and prosperous 2028. Good night, all."

-123-

Saturday, September 15, 2012
11:38 a.m.
St. Tropez, France

Pam sat in a comfortable and incredibly luxurious leather chair in the master salon of a 39-meter yacht traveling to St. Tropez, awed by the ship itself and its astoundingly opulent furnishings. Rona and Joel, her trainer/advisers, reclined on a matching couch to her right, appearing a lot less tense than Pam thought she looked ... no, KNEW she looked. After all, she was maybe about to meet, in person, the nearly-mystical top dog, head honcho, CEO, big boss of OP-US, OP-LATAM, OP-EUR-AS, OP-AUS and OP-AF, the man (or woman, possibly) who apparently had the final say on whether Pam would become a member of the inner circle at Optimum Protection. She forgave herself for being a bit nervous.

Rona had called Pam at eight a.m. two days before and arranged to pick her up at her condo in Bonita in three hours and told her to pack for a six-day overseas trip and to pile all ... ALL ... the rest of her things in the middle of the floor of her rented condo. Four hours later, Rona, Joel and Pam had taken off from Fort Myers in an OP executive jet, luxurious, but nowhere near as luxurious as this yacht.

On the flight over the Atlantic, Rona and Joel spent the first two hours going over Pam's stellar training and on-the-job performance records and then broke out a celebratory bottle of champagne for three and told Pam that they were taking her for her final orientation, but that they'd have to blindfold her for the last two hours of the flight

350

and the rest of the trip.

When the jet landed at Toulon-Hyères, France, Rona carefully led Pam off the plane to a waiting helicopter, which ferried the three of them out to the yacht, which was far offshore, on its way to St. Tropez. Once onboard, Rona gently removed Pam's blindfold and led her down to the elegantly appointed salon where the three of them now awaited the arrival of the boss, sharing more champagne, some caviar and crackers and small plates of foie gras with pickled pear. A huge platter of cold cuts, rolls and breads and a refrigerator filled with soft drinks and bottled water sat untouched and unopened on a foldout bar on one wall. An elegant bar with high-end wines and liquors filled another wall.

Ten minutes later, the sound of a larger helicopter was followed by the arrival in the salon of ten other members of Pam's class: Peter and Patty, the Sweet Peas, from Leipzig, Germany; Anja and Anna-Lena, the Cutesy Twins, from Munich, Germany; Paul and Evelyn, the Bikers, from Staten Island, USA; Vito and Danuta, the Kuzzins, from Heraklion, Crete; and Mikhael and Corinna, the Movers, from Sydney, Australia.

Another helo trip brought Molly, Melissa and Denise, the MMD Triplets, whose accent was Scottish, but who were actually from the northernmost part of England; Eileen, Elynn and Eden, the Triple-E's, from Capetown, South Africa; Kee-Kee and Mimi, the Grinners, from Naples, Florida; and Terry, Mary and Carolyn, the Merry Spinsters, from Orlando, Florida.

A third arrival brought Judy and Steve, the Survivors, from Atlanta, Georgia; Tanya and Oliver, the Players, from Lugano, Switzerland; Dixie and Wheeler, the Baptists, from near Nashville, Tennessee; Barbara and Kim, the Gigglers, also from Bonita Springs, Florida; and Jean and Tom, the Golfers, from Prescott, Arizona.

Last came Claire and Solange, the Tiny Prancers, from Brandon, Mississippi; Gavril and Magdalena, the Vampire Hunters, from Covasna, Romania; Nancy and Richard, the Readers, from Naples, Florida; Trish and Chuck, the Investors, from Hanover, Pennsylvania; and Keith and Lin, the Builders, from Elkhart, Indiana.

Ten minutes later, all of the mentor/trainers came through the salon doors, and the conversations and congratulations began.

Pam mingled with all of her classmates, gravitating naturally to the ones she'd formed the closest relationships with a year earlier, especially Barbara and Kim, Jean and Tom and Kee-Kee and Mimi.

As the volume of voices increased in direct proportion to the decrease in the quantity of food and drink on the foldout bars, an older woman and two beautiful young women entered from opposite ends of the room, the former carrying a long-range .50-caliber sniper rifle with a laser scope, which she raised in the air with an attention-grabbing, raspy, "May I have your attention, everyone?"

The voices in the room all went silent and everyone turned to see who had spoken.

"As all of you know, I'm Sharon, the Sniper, and I would like to congratulate each and every one of you on completing your initial orientation and screening last fall and the advanced courses and seminars which some of you elected to take. For those of you who elected the sniper course, a special congratulations; you all passed. And if you have had the opportunity to actually perform assignments over the past year, congratulations; you all did very well on those.

"And for those of you who took my seminar on assassination psychology and motivation, I know you all have a much deeper understanding of those threats and how to deal with them, both reactively and pre-emptively.

"Now, behind you, let me introduce Jill and Carie, the Mimosa twins, our undercover surveillance experts, who will be giving a seminar on their specialty in October."

The entire crowd spun 180 degrees to observe the newcomers. Pam looked at them and said to herself, "I knew it; pros." She shook her fingers at them, smiling, and they responded in kind, but with somewhat more knowing smiles and broad winks, which Terry, Mary and Carolyn, the Merry Spinsters, misinterpreted as meant for them; the three glanced at each other and smiled lasciviously.

"Now," Sharon continued in her raspy, smoky voice, "I know all of you have been looking forward to meeting our ultimate boss, but I'm afraid that only a select few of you will have that honor today. In fact, that select few is only one person.

"However, the boss has prepared a message for you all, and if you would turn your attention back toward me, and this screen --" at which point a wooden panel descended, revealing a huge wall-sized TV screen "-- here it is." She stepped to the screen and pressed a button in the lower right-hand corner, which brought the screen to life, showing a live but pixellated, unrecognizable figure, speaking with an electronically filtered voice, also unrecognizable.

"Ladies and gentlemen, let me begin by welcoming all of you to Optimum Protection, unequivocally the world's foremost private security company.

"I am very proud of you all for getting this far, and you all now have a job, and a career if you want to make it that, at whatever level of participation you choose, from occasional observer as a freelancer to the intense day-to-day stress of close-up bodyguarding, as well as in the security consulting and other services we offer to our clients.

"Some of you are ex-military or ex-intelligence operatives, from many, many countries, and while we value your skills deeply, there may be times when we serve clients whose interests oppose those of your native countries, and may disgust or outrage you, but you will have no obligation to work for those clients if you choose not to.

"The only thing we insist on from you is absolute confidentiality, not about O-P ... feel free to tell your spouses, friends and anyone else you want that you work for us ... but absolute confidentiality about specific missions and clients. Feel free also to discuss the non-sensitive parts of the training you've had; your trainers have let you know which parts fit that category. But I would ask that you only discuss the training in generalities. Word to the wise, okay?

"Also, any press or media inquiries must be referred to our central office ... you all know how to reach them ... and you are all forbidden from making any media appearances or giving any interviews yourselves about O-P. But if you're invited to appear on any shows or give interviews for any other reasons, feel free. Just keep O-P out of the mix. And be alert to devious invitations and what we call 'gotcha' interviews. Some so-called journalists are just trying to get at you for a feather in their cap and career advancement. Avoid them like the plague. Another word to the wise.

"With that, welcome once again to Optimum Protection. Now give yourselves a round of applause and enjoy the party. Goodbye."

Sharon pressed another button and the screen went blank, as the room erupted in applause and cheers, after which it buzzed with speculation as to who the one chosen to meet the boss might be, each one hoping and fearing he or she would be the one.

Pam immediately zeroed in on the Mimosa Twins and plowed her way through the crowd to them, smiling and shaking her fingers at them. When they saw her coming, they reciprocated with the smile and the finger-waving, which led without comment to high fives between Pam and each of the twins.

"I knew you were pros."

"We know," the twins said in unison.

"You knew I knew?"

"We knew you knew. We wanted you to know, but we didn't want you to know we knew you knew," said Jill.

"You wanted me to know, but you didn't want me to know you knew I knew or to know you wanted me to know?"

"Both."

"What?"

"We wanted you to know, but we didn't want you to know we knew you knew or wanted you to know."

"Wait. What? You wanted me to know, but you didn't want me to know you knew I knew and you didn't want me to know you wanted me to know or to know you knew I knew?"

Carie said, "Right. All three."

"What three?"

"We wanted you to know; that's one. We didn't want you to know we wanted you to know; that's two. And we didn't want you to know we knew you knew; that's three. But that was then."

"And now?"

"Now we know you knew and we know you know we knew you knew and we know you know we wanted you to know, and it's okay with us if you know we knew you knew and wanted you to know."

"Right; all four of those," Jill added.

"All four?"

"Right."

"Oh, okay." Pam gave up and shrugged. "Why?"

"Because now you're in; then you weren't in, you were out. But we were okay if you could make it in. And you have. Bravo."

"Oh ... okay."

"In fact, we were the ones who recommended you."

"Jill, I'm not sure she should know that."

"Well, now she knows. And she knows we --"

"Hold it, girls; no more knowing who knew what when, okay?

"Why did you recommend me?"

"'Cause your tradecraft was good. And because he had no idea you were testing him until that gorilla head popped up."

"You were there for – oh, right. Right. Do you know he called you the ditzy chicks?"

"No; you did."

"I did?"

"Yup; he just called us ditzy. Which was what we were trying to seem to be. But I kinda like 'ditzy chicks'; maybe we'll change our nickname.

"No, Jillybean; that would be too obvious."

"And 'Mimosa Twins' isn't obvious, CB?"

"Not as obvious as 'ditzy chicks,' JB."

"Well, I like it."

"I don't."

"Guys, guys, settle down. Guess I just need to say thanks."

"For what?"

"For recommending me; guess that's what got me here."

"No; that was the helicopter."

"Geez, JB."

"And the executive jet before that."

Pam could only nod.

"And Rona and Joel probably picked you up, right?"

"Right. But I meant that your recomm- --"

"Gotcha, Pam. I was just pulling your leg, practicing ditzy."

Pam smiled and pointed her index finger at Jill. "Got me; you do do a good ditzy."

"I do, don't I? CB can't do it quite so good."

"You mean well, JB."

"Some of the time; sometimes I don't."

"No, I meant --"

"Gotcha, Carie Berry."

"Oh, geez."

"Look, girls. I'm glad I finally got the chance to meet you, and thanks for the recommendation. I'm glad I'm here."

"So are we."

"Glad you're here?"

"No, that you are."

"Gotcha."

"Oh, Pam, that you did. Welcome. We are gonna have so much fun."

"Could be, could be. We'll see what happens next. By the way, what's the boss like?"

"Don't know; never met."

"Really? How long have you been with O-P?"

"Six years."

"Wow. And you've never met him?"

"Or her."

"Or her; hmm. Guess I've got some male stuff still kicking around in there," Pam said, tapping her temple.

"Or maybe somewhere else --"

"Ssst, Jillybean."

"Sorry. What?" Pam asked, holding a palm over an ear against the cacophony in the room.

"I said --"

"So, Pam," Carie cut in, "when are you going back to Bonita?"

"I'm not sure if I will. Rona and Joel didn't tell me; they got the tickets and had me pile all my stuff in the --"

"In the middle of the room," said Carie.

"Right."

"They're doing a cleanout; you'll get all your stuff soon."

"Oh, really? Why would --"

"We loved our time there," Jill cut in. "It's a great place."

"I love it there; it's so peaceful, most of the time. How come you left? I haven't seen you since the spring."

"Oh, we had a situation."

"A situation?"

"Yeah. Can't say anything more abou- --"

"Pamela?" A raspy, smoky voice intruded.

"Yes?"

"Could you come with me for a minute?"

"Uh ... sure, Sharon."

"Okay. Follow me."

Pam glanced back at the twins, who both held up crossed fingers and smiled, mouthing "Good luck," and winking. The Merry Spinsters moved in on them.

Pam followed Sharon, still carrying the rifle, out of the salon, down a paneled inside hallway and into a smaller, but still spacious and opulent, office-type room, where she was greeted by a woman in her late fifties, stocky, with graying hair in a loose ponytail.

"Hi, Pamela; I'm Amber. So nice to finally meet you. I've heard tremendous things about you, all good."

"Do you need anything else, Amber?"

"Nope, Sharon; thanks. Go back and enjoy the party." Sharon nodded and left.

"Sit, sit, Pamela."

"Thank you."

"I'm the boss's chief of staff, been with him for --"

"Ah-ha," Pam thought, "good."

"--nearly forty years, since we were both just young shoots."

"From what I've seen of O-P and this beautiful yacht, you've both grown up successfully."

Amber laughed, a deep, throaty laugh, and said, "Oh, good one, Pamela."

"Please, call me Pam."

"Okay. Pam," Amber said, still chuckling.

"He's got a beautiful office," Pam said, looking around.

"Oh, he doesn't use an office, Pam. This is mine."

"Wow," Pam blurted.

"It's pretty comfy for a marine setting. I'm usually in one of the onshore ones."

"More than one?"

"Oh, sure; we're worldwide, as you know."

"Ah, right. Makes sense."

"Oh, it makes more than that. We make dollars and euros, millions of them a year. But he doesn't much care about money, just what good he can do with it."

"I guess when you reach a certain point, you --"

"Exactly. He especially likes to support micro-loan programs, one in India and a couple in the States. And now he's getting into some crowd-funding things, as well."

"I've heard about those; pretty cool ideas.

"So can you tell me anything about him, what he's like?"

"Let's wait till he – oh, here he is now."

Pam turned in her chair, looked at the man who had just come in from a side door, a broad grin on his face, and gasped.

"Hi, Pam. Welcome to the inner inner inner circle."

Now Pam was totally perflutzed; she could only gape. "You?"

"Gotcha."

-124-

Friday, January 5, 2035
8:30 p.m.
The Oval Office
The White House
via a 24-hour news channel

Gordon Donne, dressed in his usual casual clothing, his fringe of hair much, much thinner and grayer, smiled into the camera. His complexion and demeanor gave a picture of general good health, even at his age of 75.

"Good evening, my fellow Americans, and Happy New Year.

"It's been a little over 23 years now that I've been working for y'all, and, as usual, I have some good news to report.

"But before I start on that, I want to take a moment to remember Wesley T. Farley, my COO at DEI, who has done phenomenally well running that company and all its subsidiaries in my absence, who passed away last month from a lingering case of vegetarian poisoning. I told him over and over again to try at least a cheeseburger or a grilled ham and cheese from time to time. Would he listen? No. But he had a wonderful and successful life, raised a happy family and left the world a better place for his time here.

"First, as usual, on the economy, I'm pleased to tell you that GDP grew at about 13 percent last year, and our unemployment rate is consistently running at about 3.1 percent, so inflation is staying below our acceptable rate.

"Our revenues amounted to eleven percent of GDP last year, and our budget is now down to a bit over eight percent of GDP. I'm now confident that we can get the total cost of your government down to less than six percent of GDP by the year after next, 2037.

"Our Sovereign Wealth Fund is now worth 15 trillion dollars, and with our population now over two billion, out of a world population of 16 billion, we are now able to reduce our income tax rates, for both individuals and businesses, by cutting them by two thirds, effective this year.

"I've also got to comment, if only briefly, on the incredible and astounding leaps and bounds our private sector has made, especially in the last seven years, in the agriculture, technology and energy sectors. We are less than a decade away from making all our roads and bridges completely obsolete and less than a year from getting a full hundred percent of our energy needs from nuclear power and sustainable resources, and building a huge export market in energy.

"I'm going to end with that and let you all know that you can find more information about the state of the country on our web site,

_____.gov.

"So I'll now simply wish you all a very happy and prosperous 2035. Good night."

-125-

Sunday, September 16, 2012
10:27 a.m.
Bonita Beach, Florida

When Norm and Janet arrived at the beach, Norm with his long-shafted drill and umbrella in hand, they noticed that Jake Devlin's three-way lounge, bag and cooler were in Jake's usual spot, but there was no Jake.

Norm glanced at Janet and said, "That's odd."

"Maybe he's taking a walk," Janet replied.

Norm, stomping on the ground and digging with his hands before positioning the drill, shrugged and said, "Ah, he'll be back soon."

But an hour later, Jake still had not returned. Janet asked, "Do you remember seeing his car in the lot?"

Norm, engrossed in his crossword, mumbled, "No idea. Hey, Janet, what's a nine-letter word for subterfuge or beguilement, D, blank, C, blank, P, ends with N?"

"I'll go check, see if it's there."

"Good luck."

A few minutes later, Janet returned, "His car isn't there. I looked all over the lot. I'm worried, Norm."

"Oh, relax; he'll be back when he's ready."

But Jake never returned. In fact, he was never seen again. Sergeant Dooley, when he was finally called in, was unable to find any clues as to his disappearance; in fact, he and his team couldn't find anything in Jake Devlin's name, no real estate, no lease, no bank or brokerage accounts, no auto registration, no passport, not even a driver's license. There were no fingerprints or DNA on his lounge, his cooler or his beach bag, all of which were left abandoned on the beach. It was as if Jake Devlin had never existed.

After that frustration and being demoted for never having checked Devlin's ID the many times he'd had the chance, now-Deputy Dooley could never hold his head high again; four years later, at the age of 43, he retired, became a mall cop and was given the nickname "Hangdog." Six years later, just before his 50th birthday, he ate his gun and was buried without honors.

-126-

Monday, September 17, 2012
Cyberspace

In the Drafts folders of nineteen different email accounts, the same message was posted: "Done; body will never be discovered. Closing payment due." By the close of business the next day, fifteen separate deposits of ten million euros each were made into fifteen different accounts scattered throughout the world. Upon receipt, each deposit was automatically moved into another account at a different bank, then another, then another and another and another, until all 150 million euros wound up in one account, with the 190 million euros already on deposit there, for a total of 340 million euros Despite two additional notices, four final payments were never sent.

Within three weeks, a London oil trader was found dead in a seriously mussed-up bed in an hourly hotel in London's East End, a used condom stuck in his mouth and a necktie, which turned out to be his, wrapped securely around his neck, his wallet, jewelry, cell phone, shoes and briefcase missing. His phone was found a day later in the bed of a lorry traveling north from Leeds to Glasgow; the driver said he had been in the East End a day earlier. The case was never solved.

A lawyer was killed in a freak automobile accident involving his top-end convertible Italian sports car and a wayward elephant that had somehow escaped from the Dothan, Alabama Zoo. A police official, who wished to remain anonymous, was quoted in the local paper as saying, "Ain't never seen a human body that'd been gored by a elephant tusk afore. Bulls? Yeah. Goats? O'course. Sheep? Yup. Even a wahld boar oncet. But a elephant? Never 'fore today. And it sho' ain't purty. In fact – 'scuse me, ma'am. Urp."

In Rome, a man later identified as a Vatican security commander by the name of Gaetano was discovered in an obscure apartment on Via Tigre, his death attributed unequivocally to twenty-nine wounds made by a large kitchen knife found protruding from his chest, bearing child-sized fingerprints which were never matched to any on file anywhere, despite exhaustive efforts by multiple law enforcement agencies, including Interpol. The case was never solved.

In Medellin, Colombia, the heads of two of the major Colombian drug cartels, despite their heavy security, were both found dead on the same day in their separate swimming pools. The COD, cause of death, in each case was ruled to be accidental drowning.

But the man with many names knew better.

-127-

Friday, January 4, 2042
8:30 p.m.
The White House
Washington, DC
via a 24-hour news channel

Gordon Olin Donne faced the camera from behind the podium in the Press Room, this time in a plain pale blue short-sleeved polo shirt, a somber look on his aged face. The room was SRO, standing room only, filled with both press and White House staff.

"Ladies and gentlemen, tonight is perhaps the most important announcement for you that I have ever made. For tonight, after more than thirty years owning this country, I am turning a good part of it back over to you, the people, with a new constitution that may ... and I can only say 'MAY' ... give the US of A the chance to continue the progress that we have made together over the last generation and a half, for which I congratulate all of you who have made it happen.

"Even with the China-India-Arab War and our ongoing embargo on Chinese imports; even with atmospheric cooling, which has ended a third of our agriculture in our northernmost states; with the loss of Western California in the Great Quake of 2036; with the devastating assaults by Hurricane Gabrielle in 2013, Hurricane Thornton in 2018, Hurricane Mitzy in 2028 and Hurricane Bitzy in 2035; with the loss of over seven billion lives in the Tofu Plague of 2037, bringing the world's total population back down to ten billion; with the Church's publicity stunt of the Antichrist in 2022 and the over six thousand infanticides that resulted; even with all that and the hundreds of other tragedies that have befallen us all, even with all that, this country and you, its people, have conquered and prospered beyond my and your own wildest expectations. Congratulations.

"You are now the proud owners of the largest economy in the world, more than the total of the seventeen next-largest economies combined, a debt of less than one trillion dollars, a continuing large trade surplus, an unemployment rate of under two percent, an annual budget surplus of nearly nine hundred and fifty billion dollars, and a government that consumes less than six percent of GDP, even with a budget of 7.8 trillion dollars. We also have the strongest, meanest and leanest military in the world, and no one has dared to challenge us since 2026, and that threat was totally eradicated in nineteen days, like a bug on a windshield of one of those antique cars that only drove on the ground.

"We have accomplished incredible things together these past

thirty years, and it is time for me to return from whence I came, and leave the future in your hopefully capable hands.

"As you can see from this face and bald, wrinkled pate, time has done its work on this now-frail body, but my spirit is still strong and will endure for many years to come.

"Now, I know the human tendency to get complacent when things are going well, and I urge all of you to guard against that trap each and every day of your lives. The freedoms and liberties that you now enjoy are always threatened by those who resent the simple fact that you have them, whether they be a foreign state or your local homeowners association board. Your government is always on alert for those threats, but it is not omnipotent. Your safety is the number one ongoing priority, but all humans are fallible. So while I encourage you to enjoy your lives, try to avoid falling into the complacency trap. Word to the wise, okay?

"In eight weeks, you will hold your first election since 2010, 32 years ago, and there are many highly qualified people who have thrown their proverbial hats in the ring and who have been given limited government funds to inform you about themselves and their positions on the issues you have told us are important to you. Any of them who indulge in any kind of negative campaigning or private funding will automatically be disqualified.

"Whoever wins the race in each of the twelve new regions created by the new Constitution to become one of my successor's senior advisers will have done so by at least a 92 percent majority, as the new Constitution mandates, and will then undergo a full year of orientation and screening before I give each of them my seal of approval to move into their new position.

"A year from today, my position as owner will be carried on by my successor, Brian Throcklegate, whom I first met a week after I bought the country, when he was a member of my social media team. He did an extraordinary job there, and I watched him move up and finally took him under my wing ten years ago, with an eye toward making him my successor when the time came, as it now has.

"He is only the second person ever to beat me at chess, and at 53 years of age, he has the endurance, experience and loyalty to you, the people, to continue with the light touch of government for another thirty years, by which time he, too, will have discovered a person to succeed him when the time comes. I'll continue to serve as his senior adviser for as long as this frail human body allows me to do so.

"His chief of staff, Melinda Galt, is someone I first learned about when she sent me a letter when she was just a little 12-year-old sprout, telling me how her mom had helped her learn to handle her own finances. Now, at an elegant 43 years of age, Melinda has a vast range of experience in the private sector, working her way up at the plastics company from which her mom recently retired, to a position as vice president of sales and then CFO, Chief Financial Officer, by the time she was 31.

"Then Wes Farley, may he rest in peace, plucked her away and gave her the first of several positions at DEI, based solely on her merit, and she moved up through the ranks to become one of DEI's top private equity managers, rescuing and restructuring over four hundred companies in all types of industries in all parts of the world over her next eight years.

"When she was 39, Wes' successor, Ben Doberstein, found out at a company party that she was the same Melinda Galt who had sent me that letter years before, and he put me in touch with her for a reunion of sorts. As soon as I met her, I knew she was going to be an important part of the White House staff, and I offered her a top-end motorcycle as a sign-on bonus, paid for from my own funds, not taxpayer funds, and she came over as Brian's executive assistant.

"I've prepared both of them over these last years to take over when my time was done. So both of them have my absolute trust, and I urge all of you watching this to give them the same support you have given me over these last three decades. I assure you that trust will be well worth it.

"With that, let me bring Brian and Melinda up here, and please give them a warm American welcome."

Brian and Melinda stepped up, one on each side of Donne, and the applause was deafening.

"Brian, Melinda, welcome, and let's make the next three decades as good for the people of the United States as the last three have been. But watch out. Even after I've gone home, if you fuck it up, I only have these seven words for you: 'Don't make me come down there ... again.'" With that, the broadcast ended.

-128-

Tuesday, September 18, 2012
Cyberspace

At noon precisely, <u>The Devlin Deception </u>had been uploaded and was immediately available on the major print-on-demand web site and other sources, including versions for all e-readers, as well as at JakeDevlin.com and TheDevlinDeception.com. Profits from all sales went directly to three private micro-loan programs in Appalachia, New Mexico and India.

-Epilogue-

Monday, November 5, 2012
10:27 p.m. local time
Nice, France

The man with many names clicked from the 24-hour news channel to the local French classical music channel, checked the time on his diamond-encrusted watch, took another sip from his glass of the most expensive wine in the world and smiled at his reflection in the window of his villa overlooking the harbor. In the light of the quarter moon, he could just make out the imposing silhouette of his 39-meter yacht, which had been sailed here a month earlier from St. Tropez. But that was not why he was smiling. What curved the corners of his mouth slightly up was the certain knowledge that he was finally permanently retired -- or so he thought.

But as he settled back into his hot tub, setting his wine glass next to his well-worn copy of Pirandello's play "Six Characters in Search of an Author," his smile turned into a full grin as his gaze took in the luscious beauty of the naked redhead reclining next to him, the water lapping at her tumescent nipples.

He kissed her gently and said, "Well, tomorrow's the American election. Business as usual continues over there: all talk, little action, more corruption, more debt, the 'fiscal cliff.' And no matter which pair of bumbleheads wins, the structural corruption will continue and 'They, the People' will keep getting screwed, especially the middle class. And I'd bet the US will be bankrupt, insolvent, whatever you want to call it, broke, in default, within three years, at the most."

"Can't win 'em all, can you?"

"Apparently not; too bad it was just fiction."

"But I do like the new title. Much better than the one I came up with."

"I'm glad you like it; I do, too."

"Do you think you accomplished anything? Anything at all?"

"Probably the only thing would be that Congress might, just MIGHT, read the bills they have before they pass 'em."

"Not before Guam tips over."

"Nor before the world ends next month ... if you're Mayan."

"Too bad we forgot to put in that Donne declared December 22nd as National Oops Day."

They both laughed.

Catching his breath, he said, "But now we've got 34 million euros to play with and give away somewhere."

"No concern about any of the clients coming at us after their money?"

"Nope; I did my job. They all just contracted for the kill, not to stop the publication. And none of them would want any disclosure of their involvement. And none of them has any idea who I really am."

"That's good." She ran a finger down his cheek, which was healing up well. "I do like your new look, sort of Charlton Heston-ey."

"It's a bit less nondescript than I usually like ... you know, for anonymity."

"Well, I do like it. But there was nothing wrong with your looks when I met you last year."

"That was more nonde- -- oh, that reminds me. Do you still want me to get us new passports with new names?"

"Might be a good idea, especially if we start on my memoirs."

"Okay; how about Paul and Evelyn Burnett, Andorran expats?"

"Sounds good to me."

"Done."

He kissed her again and said, "Give me a minute, okay?" He picked up a sat phone and dialed. "Authentication 0000001 ... Hey, Amber, it's me. ... Yup, all done ... Did you get the copy I sent you? ... Glad you liked it. Look, here's what I need you to do. First, new passports for both of us. Paul and Evelyn Burnett, B-u-r-n-e-t-t, Andorra ... Next, on that 340 million euros I deposited, 147 million should go into the hedge fund account, 146 million into the profit-sharing fund, a million each for the Mimosa twins, the KSK triplets, Wayne and Linda, Justin and Lindsay – what? They did? Oh, too bad. Well, separate checks for them, then -- Rona and Joel, Sharon and you ... Yup, per person, and you're welcome. Eight million for my personal account, eight for Pam's, six million for the micro-loan programs and the other 12 million for the foundation ... Great. And how's the cleanup guy who got hurt on the ninth step? ... Good; but too bad he didn't check the list. Make sure we take care of all his medicals, okay? ... And change the name on the yacht, will ya? 'The Devlin Deception.' Pam and I are gonna take her out for a few months, get started on her memoirs, maybe go down to Somalia, hunt some pirates. So we'll need all the weapons systems checked out, and put an extra 50 – no, make it a hundred -- RPG's on board, okay? ... Five days? That's fine ... Thanks, Amber; we will. That's it from here. Give my love to Gisele and the girls ... Will do. Bye."

He hung up and turned to the beauty in the tub. "Amber says hi, Pam. Now, where were we?"

She let loose a deep, throaty laugh, running her fingers lightly over his now-taut stomach. "Well, I was ... right about here. Amazing what a little exercise can do in a few weeks, huh?"

"Yup. Tough to get back into that after three years playing a lazy, bumbling, benign beach bum who smokes. But here's to a very successful long con. I love taking money from bad guys and hypocrites."

They clinked their glasses, took another sip and sighed contentedly.

He ran his fingers through her hair and murmured, "You're as beautiful a redhead as you were a blonde."

"It's my natural color."

. He slid his hand down to her collarbone and then a bit lower. "I know."

She giggled, nuzzling his neck and, sliding her hand further down under the water, she whispered, "Feels like Stevie Bruce is ready to play."

He slid his hand down from her belly and murmured, "Feels like Ginny May is, too."

She nuzzled him again and moaned softly. "Mmm."

He chuckled, clicked the remote, and the Bolero began to play.

(Now For Some Alternate/Additional Epilogues:)

Additional possible stuff (not too fond of this'n; JD):

He chuckled, clicked the remote, and the Bolero began to play.

Pam reached into her bag, pulled out a pair of handcuffs and cuffed his wrist to a support bar on the hot tub.

"Oh, kinky," he said, grinning.

"Sorry, Jake," Pam said, easing her naked body out of the tub and walking across the floor toward the phone. "You're under arrest. I'm with Interpol. We've been tracking the assassin known as the man with many names for decades, but until now, we never could find you. Sorry."

She reached for the phone.

Further possible stuff (which I like even less; JD)

She reached for the phone.

He opened a hidden panel on the side of the tub, just above the water line, reached in and pulled out a semi-automatic handgun, pointed and fired. Pam's head exploded in a red mist.

He then fired into the handcuffs, pulled free, crawled over to Pam's bloody, nearly headless body, held her in his arms and cried uncontrollably for the rest of the night.

In the morning, he called for a cleanup crew and checked the OP web site, looking for any new jobs he could do himself. The closer in to the target, the better.

(Now, this one I like better; JD).

She reached for the phone.

He opened a hidden panel on the side of the tub, just above the water line, reached in and pulled out a semi-automatic handgun, pointed and fired, hitting Pam in her gorgeous, perfect butt. She screamed and fell to the floor.

He then fired into the handcuffs, pulled free, crawled over to Pam, pointing the gun at her gorgeous face.

"Why, Pam, why? Interpol? What the fuck?" His finger trembled on the trigger guard.

"Just a joke, Jake, just a gotcha, like you did with the zombies. Now do something about the goddamn bullet in my fuckin' ass."

"Oh, Pam, I'm sorry. Shit, shit, shit."

"Paranoia keeps us alive, Jake. I forgot you've been living that for over four decades. Bad joke. I'm sorry." She wiped a tear from Jake's eye.

He grabbed a towel, applied pressure and called for his private doctor, who arrived twenty minutes later and tended to Pam's butt.

"Guess now I'm gonna have to shoot you in the ass, Jake Devlin, so we're still symmetrical." Then the sedative kicked in.

Jake called Amber and told her their visit to Somalia would be delayed and she should hold off on the added RPG's and put the yacht back out for charter. And leave the name as is.

(This one I like even better; JD. Hee-hee.)

She giggled, nuzzling his neck and, sliding her hand further down under the water, she whispered, "Feels like Stevie Bruce is ready to play."

He slid his hand down from her belly and murmured, "Feels like Ginny May is, too."

She nuzzled him again and moaned softly. "Mmm."

He chuckled, clicked the remote, and the Bolero began to play.

"You two going to start without me again?"

He said, "Thought you were asleep, JJ; sorry. C'mon in."

-Another Alternate Epilogue-

Jake awoke in a clean, white room, bathed in clear, white light. He was naked, his scaly skin and crested head resting on a cold, metallic surface, with his tail curled across his belly and cradled in and around his seven arms. He was completely comfortable and quickly became totally alert, opening his three eyes.

A disembodied voice surrounded him (translated as follows). "So, Zorgestal 347397458, what are your conclusions from your reconnaissance? Should we admit the planet to the Intergalactic Federation or annihilate it?"

(Just for you skee-fee junkies. Live long and proper. JD)

And Yet ANOTHER Alternate Epilogue
(For you fans of a button-down brain. JD)

Tuesday, November 6, 2012
7:06 a.m.
A luxury riverfront gated community
Bonita Springs, Florida

Marion Herman awoke to George's snoring and apparently laughing in his sleep. "George, wake up; you're dreaming again."

"Wha?"

"You're dreaming again."

After coming a bit more awake, George was able to say, "Oh, geez, Marion, this was a GREAT dream. There was this assassin who pretended to be a beach bum who was writing this book about a guy who bought the country, and then he met --"

"Oh, George, not another one of those. I am NOT letting Lurlene fix you that chocolate peanut butter turkey noodle tofu casserole ever again. The last time you had it, you dreamed about some young spy with amnesia, the one who looked like Matthew Bordrick."

"No, that was Matthew ... Dillion?"

"Whatever. No more of that casserole, ever!!! And if these dreams keep up, I'm gonna have to take you back to Dr. Deb."

"No, not Dr. Deb. Please!"

"Just a warning, George. But now we've got to get dressed and go vote. We've got to cancel out the kids' votes. And in four years, the grandkids'll be eligible, too, and they'll probably vote for that liar or his party, too; don't know what we're going to do then. Geez."

"Wait, wait. I've got to make some notes on that dream. Maybe

367

I'll write a whole book about it."

"Well, don't take too much time. I don't like long lines."

Marion rolled her eyes and climbed out of their adjustable, temperature-controlled bed. George grabbed his spiral notebook and began scribbling.

An hour later, on their way to the precinct, George piped up: "And we watched a speech on TV at Slinky Joe's." Marion rolled her eyes.

On the way back from voting, George mumbled: "No, not Dillion ... Damion?"

Marion rolled her eyes and sighed.

"Whatever."

And Yet ANOTHER Other Alternate Epilogue

Tuesday, September 25, 2012
8:23 a.m.
A small farmhouse near Lancaster, Pennsylvania

Sarah Durgenmueller stalked into the kitchen, threw an oilcloth-wrapped packet onto the wood-hewn table, placed her stolid hands on her stolid hips and planted her 180-pound, five-foot-three-inch body stolidly in front of her husband, who was sitting placidly on a stool beside the table.

"Jacob Durgenmueller, thou hast defilethed all that is holy with what thou hast writteneth there. The foul language, the rampant recreational procreative acts, spies, killers and guns, oh, my. And Pamela is not even a biblical name, not to mentioneth Mitzy, Bitsy or Ginny May. And that defilement you callethed a Suzanne? Thou musteth haveth visitethed that heathen harlot Heather again.

"I submitteth to you, as iseth my holy and sworn duty, once a year, solely for procreation, as our holy Father and our elders have proclaimethed, but that certainly iseth NOT recreational.

"And Florida, Paris, London, Vienna, Bangkok? Thou hast never travelethed further than the ten miles from this farm to the city. And all the newfangled things that thou hast includethed in there. What is a PC? A CD? A tablet? A three-way? Interpol? A bullet in the butt? And a tail and seven arms? An Alzheimer's dream? Satan's work! And what makest thou thinketh that thou knoweth anything at all abouteth nathional polithy or economicth? Thatan'th work!!!

"Thou shalt certainly getteth uth shunnethed by the elders if they findeth out what thou hast wroughteth. I cannot believeth that such dreck cometh from thy brain. And your handwriting iseth awful, too.

The Devlin Deception

"I shalleth burneth this trash immediately when the fire getteth goingeth, and thou shalt milketh the cows so I mayeth churneth the butter and maketh the ice cream for the children's monthly treat. Then thou shalt driveth the buggy into Lancaster and get the lantern repairethed, and returneth immediately to this house."

Jacob rose from the stool, picked up the packet from the table, towered momentarily over his wife, said, "I divorceth thee, I divorceth thee, I divorceth thee. Thou canst milketh thine own – oh, fucketh it. You can milk your own fuckin' cows, you fat, ugly, self-righteous bitch, and I hope one of them kicks you in the fuckin' head," and headed for the door.

"I will take with me one fifth, not half, of our savings, leaving you with eight thousand dollars for the winter. I will take the buggy into town and get Caleb to repair the lantern and return the buggy to you. He's always coveted you, and I'll let him know you're his if he still wants you. I'm outa here. And if I ever again have to add 'eth' to plain old English verbs, I think I'll puke." And he left, taking only two thousand dollars and the oilcloth-wrapped packet with him, leaving a finally speechless ex-wife spluttering behind.

When he arrived in Lancaster about eleven, he left the buggy and an explanation with Caleb at the feed store, trudged down the street to a thrift store, where he paid twelve dollars for a short-sleeved knit shirt, khakis, socks, tennis shoes and a brand new pair of underwear. He changed into all that and left his baggy coat, shirt, trousers and hat as a donation; he threw his underwear and socks into a trashcan.

He continued down the street to a barber shop, where he got his beard shaved off and his hair cut in a short, stylish cut the barber recommended, all for another twelve dollars, then sauntered another two blocks to a fast food restaurant, where he purchased a double cheeseburger, soft drink and small fries, the first in his 38-year life; he did not purchase an apple pie. He sat at the only empty table in the crowded restaurant, enjoying his first moments of freedom after years of virtual slavery on his now-ex-wife's family's farm.

Savoring a second bite of the cheeseburger, his eyes closed in delight, he did not see the source of the gentle, melodious voice that said, "Excuse me. Is this seat taken?"

Perflutzed, his mouth full of cheeseburger, his eyes opened, but he could only manage a welcoming gesture.

"Thanks."

Jacob chewed and swallowed as rapidly as he could, but then could only mumble, "You're welcome," as he watched the bewitching, perfectly figured 40-ish blonde slither into the plastic chair across from him, giving him a winning smile and batting her dazzling blues at him over her elegant sunglasses.

Jacob licked his lips, then brushed at them with his thumb.

"You missed a bit, there on the right," she said, and reached over with a napkin and wiped the last bit from his lower lip.

"Thank you," he mumbled, still perflutzed.

"No problem," she said. "By the way, I like your hair style."

"It's new, just this morning."

"Did you have a beard? Your chin and jaw are very white."

"Yup, just had that shaved off this morning, too."

"Really? Why?"

"Oh, I got divorced and left the farm."

"Oh; sorry to pry. I didn't mean --"

"It's okay."

"But you're a big, strapping guy, fairly good-looking. Why would your wife divorce you?"

"No, the other way around. I just needed some freedom."

"Really? Wow. And now what are you going to do?"

"I'm going to Florida, if I can find the bus ... uh ... station? Depot? I haven't been off the farm very much."

"Hey, I'm going to Florida, and I could use some company on the drive."

"Really?"

"You're not a serial killer or anything, are you?"

"Nope, just a simple far- – ex-farmer."

"You'll need some sunscreen on your face. I'm driving with the top down."

"Sunscreen? What --"

"Oh, you really are naïve, aren't you? It protects your skin against sunburn. I've got some in the car. So would you like to ride with me?"

"I guess so; thank you."

"I've got a condo overlooking the beach, and I'm going down for the winter. A snowbird."

"A what?"

"A – just a name for winter visitors there."

"Oh," Jacob said, taking another bite of his cheeseburger.

"I hate to leave the family, but they can always come for a visit."

"Family?" Jacob mumbled.

"My sons, Bruce and Stephen, and their wives, May and Ginny, and the brand-new grandkids, Mitzy and Bitsy."

Jacob choked on his cheeseburger.

"Are you all right?"

Jacob nodded and managed to swallow. "Sorry."

"You sure you're okay?"

"Yeah, fine. Thanks."

"Look, it's almost noon, and rush hour traffic in Baltimore can be a bitch. Okay if we go now and take this with us?"

"Sure."

"Is that all you've got for luggage?"

"Yup, just that packet."

"Good, 'cause my car is pretty full. I'll have to clear some stuff off the front seat, but you should be able to fit in."

"This is very nice of you."

"Don't sweat it. I can use the company; it's a long drive. Maybe you can spell me part of the time."

"Spell you?"

"Drive some of the time, give me a break."

"Oh. Sorry, I don't know how to drive."

"Really? Wow. Okay. Hang on while I clear the seat off."

"Okay."

Once they were settled in the car, the woman pulled her hair back into a ponytail and slid her T-shirt off, revealing a black bikini top with a golden ring in the center, fetchingly holding two perky, firm breasts.

Jacob gasped.

"Oh, sorry; I just like to feel the wind and sun when I drive."

"No problem."

"Here's the sunscreen; it's creamy, not oily. Just smear it on."

"Thanks ... uh, what should I call you?"

"Oh, my name's Pamela, Pamela Brooks, but you can call me Pam. And you?"

"Jacob Durgen- – uh, Devlin, but thou mayest – I mean you can call me Jake."

"Very nice to meet you, Jake Devlin," Pam said, holding out her hand, which Jake shook. She held his hand a bit longer than Jake thought was usual.

"So, Pam, what is it you do?"

"I'm an agent."

"What? FBI, CIA, Secret --"

She laughed, a deep, throaty, open laugh. "No, no, no, I'm a literary agent. I try to find new writers and market them."

"Really? That must be interesting."

"Only about eight percent of the time. The other 92 percent is just dreck."

"Oh."

"By the way, Jake, do you like Neapolitan ice cream?"

"Oh, yes, yes, I do," Jake said, as he leaned back in the leather seat, closed his eyes and smiled ... and smiled ... and smiled.

And the Absolutely Positively FINAL* Epilogue

Friday, October 5, 2012
1:34 p.m.
Bonita Beach, Florida

The man sitting sideways on his homemade PVC lounge, fringe free, as it always had been, took a final puff of his little light cigar and stubbed it out, putting the butt in the empty blue-and-white pack with the others, then coughed deeply for half a minute. Then he pulled a container of mostly melted chocolate ice cream out of his cooler, took a sip, swallowed slowly, then took a sip from his water bottle and applied some lip balm, SPF 45.

Lying back on his lounge, he picked up a non-spiral notebook, made some notes, set the notebook and pen back down, chuckled, reached into his cooler, popped a chocolate-and-orange-covered tofu ball into his mouth, then lay back, put his ecru beach hat over his face and fell into a deep, deep sleep, not the slightest bit perflutzed.

The notes read:

"Book 2:

"A: When Pam and Jake arrivethed in Bonita --

"B: When Pam and Jake arrived in the Indian Ocean ...

"C: When Pam's butt had healed and they arrived IO/Somalia ...

"D: When Pam and Jake and JJ arrived IO/Som ...

"E: When P/J started on her memoirs ...

"F: While Pam's butt healed, P/J started on her memoirs ...

"G: When the Mimosa twins accepted the job in ____, they had no way of knowing that ...

"H: When the phone rang, Amber ...

So you think you know Bonita?

**If you're familiar with Bonita Springs
and think you know the real names of the
places in this book, as well as some other
general stuff, you might want to visit this link:**

JakeDevlin.com/quiz

*For one more "filters-totally-off"
final epilogue, visit this link:

JakeDevlin.com/alt

**Enjoyed this read? Tell your friends.
TheDevlinDeception.com or JakeDevlin.com**

**Hated it? Tell me.
JakeDevlin@JakeDevlin.com**

22270330R00205

Made in the USA
Charleston, SC
16 September 2013